IN THE FRAME
&
DEAD CERT

Dick Francis has written over forty-one international best-sellers and is widely acclaimed as one of the world's finest thriller writers. His awards include the Crime Writers' Association's Cartier Diamond Dagger for his outstanding contribution to the crime genre, and an honorary Doctorate of Humane Letters from Tufts University of Boston. In 1996 Dick Francis was made a Mystery Writers of America Grand Master for a lifetime's achievement and in 2000 he received a CBE in the Queen's Birthday Honours list.

Dick Francis

IN THE FRAME
&
DEAD CERT

PAN BOOKS

In the Frame first published 1976 by Michael Joseph.
First published in paperback 1978 by Pan Books.
Dead Cert first published 1962 by Michael Joseph.
First published in paperback 1972 by Penguin.
First published by Pan Books 1976.

This omnibus first published 2005 by Pan Books
an imprint of Pan Macmillan Ltd
Pan Macmillan, 20 New Wharf Road, London N1 9RR
Basingstoke and Oxford
Associated companies throughout the world
www.panmacmillan.com

ISBN 0 330 44373 9

1 3 5 7 9 8 6 4 2

A CIP catalogue record for this book is available from
the British Library.

Printed and bound in Great Britain by
Mackays of Chatham plc, Chatham, Kent

IN THE FRAME

My thanks to two professional artists Michael Jeffrey of Australia and Josef Jira of Czechoslovakia who generously showed me their studios, their methods, their minds and their lives.

Also to the many art galleries whose experts gave me information and help and particularly to Peter Johnson of Oscar and Peter Johnson, London SW1, and to the Stud and Stable Gallery, Ascot.

for Caroline
sound asleep

IN THE FRAME

[INTRODUCTION]

In the Frame was conceived in Czechoslovakia, incubated in Australia and New Zealand and written in England.

We (my wife, Mary, and I) were with the remarkable lady burns-specialist doctor who translates my books into the Czech language in her spare time, when she had business to attend to with a painter friend of hers. She took us briefly to his studio, where our eyes and emotions were bombarded by massed canvases of extraordinary passion and vigorous jumbled colour, chiefly on the subject – if deciphering were possible – of the feeding of the multitude with five fishes. As the painter spoke no English nor we a word of Czech, asking for meaning was impracticable, especially as (according to my translator) he couldn't explain them to her either.

We visited her apartment and found another of his paintings on her wall: again the fishes, the thick brilliant and dark colours, the unfathomable urgent mysterious message.

I began unexpectedly to want to write about a painter, and I asked if we could go back and watch him work. To my translator's surprise he agreed, and for two fascinating silent hours the three of us watched him sticking paint on to canvas with a sort of violent divine energy, using brushes, fingers and even at one point his elbow to satisfy his vision.

I came away shaken. I couldn't imagine being *him*. I needed a less driven artist for my protagonist. I thought I could manage a painter of horses.

Later that year we went to Australia and New Zealand on a book-promotion tour, and there – arranged in advance – I met Michael Jeffrey, one of Australia's foremost horse painters. He, too, generously let me into his studio and gave great advice about the use and mixing of colours.

Back home in England, Mary and I read books about the chemical composition of oil paints and how they adhere to wood and canvas, and we filled our sunroom with easels, linseed, turps and other tools of the trade. Primed by this little knowledge, I put Charles Todd to paper as a painter of horses, alongside the flamboyant abstract genius of his long-time friend, Jik.

Mary finally painted a horse. Its neck was too long. We both learned we were never destined to be artists ourselves, but, nevertheless, *In the Frame* taught us a lot about Art.

CHAPTER ONE

I stood on the outside of disaster, looking in.

There were three police cars outside my cousin's house, and an ambulance with its blue turret light revolving ominously, and people bustling in seriously through his open front door. The chill wind of early autumn blew dead brown leaves sadly on to the driveway, and harsh scurrying clouds threatened worse to come. Six o'clock, Friday evening, Shropshire, England.

Intermittent bright white flashes from the windows spoke of photography in progress within. I slid my satchel from my shoulder and dumped both it and my suitcase on the grass verge, and with justifiable foreboding completed my journey to the house.

I had travelled by train to stay for the weekend. No cousin with car to meet me as promised, so I had started to walk the mile and a half of country road, sure he would come tearing along soon in his muddy Peugeot, full of jokes and apologies and plans.

No jokes.

He stood in the hall, dazed and grey. His body inside

1

his neat business suit looked limp, and his arms hung straight down from the shoulders as if his brain had forgotten they were there. His head was turned slightly towards the sitting-room, the source of the flashes, and his eyes were stark with shock.

'Don?' I said. I walked towards him. 'Donald!'

He didn't hear me. A policeman, however, did. He came swiftly from the sitting-room in his dark blue uniform, took me by the arm and swung me strongly and unceremoniously back towards the door.

'Out of here, sir,' he said. 'If you please.'

The strained eyes slid uncertainly our way.

'Charles . . .' His voice was hoarse.

The policeman's grip loosened very slightly. 'Do you know this man, sir?' he asked Donald.

'I'm his cousin,' I said.

'Oh.' He took his hand off, told me to stay where I was and look after Mr Stuart, and returned to the sitting-room to consult.

'What's happened?' I said.

Don was past answering. His head turned again towards the sitting-room door, drawn to a horror he could no longer see. I disobeyed the police instructions, took ten quiet steps, and looked in.

The familiar room was unfamiliarly bare. No pictures, no ornaments, no edge-to-edge floor covering of oriental rugs. Just bare grey walls, chintz-covered sofas, heavy furniture pushed awry, and a great expanse of dusty wood-block flooring.

And on the floor, my cousin's young wife, bloody and dead.

The big room was scattered with busy police, measuring, photographing, dusting for fingerprints. I knew they were there; didn't see them. All I saw was Regina lying on her back, her face the colour of cream.

Her eyes were half open, still faintly bright, and her lower jaw had fallen loose, outlining brutally the shape of the skull. A pool of urine lay wetly on the parquet around her sprawled legs, and one arm was flung out sideways with the dead white fingers curling upwards as if in supplication.

There had been no mercy.

I looked at the scarlet mess of her head and felt the blood draining from my own.

The policeman who had grabbed me before turned round from his consultation with another, saw me swaying in the doorway, and took quick annoyed strides back to my side.

'I told you to wait outside, sir,' he said with exasperation, stating clearly that my faintness was my own fault.

I nodded dumbly and went back into the hall. Donald was sitting on the stairs, looking at nothing. I sat abruptly on the floor near him and put my head between my knees.

'I . . . f . . . found . . . her,' he said.

I swallowed. What could one say? It was bad enough for me, but he had lived with her, and loved her. The faintness passed away slowly, leaving a sour feeling of sickness. I leaned back against the wall behind me and wished I knew how to help him.

'She's . . . never . . . home . . . on F . . . Fridays,' he said.

'I know.'

'S . . . six. S . . . six o'clock . . . she comes b . . . back. Always.'

'I'll get you some brandy,' I said.

'She shouldn't . . . have been . . . here . . .'

I pushed myself off the floor and went into the dining-room, and it was there that the significance of the bare sitting-room forced itself into consciousness. In the dining-room too there were bare walls, bare shelves, and empty drawers pulled out and dumped on the floor. No silver ornaments. No silver spoons or forks. No collection of antique china. Just a jumble of table mats and napkins and broken glass.

My cousin's house had been burgled. And Regina . . . Regina, who was never home on Fridays . . . had walked in . . .

I went over to the plundered sideboard, flooding with anger and wanting to smash in the heads of all greedy, callous, vicious people who cynically devastated the lives of total strangers. Compassion was all right for saints. What I felt was plain hatred, fierce and basic.

I found two intact glasses, but all the drink had gone. Furiously I stalked through the swing door into the kitchen and filled the electric kettle.

In that room too, the destruction had continued, with stores swept wholesale off the shelves. What valuables, I wondered, did thieves expect to find in kitchens? I jerkily made two mugs of tea and rummaged in Regina's spice cupboard for the cooking brandy, and felt unreasonably triumphant when it proved to be still there. The sods had missed that, at least.

Donald still sat unmoving on the stairs. I pressed the cup of strong sweet liquid into his hands and told him to drink, and he did, mechanically.

'She's never home ... on Fridays,' he said.

'No,' I agreed, and wondered just how many people knew there was no one home on Fridays.

We both slowly finished the tea. I took his mug and put it with mine on the floor, and sat near him as before. Most of the hall furniture had gone. The small Sheraton desk ... the studded leather chair ... the nineteenth-century carriage clock ...

'Christ, Charles,' he said.

I glanced at his face. There were tears, and dreadful pain. I could do nothing, nothing, to help him.

The impossible evening lengthened to midnight, and beyond. The police, I suppose, were efficient, polite, and not unsympathetic, but they left a distinct impression that they felt their job was to catch criminals, not to succour the victims. It seemed to me that there was also, in many of their questions, a faint hovering doubt, as if it were not unknown for householders to arrange their own well-insured burglaries, and for smooth-seeming swindles to go horrifically wrong.

Donald didn't seem to notice. He answered wearily, automatically, with long pauses sometimes between question and answer.

Yes, the missing goods were well insured.

Yes, they had been insured for years.

Yes, he had been to his office all day as usual.

Yes, he had been out to lunch. A sandwich in a pub.

He was a wine shipper.

His office was in Shrewsbury.

He was thirty-seven years old.

Yes, his wife was much younger. Twenty-two.

He couldn't speak of Regina without stuttering, as if his tongue and lips were beyond his control. She always s . . . spends F . . . Fridays . . . working . . . in a f . . . friend's . . . flower . . . shop.

'Why?'

Donald looked vaguely at the Detective Inspector, sitting opposite him across the dining-room table. The matched antique dining chairs had gone. Donald sat in a garden armchair brought from the sunroom. The Inspector, a constable and I sat on kitchen stools.

'What?'

'Why did she work in a flower shop on Fridays?'

'She . . . she . . . I . . . likes . . .'

I interrupted brusquely. 'She was a florist before she

married Donald. She liked to keep her hand in. She used to spend Fridays making those table arrangement things for dances and weddings and things like that . . .'

And wreaths, too, I thought, and couldn't say it.

'Thank you, sir, but I'm sure Mr Stuart can answer for himself.'

'And I'm sure he can't.'

The Detective Inspector diverted his attention my way.

'He's too shocked,' I said.

'Are you a doctor, sir?' His voice held polite disbelief, which it was entitled to, no doubt. I shook my head impatiently. He glanced at Donald, pursed his lips, and turned back to me. His gaze wandered briefly over my jeans, faded denim jacket, fawn polo-neck, and desert boots, and returned to my face, unimpressed.

'Very well, sir. Name?'

'Charles Todd.'

'Age?'

'Twenty-nine.'

'Occupation?'

'Painter.'

The constable unemotionally wrote down these scintillating details in his pocket-sized notebook.

'Houses or pictures?' asked the Inspector.

'Pictures.'

'And your movements today, sir?'

'Caught the two-thirty from Paddington and walked from the local station.'

'Purpose of visit?'

'Nothing special. I come here once or twice a year.'

'Good friends, then?'

'Yes.'

He nodded non-committally. Turned his attention again to Donald and asked more questions, but patiently and without pressure.

'And what time do you normally reach home on Fridays, sir?'

Don said tonelessly, 'Five. About.'

'And today?'

'Same.' A spasm twitched the muscles of his face. 'I saw . . . the house had been broken into . . . I telephoned . . .'

'Yes, sir. We received your call at six minutes past five. And after you had telephoned, you went into the sitting-room, to see what had been stolen?'

Donald didn't answer.

'Our sergeant found you there, sir, if you remember.'

'*Why?*' Don said in anguish. 'Why did she come home?'

'I expect we'll find out, sir.'

The careful exploratory questions went on and on, and as far as I could see achieved nothing except to bring Donald ever closer to all-out breakdown.

I, with a certain amount of shame, grew ordinarily hungry, having not bothered to eat earlier in the day. I thought with regret of the dinner I had been looking forward to, with Regina tossing in unmeasured ingredients and herbs and wine and casually producing a gourmet feast. Regina with her cap of dark hair and ready smile, chatty and frivolous and anti-blood-sports. A harmless girl, come to harm.

At some point during the evening her body was loaded into the ambulance and driven away. I heard it happen, but Donald gave no sign of interpreting the sounds. I thought that probably his mind was raising barriers against the unendurable, and one couldn't blame him.

The Inspector rose finally and stretched the kinks caused by the kitchen stool out of legs and spine. He said he would be leaving a constable on duty at the house all night, and that he would return himself in the morning. Donald nodded vaguely, having obviously not listened properly to a word, and when the police had gone still sat like an automaton in the chair, with no energy to move.

'Come on,' I said. 'Let's go to bed.'

I took his arm, persuaded him to his feet, and steered him up the stairs. He came in a daze, unprotesting.

His and Regina's bedroom was a shambles, but the twin-bedded room prepared for me was untouched. He flopped full-length in his clothes and put his arm up over his eyes, and in appalling distress asked the unanswerable question of all the world's sufferers.

'*Why?* Why did it have to happen to *us*?'

I stayed with Donald for a week, during which time some questions, but not that one, were answered.

One of the easiest was the reason for Regina's premature return home. She and the flower-shop friend, who had been repressing annoyance with each other for weeks, had erupted into a quarrel of enough bitterness to make Regina leave at once. She had driven away at about two-thirty, and had probably gone straight home, as it was considered she had been dead for at least two hours by five o'clock.

This information, expressed in semi-formal sentences, was given to Donald by the Detective Inspector on Saturday afternoon. Donald walked out into the autumnal garden and wept.

The Inspector, Frost by name and cool by nature, came quietly into the kitchen and stood beside me watching Donald with his bowed head among the apple trees.

'I would like you to tell me what you can about the relationship between Mr and Mrs Stuart.'

'You'd like *what*?'

'How did they get on?'

'Can't you tell for yourself?'

He answered neutrally after a pause. 'The intensity of grief shown is not always an accurate indication of the intensity of love felt.'

'Do you always talk like that?'

A faint smile flickered and died. 'I was quoting from a book on psychology.'

' "Not always" means it usually is,' I said.

He blinked.

'Your book is bunk,' I said.

'Guilt and remorse can manifest themselves in an excess of mourning.'

'Dangerous bunk,' I added. 'And as far as I could see, the honeymoon was by no means over.'

'After three years?'

'Why not?'

He shrugged and didn't answer. I turned away from the sight of Donald and said, 'What are the chances of getting back any of the stuff from this house?'

'Small, I should think. Where antiques are involved, the goods are likely to be halfway across the Atlantic before the owner returns from his holidays.'

'Not this time, though,' I objected.

He sighed. 'Next best thing. There have been hundreds of similar break-ins during recent years and very little has been recovered. Antiques are big business these days.'

'Connoisseur thieves?' I said sceptically.

'The prison library service reports that all their most requested books are on antiques. All the little chummies boning up to jump on the bandwagon as soon as they get out.'

He sounded suddenly quite human. 'Like some coffee?' I said.

He looked at his watch, raised his eyebrows, and accepted. He sat on a kitchen stool while I fixed the

11

mugs, a fortyish man with thin sandy hair and a well-worn grey suit.

'Are you married?' he asked.

'Nope.'

'In love with Mrs Stuart?'

'You do try it on, don't you?'

'If you don't ask, you don't find out.'

I put the milk bottle and a sugar basin on the table and told him to help himself. He stirred his coffee reflectively.

'When did you visit this house last?' he said.

'Last March. Before they went off to Australia.'

'Australia?'

'They went to see the vintage there. Donald had some idea of shipping Australian wine over in bulk. They were away for at least three months. Why didn't their house get robbed *then*, when they were safely out of the way?'

He listened to the bitterness in my voice. 'Life is full of nasty ironies.' He pursed his lips gingerly to the hot coffee, drew back, and blew gently across the top of the mug. 'What would you all have been doing today? In the normal course of events?'

I had to think what day it was. Saturday. It seemed totally unreal.

'Going to the races,' I said. 'We always go to the races when I come to stay.'

'Fond of racing, were they?' The past tense sounded

wrong. Yet so much was now past. I found it a great deal more difficult than he did, to change gear.

'Yes . . . but I think they only go . . . went . . . because of me.'

He tried the coffee again and managed a cautious sip. 'In what way do you mean?' he asked.

'What I paint,' I said, 'is mostly horses.'

Donald came in through the back door, looking red-eyed and exhausted.

'The Press are making a hole in the hedge,' he said leadenly.

Inspector Frost clicked his teeth, got to his feet, opened the door to the hall and the interior of the house, and called out loudly.

'Constable? Go and stop those reporters from breaking into the garden.'

A distant voice replied 'Sir', and Frost apologized to Donald. 'Can't get rid of them entirely, you know, sir. They have their editors breathing down their necks. They pester the life out of us at times like these.'

All day long the road outside Donald's house had been lined with cars, which disgorged crowds of reporters, photographers and plain sensation-seekers every time anyone went out of the front door. Like a hungry wolf pack they lay in wait, and I supposed that they would eventually pounce on Donald himself. Regard for his feelings was nowhere in sight.

'Newspapers listen to the radio on the police frequencies,' Frost said gloomily. 'Sometimes the Press arrive at the scene of a crime before we can get there ourselves.'

At any other time I would have laughed, but it wouldn't have been much fun for Donald if it had happened in his case. The police, of course, had thought at first that it more or less had, because I had heard that the constable who had tried to eject me forcibly had taken me for a spearheading scribbler.

Donald sat down heavily on a stool and rested his elbows wearily on the table.

'Charles,' he said, 'if you wouldn't mind heating it, I'd like some of that soup now.'

'Sure,' I said, surprised. He had rejected it earlier as if the thought of food revolted him.

Frost's head went up as if at a signal, and his whole body straightened purposefully, and I realized he had merely been coasting along until then, waiting for some such moment. He waited some more while I opened a can of Campbell's condensed, sloshed it and some water and cooking brandy into a saucepan, and stirred until the lumps dissolved. He drank his coffee and waited while Donald disposed of two platefuls and a chunk of brown bread. Then, politely, he asked me to take myself off, and when I'd gone he began what Donald afterwards referred to as 'serious digging'.

It was three hours later, and growing dark, when the Inspector left. I watched his departure from the upstairs landing window. He and his attendant plain-clothes constable were intercepted immediately outside the front door by a young man with wild hair and a microphone, and before they could dodge round him to reach their car the pack on the road were streaming in full cry into the garden and across the grass.

I went methodically round the house drawing curtains, checking windows, and locking and bolting all the outside doors.

'What are you doing?' Donald asked, looking pale and tired in the kitchen.

'Pulling up the drawbridge.'

'Oh.'

In spite of his long session with the Inspector he seemed a lot calmer and more in command of himself, and when I had finished Fort-Knoxing the kitchen-to-garden door he said, 'The police want a list of what's gone. Will you help me make it?'

'Of course.'

'It'll give us something to do . . .'

'Sure.'

'We did have an inventory, but it was in that desk in the hall. The one they took.'

'Damn silly place to keep it,' I said.

'That's more or less what *he* said. Inspector Frost.'

'What about your insurance company? Haven't they got a list?'

'Only of the more valuable things, like some of the paintings, and her jewellery.' He sighed. 'Everything else was lumped together as "contents".'

We started on the dining-room and made reasonable

progress, with him putting the empty drawers back in the sideboard while trying to remember what each had once contained, and me writing down to his dictation. There had been a good deal of solid silver tableware, acquired by Donald's family in its affluent past and handed down routinely. Donald, with his warmth for antiques, had enjoyed using it, but his pleasure in owning it seemed to have vanished with the goods. Instead of being indignant over its loss, he sounded impersonal, and by the time we had finished the sideboard, decidedly bored.

Faced by the ranks of empty shelves where once had stood a fine collection of early nineteenth-century porcelain, he baulked entirely.

'What does it matter?' he said drearily, turning away. 'I simply can't be bothered . . .'

'How about the paintings, then?'

He looked vaguely round the bare walls. The site of each missing frame showed unmistakably in lighter oblong patches of palest olive. In this room they had mostly been works of modern British painters: a Hockney, a Bratby, two Lowrys, and a Spear for openers, all painted on what one might call the artists' less exuberant days. Donald didn't like paintings which he said 'jumped off the wall and made a fuss'.

'You probably remember them better than I do,' he said. 'You do it.'

'I'd miss some.'

'Is there anything to drink?'

16

'Only the cooking brandy,' I said.

'We could have some of the wine.'

'What wine?'

'In the cellar.' His eyes suddenly opened wide. 'Good God, I'd forgotten about the cellar.'

'I didn't even know you had one.'

He nodded. 'Reason I bought the house. Perfect humidity and temperature for long-term storage. There's a small fortune down there in claret and port.'

There wasn't, of course. There were three floor-to-ceiling rows of empty racks, and a single cardboard box on a plain wooden table.

Donald merely shrugged. 'Oh well . . . that's that.'

I opened the top of the cardboard box and saw the elegant corked shapes of the tops of wine bottles.

'They've left these, anyway,' I said. 'In their rush.'

'Probably on purpose,' Don smiled twistedly. 'That's Australian wine. We brought it back with us.'

'Better than nothing,' I said disparagingly, pulling out a bottle and reading the label.

'Better than most, you know. A lot of Australian wine is superb.'

I carried the whole case up to the kitchen and dumped it on the table. The stairs from the cellar led up into the utility room among the washing machines and other domesticities, and I had always had an unclear impression that its door was just another cupboard. I looked at it thoughtfully, an unremarkable white painted panel merging inconspicuously into the general scenery.

'Do you think the burglars *knew* the wine was there?' I asked.

'God knows.'

'I would never have found it.'

'You're not a burglar, though.'

He searched for a corkscrew, opened one of the bottles, and poured the deep red liquid into two kitchen tumblers. I tasted it and it was indeed a marvellous wine, even to my untrained palate. *Wynn's Coonawarra Cabernet Sauvignon.* You could wrap the name round the tongue as lovingly as the product. Donald drank his share absent-mindedly as if it were water, the glass clattering once or twice against his teeth. There was still an uncertainty about many of his movements, as if he could not quite remember how to do things, and I knew it was because with half his mind he thought all the time of Regina, and the thoughts were literally paralysing.

The old Donald had been a man of confidence, capably running a middle-sized inherited business and adding his share to the passed-on goodies. He had a blunt uncompromising face lightened by amber eyes which smiled easily, and he had considered his money well spent on shapely haircuts.

The new Donald was a tentative man shattered with shock, a man trying to behave decently but unsure where his feet were when he walked upstairs.

18

We spent the evening in the kitchen, talking desultorily, eating a scratch meal, and tidying all the stores back on to the shelves. Donald made a good show of being busy but put half the tins back upside down.

The front door bell rang three times during the evening but never in the code pre-arranged with the police. The telephone, with its receiver lying loose beside it, rang not at all. Donald had turned down several offers of refuge with local friends and visibly shook at the prospect of talking to anyone but Frost and me.

'Why don't they go away?' he said despairingly, after the third attempt on the front door.

'They will, once they've seen you,' I said. And sucked you dry, and spat out the husk, I thought.

He shook his head tiredly. 'I simply can't.'

It felt like living through a siege.

We went eventually again upstairs to bed, although it seemed likely that Donald would sleep no more than the night before, which had been hardly at all. The police surgeon had left knock-out pills, which Donald wouldn't take. I pressed him again on that second evening, with equal non-results.

'No, Charles. I'd feel I'd deserted her. D . . . ducked out. Thought only of myself, and not of . . . of how awful it was for her . . . dying like that . . . with n . . . no one near who l . . . loved her.'

He was trying to offer her in some way the comfort

19

of his own pain. I shook my head at him, but tried no more with the pills.

'Do you mind,' he said diffidently, 'if I sleep alone tonight?'

'Of course not.'

'We could make up a bed for you in one of the other rooms.'

'Sure.'

He pulled open the linen-cupboard door on the upstairs landing and gestured indecisively at the contents. 'Could you manage?'

'Of course,' I said.

He turned away and seemed struck by one particular adjacent patch of empty wall.

'They took the Munnings,' he said.

'What Munnings?'

'We bought it in Australia. I hung it just there ... only a week ago. I wanted you to see it. It was one of the reasons I asked you to come.'

'I'm sorry,' I said. Inadequate words.

'Everything,' he said helplessly. 'Everything's gone.'

CHAPTER TWO

Frost arrived tirelessly again on Sunday morning with his quiet watchful eyes and non-committal manner. I opened the front door to his signal, and he followed me through to the kitchen, where Donald and I seemed to have taken up permanent residence. I gestured him to a stool, and he sat on it, straightening his spine to avoid future stiffness.

'Two pieces of information you might care to have, sir,' he said to Donald, his voice at its most formal. 'Despite our intensive investigation of this house during yesterday and the previous evening, we have found no fingerprints for which we cannot account.'

'Would you expect to?' I asked.

He flicked me a glance. 'No, sir. Professional house-breakers always wear gloves.'

Donald waited with a grey patient face, as if he would find whatever Frost said unimportant. Nothing, I judged, was of much importance to Donald any more.

'Second,' said Frost, 'our investigations in the district

reveal that a removal van was parked outside your front door early on Friday afternoon.'

Donald looked at him blankly.

'Dark-coloured, and dusty, sir.'

'Oh,' Donald said, meaninglessly.

Frost sighed. 'What do you know of a bronze statuette of a horse, sir? A horse rearing up on its hind legs?'

'It's in the hall,' Donald said automatically; and then, frowning slightly, 'I mean, it used to be. It's gone.'

'How do you know about it?' I asked Frost curiously, and guessed the answer before I'd finished the question. 'Oh no . . .' I stopped, and swallowed. 'I mean, perhaps you found it . . . fallen off the van . . .?'

'No, sir.' His face was calm. 'We found it in the sitting-room, near Mrs Stuart.'

Donald understood as clearly as I had done. He stood up abruptly and went to the window, and stared out for a while at the empty garden.

'It is heavy,' he said at last. 'The base of it.'

'Yes, sir.'

'It must have been . . . quick.'

'Yes, sir,' Frost said again, sounding more objective than comforting.

'P . . . poor Regina.' The words were quiet, the desolation immense. When he came back to the table, his hands were trembling. He sat down heavily and stared into space.

Frost started another careful speech about the sitting-room being kept locked by the police for a few days yet and please would neither of us try to go in there.

Neither of us would.

Apart from that, they had finished their enquiries at the house, and Mr Stuart was at liberty to have the other rooms cleaned, if he wished, where the finger-print dust lay greyish-white on every polished surface.

Mr Stuart gave no sign of having heard.

Had Mr Stuart completed the list of things stolen?

I passed it over. It still consisted only of the dining-room silver and what I could remember of the paintings. Frost raised his eyebrows and pursed his lips.

'We'll need more than this, sir.'

'We'll try again today,' I promised. 'There's a lot of wine missing, as well.'

'Wine?'

I showed him the empty cellar and he came up looking thoughtful.

'It must have taken hours to move that lot,' I said.

'Very likely, sir,' he said primly.

Whatever he was thinking, he wasn't telling. He suggested instead that Donald should prepare a short statement to read to the hungry reporters still waiting outside, so that they could go away and print it.

'No,' Don said.

'Just a short statement,' Frost said reasonably. 'We can prepare it here and now, if you like.'

He wrote it himself, more or less, and I guessed it

was as much for his own sake as Donald's that he wanted the Press to depart, as it was he who had to push through them every time. He repeated the statement aloud when he had finished. It sounded like a police account, full of jargon, but because of that so distant from Donald's own raw grief that my cousin agreed in the end to read it out.

'But no photographs,' he said anxiously, and Frost said he would see to it.

They crowded into the hall, a collection of dry-eyed fact-finders, all near the top of their digging profession and inured from sensitivity by a hundred similar intrusions into tragedy. Sure, they were sorry for the guy whose wife had been bashed, but news was news and bad news sold papers, and if they didn't produce the goods they'd lose their jobs to others more tenacious. The Press Council had stopped the brutal bullying of the past, but the leeway still allowed could be a great deal too much for the afflicted.

Donald stood on the stairs, with Frost and myself at the foot, and read without expression, as if the words applied to someone else.

'... I returned to the house at approximately five p.m. and observed that during my absence a considerable number of valuable objects had been removed ... I telephoned immediately for assistance ... My wife, who was normally absent from the house on Fridays, returned unexpectedly ... and, it is presumed, disturbed the intruders.'

He stopped. The reporters dutifully wrote down the stilted words and looked disillusioned. One of them, clearly elected by pre-arrangement, started asking questions for them all, in a gentle, coaxing, sympathetic tone of voice.

'Could you tell us which of these closed doors is the one to the room where your wife . . .'

Donald's eyes slid briefly despite himself towards the sitting-room. All the heads turned, the eyes studied the uninformative white painted panels, the pencils wrote.

'And could you tell us what exactly was stolen?'

'Silver. Paintings.'

'Who were the paintings by?'

Donald shook his head and began to look even paler.

'Could you tell us how much they were worth?'

After a pause Don said, 'I don't know.'

'Were they insured?'

'Yes.'

'How many bedrooms are there in your house?'

'What?'

'How many bedrooms?'

Donald looked bewildered. 'I suppose . . . five.'

'Do you think you could tell us anything about your wife? About her character, and about her job? And could you let us have a photograph?'

Donald couldn't. He shook his head and said, 'I'm sorry,' and turned and walked steadily away upstairs.

'That's all,' Frost said with finality.

'It's not much,' they grumbled.

'What do you want? Blood?' Frost said, opening the front door and encouraging them out. 'Put yourselves in his position.'

'Yeah,' they said cynically; but they went.

'Did you see their eyes?' I said. 'Sucking it all in?'

Frost smiled faintly. 'They'll write long stories from that little lot.'

The interview, however, produced to a great extent the desired results. Most of the cars departed, and the rest, I supposed, would follow as soon as fresher news broke.

'Why did they ask about the bedrooms?' I said.

'To estimate the value of the house.'

'Good grief.'

'They'll all get it different.' Frost was near to amusement. 'They always do.' He looked up the stairs in the direction Donald had taken, and, almost casually, said, 'Is your cousin in financial difficulties?'

I knew his catch-them-off-guard technique by now.

'I wouldn't think so,' I said unhurriedly. 'You'd better ask him.'

'I will, sir.' He switched his gaze sharply to my face and studied my lack of expression. 'What do you know?'

I said calmly, 'Only that the police have suspicious minds.'

He disregarded that. 'Is Mr Stuart worried about his business?'

'He's never said so.'

'A great many middle-sized private companies are going bankrupt these days.'

'So I believe.'

'Because of cash flow problems,' he added.

'I can't help you. You'll have to look at his company's books.'

'We will, sir.'

'And even if the firm turns out to be bust, it doesn't follow that Donald would fake a robbery.'

'It's been done before,' Frost said dryly.

'If he needed money he could simply have sold the stuff,' I pointed out.

'Maybe he had. Some of it. Most of it, maybe.'

I took a slow breath and said nothing.

'That wine, sir. As you said yourself, it would have taken a long time to move.'

'The firm is a limited company,' I said. 'If it went bankrupt, Donald's own house and private money would be unaffected.'

'You know a good deal about it, don't you?'

I said neutrally, 'I live in the world.'

'I thought artists were supposed to be unworldly.'

'Some are.'

He peered at me with narrowed eyes as if he were trying to work out a possible way in which I too might have conspired to arrange the theft.

27

I said mildly, 'My cousin Donald is an honourable man.'

'That's an out-of-date word.'

'There's quite a lot of it about.'

He looked wholly disbelieving. He saw far too much in the way of corruption, day in, day out, all his working life.

Donald came hesitantly down the stairs and Frost took him off immediately to another private session in the kitchen. I thought that if Frost's questions were to be as barbed as those he'd asked me, poor Don was in for a rough time. While they talked I wandered aimlessly round the house, looking into storage spaces, opening cupboards, seeing the inside details of my cousin's life.

Either he or Regina had been a hoarder of empty boxes. I came across dozens of them, all shapes and sizes, shoved into odd corners of shelves or drawers: brown cardboard, bright gift-wrap, beribboned chocolate boxes, all too potentially useful or too pretty to be thrown away. The burglars had opened a lot but had thrown more unopened on the floor. They must, I thought, have had a most frustrating time.

They had largely ignored the big sunroom, which held few antiques and no paintings, and I ended up there sitting on a bamboo armchair among sprawling potted plants looking out into the windy garden. Dead leaves blew in scattered showers from the drying trees and a few late roses clung hardily to thorny stems.

I hated autumn. The time of melancholy, the time of death. My spirits fell each year with the soggy leaves and revived only with crisp winter frost. Psychiatric statistics proved that the highest suicide rate occurred in the spring, the time for rebirth and growth and stretching in the sun. I could never understand it. If ever I jumped over a cliff, it would be in the depressing months of decay.

The sunroom was grey and cold. No sun, that Sunday.

I went upstairs, fetched my suitcase, and brought it down. Over years of wandering journeys I had reversed the painter's traditional luggage: my suitcase now contained the tools of my trade, and my satchel, clothes. The large toughened suitcase, its interior adapted and fitted by me, was in fact a sort of portable studio, containing besides paints and brushes a light collapsible metal easel, unbreakable containers of linseed oil and turpentine, and a rack which would hold four wet paintings safely apart. There were also a dust sheet, a large box of tissues and generous amounts of white spirit, all designed for preventing mess and keeping things clean. The organization of the suitcase had saved and made the price of many a sandwich.

I untelescoped the easel and set out my palette, and on a middling-sized canvas laid out the beginnings of a melancholy landscape, a mixture of Donald's garden as I saw it, against a sweep of bare fields and gloomy woods. Not my usual sort of picture, and not, to be honest, the sort to make headline news a century hence; but it gave me at least something to do. I worked steadily, growing ever colder, until the chillier Frost chose to depart; and he went without seeing me again, the front door closing decisively on his purposeful footsteps.

Donald, in the warm kitchen, looked torn to rags. When I went in he was sitting with his arms folded on the table and his head on his arms, a picture of absolute despair. When he heard me he sat up slowly and wearily, and showed a face suddenly aged and deeply lined.

'Do you know what he thinks?' he said.

'More or less.'

He stared at me sombrely. 'I couldn't convince him. He kept on and on. Kept asking the same questions, over and over. Why doesn't he believe me?'

'A lot of people lie to the police. I think they grow to expect it.'

'He wants me to meet him in my office tomorrow. He says he'll be bringing colleagues. He says they'll want to see the books.'

I nodded. 'Better be grateful he didn't drag you down there today.'

'I suppose so.'

I said awkwardly, 'Don, I'm sorry. I told him the wine was missing. It made him suspicious ... It was a good deal my fault that he was so bloody to you.'

He shook his head tiredly. 'I would have told him myself. I wouldn't have thought of not telling him.'

'But . . . I even pointed out that it must have taken a fair time to move so many bottles.'

'Mm. Well, he would have worked that out for himself.'

'How long, in fact, do you think it would have taken?'

'Depends how many people were doing it,' he said, rubbing his hand over his face and squeezing his tired eyes. 'They would have to have had proper wine boxes in any case. That means they had to know in advance that the wine was there, and didn't just chance on it. And that means . . . Frost says . . . that I sold it myself some time ago and am now saying it is stolen so I can claim fraudulent insurance, or, if it was stolen last Friday, that I told the thieves they'd need proper boxes, which means that I set up the whole frightful mess myself.'

We thought it over in depressed silence. Eventually, I said, 'Who *did* know you had the wine there? And who knew the house was always empty on Fridays? And was the prime target the wine, the antiques, or the paintings?'

'God, Charles, you sound like Frost.'

'Sorry.'

'Every business nowadays,' he said defensively, 'is going through a cash crisis. Look at the nationalized industries, losing money by the million. Look at the wage rises and the taxes and the inflation . . . How can any small business make the profit it used to? Of *course* we have a cash flow problem. Whoever hasn't?'

'How bad is yours?' I said.

'Not critical. Bad enough. But not within sight of liquidation. It's illegal for a limited company to carry on trading if it can't cover its costs.'

'But it could . . . if you could raise more capital to prop it up?'

He surveyed me with the ghost of a smile. 'It surprises me still that you chose to paint for a living.'

'It gives me a good excuse to go racing whenever I like.'

'Lazy sod.' He sounded for a second like the old Donald, but the lightness passed. 'The absolutely last thing I would do would be to use my own personal assets to prop up a dying business. If my firm was that rocky, I'd wind it up. It would be mad not to.'

I sucked my teeth. 'I suppose Frost asked if the stolen things were insured for more than their worth?'

'Yes, he did. Several times.'

'Not likely you'd tell him, even if they were.'

'They weren't, though.'

'No.'

'Under-insured, if anything.' He sighed. 'God knows if they'll pay up for the Munnings. I'd only arranged the insurance by telephone. I hadn't actually sent the premium.'

'It should be all right, if you can give them proof of purchase, and so on.'

He shook his head listlessly. 'All the papers to do with it were in the desk in the hall. The receipt from the gallery where I bought it, the letter of provenance, and the customs and excise receipt. All gone.'

'Frost won't like that.'

'He doesn't.'

'Well . . . I hope you pointed out that you would hardly be buying expensive pictures and going on world trips if you were down to your last farthing.'

'He said it might be *because* of buying expensive pictures and going on world trips that I might be down to my last farthing.'

Frost had built a brick wall of suspicion for Donald to batter his head against. My cousin needed hauling away before he was punch drunk.

'Have some spaghetti,' I said.

'What?'

'It's about all I can cook.'

'Oh . . .' He focused unclearly on the kitchen clock. It was half past four and long past feeding time according to my stomach.

'If you like,' he said.

The police sent a car the following morning to fetch him to his ordeal in the office. He went lifelessly, having more or less made it clear over coffee that he wouldn't defend himself.

'Don, you must,' I said. 'The only way to deal with the situation is to be firm and reasonable, and decisive, and accurate. In fact, just your own self.'

He smiled faintly. 'You'd better go instead of me. I haven't the energy. And what does it matter?' His smile broke suddenly and the ravaging misery showed deeply like black water under cracked ice. 'Without Regina . . . there's no point in making money.'

'We're not talking about making money, we're talking about suspicion. If you don't defend yourself, they'll assume you can't.'

'I'm too tired. I can't be bothered. They can think what they like.'

'Don,' I said seriously, 'they'll think what you let them.'

'I don't really care,' he said dully: and that was the trouble. He really didn't.

He was gone all day. I spent it painting.

Not the sad landscape. The sunroom seemed even greyer and colder that morning, and I had no mind any more to sink into melancholy. I left the half-finished canvas on the table there and removed myself and trappings to the source of warmth. Maybe the light wasn't so good in the kitchen, but it was the only room in the house with the pulse of life.

I painted Regina standing beside her cooker, with a wooden spoon in one hand and a bottle of wine in the other. I painted the way she held her head back to smile, and I painted the smile, shiny-eyed and guileless and unmistakably happy. I painted the kitchen behind her as I literally saw it in front of my eyes, and I painted Regina herself from the clearest of inner visions. So easily did I see her that I looked up once or twice from her face on the canvas to say something to her, and was disconcerted to find only empty space. An extraordinary feeling of the real and unreal disturbingly tangled.

I seldom ever worked for more than four hours at a stretch because for one thing the actual muscular control required was tiring, and for another the concentration always made me cold and hungry; so I knocked off at around lunch-time and dug out a tin of corned beef to eat with pickles on toast, and after that went for a walk, dodging the front-gate watchers by taking to the apple trees and wriggling through the hedge.

I tramped aimlessly for a while round the scattered shapeless village, thinking about the picture and working off the burst of physical energy I often felt after the constraint of painting. More burnt umber in the folds of the kitchen curtains, I thought; and a purplish shadow on the saucepan. Regina's cream shirt needed yellow ochre under the collar, and probably a touch of green. The cooking stove needed a lot more attention, and I had broken my general rule of working the picture as a whole, background and subject pace by pace.

This time, Regina's face stood out clearly, finished except for a gloss on the lips and a line of light along inside the lower eyelids, which one couldn't do until the under paint was dry. I had been afraid of seeing her less clearly if I took too long, but because of it the picture was now out of balance and I'd have to be very careful to get the kitchen into the same key, so that the whole thing looked harmonious and natural and as if it couldn't have been any other way.

The wind was rawly cold, the sky a hurrying jumbled mass of darkening clouds. I huddled my hands inside my anorak pockets and slid back through the hedge with the first drops of rain.

The afternoon session was much shorter because of the light, and I frustratingly could not catch the right mix of colours for the tops of the kitchen fitments. Even after years of experience, what looked right on the palette looked wrong on the painting. I got it wrong three times and decided to stop.

I was cleaning the brushes when Donald came back. I heard the scrunch of the car, the slam of the doors, and, to my surprise, the ring of the front door bell. Donald had taken his keys.

I went through and opened the door. A uniformed policeman stood there, holding Don's arm. Behind, a row of watching faces gazed on hungrily. My cousin, who had looked pale before, now seemed bloodlessly white. The eyes were as lifeless as death.

'Don!' I said, and no doubt looked as appalled as I felt.

He didn't speak. The policeman leaned forward, said, 'There we are, sir,' and transferred the support of my cousin from himself to me: and it seemed to me that the action was symbolic as much as practical, because he turned immediately on his heel and methodically drove off in his waiting car.

I helped Donald inside and shut the door. I had never seen anyone in such a frightening state of disintegration.

'I asked,' he said, 'about the funeral.'

His face was stony, and his voice came out in gasps.

'They said . . .' He stopped, dragged in air, tried again. 'They said . . . no funeral.'

'Donald . . .'

'They said . . . she couldn't be buried until they had finished their enquiries. They said . . . it might be months. They said . . . they will keep her . . . refrigerated . . .'

The distress was fearful.

'They said . . .' He swayed slightly. 'They said . . . the body of a murdered person belongs to the State.'

I couldn't hold him. He collapsed at my feet in a deep and total faint.

CHAPTER THREE

For two days Donald lay in bed, and I grew to understand what was meant by prostration.

Whether he liked it or not, this time he was heavily sedated, his doctor calling morning and evening with pills and injections. No matter that I was a hopeless nurse and a worse cook, I was appointed, for lack of anyone else, to look after him.

'I want Charles,' Donald in fact told the doctor. 'He doesn't *fuss*.'

I sat with him a good deal when he was awake, seeing him struggle dazedly to face and come to terms with the horrors in his mind. He lost weight visibly, the rounded muscles of his face slackening and the contours changing to the drawn shape of illness. The grey shadows round his eyes darkened to a permanent charcoal, and all normal strength seemed to have vanished from arms and legs.

I fed us both from tins and frozen packets, reading the instructions and doing what they said. Donald thanked me punctiliously and ate what he could, but I doubt if he tasted a thing.

In between times, while he slept, I made progress with both the paintings. The sad landscape was no longer sad but merely Octoberish, with three horses standing around in a field, one of them eating grass. Pictures of this sort, easy to live with and passably expert, were my bread and butter. They sold quite well, and I normally churned one off the production line every ten days or so, knowing that they were all technique and no soul.

The portrait of Regina, though, was the best work I'd done for months. She laughed out of the canvas, alive and glowing, and to me at least seemed vividly herself. Pictures often changed as one worked on them, and day by day the emphasis in my mind had shifted, so that the kitchen background was growing darker and less distinct and Regina herself more luminous. One could still see she was cooking, but it was the girl who was important, not the act. In the end I had painted the kitchen, which was still there, as an impression, and the girl, who was not, as the reality.

I hid that picture in my suitcase whenever I wasn't working on it. I didn't want Donald to come face to face with it unawares.

Early Wednesday evening he came shakily down to the kitchen in his dressing-gown, trying to smile and pick up the pieces. He sat at the table, drinking the

Scotch I had that day imported, and watching while I cleaned my brushes and tidied the palette.

'You're always so neat,' he said.

'Paint's expensive.'

He waved a limp hand at the horse picture which stood drying on the easel. 'How much does it cost, to paint that?'

'In raw materials, about ten quid. In heat, light, rates, rent, food, Scotch and general wear and tear on the nervous system, about the amount I'd earn in a week if I chucked it in and went back to selling houses.'

'Quite a lot, then,' he said seriously.

I grinned. 'I don't regret it.'

'No. I see that.'

I finished the brushes by washing them in soap and water under the tap, pinching them into shape, and standing them upright in a jar to dry. Good brushes were at least as costly as paint.

'After the digging into the company accounts,' Donald said abruptly, 'they took me along to the police station and tried to prove that I had actually killed her myself.'

'I don't believe it!'

'They'd worked out that I could have got home at lunch-time and done it. They said there was time.'

I picked up the Scotch from the table and poured a decent-sized shot into a tumbler. Added ice.

'They must be crazy,' I said.

'There was another man, besides Frost. A superintendent. I think his name was Wall. A thin man, with fierce eyes. He never seemed to blink. Just stared and said over and over again that I'd killed her because she'd come back and found me supervising the burglary.'

'For God's sake!' I said disgustedly. 'And anyway, she didn't leave the flower shop until half past two.'

'The girl in the flower shop now says she doesn't know to the minute when Regina left. Only that it was soon after lunch. And I didn't get back from the pub until nearly three. I went to lunch late. I was hung up with a client all morning . . .' He stopped, gripping his tumbler as if it were a support to hold on to. 'I can't tell you . . . how awful it was.'

The mild understatement seemed somehow to make things worse.

'They said,' he nodded, 'that eighty per cent of murdered married women are killed by their husbands.'

That statement had Frost stamped all over it.

'They let me come home, in the end, but I don't think . . .' His voice shook. He swallowed, visibly trying to keep tight control on his hard-won calm. 'I don't think they've finished.'

It was five days since he'd walked in and found Regina dead. When I thought of the mental hammerings he'd taken on top, the punishing assault on his emotional reserves, where common humanity would have suggested kindness and consoling help, it seemed marvellous that he had remained as sane as he had.

'Have they got anywhere with catching the thieves?'
I said.

He smiled wanly. 'I don't even know if they're
trying.'

'They must be.'

'I suppose so. They haven't said.' He drank some
whisky slowly. 'It's ironic, you know. I've always had
a regard for the police. I didn't know they could
be . . . the way they are.'

A quandary, I thought. Either they leaned on a
suspect in the hope of breaking him down, or they
asked a few polite questions and got nowhere: and
under the only effective system the innocent suffered
more than the guilty.

'I see no end to it,' Donald said. 'No end at all.'

By midday Friday the police had called twice more at
the house, but for my cousin the escalation of agony
seemed to have slowed. He was still exhausted, apa-
thetic, and as grey as smoke, but it was as if he were
saturated with suffering and could absorb little more.
Whatever Frost and his companion said to him, it
rolled off without destroying him further.

'You're supposed to be painting someone's horse,
aren't you?' he said suddenly, as we shaped up to
lunch.

'I told them I'd come later.'

He shook his head. 'I remember you saying, when

I asked you to stay, that it would fit in fine before your next commission.' He thought a bit. 'Tuesday. You should have gone to Yorkshire on Tuesday.'

'I telephoned and explained.'

'All the same, you'd better go.'

He said he would be all right alone, now, and thanks for everything. He insisted I look up the times of trains, order a taxi, and alert the people at the other end. I could see in the end that the time had indeed come for him to be by himself, so I packed up my things to depart.

'I suppose,' he said diffidently, as we waited for the taxi to fetch me, 'that you never paint portraits? People, that is, not horses.'

'Sometimes,' I said.

'I just wondered . . . Could you, one day . . . I mean, I've got quite a good photograph of Regina . . .'

I looked searchingly at his face. As far as I could see, it could do no harm. I unclipped the suitcase and took out the picture with its back towards him.

'It's still wet,' I warned. 'And not framed, and I can't varnish it for at least six months. But you can have it, if you like.'

'Let me see.'

I turned the canvas round. He stared and stared, but said nothing at all. The taxi drove up to the front door.

'See you,' I said, propping Regina against a wall.

He nodded and punched my arm, opened the door

for me, and sketched a farewell wave. Speechlessly, because his eyes were full of tears.

I spent nearly a week in Yorkshire doing my best to immortalize a patient old steeplechaser, and then went home to my noisy flat near Heathrow airport, taking the picture with me to finish.

Saturday I downed tools and went to the races, fed up with too much nose-to-the-grindstone.

Jump racing at Plumpton, and the familiar swelling of excitement at the liquid movement of racehorses. Paintings could never do justice to them: never. The moment caught on canvas was always second best.

I would love to have ridden in races, but hadn't had enough practice or skill; nor, I dare say, nerve. Like Donald, my childhood background was of middlesized private enterprise, with my father an auctioneer in business on his own account in Sussex. I had spent countless hours in my growing years watching the horses train on the Downs round Findon, and had drawn and painted them from about the age of six. Riding itself had been mostly a matter of begging the wherewithal for an hour's joy from indulgent aunts, never of a pony of my own. Art school later had been fine, but at twenty-two, alone in the world with both parents newly dead, I'd had to face the need to eat. It had been a short meant-to-be-temporary step to the estate agent's across the street, but I'd liked it well enough to stay.

Half the horse painters in England seemed to have turned up at Plumpton, which was not surprising, as the latest Grand National winner was due to make his first appearance of the new season. It was a commercial fact that a picture called, for instance, *Nijinsky on Newmarket Heath* stood a much better chance of being sold than one labelled *A Horse on Newmarket Heath*, and *The Grand National Winner at the Start* won hands down over *A Runner at Plumpton Before the Off*. The economic facts of life had brought many a would-be Rembrandt down to market research.

'Todd!' said a voice in my ear. 'You owe me fifteen smackers.'

'I bloody don't,' I said.

'You said Seesaw was a certainty for Ascot.'

'Never take sweets from a stranger.'

Billy Pyle laughed extravagantly and patted me heavily on the shoulder. Billy Pyle was one of those people you met on racecourses who greeted you as a bosom pal, plied you with drinks and bonhomie, and bored you to death. On and off I'd met Billy Pyle at the races for umpteen years, and had never yet worked out how to duck him without positive rudeness. Ordinary evasions rolled off his thick skin like mercury off glass, and I found it less wearing on the whole to get the drink over quickly than dodge him all afternoon.

I waited for him to say 'how about a beverage', as he always did.

'How about a beverage?' he said.

'Er . . . sure,' I agreed, resignedly.

'Your father would never forgive me if I neglected you.' He always said that, too. They had been business acquaintances, I knew, but I suspected the reported friendship was posthumous.

'Come along, laddie.'

I knew the irritating routine by heart. He would meet his Auntie Sal in the bar, as if by accident, and in my turn I would buy them both a drink. A double brandy and ginger for Auntie Sal.

'Why, there's Auntie Sal,' Billy said, pushing through the door. Surprise, surprise.

Auntie Sal was a compulsive racegoer in her seventies with a perpetual cigarette dangling from the corner of her mouth and one finger permanently inserted in her form book, keeping her place.

'Know anything for the two-thirty?' she demanded.

'Hello,' I said.

'What? Oh, I see. Hello. How are you? Know anything for the two-thirty?'

''Fraid not.'

'Huh.'

She peered into the form book. 'Treetops is well in at the weights, but can you trust his leg?' She looked up suddenly and with her free hand prodded her nephew, who was trying to attract service from the bar. 'Billy, get a drink for Mrs Matthews.'

'Mrs Who?'

'Matthews. What do you want, Maisie?'

She turned to a large middle-aged woman who had been standing in the shadows behind her.

'Oh . . . gin and tonic, thanks.'

'Got that, Billy? Double brandy and ginger for me, gin and tonic for Mrs Matthews.'

Maisie Matthews' clothes were noticeably new and expensive, and from lacquered hair via crocodile hand-bag to gold-trimmed shoes she shouted money without saying a word. The hand which accepted the drink carried the weight of a huge opal set in diamonds. The expression on her expertly painted face showed no joy at all.

'How do you do?' I said politely.

'Eh?' said Auntie Sal. 'Oh, yes, Maisie, this is Charles Todd. What do you think of Treetops?'

'Moderate,' I said.

Auntie Sal peered worriedly into the form book and Billy handed round the drinks.

'Cheers,' Maisie Matthews said, looking cheerless.

'Down the hatch,' said Billy, raising his glass.

'Maisie's had a bit of bad luck,' Auntie Sal said.

Billy grinned. 'Backed a loser, then, Mrs Matthews?'

'Her house burned down.'

As a light conversation stopper, it was a daisy.

'Oh . . . I say . . .' said Billy uncomfortably. 'Hard luck.'

'Lost everything, didn't you, Maisie?'

'All but what I stand up in,' she agreed gloomily.

'Have another gin,' I suggested.

'Thanks, dear.'

When I returned with the refills she was in full descriptive flood.

'. . . I wasn't there, of course, I was staying with my sister Betty up in Birmingham, and there was this policeman on the doorstep telling me what a job they'd had finding me. But by that time it was all over, of course. When I got back to Worthing there was just a heap of cinders with the chimney-breast sticking up in the middle. Well, I had a real job finding out what happened, but anyway they finally said it was a flash fire, whatever that is, but they didn't know what started it, because there'd been no one in the house for two days.'

She accepted the gin, gave me a brief unseeing smile, and returned to her story.

'Well, I was spitting mad, I'll tell you, over losing everything like that, and I said why hadn't they used sea water, what with the sea being only the other side of the tamarisk and down the shingle, because of course they said they hadn't been able to save a thing because they hadn't enough water, and this fireman, the one I was complaining to, he said they couldn't use sea water because for one thing it corroded everything and for another the pumps sucked up seaweed and shells and things, and in any case the tide was out.'

I smothered an unseemly desire to laugh. She sensed it, however.

'Well, dear, it may seem funny to you, of course, but then you haven't lost all of your treasures that you'd been collecting since heaven knows when.'

'I'm really sorry, Mrs Matthews. I don't think it's funny. It was just . . .'

'Yes, well, dear. I suppose you can see the funny side of it, all that water and not a drop to put a fire out with, but I was that mad, I can tell you.'

'I think I'll have a bit on Treetops,' Auntie Sal said thoughtfully.

Maisie Matthews looked at her uncertainly and Billy Pyle, who had heard enough of disaster, broke gratefully into geniality, clapped me again on the shoulder, and said yes, it was time to see the next contest.

Duty done, I thought with a sigh, and took myself off to watch the race from the top of the stands, out of sight and earshot.

Treetops broke down and finished last, limping. Too bad for its owner, trainer, and Auntie Sal. I wandered down to the parade ring to see the Grand National winner walk round before his race, but without any thought of drawing him. I reckoned he was just about played out as a subject, and there would shortly be a glut.

The afternoon went quickly, as usual. I won a little,

49

lost a little, and filled my eyes with something better than money. On the stands for the last race, I found myself approached by Maisie Matthews. No mistaking the bright red coat, the air of gloss, and the big, kind-looking, worldly face. She drew to a halt on the step below me, looking up. Entirely self-confident, though registering doubt.

'Aren't you,' she said, 'the young man I had a drink with, with Sal and Billy?'

'Yes, that's right.'

'I wasn't sure,' she said, the doubt disappearing. 'You look older out here.'

'Different light,' I said, agreeing. She too looked older, by about ten years. Fifty-something, I thought. Bar-light always flattered.

'They said you were an artist.' Their mild disapproval coloured the way she spoke.

'Mm,' I said, watching the runners canter past on the way to the post.

'Not very well paid, is it, dear?'

I grinned at her, liking her directness. 'It depends who you are. Picasso didn't grumble.'

'How much would you charge to paint a picture for me?'

'What sort of picture?'

'Well, dear, you may say it sounds morbid and I dare say it is, but I was just thinking this morning when I went over there, and really it makes me that mad every time I see it, I was thinking actually that it makes a crazy picture, that burnt ruin with the chimney sticking up, and the burnt hedge behind and all that sea, and I was thinking of getting the local photographer who does all the weddings and things to come along and take a colour picture, because when it's all cleared away and rebuilt, no one will believe how awful it was, and I want to hang it in the new house, just to show them.'

'But . . .'

'So how much would you charge? Because I dare say you can see I am not short of the next quid but if it would be hundreds I might as well get the photographer of course.'

'Of course,' I agreed gravely. 'How about if I came to see the house, or what's left of it, and gave you an estimate?'

She saw nothing odd in that. 'All right, dear. That sounds very businesslike. Of course, it will have to be soon, though, because once the insurance people have been I am having the rubble cleared up.'

'How soon?'

'Well, dear, as you're halfway there, could you come today?'

We discussed it. She said she would drive me in her Jaguar as I hadn't a car, and I could go home by train just as easily from Worthing as from Plumpton.

So I agreed.

One takes the most momentous steps unawares.

*

The ruin was definitely paintagenic, if there is such a word. On the way there, more or less non-stop, she had talked about her late husband, Archie, who had looked after her very well, dear.

'Well, that's to say, I looked after him too, dear, because of course I was a nurse. Private, of course. I nursed his first wife all through her illness, cancer it was, dear, of course, and then I stayed on for a bit to look after him, and, well, he asked me to stay on for life, dear, and I did. Of course he was much older, he's been gone more than ten years now. He looked after me very well, Archie did.'

She glanced fondly at the huge opal. Many a man would have liked to have been remembered as kindly.

'Since he went, and left me so well off, dear, it seemed a shame not to get some fun out of it, so I carried on with what we were doing when we were together those few years, which was going round to auction sales in big houses, dear, because you pick up such nice things there, quite cheap sometimes, and of course it's ever so much more interesting when the things have belonged to someone well known or famous.' She changed gear with a jerk and aggressively passed an inoffensive little van. 'And now all those things are burnt to cinders, of course, and all the memories of Archie and the places we went together, and I'll tell you, dear, it makes me mad.'

'It's really horrid for you.'

'Yes, dear, it is.'

I reflected that it was the second time in a fortnight that I'd been cast in the role of comforter, and I felt as inadequate for her as I had for Donald.

She stamped on the brakes outside the remains of her house and rocked us to a standstill. From the opulence of the minor mansions on either side, her property had been far from a slum; but all that was left was an extensive sprawling black heap, with jagged pieces of outside wall defining its former shape, and the thick brick chimney, as she'd said, pointing sturdily skywards from the centre. Ironic, I thought fleetingly, that the fireplace alone had survived the flames.

'There you are, dear,' Maisie said. 'What do you think?'

'A very hot fire.'

She raised her pencilled eyebrows. 'But yes, dear, all fires are hot, aren't they? And of course there was a lot of wood. So many of these old seaside houses were built with a lot of wood.'

Even before we climbed out of her big pale blue car, I could smell the ash.

'How long ago . . .?' I asked.

'Last weekend, dear. Sunday.'

While we surveyed the mess for a moment in silence a man walked slowly into view from behind the chimney. He was looking down, concentrating, taking a step at a time and then bending to poke into the rubble.

Maisie, for all her scarlet-coated bulk, was nimble on her feet.

'Hey,' she called, hopping out of the car and advancing purposefully. 'What do you think you're doing?'

The man straightened up, looking startled. About forty, I judged, with a raincoat, a crisp-looking trilby and a down-turning moustache.

He raised his hat politely. 'Insurance, madam.'

'I thought you were coming on Monday.'

'I happened to be in the district. No time like the present, don't you think?'

'Well, I suppose not,' Maisie said. 'And I hope there isn't going to be any shilly-shallying over you paying up, though of course nothing is going to get my treasures back and I'd rather have them than any amount of money, as I've got plenty of that in any case.'

The man was unused to Maisie's brand of chat.

'Er . . .' he said. 'Oh yes. I see.'

'Have you found out what started it?' Maisie demanded.

'No, madam.'

'Found anything at all?'

'No, madam.'

'Well, how soon can I get all this cleared away?'

'Any time you like, madam.'

He stepped carefully towards us, picking his way round clumps of blackened debris. He had steady greyish eyes, a strong chin, and an overall air of intelligence.

'What's your name?' Maisie asked.

'Greene, madam.' He paused slightly, and added 'With an "e".'

'Well, Mr Greene with an "e",' Maisie said good-humouredly. 'I'll be glad to have all that in writing.'

He inclined his head. 'As soon as I report back.'

Maisie said, 'Good,' and Greene, lifting his hat again, wished her good afternoon and walked along to a white Ford parked a short way along the road.

'That's all right, then,' Maisie said with satisfaction, watching him go. 'Now, how much for that picture?'

'Two hundred plus two nights' expenses in a local hotel.'

'That's a bit steep, dear. *One* hundred, and two nights, and I've got to like the results, or I don't pay.'

'No foal, no fee?'

The generous red mouth smiled widely. 'That's it, dear.'

We settled on one-fifty if she liked the picture, and fifty if she didn't, and I was to start on Monday unless it was raining.

CHAPTER FOUR

Monday came up with a bright breezy day and an echo
of summer's warmth. I went to Worthing by train and
to the house by taxi, and to the interest of the neighbours set up my easel at about the place where the
front gates would have been, had they not been
unhinged and transplanted by the firemen. The gates
themselves lay flat on the lawn, one of them still
pathetically bearing a neat painted nameboard.

Treasure Holme.

Poor Archie. Poor Maisie.

I worked over the whole canvas with an unobtrusive
coffee-coloured underpainting of raw umber much
thinned with turpentine and linseed oil, and while it
was still wet drew in, with a paintbrushful of a darker
shade of the same colour, the shape of the ruined
house against the horizontals of hedges, shingle, sea
and sky. It was easy with a tissue to wipe out mistakes
of composition at that stage, and try again: to get the
proportions right, and the perspective, and the balance
of the main masses.

That done and drying, I strolled right round the whole garden, looking at the house from different angles, and staring out over the blackened stumps of the tamarisk hedge which had marked the end of the grass and the beginning of the shingle. The sea sparkled in the morning sunshine, with the small hurrying cumulus clouds scattering patches of dark slate-grey shadow. All the waves had white frills: distant, because the tide again had receded to the far side of a deserted stretch of wet-looking, wave-rippled sand.

The sea wind chilled my ears. I turned to get back to my task and saw two men in overcoats emerge from a large station wagon and show definite signs of interest in what was left of *Treasure Holme*.

I walked back towards them, reaching them where they stood by the easel appraising my handiwork.

One, heavy and fiftyish. One lean, in the twenties. Both with firm self-confident faces and an air of purpose.

The elder raised his eyes as I approached.

'Do you have permission to be here?' he asked. An enquiry; no belligerence in sight.

'The owner wants her house painted,' I said obligingly.

'I see.' His lips twitched a fraction.

'And you?' I enquired.

He raised his eyebrows slightly. 'Insurance,' he said, as if surprised that anyone should ask.

'Same company as Mr Greene?' I asked.

57

'Mr Who?'

'Greene. With an "e".'

'I don't know who you mean,' he said. 'We are here by arrangement with Mrs Matthews to inspect the damage to her house, which is insured with us.' He looked with some depression at the extent of the so-called damage, glancing about as if expecting Maisie to materialize phoenix-like from the ashes.

'No Greene?' I repeated.

'Neither with nor without an "e".'

I warmed to him. Half an ounce of a sense of humour, as far as I was concerned, achieved results where thumb-screws wouldn't.

'Well . . . Mrs Matthews is no longer expecting you, because the aforesaid Mr Greene, who said he was in insurance, told her she could roll in the demolition squad as soon as she liked.'

His attention sharpened like a tightened violin string.

'Are you serious?'

'I was here, with her. I saw him and heard him, and that's what he said.'

'Did he show you a card?'

'No, he didn't.' I paused. 'And . . . er . . . nor have you.'

He reached into an inner pocket and did so, with the speed of a conjuror. Producing cards from pockets was a reflex action, no doubt.

'Isn't it illegal to insure the same property with two companies?' I asked idly, reading the card.

FOUNDATION LIFE AND SURETY
D. J. Lagland   Area Manager

'Fraud.' He nodded.

'Unless of course Mr Greene with an "e" had nothing to do with insurance.'

'Much more likely.'

I put the card in my trouser pocket, Arran sweaters not having been designed noticeably for business transactions. He looked at me thoughtfully, his eyes observant but judgment suspended. He was the same sort of man my father had been, middle-aged, middle-of-the-road, expert at his chosen job but unlikely to set the world on fire.

Or *Treasure Holme*, for that matter.

'Gary,' he said to his younger side-kick, 'go and find a telephone and ring the Beach Hotel. Tell Mrs Matthews we're here.'

'Will do,' Gary said. He was that sort of man.

While he was away on the errand, D. J. Lagland turned his attention to the ruin, and I, as he seemed not to object, tagged along at his side.

'What do you look for?' I asked.

He shot me a sideways look. 'Evidence of arson. Evidence of the presence of the goods reported destroyed.'

'I didn't expect you to be so frank.'

'I indulge myself, occasionally.'

I grinned. 'Mrs Matthews seems pretty genuine.'

'I've never met the lady.'

Treat in store, I thought. 'Don't the firemen,' I said, 'look for signs of arson?'

'Yes, and also the police, and we ask them for guidance.'

'And what did they say?'

'None of your business, I shouldn't think.'

'Even for a wooden house,' I said, 'it is pretty thoroughly burnt.'

'Expert, are you?' he said with irony.

'I've built a lot of Guy Fawkes bonfires, in my time.'

He turned his head.

'They burn a lot better,' I said, 'if you soak them in paraffin. Especially round the edges.'

'I've been looking at fires since before you were born,' he said. 'Why don't you go over there and paint?'

'What I've done is still wet.'

'Then if you stay with me, shut up.'

I stayed with him, silent, and without offence. He was making what appeared to be a preliminary reconnaissance, lifting small solid pieces of debris, inspecting them closely, and carefully returning them to their former positions. None of the things he chose in that way were identifiable to me from a distance of six feet, and as far as I could see none of them gave him much of a thrill.

'Permission to speak?' I said.

'Well?'

'Mr Greene was doing much what you are, though in the area behind the chimney-breast.'

He straightened from replacing yet another black lump. 'Did he take anything?' he said.

'Not while we were watching, which was a very short time. No telling how long he'd been there.'

'No.' He considered. 'Wouldn't you think he was a casual sightseer, poking around out of curiosity?'

'He hadn't the air.'

D. J. frowned. 'Then what did he want?'

A rhetorical question. Gary rolled back, and soon after him, Maisie. In her Jaguar. In her scarlet coat. In a temper.

'What do you mean,' she said, advancing upon D. J. with eyes flashing fortissimo, 'the question of arson isn't yet settled? Don't tell me you're trying to wriggle out of paying my cheque, now. Your man said on Saturday that everything was all right and I could start clearing away and rebuilding, and anyway even if it had been arson you would still have to pay up because the insurance covered arson of course.'

D. J. opened and shut his mouth several times and finally found his voice.

'Didn't our Mr Robinson tell you that the man you saw here on Saturday wasn't from us?'

Our Mr Robinson, in the shape of Gary, nodded vigorously.

'He . . . Mr Greene . . . distinctly said he *was*,' Maisie insisted.

'Well . . . what did he look like?'

'Smarmy,' said Maisie without hesitation. 'Not as young as Charles . . .' she gestured towards me, 'or as old as you.' She thought, then shrugged. 'He looked like an insurance man, that's all.'

D. J. swallowed the implied insult manfully.

'About five feet ten,' I said. 'Suntanned skin with a sallow tinge, grey eyes with deep upper eyelids, widish nose, mouth straight under heavy drooping dark moustache, straight brown hair brushed back and retreating from the two top corners of his forehead, ordinary eyebrows, greeny-brown trilby of smooth felt, shirt, tie, fawn unbuttoned raincoat, gold signet ring on little finger of right hand, suntanned hands.'

I could see him in memory as clearly as if he still stood there in the ashes before me, taking off his hat and calling Maisie 'madam'.

'Good God,' D. J. said.

'An artist's eye, dear,' said Maisie admiringly. 'Well I never.'

D. J. said he was certain they had no one like that in their poking-into-claims department, and Gary agreed.

'Well,' said Maisie, with a resurgence of crossness, 'I suppose that still means you are looking for arson, though why you think that anyone in his right senses would want to burn down my lovely home and all my treasures is something I'll never understand.'

Surely Maisie, worldly Maisie, could not be so naïve. I caught a deep glimmer of intelligence in the glance she gave me, and knew that she certainly wasn't. D. J. however, who didn't know, made frustrated little motions with his hands and voted against explaining. I smothered a few more laughs, and Maisie noticed.

'Do you want your picture,' I asked, 'to be sunny like today, or cloudy and sad?'

She looked up at the bright sky.

'A bit more dramatic, dear,' she said.

D. J. and Gary inch-by-inched over the ruin all afternoon, and I tried to infuse it with a little Gothic romance. At five o'clock, on the dot, we all knocked off.

'Union hours?' said D. J. sarcastically, watching me pack my suitcase.

'The light gets too yellow in the evenings.'

'Will you be here tomorrow?'

I nodded. 'And you?'

'Perhaps.'

I went by foot and bus along to the Beach Hotel, cleaned my brushes, thought a bit, and at seven met Maisie downstairs in the bar, as arranged.

'Well, dear,' she said, as her first gin and tonic gravitated comfortably. 'Did they find anything?'

'Nothing at all, as far as I could see.'

'Well, that's good, dear.'

I tackled my pint of draught. Put the glass down carefully.

'Not altogether, Maisie.'

'Why not?'

'What exactly were your treasures, which were burned?'

'I dare say you wouldn't think so much of them of course, but we had ever such fun buying them, and so have I since Archie's gone, and well, dear, things like an antique spear collection that used to belong to old Lord Stequers whose niece I nursed once, and a whole wall of beautiful butterflies, which professors and such came to look at, and a wrought-iron gate from Lady Tythe's old home, which divided the hall from the sitting-room, and six warming pans from a castle in Ireland, and two tall vases with eagles on the lids signed by Angelica Kaufman, which once belonged to a cousin of Mata Hari, they really did, dear, and a copper firescreen with silver bosses which was a devil to polish, and a marble table from Greece, and a silver tea urn which was once used by Queen Victoria, and really, dear, that's just the beginning, if I tell you them all I'll go on all night.'

'Did the Foundation insurance company have a full list?'

'Yes, they did, dear, and why do you want to know?'

'Because,' I said regretfully, 'I don't think many of

those things were inside the house when it burned down.'

'*What?*' Maisie, as far as I could tell, was genuinely astounded. 'But they must have been.'

'D. J. as good as told me that they were looking for traces of them, and I don't think they found any.'

'D. J.?'

'Mr Lagland. The elder one.'

Alternate disbelief and anger kept Maisie going through two more double gins. Disbelief, eventually, won.

'You got it wrong, dear,' she said finally.

'I hope so.'

'Inexperience of youth, of course.'

'Maybe.'

'Because of course everything was in its place, dear, when I went off last Friday week to stay with Betty, and I only went to Betty's with not having seen her for so long while I'd been away, which is ironic when you think of it, but of course you can't stay at home for ever on the off chance your house is going to catch fire and you can save it, can you dear, or you'd never go anywhere and I would have missed my trip to Australia.'

She paused for breath. Coincidence, I thought.

'All I can say, dear, is that it's a miracle I took most of my jewellery with me to Betty's, because I don't always, except that Archie always said it was safer and of course he was always so sensible and thoughtful and sweet.'

'Australia?' I said.

'Well, yes, dear, wasn't that nice? I went out there for a visit to Archie's sister who's lived there since heaven knows when and was feeling lonely since she'd been widowed, poor dear, and I went out for a bit of fun, dear, because of course I'd never really met her, only exchanged postcards of course, and I was out there for six weeks with her. She wanted me to stay, and of course we got on together like a house on fire ... oh dear, I didn't mean that exactly ... well, anyway, I said I wanted to come back to my little house by the sea and think it over, and of course I took my jewellery with me on that trip too, dear.'

I said idly, 'I don't suppose you bought a Munnings while you were there.'

I didn't know why I'd said it, apart from thinking of Donald in Australia. I was totally unprepared for her reaction.

Astounded she had been before: this time, pole-axed. Before, she had been incredulous and angry. This time, incredulous and frightened.

She knocked over her gin, slid off her bar stool, and covered her open mouth with four trembling red-nailed fingers.

'You didn't!' I said disbelievingly.

'How do you know?'

'I don't ...'

'Are you from Customs and Excise?'

'Of course not.'

'Oh dear. Oh dear . . .' She was shaking, almost as shattered as Donald.

I took her arm and led her over to an armchair beside a small bar table.

'Sit down,' I said coaxingly, 'and tell me.'

It took ten minutes and a refill double gin.

'Well, dear, I'm not an art expert, as you can probably guess, but there was this picture by Sir Alfred Munnings, signed and everything, dear, and it was such a bargain really, and I thought how tickled Archie would have been to have a real Munnings on the wall, what with us both liking the races, of course, and, well, Archie's sister egged me on a bit, and I felt quite . . . I suppose you might call it *high*, dear, so I bought it.'

She stopped.

'Go on,' I said.

'Well, dear, I suppose you've guessed from what I said just now.'

'You brought it into this country without declaring it?'

She sighed. 'Yes, dear, I did. Of course it was silly of me but I never gave customs duty a thought when I bought the painting, not until just before I came home, a week later, that was, and Archie's sister asked if I was going to declare it, and well, dear, I really *resent* having to pay duty on things, don't you? So anyway I thought I'd better find out just how much the duty would be, and I found it wasn't duty at all in the ordinary way, dear, there isn't duty on second-hand pictures being brought in from Australia, but would you believe it, they said I would have to pay Value Added Tax, sort of tax on buying things, you know, dear, and I would have to pay eight per cent on whatever I had bought the picture for. Well, I ask you! I was that mad, dear, I can tell you. So Archie's sister said why didn't I leave the painting with her, because then if I went back to Australia I would have paid the tax for nothing, but I wasn't sure I'd go back and anyway I did want to see Sir Alfred Munnings on the wall where Archie would have loved it, so, well, dear, it was all done up nicely in boards and brown paper so I just camouflaged it a bit with my best nightie and popped it in my suitcase, and pushed it through the "Nothing to Declare" lane at Heathrow when I got back, and nobody stopped me.'

'How much would you have had to pay?' I said.

'Well, dear, to be precise, just over seven hundred pounds. And I know that's not a fortune, dear, but it made me so mad to have to pay tax here because I'd bought something nice in Australia.'

I did some mental arithmetic. 'So the painting cost about nine thousand?'

'That's right, dear. Nine thousand.' She looked anxious. 'I wasn't done, was I? I've asked one or two people since I got back and they say lots of Munningses cost fifteen or more.'

'So they do,' I said absently. And some could be got for fifteen hundred, and others, I dared say, for less.

'Well, anyway, dear, it was only when I began to think about insurance that I wondered if I would be found out, if say, the insurance people wanted a *receipt* or anything, which they probably would, of course, so I didn't do anything about it, because of course if I *did* go back to Australia I could just take the picture with me and no harm done.'

'Awkward,' I agreed.

'So now it's burnt, and I dare say you'll think it serves me right, because the nine thousand's gone up in smoke and I won't see a penny of it back.'

She finished the gin and I bought her another.

'I know it's not my business, Maisie, but how did you happen to have nine thousand handy in Australia? Aren't there rules about exporting that much cash?'

She giggled. 'You don't know much about the world, do you, dear? But anyway, this time it was all hunky-dory. I just toddled along with Archie's sister to a jeweller's and sold him a brooch I had, a nasty sort of *toad*, dear, with a socking big diamond in the middle of its forehead, something to do with Shakespeare, I think, though I never got it clear, anyway I never wore it, it was so ugly, but of course I'd taken it with me because of it being worth so much, and I sold it for nine thousand five, though in Australian dollars of course, so there was no problem, was there?'

Maisie took it for granted I would be eating with

her, so we drifted in to dinner. Her appetite seemed healthy, but her spirits were damp.

'You won't *tell* anyone, will you, dear, about the picture?'

'Of course not, Maisie.'

'I could get into such trouble, dear.'

'I know.'

'A fine, of course,' she said. 'And I suppose that might be the least of it. People can be so beastly about a perfectly innocent little bit of smuggling.'

'No one will find out, if you keep quiet.' A thought struck me. 'Unless, that is, you've told anyone already that you'd bought it?'

'No, dear, I didn't, because of thinking I'd better pretend I'd had it for years, and of course I hadn't even hung it on the wall yet because one of the rings was loose in the frame and I thought it might fall down and be damaged, and I couldn't decide who to ask to fix it.' She paused for a mouthful of prawn cocktail. 'I expect you'll think me silly, dear, but I suppose I was feeling a bit scared of being found out, not guilty exactly because I really don't see why we *should* pay that irritating tax but anyway I didn't not only not hang it up, I hid it.'

'You hid it? Still wrapped up?'

'Well, yes, dear, more or less wrapped up. Of course I'd opened it when I got home, and that's when I found the ring coming loose with the cord through it, so I wrapped it up again until I'd decided what to do.'

I was fascinated. 'Where did you hide it?'

She laughed. 'Nowhere very much, dear. I mean, I was only keeping it out of sight to stop people asking about it, of course, so I slipped it behind one of the radiators in the lounge, and don't look so horrified dear, the central heating was turned off.'

I painted at the house all the next day, but neither D. J. nor anyone else turned up.

In between stints at the easel I poked around a good deal on my own account, searching for Maisie's treasures. I found a good many recognizable remains, durables like bed-frames, kitchen machines and radiators, all of them twisted and buckled not merely by heat but by the weight of the whole edifice from roof downwards having collapsed inwards. Occasional remains of heavy rafters lay blackly in the thick ash, but apart from these, everything combustible had totally, as one might say, combusted.

Of all the things Maisie had described, and of all the dozens she hadn't, I found only the wrought-iron gate from Lady Tythe's old home, which had divided the hall from the sitting-room. Lady Tythe would never have recognized it.

No copper warming pans, which after all had been

designed to withstand red-hot coals. No metal fire-screen. No marble table. No antique spears.

Naturally, no Munnings.

When I took my paint-stained fingers back to the Beach at five o'clock I found Maisie waiting for me in the hall. Not the kindly, basically cheerful Maisie I had come to know, but a belligerent woman in a full-blown state of rage.

'I've been waiting for you,' she said, fixing me with a furious eye.

I couldn't think how I could have offended her.

'What's the matter?' I said.

'The bar's shut,' she said. 'So come upstairs to my room. Bring all your stuff with you.' She gestured to the suitcase. 'I'm so *mad* I think I'll absolutely *burst.*'

She did indeed, in the lift, look in danger of it. Her cheeks were bright red with hard outlines of colour against the pale surrounding skin. Her blonde-rinsed hair, normally lacquered into sophistication, stuck out in wispy spikes, and for the first time since I'd met her her mouth was not glistening with lipstick.

She threw open the door of her room and stalked in. I followed, closing it after me.

'You'll never believe it,' she said forcefully, turning to face me and letting go with all guns blazing. 'I've had the police here half the day, and those insurance men here the other half, and *do you know what they're saying?*'

'Oh, Maisie.' I sighed inwardly. It had been inevitable.

'What do you think I am, I asked them,' she said. 'I was so *mad*. There they were, having the nerve to suggest I'd sold all my treasures and over-insured my house, and was trying to take the insurance people for a ride. I told them, I told them over and over, that everything was in its place when I went to Betty's and if it was over-insured it was to allow for inflation and anyway the brokers had advised me to put up the amount pretty high, and I'm glad I took their advice, but that Mr Lagland says they won't be paying out until they have investigated further and he was proper sniffy about it, and no sympathy at all for me having lost everything. They were absolutely *beastly*, and I *hate* them all.'

She paused to regather momentum, vibrating visibly with the strength of her feelings. 'They made me feel so *dirty*, and maybe I *was* screaming at them a bit, I was so mad, but they'd no call to be so *rude*, and making out I was some sort of criminal, and just what *right* have they to tell me to pull myself together when it is because of *them* and their bullying that I am yelling at them at the top of my voice?'

It must, I reflected, have been quite an encounter. I wondered in what state the police and D. J. had retired from the field.

'They say it was definitely arson and I said why did they think so now when they hadn't thought so at first, and it turns out that it was because that Lagland couldn't find any of my treasures in the ashes or any trace of them at all, and they said even if I hadn't sold the things first I had arranged for them to be stolen and the house burnt to cinders while I was away at Betty's, and they kept on and on asking me who I'd paid to do it, and I got more and more furious and if I'd had anything handy I would have *hit* them, I really would.'

'What you need is a stiff gin,' I said.

'I told them they ought to be out looking for whoever had done it instead of hounding helpless women like me, and the more I thought of someone walking into *my* house and stealing *my* treasures and then callously setting fire to everything the madder I got, and somehow that made me even *madder* with those stupid men who couldn't see any further than their stupid noses.'

It struck me after a good deal more of similar diatribe that genuine though Maisie's anger undoubtedly was, she was stoking herself up again every time her temper looked in danger of relapsing to normal. For some reason, she seemed to need to be in the position of the righteous wronged.

I wondered why; and in a breath-catching gap in the flow of hot lava, I said, 'I don't suppose you told them about the Munnings.'

The red spots on her cheeks burned suddenly brighter.

'I'm not *crazy*,' she said bitingly. 'If they found out about that, there would have been a fat chance of convincing them I'm telling the truth about the rest.'

'I've heard,' I said tentatively, 'that nothing infuriates a crook more than being had up for the one job he didn't do.'

It looked for a moment as if I'd just elected myself as the new target for hatred, but suddenly as she glared at me in rage her sense of humour reared its battered head and nudged her in the ribs. The stiffness round her mouth relaxed, her eyes softened and glimmered, and after a second or two, she ruefully smiled.

'I dare say you're right, dear, when I come to think of it.' The smile slowly grew into a giggle. 'How about that gin?'

Little eruptions continued all evening through drinks and dinner, but the red-centred volcano had subsided to manageable heat.

'You didn't seem surprised, dear, when I told you what the police thought I'd done.' She looked sideways at me over her coffee cup, eyes sharp and enquiring.

'No.' I paused. 'You see, something very much the same has just happened to my cousin. Too much the same, in too many ways. I think, if you will come, and he agrees, that I'd like to take you to meet him.'

'But why, dear?'

I told her why. The anger she felt for herself burned up again fiercely for Donald.

'How *dreadful*. How *selfish* you must think *me*, after all that that poor man has suffered.'

'I don't think you're selfish at all. In fact, Maisie, I think you're a proper trouper.'

She looked pleased and almost kittenish, and I had a vivid impression of what she had been like with Archie.

'There's one thing, though, dear,' she said awkwardly. 'After today, and all that's been said, I don't think I want that picture you're doing. I don't any more want to remember the house as it is now, only like it used to be. So if I give you just the fifty pounds, do you mind?'

CHAPTER FIVE

We went to Shropshire in Maisie's Jaguar, sharing the driving. Donald on the telephone had sounded unenthusiastic at my suggested return, but also too lethargic to raise objections. When he opened his front door to us, I was shocked.

It was two weeks since I'd left him to go to Yorkshire. In that time he had shed at least fourteen pounds and aged ten years. His skin was tinged with bluish shadows, the bones in his face showed starkly, and even his hair seemed speckled with grey.

The ghost of the old Donald put an obvious effort into receiving us with good manners.

'Come in,' he said. 'I'm in the dining-room now. I expect you'd like a drink.'

'That would be very nice, dear,' Maisie said.

He looked at her with dull eyes, seeing, as I saw, a large good-natured lady with glossy hair and expensive clothes, her smart appearance walking a tightrope between vulgarity and elegance and just making it to the safer side.

He waved to me to pour the drinks, as if it would be too much for him, and invited Maisie to sit down. The dining-room had been roughly refurnished, containing now a large rug, all the sunroom armchairs, and a couple of small tables from the bedrooms. We sat in a fairly close group round one of the tables, because I had come to ask questions, and I wanted to write down the answers. My cousin watched the production of notebook and ballpoint with no show of interest.

'Don,' I said, 'I want you to listen to a story.'

'All right.'

Maisie, for once, kept it short. When she came to the bit about buying a Munnings in Australia, Donald's head lifted a couple of inches and he looked from her to me with the first stirring of attention. When she stopped, there was a small silence.

'So,' I said finally, 'you both went to Australia, you both bought a Munnings, and soon after your return you both had your houses burgled.'

'Extraordinary coincidence,' Donald said: but he meant simply that, nothing more. 'Did you come all this way just to tell me that?'

'I wanted to see how you were.'

'Oh. I'm all right. Kind of you, Charles, but I'm all right.'

Even Maisie, who hadn't known him before, could see that he wasn't.

'Where did you buy your picture, Don? Where exactly, I mean.'

'I suppose . . . Melbourne. In the Hilton Hotel. Opposite the cricket ground.'

I looked doubtful. Although hotels quite often sold pictures by local artists, they seldom sold Munnings.

'Fellow met us there,' Don added. 'Brought it up to our room. From the gallery where we saw it first.'

'Which gallery?'

He made a slight attempt to remember. 'Might have been something like Fine Arts.'

'Would you have it on a cheque stub, or anything?'

He shook his head. 'The wine firm I was dealing with paid for it for me, and I sent a cheque to their British office when I got back.'

'Which wine firm?'

'Monga Vineyards Proprietary Limited of Adelaide and Melbourne.'

I wrote it all down.

'And what was the picture like? I mean, could you describe it?'

Donald looked tired. 'One of those "Going down to the start" things. Typical Munnings.'

'So was mine,' said Maisie, surprised. 'A nice long row of jockeys in their colours against a darker sort of sky.'

'Mine had only three horses,' Donald said.

'The biggest, I suppose you might say the *nearest* jockey in my picture had a purple shirt and green cap,' Maisie said, 'and I expect you'll think I was silly but that was one of the reasons I bought it, because when

79

Archie and I were thinking what fun it would be to buy a horse and go to the races as owners, we decided we'd like purple with a green cap for our colours, if no one else already had that, of course.'

'Don?' I said.

'Mm? Oh . . . three bay horses cantering . . . in profile . . . one in front, two slightly overlapping behind. Bright colours on the jockeys. I don't remember exactly. White racetrack rails and a lot of sunny sky.'

'What size?'

He frowned slightly. 'Not very big. About twenty-four inches by eighteen, inside the frame.'

'And yours, Maisie?'

'A bit smaller, dear, I should think.'

'Look,' Donald said. 'What are you getting at?'

'Trying to make sure that there are no more coincidences.'

He stared, but without any particular feeling.

'On the way up here,' I said, 'Maisie told me everything' (but *everything*) 'of the way she came to buy her picture. So could you possibly tell us how you came to buy yours? Did you, for example, deliberately go looking for a Munnings?'

Donald passed a weary hand over his face, obviously not wanting the bother of answering.

'Please, Don,' I said.

'Oh . . .' A long sigh. 'No. I wasn't especially wanting to buy anything at all. We just went into the Melbourne

Art Gallery for a stroll round. We came to the Munnings they have there . . . and while we were looking at it we just drifted into conversation with a woman near us, as one does in art galleries. She said there was another Munnings, not far away, for sale in a small commercial gallery, and it was worth seeing even if one didn't intend to buy it. We had time to spare, so we went.'

Maisie's mouth had fallen open. 'But dear,' she said, recovering, 'that was *just* the same as us, my sister-in-law and me, though it was Sydney Art Gallery, not Melbourne. They have this marvellous picture there, *The Coming Storm*, and we were admiring it when this man sort of drifted up to us and joined in . . .'

Donald suddenly looked a great deal more exhausted, like a sick person overdone by healthy visitors.

'Look . . . Charles . . . you aren't going to the police with all this? Because I . . . I don't think . . . I could stand . . . a whole new lot . . . of questions.'

'No, I'm not,' I said.

'Then what . . . does it matter?'

Maisie finished her gin and tonic and smiled a little too brightly.

'Which way to the girls' room, dear?' she asked, and disappeared to the cloakroom.

Donald said faintly, 'I can't concentrate . . . I'm sorry, Charles, but I can't seem to do anything . . . while they still have Regina . . . unburied . . . just *stored* . . .'

Time, far from dulling the agony, seemed to have preserved it, as if the keeping of Regina in a refrigerated drawer had stopped dead the natural progression of mourning. I had been told that the bodies of murdered people could be held in that way for six months or more in unsolved cases. I doubted whether Donald would last that long.

He stood suddenly and walked away out of the door to the hall. I followed. He crossed the hall, opened the door of the sitting-room, and went in.

Hesitantly, I went after him.

The sitting-room still contained only the chintz-covered sofas and châirs, now ranged over-tidily round the walls. The floor where Regina had lain was clean and polished. The air was cold.

Donald stood in front of the empty fireplace looking at my picture of Regina, which was propped on the mantelpiece.

'I stay in here with her, most of the time,' he said. 'It's the only place I can bear to be.'

He walked to one of the armchairs and sat down, directly facing the portrait.

'You wouldn't mind seeing yourselves out, would you Charles?' he said. 'I'm really awfully tired.'

'Take care of yourself.' Useless advice. One could see he wouldn't.

'I'm all right,' he said. 'Quite all right. Don't you worry.'

I looked back from the door. He was sitting immobile, looking at Regina. I didn't know whether it would have been better or worse if I hadn't painted her.

Maisie was quiet for the whole of the first hour of the return journey, a record in itself.

From Donald's house we had driven first to one of the neighbours who had originally offered refuge, because he clearly needed help more now than ever.

Mrs Neighbour had listened with sympathy, but had shaken her head.

'Yes, I know he should have company and get away from the house, but he won't. I've tried several times. Called. So have lots of people round here. He just tells us he's all right. He won't let anyone help him.'

Maisie drove soberly, mile after mile. Eventually she said, 'We shouldn't have bothered him. Not so soon after . . .'

Three weeks, I thought. Only three weeks. To Donald it must have seemed like three months, stretched out in slow motion. You could live a lifetime in three weeks' pain.

'I'm going to Australia,' I said.

'You're very fond of him, dear, aren't you?' Maisie said.

Fond? I wouldn't have used that word, I thought: but perhaps after all it was accurate.

'He's eight years older than me, but we've always got on well together.' I looked back, remembering. 'We were both only children. His mother and mine were sisters. They used to visit each other, with me and Donald in tow. He was always pretty patient about having a young kid under his feet.'

'He looks very ill, dear.'

'Yes.'

She drove another ten miles in silence. Then she said, 'Are you sure it wouldn't be better to tell the police? About the paintings, I mean? Because you do think they had something to do with the burglaries, don't you, dear, and the police might find out things more easily than you.'

I agreed. 'I'm sure they would, Maisie. But how can I tell them? You heard what Donald said, that he couldn't stand a new lot of questions. Seeing him today, do you think he could? And as for you, it wouldn't just be confessing to a bit of smuggling and paying a fine, but of having a conviction against your name for always, and having the customs search your baggage every time you travelled, and all sorts of other complications and humiliations. Once you get on any black-list nowadays it is just about impossible to get off.'

'I didn't know you cared, dear.' She tried a giggle, but it didn't sound right.

We stopped after a while to exchange places. I liked driving her car, particularly as for the last three years, since I'd given up a steady income, I'd owned no wheels myself. The power purred elegantly under the pale blue bonnet and ate up the southward miles.

'Can you afford the fare, dear?' Maisie said. 'And hotels, and things?'

'I've a friend out there. Another painter. I'll stay with him.'

She looked at me doubtfully. 'You can't get there by hitch-hiking, though.'

I smiled. 'I'll manage.'

'Yes, well, dear, I dare say you can, but all the same, and I don't want any silly arguments, I've got a great deal of this world's goods thanks to Archie, and you haven't, and as it's partly because of me having gone in for smuggling that you're going yourself at all, I am insisting that you let me buy your ticket.'

'No, Maisie.'

'Yes, dear. Now be a good boy, dear, and do as I say.'

You could see, I thought, why she'd been a good nurse. Swallow the medicine, dear, there's a good boy. I didn't like accepting her offer but the truth was that I would have had to borrow anyway.

'Shall I paint your picture, Maisie, when I get back?'

'That will do very nicely, dear.'

I pulled up outside the house near Heathrow whose attic was my home, and from where Maisie had picked me up that morning.

'How do you stand all this noise, dear?' she said, wincing as a huge jet climbed steeply overhead.

'I concentrate on the cheap rent.'

She smiled, opening the crocodile handbag and producing her chequebook. She wrote out and gave me the slip of paper which was far more than enough for my journey.

'If you're fussed, dear,' she said across my protests, 'you can give me back what you don't spend.' She gazed at me earnestly with grey-blue eyes. 'You will be careful dear, won't you?'

'Yes, Maisie.'

'Because of course, dear, you might turn out to be a nuisance to some really *nasty* people.'

I landed at Mascot airport at noon five days later, wheeling in over Sydney and seeing the harbour bridge and the opera house down below, looking like postcards.

Jik met me on the other side of Customs with a huge grin and a waving bottle of champagne.

'Todd the sod,' he said. 'Who'd have thought it?' His voice soared easily over the din. 'Come to paint Australia red!'

He slapped me on the back with an enthusiastic horny hand, not knowing his own strength. Jik Cassavetes, long-time friend, my opposite in almost everything.

Bearded, which I was not. Exuberant, noisy, extravagant, unpredictable; qualities I envied. Blue eyes and sun-blond hair. Muscles which left mine gasping. An outrageous way with girls. An abrasive tongue; and a wholehearted contempt for the things I painted.

We had met at art school, drawn together by mutual truancy on racetrains. Jik compulsively went racing, but strictly to gamble, never to admire the contestants, and certainly not to paint them. Horse painters, to him, were the lower orders. No *serious* artist, he frequently said, would be seen dead painting horses.

Jik's paintings, mostly abstract, were the dark reverse of the bright mind: fruits of depression, full of despair at the hatred and pollution destroying the fair world.

Living with Jik was like a toboggan run, downhill, dangerous, and exhilarating. We'd spent the last two years at art school sharing a studio flat and kicking each other out for passing girls. They would have chucked him out of school except for his prodigious talent, because he'd missed weeks in the summer for his other love, which was sailing.

I'd been out with him, deep sea, several times in the years afterwards. I reckoned he'd taken us on several occasions a bit nearer death than was strictly necessary, but it had been a nice change from the office. He was a great sailor, efficient, neat, quick and strong, with an instinctive feeling for wind and waves. I had been sorry when one day he had said he was setting off single-handed round the world. We'd had a paralytic farewell party on his last night ashore; and the next day, when he'd gone, I'd given the estate agent my notice.

He had brought a car to fetch me: his car, it turned out. A British M.G. Sports, dark blue. Both sides of him right there, extrovert and introvert, the flamboyant statement in a sombre colour.

'Are there many of these here?' I asked, surprised, loading suitcase and satchel into the back. 'It's a long way from the birth pangs.'

He grinned. 'A few. They're not popular now because petrol passes through them like salts.' The engine roared to life, agreeing with him, and he switched on the windscreen wiper against a starting shower. 'Welcome to sunny Australia. It rains all the time here. Puts Manchester in the sun.'

'But you like it?'

'Love it, mate. Sydney's like rugger, all guts and go and a bit of grace in the line-out.'

'And how's business?'

'There are thousands of painters in Australia. It's a flourishing cottage industry.' He glanced at me sideways. 'A hell of a lot of competition.'

'I haven't come to seek fame and fortune.'

'But I scent a purpose,' he said.

'How would you feel about harnessing your brawn?'

'To your brain? As in the old days?'

'Those were pastimes.'

His eyebrows rose. 'What are the risks?'

'Arson and murder, to date.'

'Jesus.'

The blue car swept gracefully into the centre of the city. Sky-scrapers grew like beanstalks.

'I live right out on the other side,' Jik said. 'God, that sounds banal. Suburban. What has become of me?'

'Contentment oozing from every pore,' I said smiling.

'Yes. So. O.K., for the first time in my life I've been actually happy. I dare say you'll soon put that right.'

The car nosed on to the expressway, pointing towards the bridge.

'If you look over your right shoulder,' Jik said, 'You'll see the triumph of imagination over economics. Like the Concorde. Long live madness, it's the only thing that gets us anywhere.'

I looked. It was the opera house, glimpsed, grey with rain.

'Dead in the day,' Jik said. 'It's a night bird. Fantastic.'

The great arch of the bridge rose above us, intricate as steel lace. 'This is the only flat bit of road in Sydney,' Jik said. We climbed again on the other side.

To our left, half seen at first behind other familiar-looking high-rise blocks, but then revealed in its full glory, stood a huge shiny red-orange building, all its sides set with regular rows of large curve-cornered square windows of bronze-coloured glass.

Jik grinned. 'The shape of the twenty-first century. Imagination and courage. I love this country.'

'Where's your natural pessimism?'

'When the sun sets, those windows glow like gold.' We left the gleaming monster behind. 'It's the water-board offices,' Jik said sardonically. 'The guy at the top moors his boat near mine.'

The road went up and down out of the city through close-packed rows of one-storey houses, whose roofs, from the air, had looked like a great red-squared carpet.

'There's one snag,' Jik said. 'Three weeks ago, I got married.'

The snag was living with him aboard his boat, which was moored among a colony of others near a headland he called the Spit: and you could see why, temporarily at least, the glooms of the world could take care of themselves.

She was not plain, but not beautiful. Oval-shaped face, mid-brown hair, so-so figure and a practical line in clothes. None of the style or instant vital butterfly quality of Regina. I found myself the critically inspected target of bright brown eyes which looked out with impact-making intelligence.

'Sarah,' Jik said. 'Todd. Todd, Sarah.'

We said hi and did I have a good flight and yes I did. I gathered she would have preferred me to stay at home.

Jik's thirty-foot ketch, which had set out from England as a cross between a studio and a chandler's warehouse, now sported curtains, cushions, and a flowering plant. When Jik opened the champagne he poured it into shining tulip glasses, not plastic mugs.

'By God,' he said. 'It's good to see you.'

Sarah toasted my advent politely, not sure that she agreed. I apologized for gatecrashing the honeymoon.

'Nuts to that,' Jik said, obviously meaning it. 'Too much domestic bliss is bad for the soul.'

'It depends,' said Sarah neutrally, 'on whether you need love or loneliness to get you going.'

For Jik, before, it had always been loneliness. I wondered what he had painted recently: but there was no sign, in the now comfortable cabin, of so much as a brush.

'I walk on air,' Jik said. 'I could bound up Everest and do a handspring on the summit.'

'As far as the galley will do,' Sarah said, 'if you remembered to buy the crayfish.'

Jik, in our shared days, had been the cook; and times, it seemed, had not changed. It was he, not Sarah, who with speed and efficiency chopped open the cray-fish, covered them with cheese and mustard, and set them under the grill. He who washed the crisp lettuce and assembled crusty bread and butter. We ate the feast round the cabin table with rain pattering on port-holes and roof and the sea water slapping against the sides in the freshening wind. Over coffee, at Jik's insist-ence, I told them why I had come to Australia.

They heard me out in concentrated silence. Then Jik, whose politics had not changed much since student pink, muttered darkly about 'pigs', and Sarah looked nakedly apprehensive.

'Don't worry,' I told her. 'I'm not asking for Jik's help, now that I know he's married.'

'You have it. You have it,' he said explosively.

I shook my head. 'No.'

Sarah said, 'What precisely do you plan to do first?'

'Find out where the two Munningses came from.'

'And after?'

'If I knew what I was looking for I wouldn't need to look.'

'That doesn't follow,' she said absently.

'Melbourne,' Jik said suddenly. 'You said one of the pictures came from Melbourne. Well, that settles it. Of course we'll help. We'll go there at once. It couldn't be better. Do you know what next Tuesday is?'

'No,' I said. 'What is it?'

'The day of the Melbourne Cup!'

His voice was triumphant. Sarah stared at me darkly across the table.

'I wish you hadn't come,' she said.

CHAPTER SIX

I slept that night in the converted boathouse which constituted Jik's postal address. Apart from a bed alcove, new-looking bathroom, and rudimentary kitchen, he was using the whole space as studio.

A huge old easel stood in the centre, with a table to each side holding neat arrays of paints, brushes, knives, pots of linseed and turpentine and cleaning fluid: all the usual paraphernalia.

No work in progress. Everything shut and tidy. Like its counterpart in England, the large rush mat in front of the easel was black with oily dirt, owing to Jik's habit of rubbing his roughly rinsed brushes on it between colours. The tubes of paint were characteristically squeezed flat in the middles, impatience forbidding an orderly progress from the bottom. The palette was a small oblong, not needed any larger because he used most colours straight from the tube and got his effects by overpainting. A huge box of rags stood under one table, ready to wipe clean everything used to apply paint to picture, not just brushes and knives, but fingers, palms, nails, wrists, anything which took his fancy. I smiled to myself. Jik's studio was as identifiable as his pictures.

Along one wall a two-tiered rack held rows of canvases, which I pulled out one by one. Dark, strong, dramatic colours, leaping to the eye. Still the troubled vision, the perception of doom. Decay and crucifixions, obscurely horrific landscapes, flowers wilting, fish dying, everything to be guessed, nothing explicit.

Jik hated to sell his paintings and seldom did, which I thought was just as well, as they made uncomfortable room-mates, enough to cause depression in a skylark. They had a vigour, though, that couldn't be denied. Everyone who saw his assembled work remembered it, and had their thoughts modified, and perhaps even their basic attitudes changed. He was a major artist in a way I would never be, and he would have looked upon easy popular acclaim as personal failure.

In the morning I walked down to the boat and found Sarah there alone.

'Jik's gone for milk and newspapers,' she said. 'I'll get you some breakfast.'

'I came to say goodbye.'

She looked at me levelly. 'The damage is done.'

'Not if I go.'

'Back to England?'

I shook my head.

'I thought not.' A dim smile appeared briefly in her eyes. 'Jik told me last night that you were the only person he knew who had a head cool enough to calculate a ship's position for a mayday call by dead reckoning at night after tossing around violently for four hours in a force ten gale with a hole in the hull and the pumps packed up, and get it right.'

I grinned. 'But he patched the hull and mended the pump, and we cancelled the mayday when it got light.'

'You were both stupid.'

'Better to stay safely at home?' I said.

She turned away. '*Men*,' she said. 'Never happy unless they're risking their necks.'

She was right, to some extent. A little healthy danger wasn't a bad feeling, especially in retrospect. It was only the nerve-breakers which gave you the shakes and put you off repetition.

'Some women, too,' I said.

'Not me.'

'I won't take Jik with me.'

Her back was still turned. 'You'll get him killed,' she said.

Nothing looked less dangerous than the small suburban gallery from which Maisie had bought her picture. It was shut for good. The bare premises could be seen nakedly through the shopfront window, and a succinct and unnecessary card hanging inside the glass door said 'Closed'.

The little shops on each side shrugged their shoulders.

'They were only open for a month or so. Never seemed to do much business. No surprise they folded.'

Did they, I asked, know which estate agent was handling the letting? No, they didn't.

'End of enquiry,' Jik said.

I shook my head. 'Let's try the local agents.'

We split up and spent a fruitless hour. None of the firms on any of the 'For Sale' boards in the district admitted to having the gallery on its books.

We met again outside the uninformative door.

'Where now?'

'Art Gallery?'

'In the Domain,' Jik said, which turned out to be a chunk of park in the city centre. The Art Gallery had a suitable façade of six pillars outside and the Munnings, when we ran it to earth, inside.

No one else was looking at it. No one approached to fall into chat and advise us we could buy another one cheap in a little gallery in an outer suburb.

We stood there for a while with me admiring the absolute mastery which set the two grey ponies in the shaft of pre-storm light at the head of the darker herd, and Jik grudgingly admitted that at least the man knew how to handle paint.

Absolutely nothing else happened. We drove back to the boat in the M.G., and lunch was an anti-climax.

'What now?' Jik said.

'A spot of work with the telephone, if I could borrow the one in the boathouse.'

It took nearly all afternoon, but alphabetically systematic calls to every estate agent as far as Holloway & Son in the classified directory produced the goods in the end. The premises in question, said Holloway & Son, had been let to North Sydney Fine Arts on a short lease.

How short?

Three months, dating from September first.

No, Holloway & Son did not know the premises were now empty. They could not re-let them until December first, because North Sydney Fine Arts had paid all the rent in advance; and they did not feel able to part with the name of any individual concerned. I blarneyed a bit, giving a delicate impression of being in the trade myself, with a client for the empty shop. Holloway & Son mentioned a Mr John Grey, with a post-office box number for an address. I thanked them. Mr Grey, they said, warming up a little, had said he wanted the gallery for a short private exhibition, and they were not really surprised he had already gone.

How could I recognize Mr Grey if I met him? They really couldn't say: all the negotiations had been done by telephone and post. I could write to him myself, if my client wanted the gallery before December first.

Ta ever so, I thought.

All the same, it couldn't do much harm. I unearthed a suitable sheet of paper, and in twee and twirly lettering in black ink told Mr Grey I had been given his name and box number by Holloway & Son, and asked him if he would sell me the last two weeks of his lease so that I could mount an exhibition of a friend's *utterly meaningful* watercolours. Name his own price, I said, within reason. Yours sincerely, I said; Peregrine Smith.

I walked down to the boat to ask if Jik or Sarah would mind me putting their own box number as a return address.

'He won't answer,' Sarah said, reading the letter. 'If he's a crook. I wouldn't.'

'The first principle of fishing,' Jik said, 'is to dangle a bait.'

'This wouldn't attract a starving piranha.'

I posted it anyway, with Sarah's grudging consent. None of us expected it to bring forth any result.

Jik's own session on the telephone proved more rewarding. Melbourne, it seemed, was crammed to the rooftops for the richest race meeting of the year, but he had been offered last-minute cancellations. Very lucky indeed, he insisted, looking amused.

'Where?' I asked suspiciously.

'In the Hilton,' he said.

I couldn't afford it, but we went anyway. Jik in his student days had lived on cautious hand-outs from a family trust, and it appeared that the source of bread was still flowing. The boat, the boathouse, the M.G. and the wife were none of them supported by paint.

We flew south to Melbourne the following morning, looking down on the Snowy Mountains en route and thinking our own chilly thoughts. Sarah's disapproval from the seat behind froze the back of my head, but she had refused to stay in Sydney. Jik's natural bent and enthusiasm for dicey adventure looked like being curbed by love, and his reaction to danger might not henceforth be uncomplicatedly practical. That was, if I could find any dangers for him to react to. The Sydney trail was dead and cold, and maybe Melbourne too would yield an unlooked-at public Munnings and a gone-away private gallery. And if it did, what then? For Donald the outlook would be bleaker than the strange puckered ranges sliding away underneath.

If I could take home enough to show beyond doubt that the plundering of his house had its roots in the sale of a painting in Australia, it should get the police off his neck, the life back to his spirit, and Regina into a decent grave.

If.

And I would have to be quick, or it would be too late to matter. Donald, staring hour after hour at a portrait in an empty house . . . Donald, on the brink.

Melbourne was cold and wet and blowing a gale. We checked gratefully into the warm plushy bosom of the

Hilton, souls cossetted from the door onwards by rich reds and purples and blues, velvety fabrics, copper and gilt and glass. The staff smiled. The lifts worked. There was polite shock when I carried my own suitcase. A long way from the bare boards of home.

I unpacked, which is to say, hung up my one suit, slightly crumpled from the squashy satchel, and then went to work again on the telephone.

The Melbourne office of the Monga Vineyards Proprietary Limited cheerfully told me that the person who dealt with Mr Donald Stuart from England was the Managing Director, Mr Hudson Taylor, and he could be found at present in his office at the vineyard itself, which was north of Adelaide. Would I like the number?

Thanks very much.

'No sweat,' they said, which I gathered was Australian shorthand for 'It's no trouble, and you're welcome.'

I pulled out the map of Australia I'd acquired on the flight from England. Melbourne, capital of the state of Victoria, lay right down in the south-east corner. Adelaide, capital of South Australia, lay about four hundred and fifty miles north-west. Correction, seven hundred and thirty kilometres: the Australians had already gone metric, to the confusion of my mental arithmetic.

Hudson Taylor was not in his vineyard office. An equally cheerful voice there told me he'd left for Melbourne to go to the races. He had a runner in the Cup. Reverence, the voice implied, was due.

Could I reach him anywhere, then?

Sure, if it was important. He would be staying with friends. Number supplied. Ring at nine o'clock.

Sighing a little I went two floors down and found Jik and Sarah bouncing around their room with gleeful satisfaction.

'We've got tickets for the races tomorrow and Tuesday,' he said, 'And a car pass, and a car. And the West Indies play Victoria at cricket on Sunday opposite the hotel and we've tickets for that too.'

'Miracles courtesy of the Hilton,' Sarah said, looking much happier at this programme. 'The whole package was on offer with the cancelled rooms.'

'So what do you want us to do this afternoon?' finished Jik expansively.

'Could you bear the Arts Centre?'

It appeared they could. Even Sarah came without forecasting universal doom, my lack of success so far having cheered her. We went in a taxi to keep her curled hair dry.

The Victoria Arts Centre was huge, modern, inventive and endowed with the largest stained-glass roof in the world. Jik took deep breaths as if drawing the living spirit of the place into his lungs and declaimed at the top of his voice that Australia was the greatest, the greatest, the only adventurous country left in the corrupt, stagnating, militant, greedy, freedom-hating, mean-minded, strait-jacketed, rotting, polluted world. Passers-by stared in amazement and Sarah showed no surprise at all.

We ran the Munnings to earth, eventually, deep in the labyrinth of galleries. It glowed in the remarkable light which suffused the whole building; the *Departure of the Hop Pickers*, with its great wide sky and the dignified gypsies with their ponies, caravans and children.

A young man was sitting at an easel slightly to one side, painstakingly working on a copy. On a table beside him stood large pots of linseed oil and turps, and a jar with brushes in cleaning fluid. A comprehensive box of paints lay open to hand. Two or three people stood about, watching him and pretending not to, in the manner of gallery-goers the world over.

Jik and I went round behind him to take a look. The young man glanced at Jik's face, but saw nothing there except raised eyebrows and blandness. We watched him squeeze flake white and cadmium yellow from tubes on to his palette and mix them together into a nice pale colour with a hogshair brush.

On the easel stood his study, barely started. The outlines were there, as precise as tracings, and a small amount of blue had been laid on the sky.

Jik and I watched in interest while he applied the pale yellow to the shirt of the nearest figure.

'Hey,' Jik said loudly, suddenly slapping him on the shoulder and shattering the reverent gallery hush into kaleidoscopic fragments, 'You're a fraud. If you're an artist I'm a gas-fitter's mate.'

Hardly polite, but not a hanging matter. The faces of the scattered onlookers registered embarrassment, not affront.

On the young man, though, the effect was galvanic. He leapt to his feet, overturning the easel and staring at Jik with wild eyes: and Jik, with huge enjoyment, put in the clincher.

'What you're doing is *criminal*,' he said.

The young man reacted to that with ruthless reptilian speed, snatching up the pots of linseed and turps and flinging the liquids at Jik's eyes.

I grabbed his left arm. He scooped up the paint-laden palette in his right and swung round fiercely, aiming at my face. I ducked instinctively. The palette missed me and struck Jik, who had his hands to his eyes and was yelling very loudly.

Sarah rushed towards him, knocking into me hard in her anxiety and loosening my grip on the young man. He tore his arm free, ran precipitously for the exit, dodged round behind two open-mouthed middle-aged spectators who were on their way in, and pushed them violently into my chasing path. By the time I'd disentangled myself, he had vanished from sight. I ran through several halls and passages, but couldn't find him. He knew his way, and I did not: and it took me long enough, when I finally gave up the hunt, to work out the route back to Jik.

A fair-sized crowd had surrounded him, and Sarah was in a roaring fury based on fear, which she unleashed on me as soon as she saw me return.

'Do something,' she screamed. 'Do something, he's going blind . . . He's going *blind* . . . I knew we should never have listened to you . . .'

I caught her wrists as she advanced in near hysteria to do at least some damage to my face in payment for Jik's. Her strength was no joke.

'Sarah,' I said fiercely. 'Jik is *not* going blind.'

'He is. He is,' she insisted, kicking my shins.

'Do you *want* him to?' I shouted.

She gasped sharply in outrage. What I'd said was at least as good as a slap in the face. Sense reasserted itself suddenly like a drench of cold water, and the manic power receded back to normal angry girl proportions.

'Linseed oil will do no harm at all,' I said positively. 'The turps is painful, but that's all. It absolutely will not affect his eyesight.'

She glared at me, pulled her wrists out of my grasp, and turned back to Jik, who was rocking around in agony and cupping his fingers over his eyes with rigid knuckles. Also, being Jik, he was exercising his tongue.

'The slimy little bugger . . . wait till I catch him . . . Jesus Christ Almighty I can't bloody see . . . Sarah . . . where's that bloody Todd . . . I'll strangle him . . . get an ambulance . . . my eyes are burning out . . . bloody buggering hell . . .'

I spoke loudly in his ear. 'Your eyes are O.K.'

'They're my bloody eyes and if I say they're not O.K. they're bloody not.'

'You know damn well you're not going blind, so stop hamming it up.'

'They're not your eyes, you sod.'

'And you're frightening Sarah,' I said.

That message got through. He took his hands away and stopped rolling about.

At the sight of his face a murmur of pleasant horror rippled through the riveted audience. Blobs of bright paint from the young man's palette had streaked one side of his jaw yellow and blue: and his eyes were red with inflammation and pouring with tears, and looked very sore indeed.

'Jesus, Sarah,' he said blinking painfully. 'Sorry, love. The bastard's right. Turps never blinded anybody.'

'Not permanently,' I said, because to do him justice he obviously couldn't see anything but tears at the moment.

Sarah's animosity was unabated. 'Get him an ambulance, then.'

I shook my head. 'All he needs is water and time.'

'You're a stupid heartless *pig*. He obviously needs a doctor, and hospital care.'

Jik, having abandoned histrionics, produced a handkerchief and gently mopped his streaming eyes.

'He's right, love. Lots of water, as the man said. Washes the sting away. Lead me to the nearest gents.'

With Sarah unconvinced but holding one arm, and a sympathetic male spectator the other, he was solicitously helped away like an amateur production of *Samson*. The chorus in the shape of the audience bent reproachful looks on me, and cheerfully awaited the next act.

I looked at the overturned mess of paints and easel which the young man had left. The onlookers looked at them too.

'I suppose,' I said slowly, 'that no one here was talking to the young artist before any of this happened?'

'We were,' said one woman, surprised at the question.

'So were we,' said another.

'What about?'

'Munnings,' said one, and 'Munnings,' said the other, both looking immediately at the painting on the wall.

'Not about his own work?' I said, bending down to pick it up. A slash of yellow lay wildly across the careful outlines, result of Jik's slap on the back.

Both of the ladies, and also their accompanying husbands, shook their heads and said they had talked with him about the pleasure of hanging a Munnings on their own walls, back home.

I smiled slowly.

'I suppose,' I said, 'that he didn't happen to know where you could get one?'

'Well, yeah,' they said. 'As a matter of fact, he sure did.'

'Where?'

'Well, look here, young fellow . . .' The elder of the husbands, a seventyish American with the unmistakable stamp of wealth, began shushing the others to silence with a practised damping movement of his right hand. Don't give information away, it said, you may lose by it. '. . . You're asking a lot of questions.'

'I'll explain,' I said. 'Would you like some coffee?'

They all looked at their watches and said doubtfully they possibly would.

'There's a coffee shop just down the hall,' I said. 'I saw it when I was trying to catch that young man . . . to make him tell why he flung turps in my friend's eyes.'

Curiosity sharpened in their faces. They were hooked.

The rest of the spectators drifted away, and I, asking the others to wait a moment, started moving the jumbled painting stuff off the centre of the floor to a tidier wallside heap.

None of it was marked with its owner's name. All regulation kit, obtainable from art shops. Artists' quality, not students' cheaper equivalents. None of it new, but not old, either. The picture itself was on a standard-sized piece of commercially prepared hardboard, not on stretched canvas. I stacked everything together, added the empty jars which had held linseed and turps, and wiped my hands on a piece of rag.

'Right,' I said. 'Shall we go?'

*

They were all Americans, all rich, retired, and fond of racing. Mr and Mrs Howard K. Petrovitch of Ridgeville, New Jersey, and Mr and Mrs Wyatt L. Minchless from Carter, Illinois.

Wyatt Minchless, the one who had shushed the others, called the meeting to order over four richly creamed iced coffees and one plain black. The black was for himself. Heart condition, he murmured, patting the relevant area of suiting. A white-haired man, black-framed specs, pale indoor complexion, pompous manner.

'Now, young fellow, let's hear it from the top.'

'Um,' I said. Where exactly was the top? 'The artist boy attacked my friend Jik because Jik called him a criminal.'

'Yuh,' Mrs Petrovitch nodded, 'I heard him. Just as we were leaving the gallery. Now why would he do that?'

'It isn't criminal to copy good painting,' Mrs Minchless said knowledgeably. 'In the Louvre in Paris, France, you can't get near the *Mona Lisa* for those irritating students.'

She had blue-rinsed puffed-up hair, uncreasable navy and green clothes, and enough diamonds to attract a top-rank thief. Deep lines of automatic disapproval ran downwards from the corner of her mouth. Thin body. Thick mind.

'It depends what you are copying *for*,' I said. 'If

you're going to try to pass your copy off as an original, then that definitely is a fraud.'

Mrs Petrovitch began to say, 'Do you think the young man was *forging* . . .' but was interrupted by Wyatt Minchless, who smothered her question both by the damping hand and his louder voice.

'Are you saying that this young artist boy was painting a Munnings he later intended to sell as the real thing?'

'Er . . .' I said.

Wyatt Minchless swept on. 'Are you saying that the Munnings picture he told us we might be able to buy is itself a forgery?'

The others looked both horrified at the possibility and admiring of Wyatt L. for his perspicacity.

'I don't know,' I said. 'I just thought I'd like to see it.'

'You don't want to buy a Munnings yourself? You are not acting as an agent for anyone else?' Wyatt's questions sounded severe and inquisitorial.

'Absolutely not,' I said.

'Well, then.' Wyatt looked round the other three, collected silent assents. 'He told Ruthie and me there was a good Munnings racing picture at a very reasonable price in a little gallery not far away . . .' He fished with forefinger and thumb into his outer breast pocket. 'Yes, here we are. Yarra River Fine Arts. Third turning off Swanston Street, about twenty yards along.'

Mr and Mrs Petrovitch looked resigned. 'He told us exactly the same.'

'He seemed such a nice young man,' Mrs Petrovitch added sadly. 'So interested in our trip. Asked us what we'd be betting on in the Cup.'

'He asked where we would be going after Melbourne,' Mr Petrovitch nodded. 'We told him Adelaide and Alice Springs, and he said Alice Springs was a Mecca for artists and to be sure to visit the Yarra River gallery there. The same firm, he said. Always had good pictures.'

Mr Petrovitch would have misunderstood if I had leaned across and hugged him. I concentrated on my fancy coffee and kept my excitement to myself.

'We're going on to Sydney,' pronounced Wyatt L. 'He didn't offer any suggestions for Sydney.'

The tall glasses were nearly empty. Wyatt looked at his watch and swallowed the last of his plain black.

'You didn't tell us,' Mrs Petrovitch said, looking puzzled, 'why your friend called the young man a criminal. I mean . . . I can see why the young man attacked your friend and ran away if he *was* a criminal, but why did your friend *think* he was?'

'Just what I was about to ask,' said Wyatt, nodding away heavily. Pompous liar, I thought.

'My friend Jik,' I said, 'is an artist himself. He didn't think much of the young man's effort. He called it criminal. He might just as well have said lousy.'

'Is that all?' said Mrs Petrovitch, looking disappointed.

'Well . . . the young man was painting with paints

which won't really mix. Jik's a perfectionist. He can't stand seeing paint misused.'

'What do you mean, won't mix?'

'Paints are chemicals,' I said apologetically. 'Most of them don't have any effect on each other, but you have to be careful.'

'What happens if you aren't?' demanded Ruthie Minchless.

'Um . . . nothing explodes,' I said, smiling. 'It's just that . . . well, if you mix flake white, which is lead, with cadmium yellow, which contains sulphur, like the young man was doing, you get a nice pale colour to start with but the two minerals react against each other and in time darken and alter the picture.'

'And your friend called this criminal?' Wyatt said in disbelief. 'It couldn't possibly make that much difference.'

'Er . . .' I said. 'Well, Van Gogh used a light bright new yellow made of chrome when he painted a picture of sunflowers. Cadmium yellow hadn't been developed then. But chrome yellow has shown that over a couple of hundred years it decomposes and in the end turns greenish black, and the sunflowers are already an odd colour, and I don't think anyone has found a way of stopping it.'

'But the young man wasn't painting for posterity,' said Ruthie with irritation. 'Unless he's another Van Gogh, surely it doesn't matter.'

I didn't think they'd want to hear that Jik hoped for

recognition in the twenty-third century. The permanence of colours had always been an obsession with
him, and he'd dragged me along once to a course on
their chemistry.

The Americans got up to go.

'All very interesting,' Wyatt said with a dismissive
smile. 'I guess I'll keep my money in regular stocks.'

CHAPTER SEVEN

Jik had gone from the gents, gone from the whole Arts Centre. I found him back with Sarah in their hotel room, being attended by the Hilton's attractive resident nurse. The door to the corridor stood open, ready for her to leave.

'Try not to rub them, Mr Cassavetes,' she was saying. 'If you have any trouble, call the reception desk, and I'll come back.'

She gave me a professional half-smile in the open doorway and walked briskly away, leaving me to go in.

'How are the eyes?' I said, advancing tentatively.

'Ruddy awful.' They were bright pink, but dry. Getting better.

Sarah said with tight lips, 'This has all gone far enough. I know that this time Jik will be all right again in a day or two, but we are not taking any more risks.'

Jik said nothing and didn't look at me.

It wasn't exactly unexpected. I said, 'O.K. . . . Well, have a nice weekend, and thanks anyway.'

'Todd . . .' Jik said.

113

Sarah leapt in fast. 'No, Jik. It's not our responsibility. Todd can think what he likes, but his cousin's troubles are nothing to do with us. We are not getting involved any further. I've been against all this silly poking around all along, and this is where it stops.'

'Todd will go on with it,' Jik said.

'Then he's a fool.' She was angry, scornful, biting.

'Sure,' I said. 'Anyone who tries to right a wrong these days is a fool. Much better not to meddle, not to get involved, not to think it's your responsibility. I really ought to be painting away safely in my attic at Heathrow, minding my own business and letting Donald rot. Much more sensible, I agree. The trouble is that I simply can't do it. I see the hell he's in. How can I just turn my back? Not when there's a chance of getting him out. True enough, I may not manage it, but what I can't face is not having tried.'

I came to a halt.

A blank pause.

'Well,' I said, raising a smile. 'Here endeth the lesson according to the world's foremost nit. Have fun at the races. I might go too, you never know.'

I sketched a farewell and eased myself out. Neither of them said a word. I shut the door quietly and took the lift up to my own room.

A pity about Sarah, I thought. She would have Jik in cotton-wool and slippers if he didn't look out; and he'd never paint those magnificent brooding pictures any more, because they sprang from a torment he would no longer be allowed. Security, to him, would be a sort of abdication; a sort of death.

I looked at my watch and decided the Yarra River Fine Arts set-up might still have its doors open. Worth trying.

I wondered, as I walked along Wellington Parade and up Swanston Street, whether the young turps-flinger would be there, and if he was, whether he would know me. I'd seen only glimpses of his face, as I'd mostly been standing behind him. All one could swear to was light-brown hair, acne on the chin, a round jaw-line and a full-lipped mouth. Under twenty. Perhaps not more than seventeen. Dressed in blue jeans, white tee-shirt, and tennis shoes. About five-foot-eight, a hundred and thirty pounds. Quick on his feet, and liable to panic. And no artist.

The gallery was open, brightly lit, with a horse paint-ing on a gilt display easel in the centre of the window. Not a Munnings. A portrait picture of an Australian horse and jockey, every detail sharp-edged, emphatic, and, to my taste, overpainted. Beside it a notice, gold embossed on black, announced a special display of distinguished equine art; and beside that, less well-produced but with larger letters, stood a display card saying 'Welcome to the Melbourne Cup'.

The gallery looked typical of hundreds of others round the world; narrow frontage, with premises stretching back a good way from the street. Two or three people were wandering about inside, looking at the merchandise on the well-lit neutral grey walls.

I had gone there intending to go in. To go in was still what I intended, but I hesitated outside in the street feeling as if I were at the top of a ski jump. Stupid, I thought. Nothing ventured, nothing gained, and all that. If you don't look, you won't see.

I took a ruefully deep breath and stepped over the welcoming threshold.

Greeny-grey carpet within, and an antique desk strategically placed near the door, with a youngish woman handing out small catalogues and large smiles.

'Feel free to look around,' she said. 'More pictures downstairs.'

She handed me a catalogue, a folded glazed white card with several typed sheets clipped into it. I flipped them over. One hundred and sixty-three items, numbered consecutively, with titles, artists' names, and asking price. A painting already sold, it said, would have a red spot on the frame.

I thanked her. 'Just passing by,' I said.

She nodded and smiled professionally, eyes sliding in a rapid summing-up over my denim clothes and general air of not belonging to the jet set. She herself wore the latest trendy fashion with careless ease and radiated tycoon-catching sincerity. Australian, assured, too big a personality to be simply a receptionist.

'You're welcome anyway,' she said.

I walked slowly down the long room, checking the

pictures against their notes. Most were by Australian artists, and I could see what Jik had meant about the hot competition. The field was just as crowded as at home, if not more so, and the standard in some respects better. As usual when faced with other people's flourishing talents I began to have doubts of my own.

At the far end of the ground-floor display there was a staircase leading downwards, adorned with a large arrow and a notice repeating 'More Pictures Downstairs'.

I went down. Same carpet, same lighting, but no scatter of customers looking from pictures to catalogues and back again.

Below stairs, the gallery was not one straight room but a series of small rooms off a long corridor, apparently the result of not being able to knock down all the dividing and load-bearing walls. A room to the rear of the stairs was an office, furnished with another distinguished desk, two or three comfortable chairs for prospective clients, and a civilized row of teak-faced filing cabinets. Heavily framed pictures adorned the walls, and an equally substantial man was writing in a ledger at the desk.

He raised his head, conscious of my presence outside his door.

'Can I help you?' he said.

'Just looking.'

He gave me an uninterested nod and went back to his work. He, like the whole place, had an air of permanence and respectability quite unlike the fly-by-night suburban affair in Sydney. This reputable business, I thought, could not be what I was looking for. I had got the whole thing wrong. I would have to wait until I could get Hudson Taylor to look up Donald's cheque and point me in a new direction.

Sighing, I continued down the line of rooms, thinking I might as well finish taking stock of the opposition. A few of the frames were adorned with red spots, but the prices on everything good were a mile from a bargain and a deterrent to all but the rich.

In the end room, which was larger than the others, I came across the Munningses. Three of them. All with horses: one racing scene, one hunting, one of gypsies.

They were not in the catalogue.

They hung without ballyhoo in a row of similar subjects, and to my eyes stuck out like thoroughbreds among hacks.

Prickles began up my spine. It wasn't just the workmanship, but one of the pictures itself. Horses going down to the start. A long line of jockeys, bright against a dark sky. The silks of the nearest rider, purple with a green cap.

Maisie's chatty voice reverberated in my inner ear, describing what I saw. '... I expect you'll think I was silly but that was one of the reasons I bought it ... because Archie and I decided we'd like purple with a green cap for our colours, if no one already had that ...'

Munnings had always used a good deal of purple and green in shadows and distances. All the same ... This picture, size, subject, and colouring, was exactly like Maisie's, which had been hidden behind a radiator, and, presumably, burned.

The picture in front of me looked authentic. The right sort of patina for the time since Munnings' death, the right excellence of draughtsmanship, the right indefinable something which separated the great from the good. I put out a gentle finger to feel the surface of canvas and paint. Nothing there that shouldn't be.

An English voice from behind me said, 'Can I help you?'

'Isn't that a Munnings?' I said casually, turning round.

He was standing in the doorway, looking in, his expression full of the guarded helpfulness of one whose best piece of stock is being appraised by someone apparently too poor to buy it.

I knew him instantly. Brown receding hair combed back, grey eyes, down-drooping moustache, suntanned skin: all last on view thirteen days ago beside the sea in Sussex, England, prodding around in a smoky ruin.

Mr Greene. With an 'e'.

It took him only a fraction longer. Puzzlement as he glanced from me to the picture and back, then the shocking realization of where he'd seen me. He took a sharp step backwards and raised his hand to the wall outside.

I was on my way to the door, but I wasn't quick enough. A steel mesh gate slid down very fast in the doorway and clicked into some sort of bolt in the floor. Mr Greene stood on the outside, disbelief still stamped on every feature and his mouth hanging open. I revised all my easy theories about danger being good for the soul and felt as frightened as I'd ever been in my life.

'What's the matter?' called a deeper voice from up the corridor.

Mr Greene's tongue was stuck. The man from the office appeared at his shoulder and looked at me through the imprisoning steel.

'A thief?' he asked with irritation.

Mr Greene shook his head. A third person arrived outside, his young face bright with curiosity, and his acne showing like measles.

'Hey,' he said in loud Australian surprise. 'He was the one at the Arts Centre. The one who chased me. I swear he didn't follow me. I swear it.'

'Shut up,' said the man from the office briefly. He stared at me steadily. I stared back.

I was standing in the centre of a brightly lit room of about fifteen feet square. No windows. No way out except through the guarded door. Nowhere to hide, no weapons to hand. A long way down the ski jump and no promise of a soft landing.

'I say,' I said plaintively. 'Just what is all this about?' I walked up to the steel gate and tapped on it. 'Open this up, I want to get out.'

'What are you doing here?' the office man said. He was bigger than Greene and obviously more senior in the gallery. Heavy dark spectacle frames over unfriendly eyes, and a blue bow tie with polka dots under a double chin. Small mouth with a full lower lip. Thinning hair.

'Looking,' I said, trying to sound bewildered. 'Just looking at pictures.' An innocent at large, I thought, and a bit dim.

'He chased me in the Arts Centre,' the boy repeated.

'You threw some stuff in that man's eyes,' I said indignantly. 'You might have blinded him.'

'Friend of yours, was he?' the office man said.

'No,' I said. 'I was just there, that was all. Same as I'm here. Just looking at pictures. Nothing wrong in that, is there? I go to lots of galleries, all the time.'

Mr Greene got his voice back. 'I saw him in England,' he said to the office man. His eyes returned to the Munnings, then he put his hand on the office man's arm and pulled him up the corridor out of my sight.

'Open the door,' I said to the boy, who still gazed in.

'I don't know how,' he said. 'And I don't reckon I'd be popular, somehow.'

The two other men returned. All three gazed in. I began to feel sympathy for creatures in cages.

'Who *are* you?' said the office man.

'Nobody. I mean, I'm just here for the racing, of course, and the cricket.'

'Name?'

'Charles Neil.' Charles Neil Todd.

'What were you doing in England?'

'I live there!' I said. 'Look,' I went on, as if trying to be reasonable under great provocation. 'I saw this man here,' I nodded to Greene, 'at the home of a woman I know slightly in Sussex. She was giving me a lift home from the races, see, as I'd missed my train to Worthing and was thumbing along the road from the Members' car park. Well, she stopped and picked me up, and then said she wanted to make a detour to see her house which had lately been burnt, and when we got there, this man was there. He said his name was Greene and that he was from an insurance company, and that's all I know about him. So what's going on?'

'It is a coincidence that you should meet here again, so soon.'

'It certainly is,' I agreed fervently. 'But that's no bloody reason to lock me up.'

I read indecision on all their faces. I hoped the sweat wasn't running visibly down my own.

I shrugged exasperatedly. 'Fetch the police or something, then,' I said. 'If you think I've done anything wrong.'

The man from the office put his hand to the switch on the outside wall and carefully fiddled with it, and the steel gate slid up out of sight, a good deal more slowly than it had come down.

'Sorry,' he said perfunctorily. 'But we have to be careful, with so many valuable paintings on the premises.'

'Well, I see that,' I said, stepping forward and resisting a strong impulse to make a dash for it. 'But all the same . . .' I managed an aggrieved tone. 'Still, no harm done, I suppose.' Magnanimous, as well.

They all walked behind me along the corridor and up the stairs and through the upper gallery, doing my nerves no slightest good. All the other visitors seemed to have left. The receptionist was locking the front door.

My throat was dry beyond swallowing.

'I thought eve.,one had gone,' she said in surprise.

'Slight delay,' I said, with a feeble laugh.

She gave me the professional smile and reversed the locks. Opened the door. Held it, waiting for me.

Six steps.

Out in the fresh air.

God almighty, it smelled good. I half turned. All four stood in the gallery watching me go. I shrugged and nodded and trudged away into the drizzle, feeling as weak as a fieldmouse dropped by a hawk.

I caught a passing tram and travelled a good way into unknown regions of the huge city, conscious only of an urgent desire to put a lot of distance between myself and that basement prison.

They would have second thoughts. They were bound to. They would wish they had found out more about me before letting me go. They couldn't be certain it wasn't a coincidence that I'd turned up at their gallery, because far more amazing coincidences did exist, like Lincoln at the time of his assassination having a secretary called Kennedy and Kennedy having a secretary called Lincoln; but the more they thought about it the less they would believe it.

If they wanted to find me, where would they look? Not at the Hilton, I thought in amusement. At the races: I had told them I would be there. On the whole I wished I hadn't.

At the end of the tramline I got off and found myself opposite a small interesting-looking restaurant with B.Y.O. in large letters on the door. Hunger as usual rearing its healthy head, I went in and ordered a steak, and asked for a look at the wine list.

The waitress looked surprised. 'It's B.Y.O.,' she said. 'What's B.Y.O.?'

Her eyebrows went still higher. 'You are a stranger? Bring Your Own. We don't sell drinks here, only food.'

'Oh.'

'If you want something to drink, there's a drive-in bottle shop a hundred yards down the road that'll still be open. I could hold the steak until you get back.'

I shook my head and settled for a teetotal dinner, grinning all through coffee at a notice on the wall saying 'We have an arrangement with our bank. They don't fry steaks and we don't cash cheques.'

When I set off back to the city centre on the tram, I passed the bottle shop, which at first sight looked so like a garage that if I hadn't known I would have thought the line of cars was queuing for petrol. I could see why Jik liked the Australian imagination: both sense and fun.

The rain had stopped. I left the tram and walked the last couple of miles through the bright streets and dark parks, asking the way. Thinking of Donald and Maisie and Greene with an 'e', and of paintings and burglaries and violent minds.

The overall plan had all along seemed fairly simple: to sell pictures in Australia and steal them back in England, together with everything else lying handy. As I had come across two instances within three weeks, I had been sure there had to be more, because it was surely impossible that I could have stumbled on the *only* two, even given the double link of racing and painting. Since I'd met the Petrovitches and the Minch-lesses, it seemed I'd been wrong to think of all the robberies taking place in England. Why not in America? Why not anywhere that was worth the risk?

Why not a mobile force of thieves shuttling containerfuls of antiques from continent to continent, selling briskly to a ravenous market? As Inspector Frost had said, few antiques were ever recovered. The demand was insatiable and the supply, by definition, limited.

Suppose I were a villain, I thought, and I didn't want to waste weeks in foreign countries finding out exactly which houses were worth robbing. I could just stay quietly at home in Melbourne selling paintings to rich visitors who could afford an impulse-buy of ten thousand pounds or so. I could chat away with them about their picture collections back home, and I could shift the conversation easily to their silver and china and objets d'art.

I wouldn't want the sort of customers who had Rembrandts or Fabergés or anything well-known and unsaleable like that. Just the middling wealthy with Georgian silver and lesser Gauguins and Chippendale chairs.

When they bought my paintings, they would give me their addresses. Nice and easy. Just like that.

I would be a supermarket type of villain, with a large turnover of small goods. I would reckon that if I kept the victims reasonably well scattered, the fact that they had been to Australia within the past year or so would mean nothing to each regional police force. I would reckon that among the thousands of burglary claims they had to settle, Australian visits would bear no significance to insurance companies.

I would not, though, reckon on a crossed wire like Charles Neil Todd.

If I were a villain, I thought, with a well-established

business and a good reputation, I wouldn't put myself at risk by selling fakes. Forged oil paintings were almost always detectable under a microscope, even if one discounted that the majority of experienced dealers could tell them at a glance. A painter left his signature all over a painting, not just in the corner, because the way he held his brush was as individual as handwriting. Brush strokes could be matched as conclusively as grooves on bullets.

If I were a villain I'd wait in my spider's web with a real Munnings, or maybe a real Picasso drawing, or a genuine work by a recently dead good artist whose output had been voluminous, and along would come the rich little flies, carefully steered my way by talkative accomplices who stood around in the states' capitals' art galleries for the purpose. Both Donald and Maisie had been hooked that way.

Supposing when I'd sold a picture to a man from England and robbed him, and got my picture back again, I then sold it to someone from America. And then robbed him, and got it back, and so on and round.

Suppose I sold a picture to Maisie in Sydney, and got it back, and started to sell it again in Melbourne . . . My supposing stopped right there, because it didn't fit.

If Maisie had left her picture in full view it would have been stolen like her other things. Maybe it even had been, and was right now glowing in the Yarra

River Fine Arts, but if so, why had the house been burnt, and why had Mr Greene turned up to search the ruins?

It only made sense if Maisie's picture had been a copy, and if the thieves hadn't been able to find it. Rather than leave it around, they'd burned the house. But I'd just decided that I wouldn't risk fakes. Except that . . . would Maisie know an expert copy if she saw one? No, she wouldn't.

I sighed. To fool even Maisie you'd have to find an accomplished artist willing to copy instead of pressing on with his own work, and they weren't that thick on the ground. All the same, she'd bought her picture in the short-lived Sydney gallery, not in Melbourne, so maybe in other places besides Melbourne they would take a risk with fakes.

The huge bulk of the hotel rose ahead of me across the last stretch of park. The night air blew cool on my head. I had a vivid feeling of being disconnected, a stranger in a vast continent, a speck under the stars. The noise and warmth of the Hilton brought the expanding universe down to imaginable size.

Upstairs, I telephoned Hudson Taylor at the number his secretary had given me. Nine o'clock on the dot. He sounded mellow and full of good dinner, his voice strong, courteous and vibrantly Australian.

'Donald Stuart's cousin? Is it true about little Regina being killed?'

'I'm afraid so.'

'It's a real tragedy. A real nice lass, that Regina.'

'Yes.'

'Lookee here, then, what can I do for you? Is it tickets for the races?'

'Er, no,' I said. 'It was just that since the receipt and provenance letter of the Munnings had been stolen along with the picture, Donald would like to get in touch with the people who had sold it to him, for insurance purposes, but he had forgotten their name. And as I was coming to Melbourne for the Cup . . .'

'That's easy enough,' Hudson Taylor said pleasantly. 'I remember the place well. I went with Donald to see the picture there, and the guy in charge brought it along to the Hilton afterwards, when we arranged the finance. Now let's see . . .' There was a pause for thought. 'I can't remember the name of the place just now. Or the manager. It was some months ago, do you see? But I've got him on record here in the Melbourne office, and I'm calling in there anyway in the morning, so I'll look them up. You'll be at the races tomorrow?'

'Yes,' I said.

'How about meeting for a drink, then? You can tell me about poor Donald and Regina, and I'll have the information he wants.'

I said that would be fine, and he gave me detailed instructions as to where I would find him, and when. 'There will be a huge crowd,' he said. 'But if you stand on that exact spot I shouldn't miss you.'

129

The spot he had described sounded public and exposed. I hoped that it would only be he who found me on it.

'I'll be there,' I said.

CHAPTER EIGHT

Jik called through on the telephone at eight next morning.

'Come down to the coffee shop and have breakfast.'

'O.K.'

I went down in the lift and along the foyer to the hotel's informal restaurant. He was sitting at a table alone, wearing dark glasses and making inroads into a mountain of scrambled egg.

'They bring you coffee,' he said, 'but you have to fetch everything else from that buffet.' He nodded towards a large well-laden table in the centre of the breezy blue and sharp green decor. 'How's things?'

'Not what they used to be.'

He made a face. 'Bastard.'

'How are the eyes?'

He whipped off the glasses with a theatrical flourish and leaned forward to give me a good look. Pink, they were, and still inflamed, but on the definite mend.

'Has Sarah relented?' I asked.

'She's feeling sick.'

'Oh?'

'God knows,' he said. 'I hope not. I don't want a kid yet. She isn't overdue or anything.'

'She's a nice girl,' I said.

He slid me a glance. 'She says she's got nothing against you personally.'

'But,' I said.

He nodded. 'The mother hen syndrome.'

'Wouldn't have cast you as a chick.'

He put down his knife and fork. 'Nor would I, by God. I told her to cheer up and get this little enterprise over as soon as possible and face the fact she hadn't married a marshmallow.'

'And she said?'

He gave a twisted grin. 'From my performance in bed last night, that she had.'

I wondered idly about the success or otherwise of their sex life. From the testimony of one or two past girls who had let their hair down to me while waiting hours in the flat for Jik's unpredictable return, he was a moody lover, quick to arousal and easily put off. 'It only takes a dog barking, and he's gone.' Not much, I dared say, had changed.

'Anyway,' he said. 'There's this car we've got. Damned silly if you didn't come with us to the races.'

'Would Sarah . . .', I asked carefully, '. . . scowl?'

'She says not.'

I accepted this offer and inwardly sighed. It looked as if he wouldn't take the smallest step henceforth without the nod from Sarah. When the wildest ones got married, was it always like that? Wedded bliss putting nets over the eagles.

'Where did you get to, last night?' he said.

'Aladdin's cave,' I said. 'Treasures galore and damned lucky to escape the boiling oil.'

I told him about the gallery, the Munnings, and my brief moment of captivity. I told him what I thought of the burglaries. It pleased him. His eyes gleamed with humour and the familiar excitement rose.

'How are we going to prove it?' he said.

He heard the 'we' as soon as he said it. He laughed ruefully, the fizz dying away. 'Well, how?'

'Don't know yet.'

'I'd like to help,' he said apologetically.

I thought of a dozen sarcastic replies and stifled the lot. It was I who was the one out of step, not them. The voice of the past had no right to break up the future.

'You'll do what pleases Sarah,' I said with finality, and as an order, not a prodding satire.

'Don't sound so bloody bossy.'

We finished breakfast amicably trying to build a suitable new relationship on the ruins of the old, and both knowing well what we were about.

When I met them later in the hall at setting-off time it was clear that Sarah too had made a reassessment and put her mind to work on her emotions. She greeted me with an attempted smile and an outstretched hand.

I shook the hand lightly and also gave her a token kiss on the cheek. She took it as it was meant.

Truce made, terms agreed, pact signed. Jik the mediator stood around looking smug.

'Take a look at him,' he said, flapping a hand in my direction. 'The complete stockbroker. Suit, tie, leather shoes. If he isn't careful they'll have him in the Royal Academy.'

Sarah looked bewildered. 'I thought that was an honour.'

'It depends,' said Jik, sneering happily. 'Passable artists with polished social graces get elected in their thirties. Masters with average social graces, in their forties; masters with no social graces, in their fifties. Geniuses who don't give a damn about being elected are ignored as long as possible.'

'Putting Todd in the first category and yourself in the last?' Sarah said.

'Of course.'

'Stands to reason,' I said. 'You never hear about young masters. Masters are always old.'

'For God's sake,' Sarah said. 'Let's go to the races.'

We went slowly, on account of a continuous stream of traffic going the same way. The car park at Flemington racecourse, when we arrived, looked like a giant picnic ground, with hundreds of full-scale lunch parties going on between the cars. Tables, chairs, cloths, china, silver, glass. Sun umbrellas optimistically raised in defiance of the rain-clouds threatening above. A lot of gaiety and booze and a giant overall statement that 'This Was The Life.'

To my mild astonishment Jik and Sarah had come prepared. They whipped out table, chairs, drinks and food from the rented car's boot and said it was easy when you knew how, you just ordered the whole works.

'I have an uncle,' Sarah said, 'who holds the title of Fastest Bar in the West. It takes him roughly ten seconds from putting the brakes on to pouring the first drink.'

She was really trying, I thought. Not just putting up with an arrangement for Jik's sake, but actually trying to make it work. If it was an effort, it didn't show. She was wearing an interesting olive-green linen coat, with a broad-brimmed hat of the same colour, which she held on from time to time against little gusts of wind. Overall, a new Sarah, prettier, more relaxed, less afraid.

'Champagne?' Jik offered, popping the cork. 'Steak and oyster pie?'

'How will I go back to cocoa and chips?'

'Fatter.'

We demolished the goodies, repacked the boot, and with a sense of taking part in some vast semi-religious ritual, squeezed along with the crowd through the gate to the holy of holies.

'It'll be much worse than this on Tuesday,' observed Sarah, who had been to these junkets several times in the past. 'Melbourne Cup day is a public holiday. The city has three million inhabitants and half of them will try to get here.' She was shouting above the crowd noises and holding grimly on to her hat against the careless buffeting all around.

'If they've got any sense they'll stay at home and watch it on the box,' I said breathlessly, receiving a hefty kidney punch from the elbow of a man fighting his way into a can of beer.

'It won't be on the television in Melbourne, only on the radio.'

'Good grief. Why ever not?'

'Because they want everyone to come. It's televised all over the rest of Australia, but not on its own doorstep.'

'Same with the golf and the cricket,' Jik said with a touch of gloom. 'And you can't even have a decent bet on those.'

We went through the bottleneck and, by virtue of the inherited badges, through a second gate and round into the calmer waters of the green oblong of Members' lawn. Much like on many a Derby Day at home, I thought. Same triumph of will over weather. Bright faces under grey skies. Warm coats over the pretty silks, umbrellas at the ready for the occasional top hat. When I painted pictures of racegoers in the rain, which I sometimes did, most people laughed. I never minded. I reckoned it meant they understood that the inner warmth of a pleasure couldn't be externally damped; that they too might play a trumpet in a thunderstorm.

Come to think of it, I thought, why didn't I paint a racegoer playing a trumpet in a thunderstorm? It might be symbolic enough even for Jik.

My friends were deep in a cross-talking assessment of the form of the first race. Sarah, it appeared, had a betting pedigree as long as her husband's, and didn't agree with him.

'I know it was soft going at Randwick last week. But it's pretty soft here too after all this rain, and he likes it on top.'

'He was only beaten by Boyblue at Randwick, and Boyblue was out of sight in the Caulfield Cup.'

'Please your silly self,' Sarah said loftily. 'But it's still too soft for Grapevine.'

'Want to bet?' Jik asked me.

'Don't know the horses.'

'As if that mattered.'

'Right.' I consulted the racecard. 'Two dollars on Generator.'

They both looked up, and they both said 'Why?'

'If in doubt, back number eleven. I once went nearly through the card on number eleven.'

They made clucking and pooh-poohing noises and told me I could make a gift of my two dollars to the bookies or the T.A.B.

'The what?'

'Totalizator Agency Board.'

137

The bookmakers, it seemed, were strictly on-course only, with no big firms as in England. All off-course betting shops were run by the T.A.B., which returned a good share of the lolly to racing. Racing was rich, rock-solid, and flourishing. Bully for Australia, Jik said.

We took our choice and paid our money, and Generator won at twenty-fives.

'Beginner's luck,' Sarah said.

Jik laughed. 'He's no beginner. He got kicked out of playschool for running a book.'

They tore up their tickets, set their minds to race two, and made expeditions to place their bets. I settled for four dollars on number one.

'Why?'

'Double my stake on half of eleven.'

'Oh God,' said Sarah. 'You're something else.'

One of the more aggressive clouds started scattering rain, and the less hardy began to make for shelter.

'Come on,' I said. 'Let's go and sit up there in the dry.'

'You two go,' Sarah said. 'I can't.'

'Why not?'

'Because those seats are only for men.'

I laughed. I thought she was joking, but it appeared it was no joke. Very unfunny, in fact. About two thirds of the best seats in the Members' stands were reserved for males.

'What about their wives and girlfriends?' I said incredulously.

'They can go up on the roof.'

Sarah, being Australian, saw nothing very odd in it. To me, and surely to Jik, it was ludicrous.

He said with a carefully straight face, 'On a lot of the bigger courses the men who run Australian racing give themselves leather armchairs behind glass to watch from, and thick-carpeted restaurants and bars to eat and drink like kings in, and let their women eat in the cafeterias and sit on hard plastic chairs on the open stands among the rest of the crowd. They consider this behaviour quite normal. All anthropological groups consider their most bizarre tribal customs quite normal.'

'I thought you were in love with all things Australian.'

Jik sighed heavily. 'Nowhere's perfect.'

'I'm getting wet,' Sarah said.

We escalated to the roof which had a proportion of two women to one man and was windy and damp, with bench seating.

'Don't worry about it,' Sarah said, amused at my aghastness on behalf of womankind. 'I'm used to it.'

'I thought this country made a big thing about equality for all.'

'For all except half the population,' Jik said.

We could see the whole race superbly from our eyrie. Sarah and Jik screamed encouragement to their fancies but number one finished in front by two lengths, at eight to one.

'It's disgusting,' Sarah said, tearing up more tickets. 'What number do you fancy for the third?'

'I won't be with you for the third. I've got an appointment to have a drink with someone who knows Donald.'

She took it in, and the lightness went out of her manner. 'More . . . investigating?'

'I have to.'

'Yes.' She swallowed and made a visible effort. 'Well . . . Good luck.'

'You're a great girl.'

She looked surprised that I should think so and suspicious that I was intending sarcasm, and also partly pleased. I returned earthwards with her multiple expression amusing my mind.

The Members' lawn was bounded on one long side by the stands and on the opposite side by the path taken by the horses on their way from the saddling boxes to the parade ring. One short side of the lawn lay alongside part of the parade ring itself: and it was at the corner of lawn where the horses' path reached the parade ring that I was to meet Hudson Taylor.

The rain had almost stopped, which was good news for my suit. I reached the appointed spot and stood there waiting, admiring the brilliant scarlet of the long bedful of flowers which lined the railing between horse-walk and lawn. Cadmium red mixtures with highlights of orange and white and maybe a streak or two of expensive vermilion . . .

'Charles Todd?'

'Yes . . . Mr Taylor?'

'Hudson. Glad to know you.' He shook hands, his grip dry and firm. Late forties, medium height, comfortable build, with affable, slightly sad eyes sloping downwards at the outer corners. He was one of the minority of men in morning suits, and he wore it as comfortably as a sweater.

'Let's find somewhere dry,' he said. 'Come this way.'

He led me steadily up the bank of steps, in through an entrance door, down a wide interior corridor running the whole length of the stands, past a uniformed guard and a notice saying 'Committee Only', and into a large square comfortable room fitted out as a small-scale bar. The journey had been one long polite push through expensively dressed cohorts, but the bar was comparatively quiet and empty. A group of four, two men, two women, stood chatting with half-filled glasses held close to their chests, and two women in furs were complaining loudly of the cold.

'They love to bring out the sables,' Hudson Taylor chuckled, fetching two glasses of Scotch and gesturing to me to sit by a small table. 'Spoils their fun, the years it's hot for this meeting.'

'Is it usually hot?'

'Melbourne's weather can change twenty degrees in an hour.' He sounded proud of it. 'Now then, this business of yours.' He delved into an inner breast pocket and surfaced with a folded paper. 'Here you are, typed out for Donald. The gallery was called Yarra River Fine Arts.'

I would have been astounded if it hadn't been.

'And the man we dealt with was someone called Ivor Wexford.'

'What did he look like?' I asked.

'I don't remember very clearly. It was back in April, do you see?'

I thought briefly and pulled a small slim sketch-book out of my pocket.

'If I draw him, might you know him?'

He looked amused. 'You never know.'

I drew quickly in soft pencil a reasonable likeness of Greene, but without the moustache.

'Was it him?'

Hudson Taylor looked doubtful. I drew in the moustache. He shook his head decisively. 'No, that wasn't him.'

'How about this?'

I flipped over the page and started again. Hudson Taylor looked pensive as I did my best with the man from the basement office.

'Maybe,' he said.

I made the lower lip fuller, added heavy-framed spectacles, and a bow tie with spots.

'That's him,' said Hudson in surprise. 'I remember the bow tie, anyway. You don't see many of those these days. How did you know? You must have met him.'

'I walked round a couple of galleries yesterday afternoon.'

'That's quite a gift you have there,' he said with interest, watching me put the notebook away.

'Practice, that's all.' Years of seeing people's faces as matters of shapes and proportions and planes, and remembering which way the lines slanted. I could already have drawn Hudson's eyes from memory. It was a knack I'd had from childhood.

'Sketching is your hobby?' Hudson asked.

'And my work. I mostly paint horses.'

'Really?' He glanced at the equine portraits decorating the wall. 'Like these?'

I nodded, and we talked a little about painting for a living.

'Maybe I can give you a commission, if my horse runs well in the Cup.' He smiled, the outer edges of his eyes crinkling finely. 'If he's down the field, I'll feel more like shooting him.'

He stood up and gestured me still to follow. 'Time for the next race. Care to watch it with me?'

We emerged into daylight in the prime part of the stands, overlooking the big square enclosure which served both for parading the runners before the race and unsaddling the winners after. I was amused to see that the front rows of seats were all for men: two couples walking in front of us split like amoebas, the husbands going down left, the women up right.

'Down here,' Hudson said, pointing.

'May we only go up there if accompanied by a lady?' I asked.

He glanced at me sideways, and smiled. 'You find our ways odd? We'll go up, by all means.'

He led the way and settled comfortably among the predominantly female company, greeting several people and introducing me companionably as his friend Charles from England. Instant first names, instant acceptance, Australian style.

'Regina hated all this division of the sexes, poor lass,' he said. 'But it has interesting historical roots.' He chuckled. 'Australia was governed nearly all last century with the help of the British Army. The officers and gentlemen left their wives back in England, but such is nature, they all set up liaisons here with women of low repute. They didn't want their fellow officers to see the vulgarity of their choice, so they invented a rule that the officers' enclosures were for men only, which effectively silenced their popsies' pleas to be taken.'

I laughed. 'Very neat.'

'It's easier to establish a tradition,' Hudson said, 'than to get rid of it.'

'You're establishing a great tradition for fine wines, Donald says.'

The sad-looking eyes twinkled with civilized pleasure. 'He was most enthusiastic. He travelled round all the big vineyards, of course, besides visiting us.'

The horses for the third race cantered away to the

start, led by a fractious chestnut colt with too much white about his head.

'Ugly brute,' Hudson said. 'But he'll win.'

'Are you backing it?'

He smiled. 'I've a little bit on.'

The race started and the field sprinted, and Hudson's knuckles whitened so much from his grip as he gazed intently through his binoculars that I wondered just how big the little bit was. The chestnut colt was beaten into fourth place. Hudson put his raceglasses down slowly and watched the unsatisfactory finish with a blank expression.

'Oh well,' he said, his sad eyes looking even sadder. 'Always another day.' He shrugged resignedly, cheered up, shook my hand, told me to remember him to Donald, and asked if I could find my own way out.

'Thank you for your help,' I said.

He smiled. 'Any time. Any time.'

With only a couple of wrong turnings I reached ground level, listening on the way to fascinating snippets of Australian conversation.

'. . . They say he's an embarrassment as a Committee man. He only opens his mouth to change feet . . .'

'. . . a beastly stomach wog, so he couldn't come . . .'

'. . . told him to stop whingeing like a bloody Pommie, and get on with it . . .'

'. . . won twenty dollars? Good on yer, Joanie . . .'

And everywhere the diphthong vowels which gave the word 'No' about five separate sounds, defying my attempts to copy it. I'd been told on the flight over, by an Australian, that all Australians spoke with one single accent. It was about as true as saying all Americans spoke alike, or all British. English was infinitely elastic; and alive, well and living in Melbourne.

Jik and Sarah, when I rejoined them, were arguing about their fancies for the Victoria Derby, next race on the card.

'Ivory Ball is out of his class and has as much chance as a blind man in a blizzard.'

Sarah ignored this. 'He won at Moonee Valley last week and two of the tipsters picked him.'

'Those tipsters must have been drunk.'

'Hello Todd,' Sarah said. 'Pick a number, for God's sake.'

'Ten.'

'Why ten?'

'Eleven minus one.'

'Jesus,' Jik said. 'You used to have more sense.'

Sarah looked it up. 'Royal Road. Compared with Royal Road, Ivory Ball's a certainty.'

We bought our tickets and went up to the roof, and none of our bets came up. Sarah disgustedly yelled at Ivory Ball who had at least managed fifth, but Royal Road fell entirely by the wayside. The winner was number twelve.

'You should have *added* eleven and one,' Sarah said. 'You make such silly mistakes.'

'What are you staring at?' Jik said.

I was looking attentively down at the crowd which had watched the race from ground level on the Members' lawn.

'Lend me your raceglasses . . .'

Jik handed them over. I raised them, took a long look, and slowly put them down.

'What is it?' Sarah said anxiously. 'What's the matter?'

'That,' I said, 'has not only torn it, but ripped the bloody works apart.'

'What has?'

'Do you see those two men . . . about twenty yards along from the parade ring railing . . . one of them in a grey morning suit?'

'What about them?' Jik said.

'The man in the morning suit is Hudson Taylor, the man I just had a drink with. He's the Managing Director of a wine-making firm, and he saw a lot of my cousin Donald when he was over here. And the other man is called Ivor Wexford, and he's the Manager of the Yarra River Fine Arts Gallery.'

'So what?' Sarah said.

'So I can just about imagine the conversation that's going on down there,' I said. 'Something like, "Excuse me, sir, but didn't I sell a picture to you recently?" "Not to me, Mr Wexford, but to my friend Donald Stuart." "And who was that young man I saw you talking to just now?" "That was Donald Stuart's cousin, Mr Wexford." "And what do you know about him?"

147

"That he's a painter by trade and drew a picture of you, Mr Wexford, and asked me for your name." '

I stopped. 'Go on,' Jik said.

I watched Wexford and Hudson Taylor stop talking, nod casually to each other, and walk their separate ways.

'Ivor Wexford now knows he made a horrible mistake in letting me out of his gallery last night.'

Sarah looked searchingly at my face. 'You really do think that's very serious.'

'Yes I really do.' I loosened a few tightened muscles and tried a smile. 'At the least, he'll be on his guard.'

'And at the most,' Jik said, 'he'll come looking for you.'

'Er . . .' I said thoughtfully. 'What do either of you feel about a spot of instant travel?'

'Where to?'

'Alice Springs?' I said.

CHAPTER NINE

Jik complained all the way to the airport on various counts. One, that he would be missing the cricket. Two, that I hadn't let him go back to the Hilton for his paints. Three, that his Derby clothes would be too hot in Alice. Four, that he wasn't missing the Melbourne Cup for any little ponce with a bow tie.

None of the colourful gripes touched on the fact that he was paying for all our fares with his credit card, as I had left my traveller's cheques in the hotel.

It had been Sarah's idea not to go back there.

'If we're going to vanish, let's get on with it,' she said. 'It's running back into fires for handbags that gets people burnt.'

'You don't have to come,' I said tentatively.

'We've been through all that. What do you think the rest of my life would be like if I stopped Jik helping you, and you came to grief?'

'You'd never forgive me.'

She smiled ruefully. 'You're dead right.'

As far as I could tell we had left the racecourse

unobserved, and certainly no one car had followed us to the airport. Neither Greene with an 'e' nor the boy non-artist appeared underfoot to trip us up, and we travelled uneventfully on a half-full aircraft on the first leg to Adelaide, and an even emptier one from there to Alice Springs.

The country beneath us from Adelaide northwards turned gradually from fresh green to grey-green, and finally to a fierce brick red.

'Gaba,' said Jik, pointing downwards.

'What?'

'G.A.B.A.,' he said. 'Gaba. Stands for Great Australian Bugger All.'

I laughed. The land did indeed look baked, deserted, and older than time, but there were track-like roads here and there, and incredibly isolated homesteads. I watched in fascination until it grew dark, the purple shadows rushing in like a tide as we swept north into the central wastelands.

The night air at Alice was hot, as if someone had forgotten to switch off the oven. The luck which had presented us with an available flight as soon as we reached Melbourne airport seemed still to be functioning: a taciturn taxi driver took us straight to a new-looking motel which proved to have room for us.

'The season is over,' he grunted, when we congratulated and thanked him. 'It will soon be too hot for tourists.'

Our rooms were air-conditioned, however. Jik and

Sarah's was down on the ground floor, their door opening directly on to a shady covered walk which bordered a small garden with a pool. Mine, in an adjacent wing across the car park, was two tall floors up, reached by an outside tree-shaded staircase and a long open gallery. The whole place looked greenly peaceful in the scattered spotlights which shone unobtrusively from palms and gums.

The motel restaurant had closed for the night at eight o'clock, so we walked along the main street to another. The road surface itself was tarmacked, but some of the side roads were not, nor were the footpaths uniformly paved. Often enough we were walking on bare fine grit, and we could see from the dust haze in the headlights of passing cars that the grit was bright red.

'Bull dust,' Sarah said. 'I've never seen it before. My aunt swore it got inside her locked trunk once when she and my uncle drove out to Ayers Rock.'

'What's Ayers Rock?' I said.

'Ignorant Pommie,' Sarah said. 'It's a chunk of sandstone two miles long and a third of a mile high left behind by some careless glacier in the ice age.'

'Miles out in the desert,' Jik added. 'A place of ancient magic regularly desecrated by the plastic society.'

'Have you been there?' I asked dryly.

He grinned. 'Nope.'

'What difference does that make?' Sarah asked.

151

'He means,' Jik said, 'our pompous friend here means that one shouldn't make judgments from afar.'

'You haven't actually got to be swallowed up by a shark before you believe it's got sharp teeth,' Sarah said. 'You can believe what other people see.'

'It depends from where they're looking.'

'Facts are not judgments, and judgments are not facts,' Jik said. 'A bit of Todd's Law from way back.'

Sarah gave me a glance. 'Have you got iced water in that head?'

'Emotion is a rotten base for politics. He used to say that too,' Jik said. 'Envy is the root of all evil. What have I left out?'

'The most damaging lies are told by those who believe they're true.'

'There you are,' Jik said. 'Such a pity you can't paint.'

'Thanks very much.'

We reached the restaurant and ate a meal of such excellence that one wondered at the organization it took to bring every item of food and clothing and everyday life to an expanding town of thirteen and a half thousand inhabitants surrounded by hundreds of miles of desert in every direction.

'It was started here, a hundred years ago, as a relay station for sending cables across Australia,' Sarah said. 'And now they're bouncing messages off the stars.'

Jik said, 'Bet the messages aren't worth the technology. Think of "See you Friday, Ethel", chattering round the eternal spheres.'

With instructions from the restaurant we walked back a different way and sought out the Yarra River Fine Arts gallery, Alice Springs variety.

It was located in a paved shopping arcade closed to traffic, one of several small but prosperous-looking boutiques. There were no lights on in the gallery, nor in the other shops. From what we could see in the single dim street light, the merchandise in the gallery window consisted of two bright orange landscapes of desert scenes.

'Crude,' said Jik, whose own colours were not noted for pastel subtlety.

'The whole place,' he said, 'will be full of local copies of Albert Namatjira. Tourists buy them by the ton.'

We strolled back to the motel more companionably than at any time since my arrival. Maybe the desert distances all around us invoked their own peace. At any rate when I kissed Sarah's cheek to say goodnight it was no longer as a sort of pact, as in the morning, but with affection.

At breakfast she said, 'You'll never guess. The main street here is Todd Street. So is the river. Todd River.'

'Such is fame,' I said modestly.

'And there are eleven art galleries.'

'She's been reading the Alice Springs Tourist Promotion Association Inc.'s handout,' Jik explained.

'There's also a Chinese takeaway.'

Jik made a face. 'Just imagine all this lot dumped down in the middle of the Sahara.'

The daytime heat, in fact, was fierce. The radio was cheerfully forecasting a noon temperature of thirty-nine, which was a hundred and two in the old Fahrenheit shade. The single step from a cool room to the sun-roasting balcony was a sensuous pleasure, but the walk to the Yarra River gallery, though less than half a mile, was surprisingly exhausting.

'I suppose one would get used to it, if one lived here,' Jik said. 'Thank God Sarah's got her hat.'

We dodged in and out of the shadows of overhanging trees and the local inhabitants marched around bareheaded as if the branding-iron in the sky was pointing another way. The Yarra River gallery was quiet and air-conditioned and provided chairs near the entrance for flaked-out visitors.

As Jik had prophesied, all visible space was knee-deep in the hard clear watercolour paintings typical of the disciples of Namatjira. They were fine if you liked that sort of thing, which on the whole I didn't. I preferred the occasional fuzzy outline, indistinct edge, shadows encroaching, suggestion, impression, and ambiguity. Namatjira, given his due as the first and greatest of the Aboriginal artists, had had a vision as sharp as a diamond. I vaguely remembered reading somewhere that he'd produced more than two thousand paintings himself, and certainly his influence on the town where he'd been born had been extraordinary.

Eleven art galleries. Mecca for artists. Tourists buying pictures by the ton. He had died, a plaque on the wall said, in Alice Springs hospital on August 8th 1959.

We had been wandering around for a good five minutes before anyone came. Then the plastic strip curtain over a recessed doorway parted, and the gallery keeper came gently through.

'See anything you fancy?' he said.

His voice managed to convey an utter boredom with tourists and a feeling that we should pay up quickly and go away. He was small, languid, long-haired and pale, and had large dark eyes with drooping tired-looking lids. About the same age as Jik and myself, though a lot less robust.

'Do you have any other pictures?' I asked.

He glanced at our clothes. Jik and I wore the trousers and shirts in which we'd gone to the races: no ties and no jackets, but more promising to picture-sellers than denims. Without discernible enthusiasm he held back half the strip curtain, inviting us to go through.

'In here,' he said.

The inner room was bright from skylights, and its walls were almost entirely covered with dozens of pictures which hung closely together. Our eyes opened wide. At first sight we were surrounded by an incredible feast of Dutch interiors, French impressionists and Gainsborough portraits. At second blink one could see that although they were original oil paintings, they were basically second rate. The sort sold as 'school of' because the artists hadn't bothered to sign them.

'All European, in this room,' the gallery keeper said. He still sounded bored. He wasn't Australian, I thought. Nor British. Maybe American. Difficult to tell.

'Do you have any pictures of horses?' I asked.

He gave me a long steady peaceful gaze. 'Yes we do, but this month we are displaying works by native Australians and lesser Europeans.' His voice had the faintest of lisps. 'If you wish to see horse paintings, they are in racks through there.' He pointed to a second plastic strip curtain directly opposite the first. 'Are you looking for anything in particular?'

I murmured the names of some of the Australians whose work I had seen in Melbourne. There was a slight brightening of the lack-lustre eyes.

'Yes, we do have a few by those artists.'

He led us through the second curtain into the third, and from our point of view, most interesting room. Half of it, as promised, was occupied by well-filled double tiers of racks. The other half was the office and packing and framing department. Directly ahead a glass door led out to a dusty parched-looking garden, but most of the lighting in here too came from the roof.

Beside the glass door stood an easel bearing a small canvas with its back towards us. Various unmistakable signs showed work currently in progress and recently interrupted.

'Your own effort?' asked Jik inquisitively, walking over for a look.

The pale gallery keeper made a fluttering movement with his hand as if he would have stopped Jik if he could, and something in Jik's expression attracted me to his side like a magnet.

A chestnut horse, three-quarters view, its elegant head raised as if listening. In the background, the noble lines of a mansion. The rest, a harmonious composition of trees and meadow. The painting, as far as I could judge, was more or less finished.

'That's great,' I said with enthusiasm. 'Is that for sale? I'd like to buy that.'

After the briefest hesitation he said, 'Sorry. That's commissioned.'

'What a pity! Couldn't you sell me that one, and paint another?'

He gave me a small regretful smile. 'I'm afraid not.'

'Do tell me your name,' I said earnestly.

He was unwillingly flattered. 'Harley Renbo.'

'Is there anything else of yours here?'

He gestured towards the racks. 'One or two. The horse paintings are all in the bottom row, against the wall.'

We all three of us pulled out the paintings one by one, making amateur-type comments.

'That's nice,' said Sarah, holding a small picture of

a fat grey pony with two old-fashioned country boys. 'Do you like that?' She showed it to Jik and me.

We looked at it.

'Very nice,' I said kindly.

Jik turned away as if uninterested. Harley Renbo stood motionless.

'Oh well,' Sarah said, shrugging. 'I just thought it looked nice.' She put it back in the rack and pulled out the next. 'How about this mare and foal? I think it's pretty.'

Jik could hardly bear it. 'Sentimental tosh,' he said.

Sarah looked downcast. 'It may not be Art, but I like it.'

We found one with a flourishing signature; Harley Renbo. Large canvas, varnished, unframed.

'Ah,' I said appreciatively. 'Yours.'

Harley Renbo inclined his head. Jik, Sarah and I gazed at his acknowledged work.

Derivative Stubbs-type. Elongated horses set in a Capability Brown landscape. Composition fair, anatomy poor, execution good, originality nil.

'Great,' I said. 'Where did you paint it?'

'Oh . . . here.'

'From memory?' Sarah said admiringly. 'How clever.'

Harley Renbo, at our urging, brought out two more examples of his work. Neither was better than the first, but one was a great deal smaller.

'How much is this?' I asked.

Jik glanced at me sharply, but kept quiet.

Harley Renbo mentioned a sum which had me shaking my head at once.

'Awfully sorry,' I said. 'I like your work, but . . .'

The haggling continued politely for quite a long time, but we came to the usual conclusion, higher than the buyer wanted, lower than the painter hoped. Jik resignedly lent his credit card and we bore our trophy away.

'Jesus Christ,' Jik exploded when we were safely out of earshot. 'You could paint better than that when you were in your cradle. Why the hell did you want to buy that rubbish?'

'Because,' I said contentedly, 'Harley Renbo is the copier.'

'But this,' Jik pointed to the parcel under my arm, 'is his own abysmal original work.'

'Like fingerprints?' Sarah said. 'You can check other things he paints against this?'

'Got brains, my wife,' Jik said. 'But that picture he wouldn't sell was nothing like any Munnings I've ever seen.'

'You never look at horse paintings if you can help it.'

'I've seen more of your pathetic daubs than I care to.'

'How about Raoul Millais?' I said.

'Jesus.'

We walked along the scorching street almost without feeling it.

'I don't know about you two,' Sarah said, 'but I'm going to buy a bikini and spend the rest of the day in the pool.'

We all bought swimming things, changed into them, splashed around for ages, and laid ourselves out on towels to dry. It was peaceful and quiet in the shady little garden. We were the only people there.

'That picture of a pony and two boys, that you thought was nice,' I said to Sarah.

'Well, it was,' she repeated defensively. 'I liked it.'

'It was a Munnings.'

She sat up abruptly on her towel.

'Why ever didn't you say so?'

'I was waiting for our friend Renbo to tell us, but he didn't.'

'A real one?' Sarah asked. 'Or a copy?'

'Real,' Jik said, with his eyes shut against the sun dappling through palm leaves.

I nodded lazily. 'I thought so, too,' I said. 'An old painting. Munnings had that grey pony for years when he was young, and painted it dozens of times. It's the same one you saw in Sydney in *The Coming Storm*.'

'You two do know a lot,' Sarah said, sighing and lying down again.

'Engineers know all about nuts and bolts,' Jik said. 'Do we get lunch in this place?'

I looked at my watch. Nearly two o'clock. 'I'll go and ask,' I said.

I put shirt and trousers on over my sun-dried trunks

and ambled from the outdoor heat into the refrigerated air of the lobby. No lunch, said the reception desk. We could buy lunch nearby at a takeaway and eat in the garden. Drink? Same thing. Buy your own at a bottle shop. There was an ice-making machine and plastic glasses just outside the door to the pool.

'Thanks,' I said.

'You're welcome.'

I looked at the ice-making machine on the way out. Beside it swung a neat notice. 'We don't swim in your toilet. Please don't pee in our pool.' I laughed across to Jik and Sarah and told them the food situation.

'I'll go and get it,' I said. 'What do you want?'

Anything, they said.

'And drink?'

'Cinzano,' Sarah said, and Jik nodded. 'Dry White.'

'O.K.'

I picked up my room key from the grass and set off to collect some cash for shopping. Walked along to the tree-shaded outside staircase, went up two storeys, and turned on to the blazing hot balcony.

There was a man walking along it towards me, about my own height, build and age; and I heard someone else coming up the stairs at my back.

Thought nothing of it. Motel guests like me. What else?

I was totally unprepared for both the attack itself, and for its ferocity.

161

CHAPTER TEN

They simply walked up to me, one from in front, one from behind.

They reached me together. They sprang into action like cats. They snatched the dangling room key out of my hand.

The struggle, if you could call it that, lasted less than five seconds. Between them, with Jik's type of strength, they simply picked me up by my legs and armpits and threw me over the balcony.

It probably takes a very short time to fall two storeys. I found it long enough for thinking that my body, which was still whole, was going to be smashed. That disaster, not yet reached, was inevitable. Very odd, and very nasty.

What I actually hit first was one of the young trees growing round the staircase. Its boughs bent and broke and I crashed on through them to the hard driveway beneath.

The monstrous impact was like being wiped out. Like fusing electrical circuits. A flash into chaos. I lay in a semi-conscious daze, not knowing if I were alive or dead.

I felt warm. Simply a feeling, not a thought.

I wasn't aware of anything else at all. I couldn't move any muscle. Couldn't remember I had muscles to move. I felt like pulp.

It was ten minutes, Jik told me later, before he came looking for me: and he came only because he wanted to ask me to buy a lemon to go with the Cinzano, if I had not gone already.

'Jesus Christ Almighty,' Jik's voice, low and horrified, near my ear.

I heard him clearly. The words made sense.

I'm alive, I thought. I think, therefore I exist.

Eventually, I opened my eyes. The light was brilliant. Blinding. There was no one where Jik's voice had been. Perhaps I'd imagined it. No I hadn't. The world began coming back fast, very sharp and clear.

I knew also that I hadn't imagined the fall. I knew, with increasing insistence, that I hadn't broken my neck and hadn't broken my back. Sensation, which had been crushed out, came flooding back with vigour from every insulted tissue. It wasn't so much a matter of which bits of me hurt, as of finding out which didn't. I remembered hitting the tree. Remembered the ripping of its branches. I felt both torn to shreds and pulverized. Frightfully jolly.

After a while I heard Jik's voice returning. 'He's alive,' he said, 'and that's about all.'

'It's impossible for anyone to fall off our balcony. It's more than waist-high.' The voice of the reception desk, sharp with anger and anxiety. A bad business for motels, people falling off their balconies.

'Don't . . . panic,' I said. It sounded a bit croaky.

'Todd!' Sarah appeared, kneeling on the ground and looking pale.

'If you give me time . . .' I said, '. . . I'll fetch . . . the Cinzano.' How much time? A million years should be enough.

'You sod,' Jik said, standing at my feet and staring down. 'You gave us a shocking fright.' He was holding a broken-off branch of tree.

'Sorry.'

'Get up, then.'

'Yeah . . . in a minute.'

'Shall I cancel the ambulance?' said the reception desk hopefully.

'No,' I said. 'I think I'm bleeding.'

Alice Springs hospital, even on a Sunday, was as efficient as one would expect from a Flying Doctor base. They investigated and X-rayed and stitched, and presented me with a list.

One broken shoulder blade. (Left.)
Two broken ribs. (Left side, no lung puncture.)

164

Large contusion, left side of head. (No skull fracture.)
Four jagged tears in skin of trunk, thigh, and left leg. (Stitched.)
Several other small cuts.
Grazes and contusions on practically all of left side of body.

'Thanks,' I said, sighing.

'Thank the tree. You'd've been in a right mess if you'd missed it.'

They suggested I stop there for the rest of the day and also all night. Better, they said, a little too meaningfully.

'O.K.' I said resignedly. 'Are my friends still here?'

They were. In the waiting-room. Arguing over my near-dead body about the favourite for the Melbourne Cup.

'Newshound *stays* . . .'

'Stays in the same place . . .'

'Jesus,' Jik said, as I shuffled stiffly in. 'He's on his feet.'

'Yeah.' I perched gingerly on the arm of a chair, feeling a bit like a mummy, wrapped in bandages from neck to waist with my left arm totally immersed, as it were, and anchored firmly inside.

'Don't damn well laugh,' I said.

'No one but a raving lunatic would fall off that balcony,' Jik said.

165

'Mm,' I agreed. 'I was pushed.'

Their mouths opened like landed fish. I told them exactly what had happened.

'Who were they?' Jik said.

'I don't know. Never seen them before. They didn't introduce themselves.'

Sarah said, definitely, 'You must tell the police.'

'Yes,' I said. 'But . . . I don't know your procedures here, or what the police are like. I wondered . . . if you would explain to the hospital, and start things rolling in an orderly and unsensational manner.'

'Sure,' she said, 'if anything about being pushed off a balcony could be considered orderly and unsensational.'

'They took my room key first,' I said. 'Would you see if they've pinched my wallet?'

They stared at me in awakening unwelcome awareness.

I nodded. 'Or that picture,' I said.

Two policemen came, listened, took notes, and departed. Very non-committal. Nothing like that had happened in The Alice before. The locals wouldn't have done it. The town had a constant stream of visitors so, by the law of averages, some would be muggers. I gathered that there would have been much more fuss if I'd been dead. Their downbeat attitude suited me fine.

By the time Jik and Sarah came back I'd been given a bed, climbed into it, and felt absolutely rotten. Shivering. Cold deep inside. Gripped by the system's aggrieved reaction to injury, or in other words, shock.

'They did take the painting,' Jik said. 'And your wallet as well.'

'And the gallery's shut,' Sarah said. 'The girl in the boutique opposite said she saw Harley close early today, but she didn't see him actually leave. He goes out the back way, because he parks his car out there.'

'The police've been to the motel,' Jik said. 'We told them about the picture being missing, but I don't think they'll do much more about it unless you tell them the whole story.'

'I'll think about it,' I said.

'So what do we do now?' Sarah asked.

'Well . . . there's no point in staying here any more. Tomorrow we'll go back to Melbourne.'

'Thank God,' she said, smiling widely. 'I thought you were going to want us to miss the Cup.'

In spite of a battery of pills and various ministering angels I spent a viciously uncomfortable and wide-awake night. Unable to lie flat. Feverishly hot on the pendulum from shock. Throbbing in fifteen places. Every little movement screechingly sticky, like an engine without oil. No wonder the hospital had told me it would be better to stay.

I counted my blessings until daybreak. It could have been so very much worse.

What was most alarming was not the murderous nature of the attackers, but the speed with which they'd found us. I'd known ever since I'd seen Regina's head that the directing mind was ruthlessly violent. The acts of the team always reflected the nature of the boss. A less savage attitude would have left Regina gagged and bound, not brutally dead.

I had to conclude that it was chiefly this pervading callousness which had led to my being thrown over the balcony. As a positive means of murder, it was too chancy. It was quite possible to survive a fall from such a height, even without a cushioning tree. The two men had not as far as I could remember bothered to see whether I was alive or dead, and they had not, while I lay half-unconscious and immobile, come along to finish the job.

So it had either been simply a shattering way of getting rid of me while they robbed my room, or they'd had the deliberate intention of injuring me so badly that I would have to stop poking my nose into their affairs.

Or both.

And how had they found us?

I puzzled over it for some time but could arrive at no definite answer. It seemed most likely that Wexford or Greene had telephoned from Melbourne and told Harley Renbo to be on his guard in case I turned up. Even the panic which would have followed the realization that I'd seen the Munnings and the fresh Millais copy, and actually carried away a specimen of Renbo's work, could not have transported two toughs from Melbourne to Alice Springs in the time available.

There had only been about four hours between purchase and attack, and some of that would have had to be spent on finding out which motel we were in, and which rooms, and waiting for me to go upstairs from the pool.

Perhaps we had after all been followed all the way from Flemington racecourse, or traced from the aeroplane passenger lists. But if that were the case, surely Renbo would have been warned we were on our way, and would never have let us see what we had.

I gave it up. I didn't even know if I would recognize my attackers again if I saw them. Certainly not the one who had been behind me, because I hadn't had a single straight look at him.

They could, though, reasonably believe they had done a good job of putting me out of action: and indeed, if I had any sense, they had.

If they wanted time, what for?

To tighten up their security, and cover their tracks, so that any investigation I might persuade the police to make into a paintings–robbery link would come up against the most respectable of brick walls.

Even if they knew I'd survived, they would not expect any action from me in the immediate future:

therefore the immediate future was the best time to act.

Right.

Easy enough to convince my brain. From the neck down, a different story.

Jik and Sarah didn't turn up until eleven, and I was still in bed. Sitting up, but not exactly perky.

'God,' Sarah said, 'You look much worse than yesterday.'

'So kind.'

'You're never going to make it to Melbourne.' She sounded despondent. 'So goodbye Cup.'

'Nothing to stop you going,' I said.

She stood beside the bed. 'Do you expect us just to leave you here . . . like this . . . and go and enjoy ourselves?'

'Why not?'

'Don't be so bloody stupid.'

Jik sprawled in a visitor's chair. 'It isn't our responsibility if he gets himself thrown from heights,' he said.

Sarah whirled on him. 'How *can* you say such a thing?'

'We don't want to be involved,' Jik said.

I grinned. Sarah heard the sardonic echo of what she'd said so passionately herself only three days ago. She flung out her arms in exasperated realization.

'You absolutely bloody beast,' she said.

Jik smiled like a cream-fed cat. 'We went round to the gallery,' he said. 'It's still shut. We also found our way round into the back garden, and looked in through the glass door, and you can guess what we saw.'

'Nothing.'

'Dead right. No easel with imitation Millais. Everything dodgy carefully hidden out of sight. Everything else, respectable and normal.'

I shifted a bit to relieve one lot of aches, and set up protests from another. 'Even if you'd got in, I doubt if you'd've found anything dodgy. I'll bet everything the least bit incriminating disappeared yesterday afternoon.'

Jik nodded. 'Sure to.'

Sarah said, 'We asked the girl in the reception desk at the motel if anyone had been asking for us.'

'And they had?'

She nodded. 'A man telephoned. She thought it was soon after ten o'clock. He asked if a Mr Charles Todd was staying there with two friends, and when she said yes, he asked for your room number. He said he had something to deliver to you.'

'Christ.' Some delivery. Express. Downwards.

'She told him the room number but said if he left the package at the desk, she would see you got it.'

'He must have laughed.'

'He wouldn't have that much sense of humour,' Jik said.

'Soon after ten?' I said, considering.

'While we were out,' Sarah said, nodding. 'It must

have been fairly soon after we'd left the gallery . . . and while we were buying the swimming things.'

'Why didn't the girl tell us someone had been enquiring for us?'

'She went off for a coffee break, and didn't see us when we came back. And after that, she forgot. She hadn't anyway thought it of any importance.'

'There aren't all that many motels in Alice,' Jik said. 'It wouldn't have taken long to find us, once they knew we were in the town. I suppose the Melbourne lot telephoned Renbo, and that set the bomb ticking.'

'They must have been apoplectic when they heard you'd bought that picture.'

'I wish I'd hidden it,' I said. The words reminded me briefly of Maisie, who had hidden her picture, and had her house burnt.

Sarah sighed. 'Well . . . what are we going to do?'

'Last chance to go home,' I said.

'Are you going?' she demanded.

I listened briefly to the fierce plea from my battered shell, and I thought too of Donald in his cold house. I didn't actually answer her at all.

She listened to my silence. 'Quite,' she said. 'So what do we do next?'

'Well . . .' I said. 'First of all, tell the girl on the reception desk at the motel that I'm in a pretty poor state and likely to be in hospital for at least a week.'

'No exaggeration,' Jik murmured.

'Tell her it's O.K. to pass on that news, if anyone

enquires. Tell her you're leaving for Melbourne, pay all our bills, confirm your bookings on the afternoon flight, and cancel mine, and make a normal exit to the airport bus.'

'But what about you?' Sarah said. 'When will you be fit to go?'

'With you,' I said. 'If between you you can think of some unobtrusive way of getting a bandaged mummy on to an aeroplane without anyone noticing.'

'Jesus,' Jik said. He looked delighted. 'I'll do that.'

'Telephone the airport and book a seat for me under a different name.'

'Right.'

'Buy me a shirt and some trousers. Mine are in the dustbin.'

'It shall be done.'

'And reckon all the time that you may be watched.'

'Put on sad faces, do you mean?' Sarah said.

I grinned. 'I'd be honoured.'

'And after we get to Melbourne, what then?' Jik said.

I chewed my lip. 'I think we'll have to go back to the Hilton. All our clothes are there, not to mention my passport and money. We don't know if Wexford and Greene ever knew we were staying there, so it may well be a hundred per cent safe. And anyway, where else in Melbourne are we likely to get beds on the night before the Melbourne Cup?'

'If you get thrown out of the Hilton's windows, you won't be alive to tell the tale,' he said cheerfully.

'They don't open far enough,' I said. 'It's impossible.'

'How reassuring.'

'And tomorrow,' Sarah said. 'What about to-morrow?'

Hesitantly, with a pause or two, I outlined what I had in mind for Cup day. When I had finished, they were both silent.

'So now,' I said. 'Do you want to go home?'

Sarah stood up. 'We'll talk it over,' she said soberly. 'We'll come back and let you know.'

Jik stood also, but I knew from the jut of his beard which way he'd vote. It had been he who'd chosen the bad-weather routes we'd taken into the Atlantic and the North Sea. At heart he was more reckless than I.

They came back at two o'clock lugging a large fruit-shop carrier with a bottle of Scotch and a pineapple sticking out of the top.

'Provisions for hospitalized friend,' said Jik, whisking them out and putting them on the end of the bed. 'How do you feel?'

'With every nerve ending.'

'You don't say. Well, Sarah says we go ahead.'

I looked searchingly at her face. Her dark eyes stared steadily back, giving assent without joy. There was no antagonism, but no excitement. She was committed, but from determination, not conviction.

'O.K.,' I said.

'Item,' said Jik, busy with the carrier, 'one pair of medium grey trousers. One light blue cotton shirt.'

'Great.'

'You won't be wearing those, though, until you get to Melbourne. For leaving Alice Springs, we bought something else.'

I saw the amusement in both their faces. I said with misgiving, 'What else?'

With rising glee they laid out what they had bought for my unobtrusive exit from Alice Springs.

Which was how I came to stroll around the little airport, in the time-gap between signing in and boarding, with the full attention of everyone in the place. Wearing faded jeans cut off and busily frayed at mid-calf. No socks. Flip-flop rope-soled sandals. A brilliant orange, red and magenta poncho-type garment which hung loosely over both arms like a cape from shoulders to crutch. A sloppy white T-shirt underneath. A large pair of sunglasses. Artificial suntan on every bit of skin. And to top it all, a large straw sunhat with a two-inch raffia fringe round the brim, the sort of hat in favour out in the bush for keeping flies away. Flies were the torment of Australia. The brushing-away-of-flies movement of the right hand was known as the great Australian salute.

175

On this hat there was a tourist-type hat-band, bright and distinctly legible. It said 'I Climbed Ayers Rock'.

Accompanying all this jazz I carried the Trans-Australian airline bag Sarah had bought on the way up. Inside it, the garments of sanity and discretion.

'No one,' Jik had said with satisfaction, laying out my wardrobe, 'will guess you're a walking stretcher case, if you're wearing these.'

'More like a nutcase.'

'Not far out,' Sarah said dryly.

They were both at the airport, sitting down and looking glum, when I arrived. They gave me a flickering glance and gazed thereafter at the floor, both of them, they told me later, fighting off terrible fits of giggles at seeing all that finery on the march.

I walked composedly down to the postcard stand and waited there on my feet, for truth to tell it was more comfortable than sitting. Most of the postcards seemed to be endless views of the huge crouching orange monolith out in the desert: Ayers Rock at dawn, at sunset, and every five minutes in between.

Alternatively with inspecting the merchandise I took stock of the room. About fifty prospective passengers, highly assorted. Some airline ground staff, calm and unhurried. A couple of Aborigines with shadowed eyes and patient black faces, waiting for the airport bus back to dreamtime. Air-conditioning doing fine, but everyone inside still moving with the slow walk of life out in the sun.

No one remotely threatening.

The flight was called. The assorted passengers, including Jik and Sarah, stood up, picked up their hand luggage and straggled out to the tarmac.

It was then, and then only, that I saw him.

The man who had come towards me on the balcony to throw me over.

I was almost sure at once, and then certain. He had been sitting among the waiting passengers, reading a newspaper which he was now folding up. He stood still, watching Jik and Sarah present their boarding passes at the door and go through to the tarmac. His eyes followed them right across to the aircraft. When they'd filed up the steps and vanished, he peeled off and made a bee-line in my direction.

My heart lurched painfully. I absolutely could not run.

He looked just the same. Exactly the same. Young, strong, purposeful, as well co-ordinated as a cat. Coming towards me.

As Jik would have said, *Jesus*.

He didn't even give me a glance. Three yards before he reached me he came to a stop beside a wall telephone, and fished in his pocket for coins.

My feet didn't want to move. I was still sure he would see me, look at me carefully, recognize me . . . and do something I would regret. I could feel the sweat prickling under the bandages.

'Last call for flight to Adelaide and Melbourne.'

I would have to, I thought. Have to walk past him to get to the door.

I unstuck my feet. Walked. Waiting for every awful step to hear his voice shouting after me. Or even worse, his heavy hand.

I got to the door, presented the boarding pass, made it out on to the tarmac.

Couldn't resist glancing back. I could see him through the glass, earnestly telephoning, and not even looking my way.

The walk to the aircraft was all the same quite far enough. God help us all, I thought, if the slightest fright is going to leave me so weak.

CHAPTER ELEVEN

I had a window seat near the rear of the aircraft, and spent the first part of the journey in the same sort of fascination as on the way up, watching the empty red miles of the ancient land roll away underneath. A desert with water underneath it in most places; with huge lakes and many rock pools. A desert which could carry dormant seed for years in its burning dust, and bloom like a garden when it rained. A place of pulverizing heat, harsh and unforgiving, and in scattered places, beautiful.

Gaba, I thought. I found it awesome, but it didn't move me in terms of paint.

After a while I took off the exaggerated hat, laid it on the empty seat beside me, and tried to find a comfortable way to sit, my main frustration being that if I leaned back in the ordinary way my broken shoulder blade didn't care for it. You wouldn't think, I thought, that one *could* break a shoulder blade. Mine, it appeared, had suffered from the full thud of my five-eleven frame hitting terra extremely firma.

Oh well ... I shut my eyes for a bit and wished I didn't still feel so shaky.

My exit from hospital had been the gift of one of the doctors, who had said he couldn't stop me if I chose to go, but another day's rest would be better.

'I'd miss the Cup,' I said, protesting.

'You're crazy.'

'Yeah ... Would it be possible for you to arrange that the hospital said I was "satisfactory", and "progressing" if anyone telephones to ask, and not on any account to say that I'd left?'

'Whatever for?'

'I'd just like those muggers who put me here to think I'm still flat out. For several days, if you don't mind. Until I'm long gone.'

'But they won't try again.'

'You never know.'

He shrugged. 'You mean you're nervous?'

'You could say so.'

'All right. For a couple of days, anyway. I don't see any harm in it, if it will set your mind at rest.'

'It would indeed,' I said gratefully.

'Whatever are these?' He gestured to Jik's shopping, still lying on the bed.

'My friend's idea of suitable travelling gear.'

'You're having me on?'

'He's an artist,' I said, as if that explained any excesses.

He returned an hour later with a paper for me to

sign before I left, Jik's credit card having again come up trumps, and at the sight of me, nearly choked. I had struggled slowly into the clothes and was trying on the hat.

'Are you going to the airport dressed like that?' he said incredulously.

'I sure am.'

'How?'

'Taxi, I suppose.'

'You'd better let me drive you,' he said, sighing. 'Then if you feel too rotten I can bring you back.'

He drove carefully, his lips twitching. 'Anyone who has the courage to go around like that shouldn't worry about a couple of thugs.' He dropped me solicitously at the airport door, and departed laughing.

Sarah's voice interrupted the memory.

'Todd?'

I opened my eyes. She had walked towards the back of the aeroplane and was standing in the aisle beside my seat.

'Are you all right?'

'Mm.'

She gave me a worried look and went on into the toilet compartment. By the time she came out, I'd assembled a few more wits, and stopped her with the flap of the hand. 'Sarah . . . You were followed to the airport. I think you'll very likely be followed from Melbourne. Tell Jik . . . tell Jik to take a taxi, spot the tail, lose him, and take a taxi back to the airport to collect the hired car. O.K?'

'Is this . . . this tail . . . on the aeroplane?' She looked alarmed at the thought.

'No. He telephoned . . . from Alice.'

'All right.'

She went away up front to her seat. The aeroplane landed at Adelaide, people got off, people got on, and we took off again for the hour's flight to Melbourne. Halfway there, Jik himself came back to make use of the facilities.

He too paused briefly beside me on the way back.

'Here are the car keys,' he said. 'Sit in it, and wait for us. You can't go into the Hilton like that, and you're not fit enough to change on your own.'

'Of course I am.'

'Don't argue. I'll lose any tail, and come back. You wait.'

He went without looking back. I picked up the keys and put them in my jeans pocket, and thought grateful thoughts to pass the time.

I dawdled a long way behind Jik and Sarah at disembarkation. My gear attracted more scandalized attention in this solemn financial city, but I didn't care in the least. Nothing like fatigue and anxiety for killing off embarrassment.

Jik and Sarah, with only hand baggage, walked without ado past the suitcase-unloading areas and straight out towards the waiting queue of taxis. The whole airport was bustling with Cup eve arrivals, but only one person, that I could see, was bustling exclusively after my fast-departing friends.

I smiled briefly. Young and eel-like, he slithered through the throng, pushing a young woman with a baby out of the way to grab the next taxi behind Jik's. They'd sent him, I supposed, because he knew Jik by sight. He'd flung turps in his eyes at the Arts Centre.

Not too bad, I thought. The boy wasn't over-intelligent, and Jik should have little trouble in losing him. I wandered around for a bit looking gormless, but as there was no one else who seemed the remotest threat, I eventually eased out to the car park.

The night was chilly after Alice Springs. I unlocked the car, climbed into the back, took off the successful hat, and settled to wait for Jik's return.

They were gone nearly two hours, during which time I grew stiffer and ever more uncomfortable and started swearing.

'Sorry,' Sarah said breathlessly, pulling open the car door and tumbling into the front seat.

'We had the devil's own job losing the little bugger,' Jik said, getting in beside me in the back. 'Are you all right?'

'Cold, hungry, and cross.'

'That's all right, then,' he said cheerfully. 'He stuck like a bloody little leech. That boy from the Arts Centre.'

'Yes, I saw him.'

'We hopped into the Victoria Royal, meaning to go straight out again by the side door and grab another cab, and there he was following us in through the front. So we peeled off for a drink in the bar and he hovered around in the lobby looking at the bookstall.'

'We thought it would be better not to let him know we'd spotted him, if we could,' Sarah said. 'So we did a re-think, went outside, called another taxi, and set off to the Naughty Ninety, which is about the only noisy big dine, dance and cabaret place in Melbourne.'

'It was absolutely packed,' Jik said. 'It cost me ten dollars to get a table. Marvellous for us, though. All dark corners and psychedelic coloured lights. We ordered and paid for some drinks, and read the menu, and then got up and danced.'

'He was still there, when we saw him last, standing in the queue for tables just inside the entrance door. We got out through an emergency exit down a passage past some cloakrooms. We'd dumped our bags there when we arrived, and simply collected them again on the way out.'

'I don't think he'll know we ducked him on purpose,' Jik said. 'It's a proper scrum there tonight.'

'Great.'

With Jik's help I exchanged Tourist, Alice Style, for Racing Man, Melbourne Cup. He drove us all back to the Hilton, parked in its car park, and we walked into the front hall as if we'd never been away.

No one took any notice of us. The place was alive

with pre-race excitement. People in evening dress flooding downstairs from the ballroom to stand in loud-talking groups before dispersing home. People returning from eating out, and calling for one more nightcap. Everyone discussing the chances of the next day's race.

Jik collected our room keys from the long desk.

'No messages,' he said. 'And they don't seem to have missed us.'

'Fair enough.'

'Todd,' Sarah said. 'Jik and I are going to have some food sent up. You'll come as well?'

I nodded. We went up in the lift and along to their rooms, and ate a subdued supper out of collective tiredness.

'Night,' I said eventually, getting up to go. 'And thanks for everything.'

'Thank us tomorrow,' Sarah said.

The night passed. Well, it passed.

In the morning I did a spot of one-handed shaving and some highly selective washing, and Jik came up, as he'd insisted, to help with my tie. I opened the door to him in underpants and dressing-gown and endured his comments when I took the latter off.

'Jesus God Almighty, is there any bit of you neither blue nor patched?'

'I could have landed face first.'

185

He stared at the thought. '*Jesus.*'

'Help me rearrange these bandages,' I said.

'I'm not touching that lot.'

'Oh come on, Jik. Unwrap the swaddling bands. I'm itching like hell underneath and I've forgotten what my left hand looks like.'

With a variety of blasphemous oaths he undid the expert handiwork of the Alice hospital. The outer bandages proved to be large strong pieces of linen, fastened with clips, and placed so as to support my left elbow and hold my whole arm statically in one position, with my hand across my chest and pointing up towards my right shoulder. Under the top layer there was a system of crêpe bandages tying my arm in that position. Also a sort of tight cummerbund of adhesive strapping, presumably to deal with the broken ribs. Also, just below my shoulder blade, a large padded wound dressing, which, Jik kindly told me after a delicate inspection from one corner, covered a mucky-looking bit of darning.

'You damn near tore a whole flap of skin off. There are four lots of stitching. Looks like Clapham Junction.'

'Fasten it up again.'

'I have, mate, don't you worry.'

There were three similar dressings, two on my left thigh and one, a bit smaller, just below the knee: all fastened both with adhesive strips and tapes with clips. We left them all untouched.

'What the eye doesn't see doesn't scare the patient,' Jik said. 'What else do you want done?'

'Untie my arm.'

'You'll fall apart.'

'Risk it.'

He laughed and undid another series of clips and knots. I tentatively straightened my elbow. Nothing much happened except that the hovering ache and soreness stopped hovering and came down to earth.

'That's not so good,' Jik observed.

'It's my muscles as much as anything. Protesting about being stuck in one position all that time.'

'What now, then?'

From the bits and pieces we designed a new and simpler sling which gave my elbow good support but was less of a strait-jacket. I could get my hand out easily, and also my whole arm, if I wanted. When we'd finished, we had a small heap of bandages and clips left over.

'That's fine,' I said.

We all met downstairs in the hall at ten-thirty.

Around us a buzzing atmosphere of anticipation pervaded the chattering throng of would-be winners, who were filling the morning with celebratory drinks. The hotel, I saw, had raised a veritable fountain of champagne at the entrance to the bar-lounge end of the lobby, and Jik, his eyes lighting up, decided it was too good to be missed.

'Free booze,' he said reverently, picking up a glass and holding it under the prodigal bubbly which flowed in delicate gold streams from a pressure-fed height. 'Not bad, either,' he added, tasting. He raised his glass. 'Here's to Art. God rest his soul.'

'Life's short. Art's long,' I said.

'I don't like that,' Sarah said, looking at me uneasily.

'It was Alfred Munnings's favourite saying. And don't worry, love, he lived to be eighty plus.'

'Let's hope you do.'

I drank to it. She was wearing a cream dress with gold buttons; neat, tailored, a touch severe. An impression of the military for a day in the front line.

'Don't forget,' I said. 'If you think you see Wexford or Greene, make sure they see you.'

'Give me another look at their faces,' she said.

I pulled the small sketch book out of my pocket and handed it to her again, though she'd studied it on and off all the previous evening through supper.

'As long as they look like this, maybe I'll know them,' she said, sighing. 'Can I take it?' She put the sketch book in her handbag.

Jik laughed. 'Give Todd his due, he can catch a likeness. No imagination, of course. He can only paint what he sees.' His voice as usual was full of disparagement.

188

Sarah said, 'Don't you mind the awful things Jik says of your work, Todd?'

I grinned. 'I know exactly what he thinks of it.'

'If it makes you feel any better,' Jik said to his wife, 'he was the star pupil of our year. The art school lacked judgment, of course.'

'You're both crazy.'

I glanced at the clock. We all finished the champagne and put down the glasses.

'Back a winner for me,' I said to Sarah, kissing her cheek.

'Your luck might run out.'

I grinned. 'Back number eleven.'

Her eyes were dark with apprehension. Jik's beard was at the bad-weather angle for possible storms ahead.

'Off you go,' I said cheerfully. 'See you later.'

I watched them through the door and wished strongly that we were all three going for a simple day out to the Melbourne Cup. The effort ahead was something I would have been pleased to avoid. I wondered if others ever quaked before the task they'd set themselves, and wished they'd never thought of it. The beginning, I supposed, was the worst. Once you were in, you were committed. But before, when there was still time to turn back, to rethink, to cancel, the temptation to retreat was demoralizing.

Why climb Everest if at its foot you could lie in the sun?

Sighing, I went to the cashier's end of the reception desk and changed a good many traveller's cheques into cash. Maisie's generosity had been far-sighted. There would be little enough left by the time I got home.

Four hours to wait. I spent them upstairs in my room calming my nerves by drawing the view from the window. Black clouds still hung around the sky like cobwebs, especially in the direction of Flemington race-course. I hoped it would stay dry for the Cup.

Half an hour before it was due to be run I left the Hilton on foot, walking unhurriedly along towards Swanston Street and the main area of shops. They were all shut, of course. Melbourne Cup Day was a national public holiday. Everything stopped for the Cup.

I had taken my left arm out of its sling and threaded it gingerly through the sleeves of my shirt and jacket. A man with his jacket hunched over one shoulder was too memorable for sense. I found that by hooking my thumb into the waistband of my trousers I got quite good support.

Swanston Street was far from its usual bustling self. People still strode along with the breakneck speed which seemed to characterize all Melbourne pedestrians, but they strode in tens, not thousands. Trams ran up and down the central tracks with more vacant seats than passengers. Cars sped along with the drivers, eyes down, fiddling dangerously with radio dials. Fifteen minutes to the race which annually stopped Australia in its tracks.

Jik arrived exactly on time, driving up Swanston Street in the hired grey car and turning smoothly around the corner where I stood waiting. He stopped outside the Yarra River Fine Arts gallery, got out, opened the boot, and put on a brown coat-overall, of the sort worn by storemen.

I walked quietly along towards him. He brought out a small radio, switched it on, and stood it on top of the car. The commentator's voice emerged tinnily, giving details of the runners currently walking round the parade ring at Flemington races.

'Hello,' he said unemotionally, when I reached him. 'All set?' I nodded, and walked to the door of the gallery. Pushed it. It was solidly shut. Jik dived again into the boot, which held further fruits of his second shopping expedition in Alice Springs.

'Gloves,' he said, handing me some, and putting some on himself. They were of white cotton, with ribbed wristbands, and looked a lot too new and clean. I wiped the backs of mine along the wings of Jik's car, and he gave me a glance and did the same with his.

'Handles and impact adhesive.'

He gave me the two handles to hold. They were simple chromium-plated handles, with flattened pieces at each end, pierced by screw holes for fixing. Sturdy handles, big enough for gripping with the whole hand. I held one steady, bottom side up, while Jik covered the screw-plate areas at each end with adhesive. We couldn't screw these handles where we wanted them. They had to be stuck.

'Now the other. Can you hold it in your left hand?'

I nodded. Jik attended to it. One or two people passed, paying no attention. We were not supposed to park there, but no one told us to move.

We walked across the pavement to the gallery. Its frontage was not one unbroken line across its whole width, but was recessed at the right-hand end to form a doorway. Between the front-facing display window and the front-facing glass door, there was a joining window at right angles to the street.

To this sheet of glass we stuck the handles, or rather, Jik did, at just above waist height. He tested them after a minute, and he couldn't pull them off. We returned to the car.

One or two more people passed, turning their heads to listen to the radio on the car roof, smiling in brotherhood at the universal national interest. The street was noticeably emptying as the crucial time drew near.

'. . . *Vinery carries the colours of Mr Hudson Taylor of Adelaide and must be in with a good outside chance. Fourth in the Caulfield Cup and before that, second at Randwick against Brain-Teaser, who went on to beat Afternoon Tea . . .*'

'Stop listening to the damn race!' Jik said sharply.

'Sorry.'

'Ready?'

'Yes.'

We walked back to the entrance to the gallery, Jik carrying the sort of glass-cutter used by, among others, picture framers. Without casting a glance around for possible onlookers, he applied the diamond cutting edge to the matter in hand, using considerable strength as he pushed the professional tool round the outside of the pane. I stood behind him to block any passing curious glances.

'Hold the right-hand handle,' he said, as he started on the last of the four sides, the left-hand vertical.

I stepped past him and slotted my hand through the grip. None of the few people left in the street paid the slightest attention.

'When it goes,' Jik said, 'for God's sake don't drop it.'

'No.'

'Put your knee against the glass. Gently, for God's sake.'

I did what he said. He finished the fourth long cut.

'Press smoothly.'

I did that. Jik's knee, too, was firmly against the glass. With his left hand he gripped the chromium handle, and with the palm of his right he began jolting the top perimeter of the heavy pane.

Jik had cut a lot of glass in his time, even if not in exactly these circumstances. The big flat sheet cracked away evenly all round under our pressure and parted with hardly a splinter. The weight fell suddenly on to the handle I held in my right hand, and Jik steadied the now free sheet of glass with hands and knees and blasphemy.

'Jesus, don't let go.'

'No.'

The heavy vibrations set up in the glass by the breaking process subsided, and Jik took over the right-hand handle from me. Without any seeming inconvenience he pivoted the sheet of glass so that it opened like a door. He stepped through the hole, lifted the glass up wholesale by the two handles, carried it several feet, and propped it against the wall to the right of the more conventional way in.

He came out, and we went over to the car. From there, barely ten feet away, one could not see that the gallery was not still securely shut. There were by now in any case very few to look.

'. . . *Most jockeys have now mounted and the horses will soon be going out on to the course . . .*'

I picked up the radio. Jik exchanged the glass-cutter for a metal saw, a hammer and a chisel, and shut the boot, and we walked through the unorthodox entrance as if it was all in the day's work. Often only the furtive manner gave away the crook. If you behaved as if you had every right, it took longer for anyone to suspect.

It would really have been best had we next been able to open the real door, but a quick inspection proved it impossible. There were two useful locks, and no keys.

'The stairs are at the back,' I said.

'Lead on.'

We walked the length of the plushy green carpet and down the beckoning stairs. There was a bank of electric switches at the top: we pressed those lighting the basement and left the upstairs lot off.

Heart-thumping time, I thought. It would take only a policeman to walk along and start fussing about a car parked in the wrong place to set Cassavetes and Todd on the road to jail.

'. . . *horses are now going out on to the course. Four-square in front, sweating up and fighting jockey Ted Nester for control . . .*'

We reached the front of the stairs. I turned back towards the office, but Jik took off fast down the corridor.

'Come back,' I said urgently. 'If that steel gate shuts down . . .'

'Relax,' Jik said. 'You told me.' He stopped before reaching the threshold of the furthest room. Stood still, and looked. Came back rapidly.

'O.K. The Munningses are all there. Three of them. Also something else which will stun you. Go and look while I get this door open.'

'. . . *cantering down to the start, and the excitement is mounting here now . . .*'

With a feeling of urgency I trekked down the passage, stopped safely short of any electric gadgets which might trigger the gate and set off alarms, and looked into the Munnings room. The three paintings still hung there, as they had before. But along the row from them was something which, as Jik had said, stunned me. Chestnut horse with head raised, listening. Stately home in the background. The Raoul Millais picture we'd seen in Alice.

I went back to Jik who with hammer and chisel had bypassed the lock on the office door.

'Which is it?' he said. 'Original or copy?'

'Can't tell from that distance. Looks like real.'

He nodded. We went into the office and started work.

'... *Derriby and Special Bet coming down to the start now, and all the runners circling while the girths are checked* ...'

I put the radio on Wexford's desk, where it sat like an hourglass, ticking away the minutes as the sands ran out.

Jik turned his practical attention to the desk drawers, but they were all unlocked. One of the waist-high line of filing cabinets, however, proved to be secure. Jik's strength and know-how soon ensured that it didn't remain that way.

In his wake I looked through the drawers. Nothing much in them except catalogues and stationery.

In the broken-open filing cabinet, a gold mine.

Not that I realized it at first. The contents looked merely like ordinary files with ordinary headings.

'... *moved very freely coming down to the start and*

is prime fit to run for that hundred-and-ten-thousand-dollar prize . . .'

There were a good many framed pictures in the office, some on the walls but even more standing in a row on the floor. Jik began looking through them at high speed, almost like flicking through a rack of record albums.

'. . . handlers are beginning to load the runners into the starting stalls, and I see Vinery playing up . . .'

Half of the files in the upper of the two drawers seemed to deal in varying ways with insurance. Letters, policies, revaluations and security. I didn't really know what I was looking for, which made it all a bit difficult.

'Jesus Almighty,' Jik said.

'What is it?'

'Look at this.'

'. . . more than a hundred thousand people here today to see the twenty-three runners fight it out over the three thousand two hundred metres . . .'

Jik had reached the end of the row and was looking at the foremost of three unframed canvases tied loosely together with string. I peered over his shoulder. The picture had Munnings written all over it. It had Alfred Munnings written large and clear in the right-hand bottom corner. It was a picture of four horses with jockeys cantering on a racecourse: and the paint wasn't dry.

'What are the others?' I said.

Jik ripped off the string. The two other pictures were exactly the same.

'God Almighty,' Jik said in awe.

'... *Vinery carries only fifty-one kilograms and has a good barrier position so it's not impossible ...*'

'Keep looking,' I said, and went back to the files.

Names. Dates. Places. I shook my head impatiently. We needed more than those Munnings copies and I couldn't find a thing.

'Jesus!' Jik said.

He was looking inside the sort of large flat two-foot by three-foot folder which was used in galleries to store prints.

'... *only Derriby now to enter the stalls ...*'

The print-folder had stood between the end of the desk and the nearby wall. Jik seemed transfixed.

Overseas Customers. My eyes flicked over the heading and then went back. Overseas Customers. I opened the file. Lists of people, sorted into countries. Pages of them. Names and addresses.

England.

A long list. Not alphabetical. Too many to read through in the shortage of time.

A good many of the names had been crossed out.

'... *They're running! This is the moment you've all been waiting for, and Special Bet is out in front ...*'

'Look at this,' Jik said.

Donald Stuart. Donald Stuart, crossed out. Shropshire, England. Crossed out.

I practically stopped breathing.

'... *as they pass the stands for the first time it's Special Bet, Foursquare, Newshound, Derriby, Wonderbug, Vinery ...*'

'Look at this,' Jik said again, insistently.

'Bring it,' I said. 'We've got less than three minutes before the race ends and Melbourne comes back to life.'

'But—'

'Bring it,' I said. 'And also those three copies.'

'... *Special Bet still making it, from Newshound close second, then Wonderbug ...*'

I shoved the filing-drawer shut.

'Put this file in the print-folder and let's get out.'

I picked up the radio and Jik's tools, as he himself had enough trouble managing all three of the untied paintings and the large print-folder.

'... *down the back stretch by the Maribyrnong River it's still Special Bet with Vinery second now ...*'

We went up the stairs. Switched off the lights. Eased round into a view of the car.

It stood there, quiet and unattended, just as we'd left it. No policeman. Everyone elsewhere, listening to the race.

Jik was calling on the Deity under his breath.

'... *rounding the turn towards home Special Bet is dropping back now and it's Derriby with Newshound ...*'

We walked steadily down the gallery.

The commentator's voice rose in excitement against a background of shouting crowds.

'. . . *Vinery in third with Wonderbug, and here comes Ringwood very fast on the stands side* . . .'

Nothing stirred out on the street. I went first through our hole in the glass and stood once more, with a great feeling of relief, on the outside of the beehive. Jik carried out the plundered honey and stacked it in the boot. He took the tools from my hands and stored them also.

'Right?'

I nodded with a dry mouth. We climbed normally into the car. The commentator was yelling to be heard.

'. . . *Coming to the line it's Ringwood by a length from Wonderbug, with Newshound third, then Derriby, then Vinery* . . .'

The cheers echoed inside the car as Jik started the engine and drove away.

'. . . *Might be a record time. Just listen to the cheers. The result again. The result of the Melbourne Cup. In the frame* . . . *first Ringwood, owned by Mr Robert Khami* . . . *second Wonderbug* . . .'

'Phew,' Jik said, his beard jaunty and a smile stretching to show an expanse of gum. 'That wasn't a bad effort. We might hire ourselves out some time for stealing politicians' papers.' He chuckled fiercely.

'It's an overcrowded field,' I said, smiling broadly myself.

We were both feeling the euphoria which follows

the safe deliverance from danger. 'Take it easy,' I said. 'We've a long way to go.'

He drove to the Hilton, parked, and carried the folder and pictures up to my room. He moved with his sailing speed, economically and fast, losing as little time as possible before returning to Sarah on the race-course and acting as if he'd never been away.

'We'll be back here as soon as we can,' he promised, sketching a farewell.

Two seconds after he'd shut my door there was a knock on it.

I opened it. Jik stood there.

'I'd better know,' he said, 'what won the Cup?'

CHAPTER TWELVE

When he'd gone I looked closely at the spoils.

The more I saw, the more certain it became that we had hit the absolute jackpot. I began to wish most insistently that we hadn't wasted time in establishing that Jik and Sarah were at the races. It made me nervous, waiting for them in the Hilton with so much dynamite in my hands. Every instinct urged immediate departure.

The list of Overseas Customers would to any other eyes have seemed the most harmless of documents. Wexford would not have needed to keep it in better security than a locked filing-cabinet, for the chances of anyone seeing its significance in ordinary circumstances were millions to one against.

Donald Stuart, Wrenstone House, Shropshire.

Crossed out.

Each page had three columns, a narrow one at each side with a broad one in the centre. The narrow left-hand column was for dates and the centre for names and addresses. In the narrow right-hand column, against each name, was a short line of apparently random letters and numbers. Those against Donald's entry, for instance, were MM3109T: and these figures had not been crossed out with his name. Maybe a sort of stock list, I thought, identifying the picture he'd bought.

I searched rapidly down all the other crossed-out names in the England sector. Maisie Matthews' name was not among them.

Damn, I thought. Why wasn't it?

I turned all the papers over rapidly. As far as I could see all the overseas customers came from basically English-speaking countries, and the proportion of crossed-out names was about one in three. If every crossing-out represented a robbery, there had been literally hundreds since the scheme began.

At the back of the file I found there was a second and separate section, again divided into pages for each country. The lists in this section were much shorter.

England.

Halfway down. My eyes positively leapt at it.

Mrs M. Matthews, Treasure Holme, Worthing, Sussex.

Crossed out.

I almost trembled. The date in the left-hand column looked like the date on which Maisie had bought her picture. The uncrossed-out numbers in the right-hand column were SMC29R.

I put down the file and sat for five minutes staring unseeingly at the wall, thinking.

My first and last conclusions were that I had a great deal to do before Jik and Sarah came back from the races, and that instincts were not always right.

The large print-folder, which had so excited Jik, lay on my bed. I opened it flat and inspected the contents.

I dare say I looked completely loony standing there with my mouth open. The folder contained a number of simplified line drawings like the one the boy-artist had been colouring in the Arts Centre. Full-sized outline drawings, on flat white canvas, as neat and accurate as tracings.

There were seven of them, all basically of horses. As they were only black and white line drawings I couldn't be sure, but I guessed that three were Munnings, two Raoul Millais, and the other two . . . I stared at the old-fashioned shapes of the horses . . . They couldn't be Stubbs, he was too well documented . . . How about Herring? Herring, I thought, nodding. The last two had a look of Herring.

Attached to one of these two canvases by an ordinary paper clip was a small handwritten memo on a piece of scrap paper.

'Don't forget to send the original. Also find out what palette he used, if different from usual.'

I looked again at the three identical finished paintings which we had also brought away. These canvases, tacked on to wooden stretchers, looked very much as if they might have started out themselves as the same sort of outlines. The canvas used was of the same weave and finish.

The technical standard of the work couldn't be faulted. The paintings did look very much like Munnings' own, and would do much more so after they had dried and been varnished. Different-coloured paints dried at different speeds, and also the drying time of paints depended very much on the amount of oil or turps used to thin them, but at a rough guess all three pictures had been completed between three and six days earlier. The paint was at the same stage on all of them. They must, I thought, have all been painted at once, in a row, like a production line. Red hat, red hat, red hat . . . It would have saved time and paint.

The brushwork throughout was painstaking and controlled. Nothing slapdash. No time skimped. The quality of care was the same as in the Millais copy at Alice.

I was looking, I knew, at the true worth of Harley Renbo.

All three paintings were perfectly legal. It was never illegal to copy: only to attempt to sell the copy as real.

I thought it all over for a bit longer, and then set rapidly to work.

The Hilton, when I went downstairs an hour later, were most amiable and helpful.

Certainly, they could do what I asked. Certainly, I

could use the photocopying machine, come this way. Certainly, I could pay my bill now, and leave later.

I thanked them for their many excellent services.

'Our pleasure,' they said: and, incredibly, they meant it.

Upstairs again, waiting for Jik and Sarah, I packed all my things. That done, I took off my jacket and shirt and did my best at rigging the spare bandages and clips back into something like the Alice shape, with my hand inside across my chest. No use pretending that it wasn't a good deal more comfortable that way than the dragging soreness of letting it all swing free. I buttoned my shirt over the top and calculated that if the traffic was bad Jik might still be struggling out of the racecourse.

A little anxiously, and still feeling faintly unwell, I settled to wait.

I waited precisely five minutes. Then the telephone by the bed rang, and I picked up the receiver.

Jik's voice, sounding hard and dictatorial.

'Charles, will you please come down to our room at once.'

'Well . . .' I said hesitantly. 'Is it important?'

'Bloody chromic oxide!' he said explosively. 'Can't you do anything without arguing?'

Christ, I thought.

I took a breath. 'Give me ten minutes,' I said. 'I

need ten minutes. I'm . . . er . . . I've just had a shower.
I'm in my underpants.'

'Thank you, Charles,' he said. The telephone clicked
as he disconnected.

A lot of Jik's great oaths galloped across my mind,
wasting precious time. If ever we needed divine help,
it was now.

Stifling a gut-twisting lurch of plain fear I picked up
the telephone and made a series of internal calls.

'Please could you send a porter up right away to
room seventeen-eighteen to collect Mr Cassavetes'
bags?'

'Housekeeper . . .? Please will you send someone
along urgently to seventeen-eighteen to clean the room
as Mr Cassavetes has been sick . . .'

'Please will you send the nurse along to seventeen-
eighteen at once as Mr Cassavetes has a severe
pain . . .'

'Please will you send four bottles of your best champagne and ten glasses up to seventeen-eighteen
immediately . . .'

'Please bring coffee for three to seventeen-eighteen
at once . . .'

'Electrician? All the electrics have fused in room
seventeen-eighteen, please come at once.'

'. . . the water is overflowing in the bathroom, please
send the plumber urgently.'

Who else was there? I ran my eye down the list of
possible services. One wouldn't be able to summon

chiropodists, masseuses, secretaries, barbers or clothes-pressers in a hurry . . . but television, why not?

'. . . Please would you see to the television in room seventeen-eighteen. There is smoke coming from the back and it smells like burning . . .'

That should do it, I thought. I made one final call for myself, asking for a porter to collect my bags. Right on, they said. Ten-dollar tip I said if the bags could be down in the hall within five minutes. No sweat, an Australian voice assured me happily. Coming right that second.

I left my door ajar for the porter and rode down two storeys in the lift to floor seventeen. The corridor outside Jik and Sarah's room was still a broad empty expanse of no one doing anything in a hurry.

The ten minutes had gone.

I fretted.

The first to arrive was the waiter with the champagne, and he came not with a tray but a trolley, complete with ice buckets and spotless white cloths. It couldn't possibly have been better.

As he slowed to a stop outside Jik's door, two other figures turned into the corridor, hurrying, and behind them, distantly, came a cleaner slowly pushing another trolley of linen and buckets and brooms.

I said to the waiter, 'Thank you so much for coming so quickly.' I gave him a ten-dollar note, which surprised him. 'Please go and serve the champagne straight away.'

He grinned, and knocked on Jik's door.

After a pause, Jik opened it. He looked tense and strained.

'Your champagne, sir,' said the waiter.

'But I didn't . . .' Jik began. He caught sight of me suddenly, where I stood a little back from his door. I made waving-in motions with my hand, and a faint grin appeared to lighten the anxiety.

Jik retreated into the room followed by trolley and waiter.

At a rush, after that, came the electrician, the plumber and the television man. I gave them each ten dollars and thanked them for coming so promptly. 'I had a winner,' I said. They took the money with more grins and Jik opened the door to their knock.

'Electrics . . . plumbing . . . television . . .' His eyebrows rose. He looked across to me in rising comprehension. He flung wide his door and invited them in with all his heart.

'Give them some champagne,' I said.

'God Almighty.'

After that, in quick succession, came the porter, the man with the coffee, and the nurse. I gave them all ten dollars from my mythical winnings and invited them to join the party. Finally came the cleaner, pushing her top-heavy-looking load. She took the ten dollars, congratulated me on my good fortune, and entered the crowded and noisy fray.

It was up to Jik, I thought. I couldn't do any more.

He and Sarah suddenly popped out like the corks from the gold-topped bottles, and stood undecided in the corridor. I gripped Sarah's wrist and tugged her towards me.

'Push the cleaning trolley through the door, and turn it over,' I said to Jik.

He wasted no time deliberating. The brooms crashed to the carpet inside the room, and Jik pulled the door shut after him.

Sarah and I were already running on ourselves to the lifts. She looked extremely pale and wild-eyed, and I knew that whatever had happened in their room had been almost too much for her.

Jik sprinted along after us. There were six lifts from the seventeenth floor, and one never had to wait more than a few seconds for one to arrive. The seconds this time seemed like hours but were actually very few indeed. The welcoming doors slid open, and we leapt inside and pushed the 'doors closed' button like maniacs.

The doors closed.

The lift descended, smooth and fast.

'Where's the car?' I said.

'Car park.'

'Get it and come round to the side door.'

'Right.'

'Sarah . . .'

She stared at me in fright.

'My satchel will be in the hall. Will you carry it for me?'

She looked vaguely at my one-armed state, my jacket swinging loosely over my left shoulder.

'Sarah!'

'Yes . . . all right.'

We erupted into the hall, which had filled with people returning from the Cup. Talkative groups mixed and mingled, and it was impossible to see easily from one side to the other. All to the good, I thought.

My suitcase and satchel stood waiting near the front entrance, guarded by a young man in porter's uniform.

I parted with the ten dollars. 'Thank you very much,' I said.

'No sweat,' he said cheerfully. 'Can I get you a taxi?'

I shook my head. I picked up the suitcase and Sarah the satchel and we headed out of the door.

Turned right. Hurried. Turned right again, round to the side where I'd told Jik we'd meet him.

'He's not here,' Sarah said with rising panic.

'He'll come,' I said encouragingly. 'We'll just go on walking to meet him.'

We walked. I kept looking back nervously for signs of pursuit, but there were none. Jik came round the corner on two wheels and tore millimetres off the tyres stopping beside us. Sarah scrambled into the front and I and my suitcase filled the back. Jik made a hair-raising U-turn and took us away from the Hilton at an illegal speed.

'Wowee,' he said, laughing with released tension. 'Whatever gave you that idea?'

'The Marx Brothers.'

He nodded. 'Pure crazy comedy.'

'Where are we going?' Sarah said.

'Have you noticed,' Jik said, 'how my wife always brings us back to basics?'

The city of Melbourne covered a great deal of land.

We drove randomly north and east through seemingly endless suburban developments of houses, shops, garages and light industry, all looking prosperous, haphazard, and, to my eyes, American.

'Where are we?' Jik said.

'Somewhere called Box Hill,' I said, reading it on shop fronts.

'As good as anywhere.'

We drove a few miles further and stopped at a modern middle-rank motel which had bright coloured strings of triangular flags fluttering across the forecourt. A far cry from the Hilton, though the rooms we presently took were cleaner than nature intended.

There were plain divans, a square of thin carpet nailed at the edges, and a table lamp screwed to an immovable table. The looking glass was stuck flat to the wall and the swivelling armchair was bolted to the floor. Apart from that, the curtains were bright and the hot tap ran hot in the shower.

'They don't mean you to pinch much,' Jik said. 'Let's paint them a mural.'

'No!' Sarah said, horror-struck.

'There's a great Australian saying,' Jik said. 'If it moves, shoot it, and if it grows, chop it down.'

'What's that got to do with it?' Sarah said.

'Nothing. I just thought Todd might like to hear it.'

'Give me strength.'

We were trying to, in our inconsequential way.

Jik sat in the armchair in my room, swivelling. Sarah sat on one of the divans, I on the other. My suitcase and satchel stood side by side on the floor.

'You do realize we skipped out of the Hilton without paying,' Sarah said.

'No, we didn't,' Jik said. 'According to our clothes, we are still resident. I'll ring them up later.'

'But Todd . . .'

'I did pay,' I said. 'Before you got back.'

She looked slightly happier.

'How did Greene find you?' I said.

'God knows,' Jik said gloomily.

Sarah was astonished. 'How did you know about Greene? How did you know there was anyone in our room besides Jik and me? How did you know we were in such awful trouble?'

'Jik told me.'

'But he couldn't! He couldn't risk warning you. He just had to tell you to come. He really did . . .' Her voice quivered. The tears weren't far from the surface. 'They made him . . .'

'Jik told me,' I said matter-of-factly. 'First, he called me Charles, which he never does, so I knew something was wrong. Second, he was rude to me, and I know you think he is most of the time, but he isn't, not like that. And third, he told me the name of the man who I was to guess was in your room putting pressure on you both to get me to come down and walk into a nasty little hole. He told me it was chromic oxide, which is the pigment in green paint.'

'Green paint!' The tearful moment passed. 'You really are both extraordinary,' she said.

'Long practice,' Jik said cheerfully.

'Tell me what happened,' I said.

'We left before the last race, to avoid the traffic, and we just came back normally to the Hilton. I parked the car, and we went up to our room. We'd only been there about a minute when there was this knock on the door, and when I opened it they just pushed in . . .'

'They?'

'Three of them. One was Greene. We both knew him straightaway, from your drawing. Another was the boy from the Arts Centre. The third was all biceps and beetle brows, with his brains in his fists.'

He absent-mindedly rubbed an area south of his heart.

'He punched you?' I said.

'It was all so quick . . .' he said apologetically. 'They

just crammed in . . . and biff bang . . . The next thing I knew they'd got hold of Sarah and were twisting her arm and saying that she wouldn't just get turps in her eyes if I didn't get you to come at once.'

'Did they have a gun?' I asked.

'No . . . a cigarette lighter. Look, I'm sorry, mate. I guess it sounds pretty feeble, but Beetle-brows had her in a pretty rough grasp and the boy had this ruddy great cigarette lighter with a flame like a blowtorch just a couple of inches from her cheek . . . and I was a bit groggy . . . and Greene said they'd burn her if I didn't get you . . . and I couldn't fight them all at once.'

'Stop apologizing,' I said.

'Yeah . . . well, so I rang you. I told Greene you'd be ten minutes because you were in your underpants, but I think he heard you anyway because he was stand-ing right beside me, very wary and sharp. I didn't know really whether you'd cottoned on, but I hoped to God . . . and you should have seen their faces when the waiter pushed the trolley in. Beetle-brows let go of Sarah and the boy just stood there with his mouth open and the cigarette lighter flaring up like an oil refinery . . .'

'Greene said we didn't want the champagne and to take it away,' Sarah said. 'But Jik and I said yes we did, and Jik asked the waiter to open it at once.'

'Before he got the first cork out the others all began coming . . . and then they were all picking up glasses . . . and the room was filling up . . . and Greene and the

boy and Beetle-brows were all on the window side of
the room, sort of pinned in by the trolley and all those
people ... and I just grabbed Sarah and we ducked
round the edge. The last I saw, Greene and the others
were trying to push through, but our guests were pretty
thick on the ground by then and keen to get their
champagne ... and I should think the cleaning trolley
was just about enough to give us that start to the lift.'

'I wonder how long the party lasted,' I said.

'Until the bubbles ran out.'

'They must all have thought you mad,' Sarah said.

'Anything goes on Cup day,' I said, 'and the staff of
the Hilton would be used to eccentric guests.'

'What if Greene had had a gun?' Sarah said.

I smiled at her twistedly. 'He would have had to
wave it around in front of a hell of a lot of witnesses.'

'But he might have done.'

'He might ... but he was a long way from the front
door.' I bit my thumbnail. 'Er ... how did he know I
was in the Hilton?'

There was a tangible silence.

'I told him,' Sarah said finally, in a small mixed
outburst of shame and defiance. 'Jik didn't tell you it
all, just now. At first they said ... Greene said ...
they'd burn my face if Jik didn't tell them where you
were. He didn't want to ... but he had to ... so I told
them, so that it wouldn't be him ... I suppose that
sounds stupid.'

I thought it sounded extraordinarily moving. Love of an exceptional order, and a depth of understanding.

I smiled at her. 'So they didn't know I was there, to begin with?'

Jik shook his head. 'I don't think they knew you were even in Melbourne. They seemed surprised when Sarah said you were upstairs. I think all they knew was that you weren't still in hospital in Alice Springs.'

'Did they know about our robbery?'

'I'm sure they didn't.'

I grinned. 'They'll be schizophrenic when they find out.'

Jik and I both carefully shied away from what would have happened if I'd gone straight down to their room, though I saw from his eyes that he knew. With Sarah held as a hostage I would have had to leave the Hilton with Greene and taken my chance. The uncomfortably slim chance that they would have let me off again with my life.

'I'm hungry,' I said.

Sarah smiled. 'Whenever are you not?'

We ate in a small Bring Your Own restaurant nearby, with people at tables all around us talking about what they'd backed in the Cup.

'Good heavens,' Sarah exclaimed. 'I'd forgotten about that.'

'About what?'

'Your winnings,' she said. 'On Ringwood.'

'But . . .' I began.

'It was number eleven!'

'I don't believe it.'

She opened her handbag and produced a fat wad of notes. Somehow, in all the mêlée in the Hilton, she had managed to emerge from fiery danger with the cream leather pouch swinging from her arm. The strength of the instinct which kept women attached to their handbags had often astounded me, but never more than that day.

'It was forty to one,' she said. 'I put twenty dollars on for you, so you've got eight hundred dollars, and I think it's disgusting.'

'Share it,' I said, laughing.

She shook her head. 'Not a cent . . . To be honest, I thought it had no chance at all, and I thought I'd teach you not to bet that way by losing you twenty dollars, otherwise I'd only have staked you ten.'

'I owe most of it to Jik, anyway,' I said.

'Keep it,' he said. 'We'll add and subtract later. Do you want me to cut your steak?'

'Please.'

He sliced away neatly at my plate, and pushed it back with the fork placed ready.

'What else happened at the races?' I said, spearing the first succulent piece. 'Who did you see?' The steak tasted as good as it looked, and I realized that in spite of all the sore patches I had at last lost the overall feeling of unsettled shaky sickness. Things were on the mend, it seemed.

'We didn't see Greene,' Jik said. 'Or the boy, or Beetle-brows.'

'I guess they saw you.'

'Do you think so?' Sarah said worriedly.

'I'd guess,' I said, 'that they saw you at the races and simply followed you back to the Hilton.'

'Jesus,' Jik groaned. 'We never spotted them. There was a whole mass of traffic.'

I nodded. 'And all moving very slowly. If Greene was perhaps three cars behind you, you'd never have seen him, but he could have kept you in sight easily.'

'I'm bloody sorry, Todd.'

'Don't be silly. And no harm done.'

'Except for the fact,' Sarah said, 'that I've still got no clothes.'

'You look fine,' I said absently.

'We saw a girl I know in Sydney,' Sarah said. 'We watched the first two races together and talked to her aunt. And Jik and I were talking to a photographer we both knew just after he got back ... so it would be pretty easy to prove Jik was at the races all afternoon, like you wanted.'

'No sign of Wexford?'

'Not if he looked like your drawing,' Sarah said. 'Though of course he might have been there. It's awfully difficult to recognize a complete stranger just from a drawing, in a huge crowd like that.'

'We talked to a lot of people,' Jik said. 'To everyone Sarah knew even slightly. She used the excuse of introducing me as her newly bagged husband.'

'We even talked to that man you met on Saturday,' Sarah agreed, nodding. 'Or rather, he came over and talked to us.'

'Hudson Taylor?' I asked.

'The one you saw talking to Wexford,' Jik said.

'He asked if you were at the Cup,' Sarah said. 'He said he'd been going to ask you along for another drink. We said we'd tell you he'd asked.'

'His horse ran quite well, didn't it?' I said.

'We saw him earlier than that. We wished him luck and he said he'd need it.'

'He bets a bit,' I said, remembering.

'Who doesn't?'

'Another commission down the drain,' I said. 'He would have had Vinery painted if he'd won.'

'You hire yourself out like a prostitute,' Jik said. 'It's obscene.'

'And anyway,' added Sarah cheerfully, 'you won more on Ringwood than you'd've got for the painting.'

I looked pained, and Jik laughed.

We drank coffee, went back to the motel, and divided to our separate rooms. Five minutes later Jik knocked on my door.

'Come in,' I said, opening it.

He grinned. 'You were expecting me.'

'Thought you might come.'

He sat in the armchair and swivelled. His gaze fell on my suitcase, which lay flat on one of the divans.

'What did you do with all the stuff we took from the gallery?'

I told him.

He stopped swivelling and sat still.

'You don't mess about, do you?' he said eventually.

'A few days from now,' I said, 'I'm going home.'

'And until then?'

'Um . . . until then, I aim to stay one jump ahead of Wexford, Greene, Beetle-brows, the Arts Centre boy, and the toughs who met me on the balcony at Alice.'

'Not to mention our copy artist, Harley Renbo.'

I considered it. 'Him too,' I said.

'Do you think we can?'

'Not we. Not from hereon. This is where you take Sarah home.'

He slowly shook his head. 'I don't reckon it would be any safer than staying with you. We're too easy to find. For one thing, we're in the Sydney phone book. What's to stop Wexford from marching on to the boat with a bigger threat than a cigarette lighter?'

'You could tell him what I've just told you.'

'And waste all your efforts.'

'Retreat is sometimes necessary.'

He shook his head. 'If we stay with you, retreat may never be necessary. It's the better of two risks. And anyway . . .' the old fire gleamed in his eye . . . 'It will be a great game. Cat and mouse. With cats who don't know they are mice chasing a mouse who knows he's a cat.'

More like a bull fight, I thought, with myself waving the cape to invite the charge. Or a conjuror, attracting attention to one hand while he did the trick with the other. On the whole I preferred the notion of the conjuror. There seemed less likelihood of being gored.

CHAPTER THIRTEEN

I spent a good deal of the night studying the list of Overseas Customers, mostly because I still found it difficult to lie comfortably to sleep, and partly because I had nothing else to read.

It became more and more obvious that I hadn't really pinched *enough*. The list I'd taken was fine in its way, but would have been doubly useful with a stock list to match the letters and numbers in the right-hand column.

On the other hand, all stock numbers were a form of code, and if I looked at them long enough, maybe some sort of recognizable pattern might emerge.

By far the majority began with the letter M, particularly in the first and much larger section. In the smaller section, which I had found at the back of the file, the M prefixes were few, and S, A, W and B were much commoner.

Donald's number began with M. Maisie's began with S.

Suppose, I thought, that the M simply stood for

Melbourne, and the S for Sydney, the cities where each had bought their pictures.

Then A, W and B were where? Adelaide, Wagga Wagga and Brisbane?

Alice?

In the first section the letters and numbers following the initial M seemed to have no clear pattern. In the second section, though, the third letter was always C, the last letter always R, and the numbers, divided though they were between several countries, progressed more or less consecutively. The highest number of all was 54, which had been sold to a Mr Norman Updike, living in Auckland, New Zealand. The stock number against his name was WHC54R. The date in the left-hand column was only a week old, and Mr Updike had not been crossed out.

All the pictures in the shorter section had been sold within the past three years. The first dates in the long first section were five and a half years old.

I wondered which had come first, five and a half years ago: the gallery or the idea. Had Wexford originally been a full-time crook deliberately setting up an imposing front, or a formerly honest art dealer struck by criminal possibilities? Judging from the respectable air of the gallery and what little I'd seen of Wexford himself, I would have guessed the latter. But the violence lying just below the surface didn't match.

I sighed, put down the lists, and switched off the

light. Lay in the dark, thinking of the telephone call I'd made after Jik had gone back to Sarah.

It had been harder to arrange from the motel than it would have been from the Hilton, but the line had been loud and clear.

'You got my cable?' I said.

'I've been waiting for your call for half an hour.'

'Sorry.'

'What do you want?'

'I've sent you a letter,' I said. 'I want to tell you what's in it.'

'But . . .'

'Just listen,' I said. 'And talk after.' I spoke for quite a long time to a response of grunts from the far end.

'Are you sure of all this?'

'Positive about most,' I said. 'Some of it's a guess.'

'Repeat it.'

'Very well.' I did so, at much the same length.

'I have recorded all that.'

'Good.'

'Hm . . . What do you intend doing now?'

'I'm going home soon. Before that, I think I'll keep looking into things that aren't my business.'

'I don't approve of that.'

I grinned at the telephone. 'I don't suppose you do, but if I'd stayed in England we wouldn't have got this far. There's one other thing . . . Can I reach you by telex if I want to get a message to you in a hurry?'

'Telex? Wait a minute.'

I waited.

'Yes, here you are.' A number followed. I wrote it down. 'Address any message to me personally and head it urgent.'

'Right,' I said. 'And could you get answers to three questions for me?' He listened and said he could. 'Thank you very much,' I said. 'And goodnight.'

Sarah and Jik both looked heavy-eyed and languorous in the morning. A successful night, I judged.

We checked out of the motel, packed my suitcase into the boot of the car, and sat in the passenger seats to plan the day.

'Can't we please get our clothes from the Hilton?' Sarah said, sounding depressed.

Jik and I said 'No' together.

'I'll ring them now,' Jik said. 'I'll get them to pack all our things and keep them safe for us, and I'll tell them I'll send a cheque for the bill.' He levered himself out of the car again and went off on the errand.

'Buy what you need out of my winnings,' I said to Sarah.

She shook her head. 'I've got some money. It's not that. It's just . . . I wish all this was over.'

'It will be, soon,' I said neutrally. She sighed heavily. 'What's your idea of a perfect life?' I asked.

'Oh . . .' she seemed surprised. 'I suppose right now

I just want to be with Jik on the boat and have fun, like before you came.'

'And for ever?'

She looked at me broodingly. 'You may think, Todd, that I don't know Jik is a complicated character, but you've only got to look at his paintings . . . They make me shudder. They're a side of Jik I don't know because he hasn't painted anything since we met. You may think that this world will be worse off if Jik is happy for a bit, but I'm no fool, I know that in the end whatever it is that drives him to paint like that will come back again . . . I think these first few months together are frantically precious . . . and it isn't just the physical dangers you've dragged us into that I hate, but the feeling that I've lost the rest of that golden time . . . that you remind him of his painting, and that after you've gone he'll go straight back to it . . . weeks and weeks before he might have done.'

'Get him to go sailing,' I said. 'He's always happy at sea.'

'You don't care, do you?'

I looked straight into her clouded brown eyes. 'I care for you both, very much.'

'Then God help the people you hate.'

And God help me, I thought, if I become any fonder of my oldest friend's wife. I looked away from her, out of the window. Affection wouldn't matter. Anything else would be a mess.

Jik came back with a satisfied air. 'That's all fixed.

They said there's a letter for you, Todd, delivered by hand a few minutes ago. They asked me for a forwarding address.'

'What did you say?'

'I said you'd call them yourself.'

'Right . . . Well, let's get going.'

'Where to?'

'New Zealand, don't you think?'

'That should be far enough,' Jik said dryly.

He drove us to the airport, which was packed with people going home from the Cup.

'If Wexford and Greene are looking for us,' Sarah said, 'they will surely be watching at the airport.'

If they weren't, I thought, we'd have to lay a trail: but Jik, who knew that, didn't tell her.

'They can't do much in public,' he said comfortingly.

We bought tickets and found we could either fly to Auckland direct at lunch-time, or via Sydney leaving within half an hour.

'Sydney,' said Sarah positively, clearly drawing strength from the chance of putting her feet down on her own safe doorstep.

I shook my head. 'Auckland direct. Let's see if the restaurant's still open for breakfast.'

We squeezed in under the waitresses' pointed consultation of clocks and watches and ordered bacon and eggs lavishly.

'Why are we going to New Zealand?' Sarah said.

'To see a man about a painting and advise him to take out extra insurance.'

'Are you actually making sense?'

'Actually,' I said, 'yes.'

'I don't see why we have to go so far, when Jik said you found enough in the gallery to blow the whole thing wide open.'

'Um . . .' I said. 'Because we don't want to blow it wide open. Because we want to hand it to the police in full working order.'

She studied my face. 'You are very devious.'

'Not on canvas,' Jik said.

After we'd eaten we wandered around the airport shops, buying yet more toothbrushes and so on for Jik and Sarah, and another airline bag. There was no sign of Wexford or Greene or the boy or Beetle-brows or Renbo, or the tough who'd been on watch at Alice Springs. If they'd seen us without us seeing them, we couldn't tell.

'I think I'll ring the Hilton,' I said.

Jik nodded. I put the call through with him and Sarah sitting near, within sound and sight.

'I called about a forwarding address . . .' I told the reception desk. 'I can't really give you one. I'll be in New Zealand. I'm flying to Auckland in an hour or two.'

They asked for instructions about the hand-delivered letter.

229

'Er . . . Would you mind opening it, and reading it to me?'

Certainly, they said. Their pleasure. The letter was from Hudson Taylor saying he was sorry to have missed me at the races, and that if while I was in Australia I would like to see round a vineyard, he would be pleased to show me his.

Thanks, I said. Our pleasure, sir, they said. If anyone asked for me, I said, would they please mention where I'd gone. They would. Certainly. Their pleasure.

During the next hour Jik called the car-hire firm about settling their account and leaving the car in the airport car park, and I checked my suitcase through with Air New Zealand. Passports were no problem: I had mine with me in any case, but for Jik and Sarah they were unnecessary, as passage between New Zealand and Australia was as unrestricted as between England and Ireland.

Still no sign of Wexford or Greene. We sat in the departure bay thinking private thoughts.

It was again only when our flight was called that I spotted a spotter. The prickles rose again on my skin. I'd been blind, I thought. Dumb and blind.

Not Wexford, nor Greene, nor the boy, nor Renbo, nor any rough set of muscles. A neat day dress, neat hair, unremarkable handbag and shoes. A calm concentrated face. I saw her because she was staring at Sarah. She was standing outside the departure bay, looking in. The woman who had welcomed me into the Yarra

River Fine Arts, and given me a catalogue, and let me out again afterwards.

As if she felt my eyes upon her she switched her gaze abruptly to my face. I looked away instantly, blankly, hoping she wouldn't know I'd seen her, or wouldn't know at least that I'd recognized her.

Jik, Sarah and I stood up and drifted with everyone else towards the departure doors. In their glass I could see the woman's reflection: standing still, watching us go. I walked out towards the aircraft and didn't look back.

Mrs Norman Updike stood in her doorway, shook her head, and said that her husband would not be home until six.

She was thin and sharp-featured and talked with tight New Zealand vowels. If we wanted to speak to her husband, we would have to come back.

She looked us over; Jik with his rakish blond beard, Sarah in her slightly crumpled but still military cream dress, I with my arm in its sling under my shirt, and jacket loose over my shoulder. Hardly a trio one would easily forget. She watched us retreat down her front path with a sharply turned-down mouth.

'Dear gentle soul,' murmured Jik.

We drove away in the car we had hired at the airport.

'Where now?' Jik said.

'Shops.' Sarah was adamant. 'I must have some clothes.'

The shops, it appeared, were in Queen Street, and still open for another half-hour. Jik and I sat in the car, waiting and watching the world go by.

'The dolly-birds fly out of their office cages about now,' Jik said happily.

'What of it?'

'I sit and count the ones with no bras.'

'And you a married man.'

'Old habits die hard.'

We had counted eight definites and one doubtful by the time Sarah returned. She was wearing a light olive skirt with a pink shirt, and reminded me of pistachio ice cream.

'That's better,' she said, tossing two well-filled carriers on to the back seat. 'Off we go, then.'

The therapeutic value of the new clothes lasted all the time we spent in New Zealand and totally amazed me. She seemed to feel safer if she looked fresh and clean, her spirits rising accordingly. Armour-plated cotton, I thought. Drip-dry bullet-proofing. Security is a new pin.

We dawdled back to the hill overlooking the bay where Norman Updike's house stood in a crowded suburban street. The Updike residence was large but squashed by neighbours, and it was not until one was inside that one realized that the jostling was due to the view. As many houses as could be crammed on to the land had been built to share it. The city itself seemed to sprawl endlessly round miles of indented coastline, but all the building plots looked tiny.

Norman Updike proved as expansive as his wife was closed in. He had a round shiny bald head on a round short body, and he called his spouse Chuckles without apparently intending satire.

We said, Jik and I, that we were professional artists who would be intensely interested and grateful if we could briefly admire the noted picture he had just bought.

'Did the gallery send you?' he asked, beaming at the implied compliments to his taste and wealth.

'Sort of,' we said, and Jik added: 'My friend here is well known in England for his painting of horses, and is represented in many top galleries, and has been hung often at the Royal Academy . . .'

I thought he was laying it on a bit too thick, but Norman Updike was impressed and pulled wide his door.

'Come in then. Come in. The picture's in the lounge. This way, lass, this way.'

He showed us into a large over-stuffed room with dark ankle-deep carpet, big dark cupboards, and the glorious view of sunlit water.

Chuckles, sitting solidly in front of a television busy with a moronic British comic show, gave us a sour look and no greeting.

'Over here,' Norman Updike beamed, threading his

portly way round a battery of fat armchairs. 'What do you think of that, eh? He waved his hand with proprietorial pride at the canvas on his wall.

A smallish painting, fourteen inches by eighteen. A black horse, with an elongated neck curving against a blue and white sky; a chopped-off tail; the grass in the foreground yellow; and the whole covered with an old-looking varnish.

'Herring,' I murmured reverently.

Norman Updike's beam broadened. 'I see you know your stuff. Worth a bit, that is.'

'A good deal,' I agreed.

'I reckon I got a bargain. The gallery said I'd always make a profit if I wanted to sell.'

'May I look at the brushwork?' I asked politely.

'Go right ahead.'

I looked closely. It was very good. It did look like Herring, dead since 1865. It also, indefinably, looked like the meticulous Renbo. One would need a microscope and chemical analysis to make sure.

I stepped back and glanced round the rest of the room. There was nothing of obvious value, and the few other pictures were all prints.

'Beautiful,' I said admiringly, turning back to the Herring. 'Unmistakable style. A real master.'

Updike beamed.

'You'd better beware of burglars,' I said.

He laughed. 'Chuckles, dear, do you hear what this

young man says? He says we'd better beware of
burglars!'

Chuckles' eyes gave me two seconds' sour attention
and returned to the screen.

Updike patted Sarah on the shoulder. 'Tell your
friend not to worry about burglars.'

'Why not?' I said.

'We've got alarms all over this house,' he beamed.
'Don't you worry, a burglar wouldn't get far.'

Jik and Sarah, as I had done, looked round the
room and saw nothing much worth stealing. Nothing,
certainly, worth alarms all over the house. Updike
watched them looking and his beam grew wider.

'Shall I show these young people our little treasures,
Chuckles?' he said.

Chuckles didn't even reply. The television cackled
with tinned laughter.

'We'd be most interested,' I said.

He smiled with the fat anticipatory smirk of one
about to show what will certainly be admired. Two or
three steps took him to one of the big dark cupboards
which seemed built into the walls, and he pulled open
the double doors with a flourish.

Inside, there were about six deep shelves, each bearing several complicated pieces of carved jade. Pale
pink, creamy-white and pale green, smooth, polished,
intricate, expensive; each piece standing upon its own
heavy-looking black base-support. Jik, Sarah and I

made appreciative noises and Norman Updike smiled even wider.

'Hong Kong, of course,' he said. 'I worked there for years, you know. Quite a nice little collection, eh?' He walked along to the next dark cupboard and pulled open a duplicate set of doors. Inside, more shelves, more carvings, as before.

'I'm afraid I don't know much about jade,' I said, apologetically. 'Can't appreciate your collection to the full.'

He told us a good deal more about the ornate goodies than we actually wanted to know. There were four cupboards full in the lounge and overflows in bedroom and hall.

'You used to be able to pick them up very cheap in Hong Kong,' he said. 'I worked there more than twenty years, you know.'

Jik and I exchanged glances. I nodded slightly.

Jik immediately shook Norman Updike by the hand, put his arm round Sarah, and said we must be leaving. Updike looked enquiringly at Chuckles, who was still glued to the telly and still abdicating from the role of hostess. When she refused to look our way he shrugged good-humouredly and came with us to his front door. Jik and Sarah walked out as soon as he opened it, and left me alone with him in the hall.

'Mr Updike,' I said. 'At the gallery . . . which man was it who sold you the Herring?'

'Mr Grey,' he said promptly.

Mr Grey ... Mr Grey ...

I frowned.

'Such a pleasant man,' nodded Updike, beaming. 'I told him I knew very little about pictures, but he assured me I would get as much pleasure from my little Herring as from all my jade.'

'You did tell him about your jade, then?'

'Naturally I did. I mean ... if you don't know anything about one thing, well ... you try and show you do know about something else. Don't you? Only human, isn't it?'

'Only human,' I agreed, smiling. 'What was the name of Mr Grey's gallery?'

'Eh?' He looked puzzled. 'I thought you said he sent you, to see my picture.'

'I go to so many galleries, I've foolishly forgotten which one it was.'

'Ruapehu Fine Arts,' he said. 'I was down there last week.'

'Down ...?'

'In Wellington.' His smile was slipping. 'Look here, what is all this?' Suspicion flitted across his rounded face. 'Why did you come here? I don't think Mr Grey sent you at all.'

'No,' I said. 'But Mr Updike, we mean you no harm. We really are painters, my friend and I. But ... now we've seen your jade collection ... we do think we must warn you. We've heard of several people who've bought paintings and had their houses burgled soon

237

after. You say you've got burglar alarms fitted, so if I were you I'd make sure they are working properly.'

'But . . . good gracious . . .'

'There's a bunch of thieves about,' I said. 'Who follow up the sales of paintings and burgle the houses of those who buy. I suppose they reckon that if anyone can afford, say, a Herring, they have other things worth stealing.'

He looked at me with awakening shrewdness. 'You mean, young man, that I told Mr Grey about my jade . . .'

'Let's just say,' I said, 'that it would be sensible to take more precautions than usual.'

'But . . . for how long?'

I shook my head. 'I don't know, Mr Updike. Maybe for ever.'

His round jolly face looked troubled.

'Why did you bother to come and tell me all this?' he said.

'I'd do a great deal more to break up this bunch.'

He asked 'Why?' again, so I told him. 'My cousin bought a painting. My cousin's house was burgled. My cousin's wife disturbed the burglars, and they killed her.'

Norman Updike took a long slow look at my face. I couldn't have stopped him seeing the abiding anger, even if I'd tried. He shivered convulsively.

'I'm glad you're not after *me*,' he said.

I managed a smile. 'Mr Updike . . . please take care.

And one day, perhaps, the police may come to see your picture, and ask where you bought it ... anyway, they will if I have anything to do with it.'

The round smile returned with understanding and conviction. 'I'll expect them,' he said.

CHAPTER FOURTEEN

Jik drove us from Auckland to Wellington; eight hours in the car.

We stopped overnight in a motel in the town of Hamilton, south of Auckland, and went on in the morning. No one followed us, molested us or spied on us. As far as I could be, I was sure no one had picked us up in the northern city, and no one knew we had called at the Updikes.

Wexford must know, all the same, that I had the Overseas Customers list, and he knew there were several New Zealand addresses on it. He couldn't guess which one I'd pick to visit, but he could and would guess that any I picked with the prefix W would steer me straight to the gallery in Wellington.

So in the gallery in Wellington, he'd be ready . . .

'You're looking awfully grim, Todd,' Sarah said.

'Sorry.'

'What were you thinking?'

'How soon we could stop for lunch.'

She laughed. 'We've only just had breakfast.'

We passed the turning to Rotorua and the land of hot springs. Anyone for a boiling mud pack? Jik asked. There was a power station further on run by steam jets from underground, Sarah said, and horrid black craters stinking of sulphur, and the earth's crust was so thin in places that it vibrated and sounded hollow. She had been taken round a place called Waiotapu when she was a child, she said, and had had terrible nightmares afterwards, and she didn't want to go back.

'Pooh,' Jik said dismissively. 'They only have earthquakes every other Friday.'

'Somebody told me they have so many earthquakes in Wellington that all the new office blocks are built in cradles,' Sarah said.

'Rock-a-bye sky-scraper . . .' sang Jik, in fine voice.

The sun shone bravely, and the countryside was green with leaves I didn't know. There were fierce bright patches and deep mysterious shadows; gorges and rocks and heaven-stretching tree trunks; feathery waving grasses, shoulder-high. An alien land, wild and beautiful.

'Get that chiaroscuro,' Jik said, as we sped into one particularly spectacular curving valley.

'What's chiaroscuro?' Sarah said.

'Light and shade,' Jik said. 'Contrast and balance. Technical term. All the world's a chiaroscuro, and all the men and women merely blobs of light and shade.'

'Every life's a chiaroscuro,' I said.

'And every soul.'

'The enemy,' I said, 'is grey.'

'And you get grey,' Jik nodded, 'by muddling together red, white and blue.'

'Grey lives, grey deaths, all levelled out into equal grey nothing.'

'No one,' Sarah sighed, 'would ever call you two grey?'

'Grey!' I said suddenly. 'Of bloody course.'

'What are you on about?' Jik said.

'Grey was the name of the man who hired the suburban art gallery in Sydney, and Grey is the name of the man who sold Updike his quote Herring unquote.'

'Oh dear.' Sarah's sigh took the lift out of the spirits and the dazzle from the day.

'Sorry,' I said.

There were so many of them, I thought. Wexford and Greene. The boy. The woman. Harley Renbo. Two toughs at Alice Springs, one of whom I knew by sight, and one (the one who'd been behind me) whom I didn't. The one I didn't know might, or might not, be Beetle-brows. If he wasn't, Beetle-brows was extra.

And now Grey. And another one, somewhere.

Nine at least. Maybe ten. How could I possibly tangle all that lot up without getting crunched? Or worse, getting Sarah crunched, or Jik. Every time I moved, the serpent grew another head.

I wondered who did the actual robberies. Did they

send their own two (or three) toughs overseas, or did they contract out to local labour, so to speak?

If they sent their own toughs, was it one of them who had killed Regina?

Had I already met Regina's killer? Had he thrown me over the balcony at Alice?

I pondered uselessly, and added one more twist . . .

Was he waiting ahead in Wellington?

We reached the capital in the afternoon and booked into the Townhouse Hotel because of its splendid view over the harbour. With such marvellous coastal scenery, I thought, it would have been a disgrace if the cities of New Zealand had been ugly. I still thought there were no big towns more captivating than flat old marshy London, but that was another story. Wellington, new and cared for, had life and character to spare.

I looked up the Ruapehu Fine Arts in the telephone directory and asked the hotel's reception desk how to get there. They had never heard of the gallery, but the road it was in, that must be up past the old town, they thought: past Thorndon.

They sold me a local area road map, which they said would help, and told me that Mount Ruapehu was a (with luck) extinct volcano, with a warm lake in its crater. If we'd come from Auckland, we must have passed nearby.

I thanked them and carried the map to Jik and Sarah upstairs in their room.

'We could find the gallery,' Jik said. 'But what would we do when we got there?'

'Make faces at them through the window?'

'You'd be crazy enough for that, too,' Sarah said.

'Let's just go and look,' I said. 'They won't see us in the car, if we simply drive past.'

'And after all,' Jik said incautiously, 'we do want them to know we're here.'

'Why?' asked Sarah in amazement.

'Oh Jesus,' Jik said.

'Why?' she demanded, the anxiety crowding back.

'Ask Todd, it's his idea.'

'You're a sod,' I said.

'Why, Todd?'

'Because,' I said, 'I want them to spend all their energies looking for us over here and not clearing away every vestige of evidence in Melbourne. We do want the police to deal with them finally, don't we, because we can't exactly arrest them ourselves? Well ... when the police start moving, it would be hopeless if there was no one left for them to find.'

She nodded. 'That's what you meant by leaving it all in working order. But ... you didn't say anything about deliberately enticing them to follow us.'

'Todd's got that list, and the pictures we took,' Jik said, 'and they'll want them back. Todd wants them to concentrate exclusively on getting them back, because if they think they can get them back and shut us up . . .'

'Jik,' I interrupted. 'You do go on a bit.'

Sarah looked from me to him and back again. A sort of hopeless calm took over from the anxiety.

'If they think they can get everything back and shut us up,' she said, 'they will be actively searching for us in order to kill us. And you intend to give them every encouragement. Is that right?'

'No,' I said. 'Or rather, yes.'

'They'd be looking for us anyway,' Jik pointed out.

'And we are going to say "Coo-ee, we're over here"?'

'Um,' I said. 'I think they may know already.'

'God give me strength,' she said. 'All right. I see what you're doing, and I see why you didn't tell me. And I think you're a louse. But I'll grant you you've been a damn sight more successful than I thought you'd be, and here we all still are, safe and moderately sound, so all right, we'll let them know we're definitely here. On the strict understanding that we then keep our heads down until you've fixed the police in Melbourne.'

I kissed her cheek. 'Done,' I said.

'So how do we do it?'

I grinned at her. 'We address ourselves to the telephone.'

In the end Sarah herself made the call, on the basis that her Australian voice would be less remarkable than Jik's Englishness, or mine.

245

'Is that the Ruapehu Fine Arts gallery? It is? I wonder if you can help me . . .' she said. 'I would like to speak to whoever is in charge. Yes, I know, but it is important. Yes, I'll wait.' She rolled her eyes and put her hand over the mouthpiece. 'She sounded like a secretary. New Zealand, anyway.'

'You're doing great,' I said.

'Oh . . . Hello? Yes. Could you tell me your name, please?' Her eyes suddenly opened wide. '*Wexford.* Oh, er . . . Mr Wexford, I've just had a visit from three extraordinary people who wanted to see a painting I bought from you some time ago. Quite extraordinary people. They said you'd sent them. I didn't believe them. I wouldn't let them in. But I thought perhaps I'd better check with you. Did you send them to see my painting?'

There was some agitated squawking from the receiver.

'Describe them? A young man with fair hair and a beard, and another young man with an injured arm, and a bedraggled-looking girl. I sent them away. I didn't like the look of them.'

She grimaced over the phone and listened to some more squawks.

'No of course I didn't give them any information. I told you I didn't like the look of them. Where do I live? Why, right here in Wellington. Well, thank you so much Mr Wexford, I am so pleased I called you.'

She put the receiver down while it was still squawking.

'He was asking me for my name,' she said.

'What a girl,' Jik said. 'What an actress, my wife.'

Wexford. Wexford himself.

It had *worked*.

I raised a small internal cheer.

'So now that they know we're here,' I said, 'would you like to go off somewhere else?'

'Oh no,' Sarah said instinctively. She looked out of the window across the busy harbour. 'It's lovely here, and we've been travelling all day already.'

I didn't argue. I thought it might take more than a single telephone call to keep the enemy interested in Wellington, and it had only been for Sarah's sake that I would have been prepared to move on.

'They won't find us just by checking the hotels by telephone,' Jik pointed out. 'Even if it occurred to them to try the Townhouse, they'd be asking for Cassavetes and Todd, not Andrews and Peel.'

'Are we Andrews and Peel?' Sarah asked.

'We're Andrews. Todd's Peel.'

'So nice to know,' she said.

Mr and Mrs Andrews and Mr Peel took dinner in the hotel restaurant without mishap, Mr Peel having discarded his sling for the evening on the grounds that it was in general a bit too easy to notice. Mr Andrews had declined, on the same consideration, to remove his beard.

We went in time to our separate rooms, and so to bed. I spent a jolly hour unsticking the Alice bandages from my leg and admiring the hemstitching. The tree had made tears that were far from the orderly cuts of operations, and as I inspected the long curving railway lines on a ridged backing of crimson, black and yellow skin, I reckoned that those doctors had done an expert job. It was four days since the fall, during which time I hadn't exactly led an inactive life, but none of their handiwork had come adrift. I realized I had progressed almost without noticing it from feeling terrible all the time to scarcely feeling anything worth mentioning. It was astonishing, I thought, how quickly the human body repaired itself, given the chance.

I covered the mementoes with fresh adhesive plaster bought that morning in Hamilton for the purpose, and even found a way of lying in bed that drew no strike action from mending bones. Things, I thought complacently as I drifted to sleep, were altogether looking up.

I suppose one could say that I underestimated on too many counts. I underestimated the desperation with which Wexford had come to New Zealand. Underestimated the rage and the thoroughness with which he searched for us.

Underestimated the effect of our amateur robbery on professional thieves. Underestimated our success. Underestimated the fear and the fury we had unleashed.

My picture of Wexford tearing his remaining hair in almost comic frustration was all wrong. He was pursuing us with a determination bordering on obsession, grimly, ruthlessly, and fast.

In the morning I woke late to a day of warm windy spring sunshine and made coffee from the fixings provided by the hotel in each room; and Jik rang through on the telephone.

'Sarah says she must wash her hair today. Apparently it's sticking together.'

'It looks all right to me.'

His grin came down the wire. 'Marriage opens vast new feminine horizons. Anyway, she's waiting down in the hall for me to drive her to the shops to buy some shampoo, but I thought I'd better let you know we were going.'

I said uneasily, 'You will be careful . . .'

'Oh sure,' he said. 'We won't go anywhere near the gallery. We won't go far. Only as far as the nearest shampoo shop. I'll call you as soon as we get back.'

He disconnected cheerfully, and five minutes later the bell rang again. I lifted the receiver.

It was the girl from the reception desk. 'Your friends say would you join them downstairs in the car.'

'O.K.,' I said.

I went jacketless down in the lift, left my room key at the desk, and walked out through the front door to the sun-baked and windy car park. I looked around for Jik and Sarah; but they were not, as it happened, the friends who were waiting.

It might have been fractionally better if I hadn't had my left arm slung up inside my shirt. As it was they simply clutched my clothes, lifted me off balance and off my feet, and ignominiously bundled me into the back of their car.

Wexford was sitting inside it; a one-man reception committee. The eyes behind the heavy spectacles were as hostile as forty below, and there was no indecision this time in his manner. This time he as good as had me again behind his steel mesh door, and this time he was intent on not making mistakes.

He still wore a bow tie. The jaunty polka dots went oddly with the unfunny matter in hand.

The muscles propelling me towards him turned out to belong to Greene with an 'e', and to a thug I'd never met but who answered the general description of Beetle-brows.

My spirits descended faster than the Hilton lifts. I ended up sitting between Beetle-brows and Wexford, with Greene climbing in front into the driving seat.

'How did you find me?' I said.

Greene, with a wolfish smile, took a Polaroid photograph from his pocket and held it for me to see. It was a picture of the three of us, Jik, Sarah and me, standing by the shops in Melbourne airport. The woman from the gallery, I guessed, had not been wasting the time she spent watching us depart.

'We went round asking the hotels,' Greene said. 'It was easy.'

There didn't seem to be much else to say, so I didn't say anything. A slight shortage of breath might have had something to do with it.

None of the others, either, seemed over-talkative. Greene started the car and drove out into the city. Wexford stared at me with a mixture of anger and satisfaction: and Beetle-brows began twisting my free right arm behind my back in a grip which left no room for debate. He wouldn't let me remain upright. My head went practically down to my knees. It was all most undignified and excruciating.

Wexford said finally, 'We want our list back.'

There was nothing gentlemanly in his voice. He wasn't making light conversation. His heavy vindictive rage had no trouble at all in communicating itself to me without possibility of misunderstanding.

Oh Christ, I thought miserably; I'd been such a bloody fool, just walking into it like that.

'Do you hear? We want our list back, and everything else you took.'

I didn't answer. Too busy suffering.

From external sounds I guessed we were travelling through busy workaday Friday-morning city streets, but as my head was below window level, I couldn't actually see.

After some time the car turned sharply left and ground uphill for what seemed like miles. The engine

sighed from overwork at the top, and the road began
to descend.

Almost nothing was said on the journey. My
thoughts about what very likely lay at the end of it
were so unwelcome that I did my best not to allow
them houseroom. I could give Wexford his list back,
but what then? What then, indeed.

After a long descent the car halted briefly and then
turned to the right. We had exchanged city sounds for
those of the sea. There were also no more Doppler
effects from cars passing us from the opposite direction. I came to the sad conclusion that we had turned
off the highway and were on our way along an
infrequently used side road.

The car stopped eventually with a jerk.

Beetle-brows removed his hands. I sat up stiffly,
wrenched and unenthusiastic.

They could hardly have picked a lonelier place. The
road ran along beside the sea so closely that it was
more or less part of the shore, and the shore was a
jungle of sharply pointed rough black rocks, with frothy
white waves slapping among them, a far cry from the
gentle beaches of home.

On the right rose jagged cliffs, steeply towering.
Ahead, the road ended blindly in some workings which
looked like a sort of quarry. Slabs had been cut from
the cliffs, and there were dusty clearings, and huge
heaps of small jagged rocks, and graded stones and
sifted chips. All raw and harsh and blackly volcanic.

No people. No machinery. No sign of occupation.

'Where's the list?' Wexford said.

Greene twisted round in the driving seat and looked seriously at my face.

'You'll tell us,' he said. 'With or without a beating. And we won't hit you with our fists, but with pieces of rock.'

Beetle-brows said aggrievedly, 'What's wrong with fists?' But what was wrong with Greene's fists was the same as with mine: I would never have been able to hit anyone hard enough to get the desired results. The local rocks, by the look of them, were something else.

'What if I tell you?' I said.

They hadn't expected anything so easy. I could see the surprise on their faces, and it was flattering, in a way. There was also a furtiveness in their expressions which boded no good at all. Regina, I thought. Regina, with her head bashed in.

I looked at the cliffs, the quarry, the sea. No easy exit. And behind us, the road. If I ran that way, they would drive after me, and mow me down. If I could run. And even that was problematical.

I swallowed and looked dejected, which wasn't awfully difficult.

'I'll tell you . . .' I said. 'Out of the car.'

There was a small silence while they considered it; but as they weren't anyway going to have room for much crashing around with rocks in that crowded interior, they weren't entirely against it.

Greene leaned over towards the glove compartment on the passenger side, opened it, and drew out a pistol. I knew just about enough about firearms to distinguish a revolver from an automatic, and this was a revolver, a gun whose main advantage, I had read, was that it never jammed.

Greene handled it with a great deal more respect than familiarity. He showed it to me silently, and returned it to the glove compartment, leaving the hinged flap door open so that we all had a clear view of his ultimate threat.

'Get out, then,' Wexford said.

We all got out, and I made sure that I ended up on the side of the sea. The wind was much stronger on this exposed coast, and chilling in the bright sunshine. It lifted the thin carefully combed hair away from Wexford's crown, and left him straggly bald, and intensified the stupid look of Beetle-brows. Greene's eyes stayed as watchful and sharp as the harsh terrain around us.

'All right then,' Wexford said roughly, shouting a little to bring his voice above the din of sea and sky. 'Where's the list?'

I whirled away from them and did my best to sprint for the sea.

I thrust my right hand inside my shirt and tugged at the sling-forming bandages.

Wexford, Greene and Beetle-brows shouted furiously and almost trampled on my heels.

I pulled the lists of Overseas Customers out of the sling, whirled again with them in my hand, and flung them with a bowling action as far out to sea as I could manage.

The pages fluttered apart in mid-air, but the offshore winds caught most of them beautifully and blew them like great leaves out to sea.

I didn't stop at the water's edge. I went straight on into the cold inhospitable battlefield of shark-teeth rocks and green water and white foaming waves. Slipping, falling, getting up, staggering on, finding that the current was much stronger than I'd expected, and the rocks more abrasive, and the footing more treacherous. Finding I'd fled from one deadly danger to embrace another.

For one second, I looked back.

Wexford had followed me a step or two into the sea, but only, it seemed, to reach one of the pages which had fallen shorter than the others. He was standing there with the frothy water swirling round his trouser legs, peering at the sodden paper.

Greene was beside the car, leaning in; by the front passenger seat.

Beetle-brows had his mouth open.

I reapplied myself to the problem of survival.

The shore shelved, as most shores do. Every forward step led into a stronger current, which sucked and pulled and shoved me around like a piece of flotsam. Hip-deep between waves, I found it difficult to stay on my feet, and every time I didn't I was in dire trouble, because of the black needle-sharp rocks waiting in ranks above and below the surface to scratch and tear.

The rocks were not the kind I was used to: not the hard familiar lumpy rocks of Britain, polished by the sea. These were the raw stuff of volcanoes, as scratchy as pumice. One's groping hand didn't slide over them: one's skin stuck to them, and tore off. Clothes fared no better. Before I'd gone thirty yards I was running with blood from a dozen superficial grazes: and no blood vessels bleed more convincingly than the small surface capillaries.

My left arm was still tangled inside the sling, which had housed the Overseas Customers since Cup Day as an insurance against having my room robbed, as at Alice. Soaking wet, the bandages now clung like leeches, and my shirt also. Muscles weakened by a fracture and inactivity couldn't deal with them. I rolled around a lot from not having two hands free.

My foot stepped awkwardly on the side of a submerged rock and I felt it scrape my shin: lost my balance, fell forward, tried to save myself with my hand, failed, crashed chest first against a small jagged peak dead ahead, and jerked my head sharply sideways to avoid connecting with my nose.

The rock beside my cheek splintered suddenly as if exploding. Slivers of it prickled in my face. For a flicker of time I couldn't understand it: and then I struggled round and looked back to the shore with a flood of foreboding.

Greene was standing there, aiming the pistol, shooting to kill.

CHAPTER FIFTEEN

Thirty to thirty-five yards is a long way for a pistol; but Greene seemed so close.

I could see his drooping moustache and the lanky hair blowing in the wind. I could see his eyes and the concentration in his body. He was standing with his legs straddled and his arms out straight ahead, aiming the pistol with both hands.

I couldn't hear the shots above the crash of the waves on the rocks. I couldn't see him squeeze the trigger. But I did see the upward jerk of the arms at the recoil, and I reckoned it would be just plain silly to give him a stationary target.

I was, in all honesty, pretty frightened. I must have looked as close to him as he to me. He must have been quite certain he would hit me, even though his tenderness with the pistol in the car had made me think he was not an expert.

I turned and stumbled a yard or two onwards, though the going became even rougher, and the relentless fight against current and waves and rocks was draining me to dish-rags.

There would have to be an end to it.

Have to be.

I stumbled and fell on a jagged edge and gashed the inside of my forearm, and out poured more good red life. Christ, I thought, I must be scarlet all over, leaking from a hundred tiny nicks.

It gave me at least an idea.

I was waist-deep in dangerous green water, with most of the shore-line rocks now submerged beneath the surface. Close to one side a row of bigger rock-teeth ran out from the shore like a nightmarish breakwater, and I'd shied away from it, because of the even fiercer waves crashing against it. But it represented the only cover in sight. Three stumbling efforts took me nearer; and the current helped.

I looked back at Greene. He was reloading the gun. Wexford was practically dancing up and down beside him, urging him on; and Beetle-brows, from his disinclination to chase me, probably couldn't swim.

Greene slapped shut the gun and raised it again in my direction.

I took a frightful chance.

I held my fast-bleeding forearm close across my chest: and I stood up, swaying in the current, visible to him from the waist up.

I watched him aim, with both arms straight. It would take a marksman, I believed, to hit me with that pistol from that distance, in that wind. A marksman whose arms didn't jerk upwards when he fired.

The gun was pointing straight at me.

I saw the jerk as he squeezed the trigger.

For an absolutely petrifying second I was convinced he had shot accurately; but I didn't feel or see or even hear the passing of the flying death.

I flung my own right arm wide and high, and paused there facing him for a frozen second, letting him see that most of the front of my shirt was scarlet with blood.

Then I twisted artistically and fell flat, face downwards, into the water; and hoped to God he would think he had killed me.

The sea wasn't much better than bullets. Nothing less than extreme fear of the alternative would have kept me down in it, tumbling and crashing against the submerged razor edges like a piece of cheese in a grater.

The waves themselves swept me towards the taller breakwater teeth, and with a fair amount of desperation I tried to get a grip on them, to avoid being alternately sucked off and flung back, and losing a lot more skin.

There was also the problem of not struggling too visibly. If Wexford or Greene saw me threshing about, all my histrionics would have been in vain.

As much by luck as trying I found the sea shoving

me into a wedge-shaped crevice between the rocks, from where I was unable to see the shore. I clutched for a hand-hold, and then with bent knees found a good foothold, and clung there precariously while the sea tried to drag me out again. Every time the wave rolled in it tended to float my foot out of the niche it was lodged in, and every time it receded it tried to suck me with it, with a syphonic action. I clung, and see-sawed in the chest-high water, and clung, and see-sawed, and grew progressively more exhausted.

I could hear nothing except the waves on the rocks. I wondered forlornly how long Wexford and Greene would stay there, staring out to sea for signs of life. I didn't dare to look, in case they spotted my moving head.

The water was cold, and the grazes gradually stopped bleeding, including the useful gash on my forearm. Absolutely nothing, I thought, like having a young strong healthy body. Absolutely nothing like having a young strong healthy body on dry land with a paintbrush in one hand and a beer in the other, with the nice friendly airliners thundering overhead and no money to pay the gas.

Fatigue, in the end, made me look. It was either that or cling like a limpet until I literally fell off nervelessly, too weak to struggle back to life.

To look, I had to leave go. I tried to find other holds, but they weren't as good. The first out-going wave took me with it in no uncertain terms; and its incoming fellow threw me back.

In the tumbling interval I caught a glimpse of the shore.

The road, the cliffs, the quarry, as before. Also the car. Also people.

Bloody damn, I thought.

My hand scrambled for its former hold. My fingers were cramped, bleeding again, and cold. Oh Christ, I thought. How much longer.

It was a measure of my tiredness that it took the space of three in and out waves for me to realize that it wasn't Wexford's car, and it wasn't Wexford standing on the road.

If it wasn't Wexford, it didn't matter who it was.

I let go again of the hand-hold and tried to ride the wave as far out of the crevice as possible, and to swim away from the return force flinging me back. All the other rocks were still there under the surface. A few yards was a heck of a long way.

I stood up gingerly, feeling for my footing more carefully than on the outward flight, and took a longer look at the road.

A grey-white car. A couple beside it, standing close, the man with his arms round the girl.

A nice quiet spot for it, I thought sardonically. I hoped they would drive me somewhere dry.

They moved apart and stared out to sea.

I stared back.

For an instant it seemed impossible. Then they started waving their arms furiously and ran towards the water; and it was Sarah and Jik.

Throwing off his jacket, Jik ploughed into the waves with enthusiasm, and came to a smart halt as the realities of the situation scraped his legs. All the same, he came on after a pause towards me, taking care.

I made my slow way back. Even without haste driving like a fury, any passage through those wave-swept rocks was ruin to the epidermis. By the time we met we were both streaked with red.

We looked at each other's blood. Jik said 'Jesus' and I said 'Christ', and it occurred to me that maybe the Almighty would think we had been calling for His help a bit too often.

Jik put his arm round my waist and I held on to his shoulders, and together we stumbled slowly to land. We fell now and then. Got up gasping. Reclutched, and went on.

He let go when we reached the road. I sat down on the edge of it with my feet pointing out to sea, and positively drooped.

'Todd,' Sarah said anxiously. She came nearer. '*Todd.*' Her voice was incredulous. 'Are you *laughing*?'

'Sure.' I looked up at her, grinning. 'Why ever not?'

Jik's shirt was torn, and mine was in tatters. We took them off and used them to mop up the grazes which were still persistently oozing. From the expression on Sarah's face, we must have looked crazy.

'What a damn silly place to bathe,' Jik said.

'Free back-scratchers,' I said.

He glanced round behind me. 'Your Alice Springs dressing has come off.'

'How're the stitches?'

'Intact.'

'Bully for them.'

'You'll both get pneumonia, sitting there,' Sarah said.

I took off the remnants of the sling. All in all, I thought, it had served me pretty well. The adhesive rib-supporting cummerbund was still more or less in place, but had mostly come unstuck through too much immersion. I pulled that off also. That only left the plasters on my leg, and they too, I found, had floated off in the mêlée. The trousers I'd worn over them had windows everywhere.

'Quite a dust-up,' Jik observed, pouring water out of his shoes and shivering.

'We need a telephone,' I said, doing the same.

'Give me strength,' Sarah said. 'What you need is hot baths, warm clothes, and half a dozen psychiatrists.'

'How did you get here?' I asked.

'How come you aren't dead?' Jik said.

'You first.'

'I came out of the shop where I'd bought the shampoo,' Sarah said, 'and I saw Greene drive past. I nearly died on the spot. I just stood still, hoping he wouldn't look my way, and he didn't . . . The car turned to the left just past where I was . . . and I could see there were two other people in the back . . . and I went back to our car and told Jik.'

'We thought it damn lucky he hadn't spotted her,' Jik said, dabbing at persistent scarlet trickles. 'We went back to the hotel, and you weren't there, so we asked the girl at the desk if you'd left a message, and she said you'd gone off in a car with some friends . . . With a man with a droopy moustache.'

'Friends!' Sarah said.

'Anyway,' Jik continued, 'choking down our rage, sorrow, indignation and what not, we thought we'd better look for your body.'

'Jik!' Sarah protested.

He grinned. 'And who was crying?'

'Shut up.'

'Sarah hadn't seen any sign of you in Greene's car but we thought you might be imitating a sack of potatoes in the boot or something, so we got out the road map, applied our feet to the accelerator, and set off in pursuit. Turned left where Greene had gone, and found ourselves climbing a ruddy mountain.'

I surveyed our extensive grazes and scratches. 'I think we'd better get some disinfectant,' I said.

'We could bath in it.'

'Good idea.'

I could hear his teeth chattering even above the din of my own.

'Let's get out of this wind,' I said. 'And bleed in the car.'

We crawled stiffly into the seats. Sarah said it was lucky the upholstery was plastic. Jik automatically took his place behind the wheel.

'We drove for miles,' he said. 'Growing, I may say, a little frantic. Over the top of the mountain and down this side. At the bottom of the hill the road swings round to the left and we could see from the map that it follows the coastline round a whole lot of bays and eventually ends up right back in Wellington.'

He started the car, turned it, and rolled gently ahead. Naked to the waist, wet from there down, and still with beads of blood forming and overflowing, he looked an unorthodox chauffeur. The beard, above, was undaunted.

'We went that way,' Sarah said. 'There was nothing but miles of craggy rocks and sea.'

'I'll paint those rocks,' Jik said.

Sarah glanced at his face, and then at me. She'd heard the fervour in that statement of intent. The golden time was almost over.

'After a bit we turned back,' Jik said. 'There was this bit of road saying "No through road", so we came down it. No you, of course. We stopped here on this spot and Sarah got out of the car and started bawling her eyes out.'

'You weren't exactly cheering yourself,' she said.

'Huh,' he smiled. 'Anyway, I kicked a few stones about, wondering what to do next, and there were those cartridges.'

'Those what?'

'On the edge of the road. All close together. Maybe dropped out of one of those spider-ejection revolvers, or something like that.'

'When we saw them,' Sarah said, 'we thought . . .'

'It could have been anyone popping off at seabirds,' I said. 'And I think we might go back and pick them up.'

'Are you serious?' Jik said.

'Yeah.'

We stopped, turned again, and retraced our tyre treads.

'No one shoots seabirds with a revolver,' he said. 'But bloody awful painters of slow horses, that's different.'

The quarry came in sight again. Jik drew up and stopped, and Sarah, hopping out quickly, told us to stay where we were, she would fetch the bullet cases.

'They really did shoot at you?' Jik said.

'Greene. He missed.'

'Inefficient.' He shifted in his seat, wincing. 'They must have gone back over the hill while we were looking for you round the bays.' He glanced at Sarah as she searched along the side of the road. 'Did they take the list?'

'I threw it in the sea.' I smiled lopsidedly. 'It seemed too tame just to hand it over . . . and it made a handy diversion. They salvaged enough to see that they'd got what they wanted.'

'It must all have been a bugger.'

'Hilarious.'

Sarah found the cases, picked them up, and came running back. 'Here they are . . . I'll put them in my handbag.' She slid into the passenger seat. 'What now?'

'Telephone,' I said.

'Like that?' She looked me over. 'Have you any idea . . .' She stopped. 'Well,' she said. 'I'll buy you each a shirt at the first shop we come to.' She swallowed. 'And don't say what if it's a grocery.'

'What if it's a grocery?' Jik said.

We set off again, and at the intersection turned left to go back over the hill, because it was about a quarter of the distance.

Near the top there was a large village with the sort of store which sold everything from hammers to hairpins. Also groceries. Also, upon enquiry, shirts. Sarah made a face at Jik and vanished inside.

I pulled on the resulting navy tee-shirt and made wobbly tracks for the telephone, clutching Sarah's purse.

'Operator . . . which hotels have a telex?'

She told me three. One was the Townhouse. I thanked her and rang off.

I called the Townhouse. Remembered, with an effort, that my name was Peel.

'But, Mr Peel . . .' said the girl, sounding bewildered. 'Your friend . . . the one with the moustache, not the one with the beard . . . He paid your account not half an hour ago and collected all your things . . . Yes, I suppose it is irregular, but he brought your note, asking us to let him have your room key . . . I'm sorry but I didn't know you hadn't written it . . . Yes, he took all your things, the room's being cleaned at this minute . . .'

'Look,' I said, 'can you send a telex for me? Put it on my friend Mr . . . er . . . Andrews' bill.'

She said she would. I dictated the message. She repeated it, and said she would send it at once.

'I'll call again soon for the reply,' I said.

Sarah had bought jeans for us, and dry socks. Jik drove out of the village to a more modest spot, and we put them on: hardly the world's best fit, but they hid the damage.

'Where now?' he said. 'Intensive Care Unit?'

'Back to the telephone.'

'Jesus God Almighty.'

He drove back and I called the Townhouse. The girl said she'd received an answer, and read it out. 'Telephone at once, reverse charges,' she said, 'and there's a number . . .' She read it out, twice. I repeated it. 'That's right.'

I thanked her.

'No sweat,' she said. 'Sorry about your things.'

269

I called the international exchange and gave them the number. It had a priority rating, they said. The call would be through in ten minutes. They would ring back.

The telephone was on the wall of a booth inside the general store. There was nothing to sit on. I wished to God there was.

The ten minutes dragged slowly by. Nine and a half, to be exact.

The bell rang, and I picked up the receiver.

'Your call to England . . .'

The modern miracle. Half-way round the world, and I was talking to Inspector Frost as if he were in the next room. Eleven-thirty in the morning at Wellington: eleven-thirty at night in Shropshire.

'Your letter arrived today, sir,' he said. 'And action has already been started.'

'Stop calling me sir. I'm used to Todd.'

'All right. Well, we telexed Melbourne to alert them and we've started checking on all the people on the England list. The results are already incredible. All the crossed-out names we've checked so far have been the victims of break-ins. We're alerting the police in all the other countries concerned. The only thing is, we see the list you sent us is a photocopy. Do you have the original?'

'No . . . Most of it got destroyed. Does it matter?'

'Not really. Can you tell us how it came into your possession?'

'Er . . . I think we'd better say it just did.'

A dry laugh travelled twelve thousand miles.

'All right. Now what's so urgent that you're keeping me from my bed?'

'Are you at home?' I said contritely.

'On duty, as it happens. Fire away.'

'Two things . . . One is, I can save you time with the stock list numbers. But first . . .' I told him about Wexford and Greene being in Wellington, and about them stealing my things. 'They've got my passport and traveller's cheques, and also my suitcase which contains painting equipment.'

'I saw it at your cousin's,' he said.

'That's right. I think they may also have a page or two of the list . . .'

'Say that again.'

I said it again. 'Most of it got thrown into the sea, but I know Wexford regained at least one page. Well . . . I thought . . . they'd be going back to Melbourne, probably today, any minute really, and when they land there, there's a good chance they'll have at least some of those things with them . . .'

'I can fix a Customs search,' he said. 'But why should they risk stealing . . . ?'

'They don't know I know,' I said. 'I think they think I'm dead.'

'Good God. Why?'

'They took a pot-shot at me. Would bullet cases be

271

of any use? Fortunately I didn't collect a bullet, but I've got six shells.'

'They may be . . .' He sounded faint. 'What about the stock list?'

'In the shorter list . . . Got it?'

'Yes, in front of me.'

'Right. The first letter is for the city the painting was sold in; M for Melbourne, S for Sydney, W for Wellington. The second letter identifies the painter; M for Munnings, H for Herring, and I think R for Raoul Millais. The letter C stands for copy. All the paintings on that list are copies. All the ones on the longer list are originals. Got that?'

'Yes. Go on.'

'The numbers are just numbers. They'd sold 54 copies when I . . . er . . . when the list reached me. The last letter R stands for Renbo. That's Harley Renbo, who was working at Alice Springs. If you remember, I told you about him last time.'

'I remember,' he said.

'Wexford and Greene have spent the last couple of days chasing around in New Zealand, so with a bit of luck they will not have destroyed anything dodgy in the Melbourne gallery. If the Melbourne police can arrange a search, there might be a harvest.'

'It's their belief that the disappearance of the list from the gallery will have already led to the immediate destruction of anything else incriminating.'

'They may be wrong. Wexford and Green don't

know I photocopied the list and sent it to you. They think the list is floating safely out to sea, and me with it.'

'I'll pass your message to Melbourne.'

'There's also another gallery here in Wellington, and an imitation Herring they sold to a man in Auckland . . .'

'For heaven's sake . . .'

I gave him the Ruapehu address, and mentioned Norman Updike.

'There's also a recurring B on the long stock list, so there's probably another gallery. In Brisbane, maybe. There may also be another one in Sydney. I shouldn't think the suburban place I told you about had proved central enough, so they shut it.'

'Stop,' he said.

'Sorry,' I said. 'But the organization is like a mushroom . . . it burrows along underground and pops up everywhere.'

'I only said stop so I could change the tape on the recorder. You can carry right on now.'

'Oh.' I half laughed. 'Well . . . did you get any answers from Donald to my questions?'

'Yes, we did.'

'Carefully?'

'Rest assured,' he said dryly. 'We carried out your wishes to the letter. Mr Stuart's answers were "Yes, of course" to the first question, and "No, why ever should I" to the second, and "Yes" to the third.'

'Was he absolutely certain?'

'Absolutely.' He cleared his throat. 'He seems distant and withdrawn. Uninterested. But quite definite.'

'How is he?' I asked.

'He spends all his time looking at a picture of his wife. Every time we call at his house, we can see him through the front window, just sitting there.'

'He is still . . . sane?'

'I'm no judge.'

'You can at least let him know that he's no longer suspected of engineering the robbery and killing Regina.'

'That's a decision for my superiors,' he said.

'Well, kick them into it,' I said. 'Do the police positively yearn for bad publicity?'

'You were quick enough to ask our help,' he said tartly.

To do your job, I thought. I didn't say it aloud. The silence spoke for itself.

'Well . . .' his voice carried a mild apology. 'Our co-operation, then.' He paused. 'Where are you now? When I've telexed Melbourne, I may need to talk to you again.'

'I'm in a phone booth in a country store in a village on the hills above Wellington.'

'Where are you going next?'

'I'm staying right here. Wexford and Greene are still around in the city and I don't want to risk the outside chance of their seeing me.'

'Give me the number, then.'

I read it off the telephone.

'I want to come home as soon as possible,' I said. 'Can you do anything about my passport?'

'You'll have to find a consul.'

Oh ta, I though tiredly. I hung up the receiver and wobbled back to the car.

'Tell you what,' I said, dragging into the back seat, 'I could do with a double hamburger and a bottle of brandy.'

We sat in the car for two hours.

The store didn't sell liquor or hot food. Sarah bought a packet of biscuits. We ate them.

'We can't stay here all day,' she said explosively, after a lengthy glum silence.

I couldn't be sure that Wexford wasn't out searching for her and Jik with murderous intent, and I didn't think she'd be happy to know it.

'We're perfectly safe here,' I said.

'Just quietly dying of blood-poisoning,' Jik agreed.

'I left my pills in the Hilton,' Sarah said.

Jik stared. 'What's that got to do with it?'

'Nothing. I just thought you might like to know.'

'*The* pill?' I asked.

'Yes.'

'Jesus,' Jik said.

A delivery van struggled up the hill and stopped

275

outside the shop. A man in an overall opened the back, took out a large bakery tray, and carried it in.

'Food,' I said hopefully.

Sarah went in to investigate. Jik took the opportunity to unstick his tee-shirt from his healing grazes, but I didn't bother.

'You'll be glued to those clothes, if you don't,' Jik said, grimacing over his task.

'I'll soak them off.'

'All those cuts and things didn't feel so bad when we were in the sea.'

'No.'

'Catches up with you a bit, doesn't it?'

'Mm.'

He glanced at me. 'Why don't you just scream or something?'

'Can't be bothered. Why don't you?'

He grinned. 'I'll scream in paint.'

Sarah came back with fresh doughnuts and cans of Coke. We made inroads, and I at least felt healthier.

After another half-hour, the storekeeper appeared in the doorway, shouting and beckoning.

'A call for you . . .'

I went stiffly to the telephone. It was Frost, clear as a bell.

'Wexford, Greene and Snell have booked a flight to Melbourne. They will be met at Melbourne airport . . .'

'Who's Snell?' I said.

'How do I know? He was travelling with the other two.'

Beetle-brows, I thought.

'Now listen,' Frost said. 'The telex has been red-hot between here and Melbourne, and the police there want your co-operation, just to clinch things . . .' He went on talking for a long time. At the end he said, 'Will you do that?'

I'm tired, I thought. I'm battered, and I hurt. I've done just about enough.

'All right.'

Might as well finish it, I supposed.

'The Melbourne police want to know for sure that the three Munnings copies you . . . er . . . acquired from the gallery are still where you told me.'

'Yes, they are.'

'Right. Well . . . good luck.'

CHAPTER SIXTEEN

We flew Air New Zealand back to Melbourne, tended by angels in sea green. Sarah looked fresh, Jik definitely shop-worn, and I apparently like a mixture (Jik said) of yellow ochre, Payne's grey, and white, which I didn't think was possible.

Our passage had been oiled by telexes from above. When we arrived at the airport after collecting Sarah's belongings in their carrier bags from the Townhouse, we found ourselves whisked into a private room, plied with strong drink, and subsequently taken by car straight out across the tarmac to the aeroplane.

A thousand miles across the Tasman Sea and an afternoon tea later we were driven straight from the aircraft's steps to another small airport room, which contained no strong drink but only a large hard Australian plain-clothes policeman.

'Porter,' he said, introducing himself and squeezing our bones in a blacksmith's grip. 'Which of you is Charles Todd?'

'I am.'

'Right on, Mr Todd.' He looked at me without favour. 'Are you ill, or something?' He had a strong rough voice and a strong rough manner, natural aids to putting the fear of God into chummy and bringing on breakdowns in the nervous. To me, I gradually gathered, he was grudgingly offering the status of temporary inferior colleague.

'No,' I said, sighing slightly. Time and airline schedules waited for no man. If I'd spent time on first aid we'd have missed the only possible flight.

'His clothes are sticking to him,' Jik observed, giving the familiar phrase the usual meaning of being hot. It was cool in Melbourne. Porter looked at him uncertainly.

I grinned. 'Did you manage what you planned?' I asked him. He decided Jik was nuts and switched his gaze back to me.

'We decided not to go ahead until you had arrived,' he said, shrugging. 'There's a car waiting outside.' He wheeled out of the door without holding it for Sarah and marched briskly off.

The car had a chauffeur. Porter sat in front, talking on a radio, saying in stiltedly guarded sentences that the party had arrived and the proposals should be implemented.

'Where are we going?' Sarah said.

'To reunite you with your clothes,' I said.

Her face lit up. 'Are we really?'

'And what for?' Jik asked.

'To bring the mouse to the cheese.' And the bull to the sword, I thought: and the moment of truth to the conjuror.

'We got your things back, Todd,' Porter said with satisfaction. 'Wexford, Greene and Snell were turned over on entry, and they copped them with the lot. The locks on your suitcase were scratched and dented but they hadn't burst open. Everything inside should be O.K. You can collect everything in the morning.'

'That's great,' I said. 'Did they still have any of the lists of customers?'

'Yeah. Damp but readable. Names of guys in Canada.'

'Good.'

'We're turning over that Yarra gallery right this minute, and Wexford is there helping. We've let him overhear what we wanted him to, and as soon as I give the go-ahead we'll let him take action.'

'Do you think he will?' I said.

'Look, mister, wouldn't you?'

I thought I might be wary of gifts from the Greeks, but then I wasn't Wexford, and I didn't have a jail sentence breathing down my neck.

We pulled up at the side door of the Hilton. Porter raised himself agilely to the pavement and stood like a solid pillar, watching with half-concealed impatience while Jik, Sarah, and I eased ourselves slowly out. We all went across the familiar red-and-blue opulence of the great entrance hall, and from there through a gate in the reception desk, and into the hotel manager's office at the rear.

A tall dark-suited member of the hotel staff there offered us chairs, coffee, and sandwiches. Porter looked at his watch and offered us an indeterminate wait.

It was six o'clock. After ten minutes a man in shirt and necktie brought a two-way personal radio for Porter, who slipped the ear-plug into place and began listening to disembodied voices.

The office was a working room, lit by neon strips and furnished functionally, with a wall-papering of charts and duty rosters. There were no outside windows: nothing to show the fade of day to night.

We sat, and drank coffee, and waited. Porter ate three of the sandwiches simultaneously. Time passed.

Seven o'clock.

Sarah was looking pale in the artificial light, and tired also. So was Jik, his beard on his chest. I sat and thought about life and death and polka dots.

At seven-eleven Porter clutched his ear and concentrated intently on the ceiling. When he relaxed, he passed to us the galvanic message.

'Wexford did just what we reckoned he would, and the engine's turning over.'

'What engine?' Sarah said.

Porter stared at her blankly. 'What we planned,' he said painstakingly, 'is happening.'

'Oh.'

Porter listened again to his private ear and spoke directly to me. 'He's taken the bait.'

'He's a fool,' I said.

Porter came as near to a smile as he could. 'All crooks are fools, one way or another.'

Seven-thirty came and went. I raised my eyebrows at Porter. He shook his head.

'We can't say too much on the radio,' he said. 'Because you get all sorts of ears listening in.'

Just like England, I thought. The Press could turn up at a crime before the police; and the mouse might hear of the trap.

We waited. The time dragged. Jik yawned and Sarah's eyes were dark with fatigue. Outside, in the lobby, the busy rich life of the hotel chattered on unruffled, with guests' spirits rising towards the next day's race meeting, the last of the carnival.

The Derby on Saturday, the Cup on Tuesday, the Oaks (which we'd missed) on Thursday, and the International on Saturday. No serious racegoers went home before the end of things, if they could help it.

Porter clutched his ear again, and stiffened.

'He's here,' he said.

My heart, for some unaccountable reason, began beating overtime. We were in no danger that I could see, yet there it was, thumping away like a steam organ.

Porter disconnected himself from the radio, put it on the Manager's desk, and went out into the foyer.

'What do we do?' Sarah said.

'Nothing much except listen.'

We all three went over to the door and held it six inches open. We listened to people asking for their room keys, asking for letters and messages, asking for Mr and Mrs So-and-So, and which way to Toorak, and how did you get to Fanny's.

Then suddenly, the familiar voice, sending electric fizzes to my fingertips. Confident: not expecting trouble. 'I've come to collect a package left here last Tuesday by a Mr Charles Todd. He says he checked it into the baggage-room. I have a letter here from him, authorizing you to release it to me.'

There was a crackle of paper as the letter was handed over. Sarah's eyes were round and startled.

'Did you write it?' she whispered.

I shook my head. 'No.'

The desk clerk outside said, 'Thank you, sir. If you'll just wait a moment I'll fetch the package.'

There was a long pause. My heart made a lot of noise, but nothing much else happened.

The desk clerk came back. 'Here you are, sir. Paintings, sir.'

'That's right.'

There were vague sounds of the bundle of paintings and the print-folder being carried along outside the door.

'I'll bring them round for you,' said the clerk, suddenly closer to us. 'Here we are, sir.' He went past the office, through the door in the desk, and round to the front. 'Can you manage them, sir?'

'Yes. Yes. Thank you.' There was a haste in his voice, now that he'd got his hands on the goods. 'Thank you. Goodbye.'

Sarah had begun to say 'Is that all?' in disappointment when Porter's loud voice chopped into the Hilton velvet like a hatchet.

'I guess we'll take care of those paintings, if you don't mind,' he said. 'Porter, Melbourne City Police.'

I opened the door a little, and looked out. Porter stood four-square in the lobby, large and rough, holding out a demanding hand.

At his elbows, two plain-clothes policemen. At the front door, two more, in uniform. There would be others, I supposed, at the other exits. They weren't taking any chances.

'Why . . . er . . . Inspector . . . I'm only on an errand . . . er . . . for my young friend, Charles Todd.'

'And these paintings?'

'I've no idea what they are. He asked me to fetch them for him.'

I walked quietly out of the office, through the gate and round to the front. I leaned a little wearily against the reception desk. He was only six feet away, in front of me to my right. I could have stretched forward and touched him. I hoped Porter would think it near enough, as requested.

A certain amount of unease had pervaded the

Hilton guests. They stood around in an uneven semi-circle, eyeing the proceedings sideways.

'Mr Charles Todd asked you to fetch them?' Porter said loudly.

'Yes, that's right.'

Porter's gaze switched abruptly to my face.

'Did you ask him?'

'No,' I said.

The explosive effect was all that the Melbourne police could have asked, and a good deal more than I expected. There was no polite quiet identification followed by a polite quiet arrest. I should have remembered all my own theories about the basic brutality of the directing mind.

I found myself staring straight into the eyes of the bull. He realized that he'd been tricked. Had convicted himself out of his own mouth and by his own presence on such an errand. The fury rose in him like a geyser and his hands reached out to grab my neck.

'*You're dead,*' he yelled. '*You're fucking dead.*'

His plunging weight took me off balance and down on to one knee, smothering under his choking grip and two hundred pounds of city suiting; trying to beat him off with my fists and not succeeding. His anger poured over me like lava. Heaven knows what he intended, but Porter's men pulled him off before he did bloody murder on the plushy carpet. As I got creakily to my feet, I heard the handcuffs click.

He was standing there, close to me, quivering in the

restraining hands, breathing heavily, dishevelled and bitter-eyed. Civilized exterior all stripped away by one instant of ungovernable rage. The violent core plain to see.

'Hello, Hudson,' I said.

'Sorry,' Porter said perfunctorily. 'Didn't reckon he'd turn wild.'

'Revert,' I said.

'Uh?'

'He always was wild,' I said, 'underneath.'

'You'd know,' he said. 'I never saw the guy before.' He nodded to Jik and Sarah and finally to me, and hurried away after his departing prisoner.

We looked at each other a little blankly. The hotel guests stared at us curiously and began to drift away. We sat down weakly on the nearest blue velvet seat, Sarah in the middle.

Jik took her hand and squeezed it. She put her fingers over mine.

It had taken nine days.

It had been a long haul.

'Don't know about you,' Jik said. 'But I could do with a beer.'

'Todd,' said Sarah, 'start talking.'

We were upstairs in a bedroom (mine) with both of

them in a relaxed mood, and me in Jik's dressing-gown, and he and I in a cloud of Dettol.

I yawned. 'About Hudson?'

'Who else? And don't go to sleep before you've told us.'

'Well . . . I was looking for him, or someone like him, before I ever met him.'

'But why?'

'Because of the wine,' I said. 'Because of the wine which was stolen from Donald's cellar. Whoever stole it not only knew it was there, down some stairs behind an inconspicuous cupboard-like door . . . and I'd stayed several times in the house and never knew the cellar existed . . . but according to Donald they would have had to come prepared with proper cases to pack it in. Wine is usually packed twelve bottles in a case . . . and Donald had two thousand or more bottles stolen. In bulk alone it would have taken a lot of shifting. A lot of time, too, and time for housebreakers is risky. But also it was special wine. A small fortune, Donald said. The sort of wine that's bought and sold as an asset and ends up at a week's wage a bottle, if it's ever drunk at all. Anyway, it was the sort of wine that needed expert handling and marketing if it was to be worth the difficulty of stealing it in the first place . . . and as Donald's business is wine, and the reason for his journey to Australia was wine, I started looking right away for someone who knew Donald, knew he'd bought a Munnings, and knew about good wine and how to sell

287

it. And there, straightaway, was Hudson Taylor, who matched like a glove. But it seemed too easy . . . because he didn't *look* right.'

'Smooth and friendly,' said Sarah, nodding.

'And rich,' Jik added.

'Probably a moneyholic,' I said, pulling open the bed and looking longingly at the cool white sheets.

'A what?'

'Moneyholic. A word I've just made up to describe someone with an uncontrollable addiction to money.'

'The world's full of them,' Jik said, laughing.

I shook my head. 'The world is full of drinkers, but alcoholics are obsessive. Moneyholics are obsessive. They never have enough. They *cannot* have enough. However much they have, they want more. And I'm not talking about the average hard-up man, but about real screwballs. Money, money, money. Like a drug. Moneyholics will do anything to get it . . . Kidnap, murder, cook the computer, rob banks, sell their grandmothers . . . You name it.'

I sat on the bed with my feet up, feeling less than fit. Sore from too many bruises, on fire from too many cuts. Jik too, I guessed. They had been wicked rocks.

'Moneyholism,' Jik said, like a lecturer to a dimmish class, 'is a widespread disease easily understood by everyone who has ever felt a twinge of greed, which is everyone.'

'Go on about Hudson,' Sarah said.

'Hudson had the organizing ability . . . I didn't know

when I came that the organization was so huge, but I did know it was *organized*, if you see what I mean. It was an overseas operation. It took some doing. Know-how.'

Jik tugged the ring off a can of beer and passed it to me, wincing as he stretched.

'But he convinced me I was wrong about him,' I said, drinking through the triangular hole. 'Because he was so careful. He pretended he had to look up the name of the gallery where Donald bought his picture. He didn't think of me as a threat, of course, but just as Donald's cousin. Not until he talked to Wexford down on the lawn.'

'I remember,' Sarah said. 'When you said it had ripped the whole works apart.'

'Mm . . . I thought it was only that he had told Wexford I was Donald's cousin, but of course Wexford also told *him* that I'd met Greene in Maisie's ruins in Sussex and then turned up in the gallery looking at the original of Maisie's burnt painting.'

'Jesus Almighty,' Jik said. 'No wonder we beat it to Alice Springs.'

'Yes, but by then I didn't think it could be Hudson I was looking for. I was looking for someone brutal, who passed on his violence through his employees. Hudson didn't look or act brutal.' I paused. 'The only slightest crack was when his gamble went down the drain at the races. He gripped his binoculars so hard that his knuckles showed white. But you can't think a man is a big-time thug just because he gets upset over losing a bet.'

Jik grinned. 'I'd qualify.'

'In spades, redoubled,' Sarah said.

'I was thinking about it in the Alice Springs hospital . . . There hadn't been time for the musclemen to get to Alice from Melbourne between us buying Renbo's picture and me diving off the balcony, but there had been time for them to come from *Adelaide*, and Hudson's base was at Adelaide . . . but it was much too flimsy.'

'They might have been in Alice to start with,' Jik said reasonably.

'They might, but what for?' I yawned. 'Then on the night of the Cup you said Hudson had made a point of asking you about me . . . and I wondered how he knew you.'

'Do you know,' Sarah said, 'I did wonder too at the time, but it didn't seem important. I mean, *we'd* seen *him* from the top of the stands, so it didn't seem impossible that somewhere he'd seen you with us.'

'The boy knew you,' I said. 'And he was at the races, because he followed you, with Greene, to the Hilton. The boy must have pointed you out to Greene.'

'And Greene to Wexford, and Wexford to Hudson?' Jik asked.

'Quite likely.'

'And by then,' he said, 'they all knew they wanted to silence you pretty badly, and they'd had a chance and muffed it . . . I'd love to have heard what happened when they found we'd robbed the gallery.' He chuckled, tipping up his beer can to catch the last few drops.

'On the morning after,' I said, 'a letter from Hudson was delivered by hand to the Hilton. How did he know we were there?'

They stared. 'Greene must have told him,' Jik said. 'We certainly didn't. We didn't tell anybody. We were careful about it.'

'So was I,' I said. 'That letter offered to show me round a vineyard. Well . . . if I hadn't been so doubtful of him, I might have gone. He was a friend of Donald's . . . and a vineyard would be interesting. From his point of view, anyway, it was worth a try.'

'Jesus!'

'On the night of the Cup, when we were in that motel near Box Hill, I telephoned the police in England and spoke to the man in charge of Donald's case, Inspector Frost. I asked him to ask Donald some questions . . . and this morning outside Wellington I got the answers.'

'This morning seems several light years away,' Sarah said.

'Mm . . .'

'What questions and what answers?' Jik said.

'The questions were, did Donald tell Hudson all about the wine in his cellar, and did Donald tell *Wexford* about the wine in the cellar, and was it Hudson

who had suggested to Donald that he and Regina
should go and look at the Munnings in the Arts
Centre? And the answers were "Yes, of course", and
"No, why ever should I?", and "Yes".'

They thought about it in silence. Jik fiddled with
the dispenser in the room's in-built refrigerator and
liberated another can of Foster's.

'So what then?' Sarah said.

'So the Melbourne police said it was too insubstan-
tial, but if they could tie Hudson in definitely with the
gallery they might believe it. So they dangled in front
of Hudson the pictures and stuff we stole from the
gallery, and along he came to collect them.'

'How? How did they dangle them?'

'They let Wexford accidentally overhear snippets
from a fake report from several hotels about odd
deposits in their baggage rooms, including the paintings
at the Hilton. Then after we got here they gave him
an opportunity to use the telephone when he thought
no one was listening, and he rang Hudson at the house
e's been staying in here for the races, and told him. So
Hudson wrote himself a letter to the Hilton from me,
and zoomed along to remove the incriminating
evidence.'

'He must have been crazy.'

'Stupid. But he thought I was dead ... and he'd no
idea anyone suspected him. He should have had the
sense to know that Wexford's call to him would be

bugged by the police . . . but Frost told me that Wexford would think he was using a public phone booth.'

'Sneaky,' Sarah said.

I yawned. 'It takes a sneak to catch a sneak.'

'You'd never have thought Hudson would blaze up like that,' she said. 'He looked so . . . so dangerous.' She shivered. 'You wouldn't think people could hide such really frightening violence under a friendly public face.'

'The nice Irish bloke next door,' Jik said, standing up, 'can leave a bomb to blow the legs off children.'

He pulled Sarah to her feet. 'What do you think I paint?' he said. 'Vases of flowers?' He looked down at me. 'Horses?'

We parted the next morning at Melbourne airport, where we seemed to have spent a good deal of our lives.

'It seems strange, saying goodbye,' Sarah said.

'I'll be coming back,' I said.

They nodded.

'Well . . .' We looked at watches.

It was like all partings. There wasn't much to say. I saw in their eyes, as they must have seen in mine, that the past ten days would quickly become a nostalgic memory. Something we did in our crazy youth. Distant.

'Would you do it all again?' Jik said.

I thought inconsequentially of surviving wartime

pilots looking back from forty years on. Had their achievements been worth the blood and sweat and risk of death: did they regret?

I smiled. Forty years on didn't matter. What the future made of the past was its own tragedy. What we ourselves did on the day was all that counted.

'I guess I would.'

I leaned forward and kissed Sarah, my oldest friend's wife.

'Hey,' he said. 'Find one of your own.'

CHAPTER SEVENTEEN

Maisie saw me before I saw her, and came sweeping down like a great scarlet bird, wings outstretched.

Monday lunch-time at Wolverhampton races, misty and cold.

'Hello, dear, I'm so glad you've come. Did you have a good trip back, because of course it's such a long way, isn't it, with all that wretched jet lag?' She patted my arm and peered acutely at my face. 'You don't really look awfully well, dear, if you don't mind me saying so, and you don't seem to have collected any suntan, though I suppose as you haven't been away two weeks it isn't surprising, but those are nasty gashes on your hand, dear, aren't they, and you were walking very *carefully* just now.'

She stopped to watch a row of jockeys canter past on their way to the start. Bright shirts against the thin grey mist. A subject for Munnings.

'Have you backed anything, dear? And are you sure you're warm enough in that anorak? I never think jeans are good for people in the winter, they're only cotton, dear, don't forget, and how did you get on in Australia? I mean, dear, did you find out anything useful?'

'It's an awfully long story...'

'Best told in the bar, then, don't you think, dear?'

She bought us immense brandies with ginger ale and settled herself at a small table, her kind eyes alert and waiting.

I told her about Hudson's organization, about the Melbourne gallery, and about the list of robbable customers.

'Was I on it?'

I nodded. 'Yes, you were.'

'And you gave it to the police?' she said anxiously.

I grinned. 'Don't look so worried, Maisie. Your name was crossed out already. I just crossed it out more thoroughly. By the time I'd finished, no one could ever disentangle it, particularly on a photocopy.'

She smiled broadly. 'No one could call you a fool, dear.'

I wasn't so sure about that. 'I'm afraid, though,' I said, 'that you've lost your nine thousand quid.'

'Oh yes, dear,' she said cheerfully. 'Serves me right, doesn't it, for trying to cheat the Customs, though frankly, dear, in the same circumstances I'd probably do it again, because that tax makes me so mad, dear. But I'm ever so glad, dear, that they won't come knocking on my door this time, or rather my sister Betty's, because of course I'm staying with her again up here at the moment, as of course the Beach told you, until my house is ready.'

I blinked. 'What house?'

'Well, dear, I decided not to rebuild the house at Worthing because it wouldn't be the same without the things Archie and I bought together, so I'm selling that plot of seaside land for a fortune, dear, and I've chosen a nice place just down the road from Sandown Park racecourse.'

'You're not going to live in Australia?'

'Oh no, dear, that would be too far away. From Archie, you see, dear.'

I saw. I liked Maisie very much.

'I'm afraid I spent all your money,' I said.

She smiled at me with her well-kept head on one side and absent-mindedly stroked her crocodile handbag.

'Never mind, dear. You can paint me *two* pictures. One of me, and one of my new house.'

I left after the third race, took the train along the main line to Shrewsbury, and from there travelled by bus to Inspector Frost's official doorstep.

He was in an office, chin-deep in papers. Also present, the unblinking Superintendent Wall, who had so unnerved Donald, and whom I'd not previously met. Both men shook hands in a cool and businesslike manner, Wall's eyes traversing the anorak, jeans and desert boots, and remaining unimpressed. They offered me a chair, moulded plastic and armless.

Frost said, faintly smiling, 'You sure kicked open an ant-hill.'

Wall frowned, disliking such frivolity. 'It appears you stumbled on an organization of some size.'

The gaze of both men swept the mountain of paper.

'What about Donald?' I asked.

Frost kept his eyes down. His mouth twitched.

Wall said, 'We have informed Mr Stuart that we are satisfied the break-in at his house and the death of Mrs Stuart were the work of outside agencies, beyond his knowledge or control.'

Cold comfort words. 'Did he understand what he was hearing?'

The Wall eyebrows rose. 'I went to see him myself, this morning. He appeared to understand perfectly.'

'And what about Regina?'

'The body of Mrs Stuart,' Wall said correctively.

'Donald wants her buried,' I said.

Frost looked up with an almost human look of compassion. 'The difficulty is,' he said, 'that in a murder case, one has to preserve the victim's body in case the defence wishes to call for its own post-mortem. In this case, we have not been able to accuse anyone of her murder, let alone get as far as them arranging a defence.' He cleared his throat. 'We'll release Mrs Stuart's body for burial as soon as official requirements have been met.'

I looked at my fingers, interlacing them.

Frost said, 'Your cousin already owes you a lot. You can't be expected to do more.'

I smiled twistedly and stood up. 'I'll go and see him,' I said.

Wall shook hands again, and Frost came with me through the hall and out into the street. The lights shone bright in the early winter evening.

'Unofficially,' he said, walking slowly with me along the pavement, 'I'll tell you that the Melbourne police found a list of names in the gallery which it turns out are of known housebreakers. Divided into countries, like the Overseas Customers. There were four names for England. I suppose I shouldn't guess and I certainly ought not to be saying this to you, but there's a good chance Mrs Stuart's killer may be one of them.'

'Really?'

'Yes. But don't quote me.' He looked worried.

'I won't,' I said. 'So the robberies were local labour?'

'It seems to have been their normal method.'

Greene, I thought. With an 'e'. Greene could have recruited them. And checked afterwards, in burnt houses, on work done.

I stopped walking. We were standing outside the flower shop where Regina had worked. Frost looked at the big bronze chrysanthemums in the brightly lit window, and then enquiringly at my face.

I put my hand in my pocket and pulled out the six revolver shell cases. Gave them to Frost.

'These came from the gun which the man called Greene fired at me,' I said. 'He dropped them when he was reloading. I told you about them on the telephone.'

He nodded.

'I don't imagine they're of much practical use,' I said. 'But they might persuade you that Greene is capable of murder.'

'Well... what of it?'

'It's only a feeling...'

'Get on with it.'

'Greene,' I said, 'was in England at about the time Regina died.'

He stared.

'Maybe Regina knew him,' I said. 'She had been in the gallery in Australia. Maybe she saw him helping to rob her house... supervising, perhaps... and maybe that's why she was killed, because it wouldn't have been enough just to tie her up and gag her... she could identify him for certain if she was alive.'

He looked as if he was trying to draw breath.

'That's all... guessing,' he said.

'I know for certain that Greene was in England two weeks after Regina's death. I know for certain he was up to his neck in selling paintings and stealing them back. I know for certain that he would kill someone who could get him convicted. The rest... well... it's over to you.'

'My God,' Frost said. 'My God.'

I started off again, towards the bus-stop. He came with me, looking glazed.

'What everyone wants to know,' he said, 'is what put you on to the organization in the first place.'

I smiled. 'A hot tip from an informer.'

'What informer?'

A smuggler in a scarlet coat, glossy hair-do and crocodile handbag. 'You can't grass on informers,' I said.

He sighed, shook his head, stopped walking, and pulled a piece of torn-off telex paper out of his jacket.

'Did you meet an Australian policeman called Porter?'

'I sure did.'

'He sent you a message.' He handed me the paper. I read the neatly typed words.

'*Tell that Pommie painter Thanks.*'

'Will you send a message back?'

He nodded. 'What is it?'

'No sweat,' I said.

I stood in the dark outside my cousin's house, looking in.

He sat in his lighted drawing-room, facing Regina, unframed on the mantelshelf. I sighed, and rang the bell.

Donald came slowly. Opened the door.

'Charles!' He was mildly surprised. 'I thought you were in Australia.'

'Got back yesterday.'

'Come in.'

We went into the kitchen, where at least it was warm, and sat one each side of the table. He looked gaunt and fifty, a shell of a man, retreating from life.

'How's business?' I said.

'Business?'

'The wine trade.'

'I haven't been to the office.'

'If you didn't have a critical cash flow problem before,' I said, 'you'll have one soon.'

'I don't really care.'

'You've got stuck,' I said. 'Like a needle in a record. Playing the same little bit of track over and over again.'

He looked blank.

'The police know you didn't fix the robbery,' I said.

He nodded slowly. 'That man Wall . . . came and told me so. This morning.'

'Well, then.'

'It doesn't seem to make much difference.'

'Because of Regina?'

He didn't answer.

'You've got to stop it, Donald,' I said. 'She's dead. She's been dead five weeks and three days. Do you want to see her?'

He looked absolutely horrified. 'No! Of course not.'

'Then stop thinking about her body.'

'Charles!' He stood up violently, knocking over his chair. He was somewhere between outrage and anger, and clearly shocked.

'She's in a cold drawer,' I said, 'and you want her in a box in the cold ground. So where's the difference?'

'Get out,' he said loudly. 'I don't want to hear you.'

'The bit of Regina you're obsessed about,' I said, not moving, 'is just a collection of minerals. That . . . that *shape* lying in storage isn't Regina. The real girl is in your head. In your memory. The only life you can give her is to remember her. That's her immortality, in your head. You're killing her all over again with your refusal to go on living.'

He turned on his heel and walked out. I heard him go across the hall, and guessed he was making for the sitting-room.

After a minute I followed him. The white-panelled door was shut.

I opened the door. Went in.

He was sitting in his chair, in the usual place.

'Go away,' he said.

What did it profit a man, I thought, if he got flung over balconies and shot at and mangled by rocks, and couldn't save his cousin's soul.

'I'm taking that picture with me to London,' I said.

He was alarmed. He stood up. 'You're *not*.'

'I am.'

'You can't. You gave it to me.'

'It needs a frame,' I said. 'Or it will warp.'

303

'You can't take it.'

'You can come as well.'

'I can't leave here,' he said.

'Why not?'

'Don't be stupid,' he said explosively. 'You know why not. Because of . . .' His voice died away.

I said, 'Regina will be with you wherever you are. Whenever you think of her, she'll be there.'

Nothing.

'She isn't in this room. She's in your head. You can go out of here and take her with you.'

Nothing.

'She was a great girl. It must be bloody without her. But she deserves the best you can do.'

Nothing.

I went over to the fireplace and picked up the picture. Regina's face smiled out, vitally alive. I hadn't done her left nostril too well, I thought.

Donald didn't try to stop me.

I put my hand on his arm.

'Let's get your car out,' I said, 'and drive down to my flat. Right this minute.'

A little silence.

'Come on,' I said.

He began, with difficulty, to cry.

I took a long breath and waited. 'O.K.,' I said. 'How are you off for petrol?'

'We can get some more . . .' he said, sniffing, '. . . on the motorway.'

DEAD CERT

DEAD CERT

CHAPTER ONE

The mingled smells of hot horse and cold river mist filled my nostrils. I could hear only the swish and thud of galloping hooves and the occasional sharp click of horseshoes striking against each other. Behind me, strung out, rode a group of men dressed like myself in white silk breeches and harlequin jerseys, and in front, his body vividly red and green against the pale curtain of fog, one solitary rider steadied his horse to jump the birch fence stretching blackly across his path.

All, in fact, was going as expected. Bill Davidson was about to win his ninety-seventh steeplechase. Admiral, his chestnut horse, was amply proving he was still the best hunter 'chaser in the kingdom, and I, as often before, had been admiring their combined back view for several minutes.

Ahead of me the powerful chestnut hindquarters bunched, tensed, sprang: Admiral cleared the fence with the effortlessness of the really good performer. And he'd gained another two lengths, I saw, as I followed him over. We were down at the far end of Maidenhead racecourse with more than half a mile to go to the winning post. I hadn't a hope of catching him.

The February fog was getting denser. It was now impossible to see much farther than from one fence to the next, and the silent surrounding whiteness seemed to shut us, an isolated string of riders, into a private lonely limbo. Speed was the only reality. Winning post, crowds, stands, and stewards, left behind in the mist, lay again invisibly ahead, but on the long deserted mile and a half circuit it was quite difficult to believe they were really there.

It was an eerie, severed world in which anything might happen. And something did.

We rounded the first part of the bend at the bottom of the racecourse and straightened to jump the next fence. Bill was a good ten lengths in front of me and the other horses, and hadn't exerted himself. He seldom needed to.

The attendant at the next fence strolled across the course from the outside to the inside, patting the top of the birch as he went, and ducked under the rails. Bill glanced back over his shoulder and I saw the flash of his teeth as he smiled with satisfaction to see me so far behind. Then he turned his head towards the fence and measured his distance.

Admiral met the fence perfectly. He rose to it as if flight were not only for the birds.

And he fell.

Aghast, I saw the flurry of chestnut legs threshing the air as the horse pitched over in a somersault. I had a glimpse of Bill's bright-clad figure hurtling head downwards from the highest point of his trajectory, and I heard the crash of Admiral landing upside down after him.

Automatically I swerved over to the right and kicked my horse into the fence. In mid-air, as I crossed it, I looked down at Bill. He lay loosely on the ground with one arm outstretched. His eyes were shut. Admiral had fallen solidly, back downwards, across Bill's unprotected abdomen, and he was rolling backwards and forwards in a frantic effort to stand up again.

I had a brief impression that something lay beneath them. Something incongruous, which ought not to be there. But I was going too fast to see properly.

As my horse pressed on away from the fence, I felt as sick as if I'd been kicked in the stomach myself. There had been a quality about that fall which put it straight into the killing class.

I looked over my shoulder. Admiral succeeded in getting to his feet and cantered off loose, and the attendants stepped forward and bent over Bill, who still lay motionless on the ground. I turned back to attend to the race. I had been left in front and I ought to stay there. At the side of the course a black-suited, white-sashed First-Aid man was running towards and past me.

He had been standing at the fence I was now approaching, and was on his way to help Bill.

I booted my horse into the next three fences, but my heart was no longer in it, and when I emerged as the winner into the full view of the crowded stands, the mixed gasp and groan which greeted me seemed an apt enough welcome. I passed the winning post, patted my mount's neck, and looked at the stands. Most heads were still turned towards the last fence, searching the impenetrable mist for Admiral, the odds-on certainty who had lost his first race for two years.

Even the pleasant middle-aged woman whose horse I was riding met me with the question 'What happened to Admiral?'

'He fell,' I said.

'How lucky,' said Mrs Mervyn, laughing happily.

She took hold of the bridle and led her horse into the winner's unsaddling enclosure. I slid off and undid the girth buckles with fingers clumsy from shock. She patted the horse and chattered on about how delighted she was to have won, and how unexpected it was, and how fortunate that Admiral had tripped up for a change, though a great pity in another way, of course.

I nodded and smiled at her and didn't answer, because what I would have said would have been savage and unkind. Let her enjoy her win, I thought. They come seldom enough. And Bill might, after all, be all right.

I tugged the saddle off the horse and, leaving a beaming Mrs Mervyn receiving congratulations from all around, pressed through the crowd into the weighing room. I sat on the scales, was passed as correct, walked into the changing room, and put my gear down on the bench.

Clem, the racecourse valet who looked after my stuff, came over. He was a small elderly man, very spry and tidy, with a weatherbeaten face and wrists whose tendons stood out like tight strung cords.

He picked up my saddle and ran his hand caressingly over the leather. It was a habit he had grown into, I imagined, from long years of caring for fine-grained skins. He stroked a saddle as another man would a pretty girl's cheek, savouring the suppleness, the bloom.

'Well done, sir,' he said; but he didn't look overjoyed.

I didn't want to be congratulated. I said abruptly, 'Admiral should have won.'

'Did he fall?' asked Clem anxiously.

'Yes,' I said. I couldn't understand it, thinking about it.

'Is Major Davidson all right, sir?' asked Clem. He valeted Bill too and, I knew, looked upon him as a sort of minor god.

'I don't know,' I said. But the hard saddle-tree had hit him plumb in the belly with the weight of a big horse falling at thirty miles an hour behind it. What chance has he got, poor beggar, I thought.

I shrugged my arms into my sheepskin coat and went

along to the First-Aid room. Bill's wife, Scilla, was standing outside the door there, pale and shaking and doing her best not to be frightened. Her small neat figure was dressed gaily in scarlet, and a mink hat sat provocatively on top of her cloudy dark curls. They were clothes for success, not sorrow.

'Alan,' she said, with relief, when she saw me. 'The doctor's looking at him and asked me to wait here. What do you think? Is he bad?' She was pleading, and I hadn't much comfort to give her. I put my arm round her shoulders.

She asked me if I had seen Bill fall, and I told her he had dived on to his head and might be slightly concussed.

The door opened, and a tall slim well-groomed man came out. The doctor.

'Are you Mrs Davidson?' he said to Scilla. She nodded.

'I'm afraid your husband will have to go along to the hospital,' he said. 'It wouldn't be sensible to send him home without an X-ray.' He smiled reassuringly, and I felt some of the tension go out of Scilla's body.

'Can I go in and see him?' she said.

The doctor hesitated. 'Yes,' he said finally, 'but he's almost unconscious. He had a bit of a bang on the head. Don't try to wake him.'

When I started to follow Scilla into the First-Aid room the doctor put his hand on my arm to stop me.

'You're Mr York, aren't you?' he asked. He had given me a regulation check after an easy fall I'd had the day before.

'Yes.'

'Do you know these people well?'

'Yes. I live with them most of the time.'

The doctor closed his lips, tight, thinking. Then he said, 'It's not good. The concussion's not much, but he's bleeding internally, possibly from a ruptured spleen. I've telephoned the hospital to take him in as an emergency case as soon as we can get him there.'

As he spoke, one of the racecourse ambulances backed up towards us. The men jumped out, opened the rear doors, took out a big stretcher and carried it into the First-Aid room. The doctor went in after them. Soon they all reappeared with Bill on the stretcher. Scilla followed, the anxiety plain on her face, deep and well-founded.

Bill's firm brown humorous face now lolled flaccid, bluish-white, and covered with fine beads of sweat. He was gasping slightly through his open mouth, and his hands were restlessly pulling at the blanket which covered him. He was still wearing his green and red checked racing colours, the most ominous sign of all.

Scilla said to me, 'I'm going with him in the ambulance. Can you come?'

'I've a ride in the last race,' I said. 'I'll come along to

7

the hospital straight after that. Don't worry, he'll be all right.' But I didn't believe it, and nor did she.

After they had gone I walked along beside the weighing room building and down through the car park until I came to the bank of the river. Swollen from the recently melted snow, the Thames was flowing fast, sandy brown and grey with froths of white. The water swirled out of a mist a hundred yards to my right, churned round the bend where I stood and disappeared again into the fog. Troubled, confused, not seeing a clear course ahead. Just like me.

For there was something wrong about Bill's accident.

Back in Bulawayo where I got my schooling, the mathematics master spent hours (too many, I thought in my youth) teaching us to draw correct inferences from a few known facts. But deduction was his hobby as well as his job, and occasionally we had been able to side-track him from problems of geometry or algebra to those of Sherlock Holmes. He produced class after class of boys keenly observant of well-worn toe-caps on charwomen and vicars and calluses on the finger tips of harpists; and the mathematics standard of the school was exceptionally high.

Now, thousands of miles and seven years away from the sunbaked schoolroom, standing in an English fog and growing very cold, I remembered my master and took out my facts, and had a look at them.

Known facts ... Admiral, a superb jumper, had

fallen abruptly in full flight for no apparent reason. The racecourse attendant had walked across the course behind the fence as Bill and I rode towards it, but this was not at all unusual. And as I had cleared the fence, and while I was looking down at Bill, somewhere on the edge of my vision there had been a dull damp gleam from something grey and metallic. I thought about these things for a long time.

The inference was there all right, but unbelievable. I had to find out if it was the correct one.

I went back into the weighing room to collect my kit and weigh out for the last race, but as I packed the flat lead pieces into my weight cloth to bring my weight up to that set by the handicapper, the loudspeakers were turned on and it was announced that owing to the thickening fog the last race had been abandoned.

There was a rush then in the changing room and the tea and fruit-cake disappeared at a quickened tempo. It was a long time since breakfast, and I stuffed a couple of beef sandwiches into my mouth while I changed. I arranged with Clem for my kit to go to Plumpton, where I was due to ride four days later, and set off on an uninviting walk. I wanted to have a close look at the place where Bill had fallen.

It is a long way on foot from the stands to the far end of Maidenhead racecourse, and by the time I got there my shoes, socks, and trouser legs were wet through from the long sodden grass. It was very cold, very foggy. There was no one about.

I reached the fence, the harmless, softish, easy-to-jump fence, made of black birch twigs standing upright. Three feet thick at the bottom slanting to half that size at the top, four feet six inches tall, about ten yards wide. Ordinary, easy.

I looked carefully along the landing side of the fence. There was nothing unusual. Round I went to the take-off side. Nothing. I poked around the wing which guides the horses into the fence, the one on the inside of the course, the side Bill had been when he fell. Still nothing.

It was down underneath the wing on the outside of the course that I found what I was looking for. There it lay in the long grass, half hidden, beaded with drops of mist, coiled and deadly.

Wire.

There was a good deal of it, a pale silver grey, wound into a ring about a foot across, and weighted down with a piece of wood. One end of it led up the main side post of the wing and was fastened round it two feet above the level of the top of the birch. Fastened, I saw, very securely indeed. I could not untwist it with my fingers.

I went back to the inside wing and had a look at the post. Two feet above the fence there was a groove in the wood. This post had once been painted white, and the mark showed clearly.

It was clear to me that only one person could have

fixed the wire in place. The attendant. The man whom I myself had seen walk across from one side of the course to the other. The man, I thought bitterly, whom I had left to *help* Bill.

In a three mile 'chase at Maidenhead one rode twice round the course. On the first circuit there had been no trouble at this fence. Nine horses had jumped it safely, with Admiral lying third and biding his time, and me riding alongside telling Bill I didn't think much of the English climate.

Second time round, Admiral was lengths out in front. As soon as the attendant had seen him land over the fence before this one, he must have walked over holding the free end of the wire and wound it round the opposite post so that it stretched there taut in the air, almost invisible, two feet above the birch. At that height it would catch the high-leaping Admiral straight across the shoulders.

The callousness of it awoke a slow deep anger which, though I did not then know it, was to remain with me as a spur for many weeks to come.

Whether the horse had snapped the wire when he hit it, or pulled it off the post, I could not be sure. But as I could find no separate pieces, and the coil by the outer wing was all one length, I thought it likely that the falling horse had jerked the less secure end down with him. None of the seven horses following me had been

11

brought down. Like me, they must have jumped clear over the remains of the trap.

Unless the attendant was a lunatic, which could by no means be ruled out, it was a deliberate attack on a particular horse and rider. Bill on Admiral had normally reached the front by this stage in a race, often having opened up a lead of twenty lengths, and his red and green colours, even on a misty day, were easy to see.

At this point, greatly disturbed, I began to walk back. It was already growing dark. I had been longer at the fence than I had realized, and when I at length reached the weighing room, intending to tell the Clerk of the Course about the wire, I found everyone except the caretaker had gone.

The caretaker, who was old and bad-tempered, and incessantly sucking his teeth, told me he did not know where the Clerk of the Course could be found. He said the racecourse manager had driven off towards the town five minutes earlier. He did not know where the manager had been going, nor when he would be back; and with a grumbling tale that he had five separate stoves besides the central boiler to see to, and that the fog was bad for his bronchitis, the caretaker shuffled purposefully off towards the dim murky bulk of the grandstand.

Undecided, I watched him go. I ought, I knew, to tell someone in authority about the wire. But who? The

Stewards who had been at the meeting were all on their way home, creeping wearily through the fog, unreachable. The manager was gone; the Clerk of the Course's office, I discovered, was locked. It would take me a long time to locate any of them, persuade them to return to the racecourse and get them to drive down the course over the rough ground in the dark; and after that there would be discussion, repetition, statements. It would be hours before I could get away.

Meanwhile Bill was fighting for his life in Maidenhead hospital, and I wanted profoundly to know if he were winning. Scilla faced racking hours of anxiety and I had promised to be with her as soon as I could. Already I had delayed too long. The wire, fogbound and firmly twisted round the post, would keep until tomorrow, I thought; but Bill might not.

Bill's Jaguar was alone in the car park. I climbed in, switched on the side lights and the fog lights and drove off. I turned left at the gates, went gingerly along the road for two miles, turned left again over the river, twisted through Maidenhead's one way streets, and finally arrived at the hospital.

There was no sign of Scilla in the brightly lit busy hall. I asked the porter.

'Mrs Davidson? Husband a jockey? That's right, she's down there in the waiting room. Fourth door on the left.'

I found her. Her dark eyes looked enormous,

13

shadowed with grey smudges beneath them. All other colour had gone from her sad strained face, and she had taken off her frivolous hat.

'How is he?' I asked.

'I don't know. They just tell me not to worry.' She was very close to tears.

I sat down beside her and held her hand.

'You're a comfort, Alan,' she said.

Presently the door opened and a fair young doctor came in, stethoscope dangling.

'Mrs Davidson, I think . . .' he paused, 'I think you should come and sit with your husband.'

'How is he?'

'Not . . . very well. We are doing all we can.' Turning to me he said, 'Are you a relative?'

'A friend. I am going to drive Mrs Davidson home.'

'I see,' he said. 'Will you wait, or come back for her? Later this evening.' There was meaning in his careful voice, his neutral words. I looked closely into his face, and I knew that Bill was dying.

'I'll wait.'

'Good.'

I waited for four hours, getting to know intimately the pattern of the curtains and the cracks in the brown linoleum. Mostly, I thought about wire.

At last a nurse came, serious, young, pretty.

'I am so sorry . . . Major Davidson is dead.'

Mrs Davidson would like me to go and see him, she

14

said, if I would follow her. She took me down the long corridors, and into a white room, not very big, where Scilla sat beside the single bed.

Scilla looked up at me. She couldn't speak.

Bill lay there, grey and quiet, finished. The best friend a man could wish for.

CHAPTER TWO

Early next morning I drove Scilla, worn out from the vigil she had insisted on keeping all night beside Bill's body, and heavily drugged now with sedatives, home to the Cotswolds. The children came out and met her on the doorstep, their three faces solemn and round-eyed. Behind them stood Joan, the briskly competent girl who looked after them, and to whom I had telephoned the news the evening before.

There on the step Scilla sat down and wept. The children knelt and sat down beside her, putting their arms round her, doing their best to comfort a grief they could only dimly understand.

Presently Scilla went upstairs to bed. I drew the curtains for her and tucked her in, and kissed her cheek. She was exhausted and very sleepy, and I hoped it would be many hours before she woke again.

I went along to my own room and changed my clothes. Downstairs I found Joan putting coffee, bacon and eggs, and hot rolls for me on the kitchen table. I gave the children the chocolate bars I had bought for them the previous morning (how very long ago it seemed) and they sat with me, munching, while I ate my breakfast. Joan poured herself some coffee.

'Alan?' said William. He was five, the youngest, and he would never go on speaking until you said 'Yes?' to show you were listening.

'Yes?' I said.

'What happened to Daddy?'

So I told them about it, all of it except the wire.

They were unusually silent for a while. Then Henry, just eight, asked calmly, 'Is he going to be buried or burnt?'

Before I could answer, he and his elder sister Polly launched into a heated and astonishingly well-informed discussion about the respective merits of burial or cremation. I was horrified, but relieved too, and Joan, catching my eye, was hard put to it not to laugh.

The innocent toughness of their conversation started me on my way back to Maidenhead in a more cheerful frame of mind. I put Bill's car in the garage and set off in my own little dark blue Lotus. The fog had completely gone, but I drove slowly (for me), working out what was best to do.

First I called at the hospital. I collected Bill's clothes, signed forms, made arrangements. There was to be a routine post mortem examination the next day.

It was Sunday. I drove to the racecourse, but the

gates were locked. Back in the town the Clerk of the Course's office was shut and empty. I telephoned his home, but there was no answer.

After some hesitation I rang up the Senior Steward of the National Hunt Committee, going straight to the top steeplechase authority. Sir Creswell Stampe's butler said he would see if Sir Creswell was available. I said it was very important that I should speak with him. Presently he came on the line.

'I certainly hope what you have to say *is* very important, Mr York. I am in the middle of luncheon with my guests.'

'Have you heard, sir, that Major Davidson died yesterday evening?'

'Yes, I'm very sorry about it, very sorry indeed.' He waited. I took a deep breath.

'His fall wasn't an accident,' I said.

'What do you mean?'

'Major Davidson's horse was brought down by wire,' I said.

I told him about my search at the fence, and what I had found there.

'You have let Mr Dace know about this?' he asked. Mr Dace was the Clerk of the Course.

I explained that I had been unable to find him.

'So you rang me. I see.' He paused. 'Well, Mr York, if you are right, this is too serious to be dealt with entirely by the National Hunt Committee. I think you should inform the police in Maidenhead without delay. Let me know this evening, without fail, what is happening. I will try to get in touch with Mr Dace.'

I put down the receiver. The buck had been passed, I thought. I could imagine the Stampe roast beef congealing on the plate while Sir Creswell set the wires humming.

The police station in the deserted Sunday street was dark, dusty-looking and uninviting. I went in. There were three desks behind the counter, and at one of them sat a young constable reading a newspaper of the juicier sort. Keeping up with his crime, I reflected.

'Can I help you, sir?' he said, getting up.

'Is there someone here?' I asked. 'I mean, someone senior? It's about a . . . a death.'

'Just a minute, sir.' He went out of a door at the back, and returned to say, 'Will you come in here, please?'

He stood aside to let me into a little inner office, and shut the door behind me.

The man who rose to his feet was small for a policeman, thick-set, dark, and in his late thirties. He looked more of a fighter than a thinker, but I found later that his brain matched his physique. His desk was littered with papers and heavy-looking law books. The gas fire had made a comfortable warm fug, and his ashtray was overflowing. He, too, was spending his Sunday afternoon reading up crime.

'Good afternoon. I am Inspector Lodge,' he said. He

19

gestured to a chair facing his desk, asking me to sit down. He sat down again himself, and began to shape his papers into neat piles.

'You have come about a death?' My own words, repeated, sounded foolish, but his tone was matter-of-fact.

'It's about a Major Davidson . . .' I began.

'Oh yes. We had a report. He died in the hospital last night after a fall at the races.' He waited politely for me to go on.

'That fall was engineered,' I said bluntly.

Inspector Lodge looked at me steadily, then drew a sheet of paper out of a drawer, unscrewed his fountain pen, and wrote, I could see, the date and the time. A methodical man.

'I think we had better start at the beginning,' he said. 'What is your name?'

'Alan York.'

'Age?'

'Twenty-four.'

'Address?'

I gave Davidson's address, explaining whose it was, and that I lived there a good deal.

'Where is your own home?'

'In Southern Rhodesia,' I said. 'On a cattle station near a village called Induna, about fifteen miles from Bulawayo.'

'Occupation?'

'I represent my father in his London office.'

'And your father's business?'

'The Bailey York Trading Company.'

'What do you trade in?' asked Lodge.

'Copper, lead, cattle. Anything and everything. We're transporters mainly,' I said.

He wrote it all down, in quick distinctive script.

'Now then,' he put down the pen, 'what is all this about?'

'I don't know what it's about,' I said, 'but this is what happened.' I told him the whole thing. He listened without interrupting, then he said, 'What made you even begin to suspect that this was not a normal fall?'

'Admiral is the safest jumper there is. He's sure-footed, like a cat. He doesn't make mistakes.'

But I could see from his politely surprised expression that he knew little, if anything, about steeplechasing, and thought that one horse was as likely to fall as another.

I tried again. 'Admiral is brilliant over fences. He would never fall like that, going into an easy fence in his own time, not being pressed. He took off perfectly. I saw him. That fall was unnatural. It looked to me as though something had been used to bring him down. I thought it might be wire, and I went back to look and it was. That's all.'

'Hm. Was the horse likely to win?' asked Lodge.

'Certain,' I said.

'And who did win?'

'I did,' I said.

Lodge paused, and bit the end of his pen.

'How do the racecourse attendants get their jobs?' he asked.

'I don't really know. They are casual staff, taken on for the meeting, I think,' I said.

'Why would a racecourse attendant wish to harm Major Davidson?' He said this naïvely, and I looked at him sharply.

'Do you think I have made it all up?' I asked.

'No.' He sighed. 'I suppose I don't. Perhaps I should have said, how difficult would it be for someone who wished to harm Major Davidson to get taken on as a racecourse attendant?'

'Easy,' I said.

'We'll have to find out.' He reflected. 'It's a very chancy way to murder a man.'

'Whoever planned it can't have meant to kill him,' I said flatly.

'Why not?'

'Because it was so unlikely that he would die. I should think it was simply meant to stop him winning.'

'Why was such a fall unlikely to result in death?' said Lodge. 'It sounds highly dangerous to me.'

I said: 'It could have been meant to injure him, I suppose. Usually when a horse is going fast and hits a fence hard when you're not expecting it, you get cata-

pulted out of the saddle. You fly through the air and hit
the ground way out in front of where your horse falls.
That may do a lot of damage, but it doesn't often kill.
But Bill Davidson wasn't flung off forwards. His toe
may have stuck in his stirrup, though that's not very
likely. Perhaps the wire caught round his leg and pulled
him back. Anyway, he fell straight down and his horse
crashed on top of him. Even then it was sheer bad luck
that the saddle tree hit him in the stomach. You
couldn't even hope to kill a man like that on purpose.'

'I see. You seem to have given it some thought.'

'Yes.' The pattern of the hospital waiting room curtains, the brown linoleum, came back into my mind in
association.

'Can you think of anyone who might wish to hurt
Major Davidson?' asked Lodge.

'No,' I said. 'He was very well liked.'

Lodge got up and stretched. 'We'll go and have a
look at your wire,' he said. He put his head out into the
big office. 'Wright, go and see if Hawkins is there, and
tell him I want a car if there's one available.'

There was a car. Hawkins (I presumed) drove; I sat
in the back with Lodge. The main gates of the racecourse were still locked, but there were ways and
means, I found. A police key opened another, inconspicuous gate in the wooden fence.

'In case of fire,' said Lodge, seeing my sideways look.

There was no one about in the racecourse buildings:

the manager was out. Hawkins drove over the course into the centre and headed down towards the farthest fence. We bumped a good deal on the uneven ground. The car drew up just short of the inside wing, and Lodge and I climbed out.

I led the way past the fence to the outer wing.

'The wire is over here,' I said.

But I was wrong.

There was the post, the wing, the long grass, the birch fence. And no coil of wire.

'Are you sure this is the right fence?' said Lodge.

'Yes,' I said. We stood looking at the course set out in front of us. We were at the very far end, the stands a blurred massive block in the distance. The fence by which we stood was alone on a short straight between two curves, and the nearest fence to us was three hundred yards to the left, round a shallow bend.

'You jump that fence,' I said, pointing away to it. 'Then there's quite a long run, as you can see, to this one.' I patted the fence beside us. 'Then twenty yards after we land over this one there is that sharpish left turn into the straight. The next fence is some way up the straight, to allow the horses to balance themselves properly after coming round the bend, before they have to jump. It's a good course.'

'You couldn't have made a mistake in the mist?'

'No. This is the fence,' I said.

Lodge sighed. 'Well, we'll take a closer look.'

But all there was to be seen was a shallow groove on the once white inner post, and a deeper groove on the outer post, where the wire had bitten into the wood. Both grooves needed looking for and would ordinarily have been unnoticed. Both were at the same level, six feet six inches, from the ground.

'Very inconclusive indeed,' said Lodge.

We went back to Maidenhead in silence. Glum and feeling foolish, I knew now that even though I could reach no one in authority, I should have found someone, anyone, even the caretaker, the day before, to go back to the fence with me, after I had found the wire, to see it in its place. A witness who had seen wire fastened to a fence, even though it would have been dark and foggy, even though perhaps he could not swear at which fence he had seen it, would definitely have been better than no witness at all. I tried to console myself with the possibility that the attendant had been returning to the fence with his wire clippers at the same time that I was walking back to the stands, and that even if I had returned at once with a witness, if would already have been too late.

From Maidenhead police station I called Sir Creswell Stampe. I had parted him this time, he said, from his toasted muffins. The news that the wire had disappeared didn't please him either.

'You should have got someone else to see it at once. Photographed it. Removed it. We can't proceed without evidence. I can't think why you didn't have sense enough to act more quickly, either. You have been very irresponsible, Mr York.' And with these few kind words he put down the receiver.

Depressed, I drove home.

I put my head quietly round Scilla's door. Her room was dark, but I could hear her even breathing. She was still sound asleep.

Downstairs Joan and the children were sitting on the floor in front of the welcoming log fire playing poker. I had introduced them to the game one rainy day when the children were tired of snap and rummy and had been behaving very badly, quarrelling and shouting and raising tempers all round. Poker, the hitherto mysterious game of the cowboys in Westerns, had worked a miracle.

Henry developed in a few weeks into the sort of player you wouldn't sit down with twice without careful thought. His razor-sharp mathematical mind knew the odds to a fraction against any particular card turning up; his visual memory was formidable; and his air of slight bewilderment, calculated to be misleading, led many an unsuspecting adult straight into his traps. I admired Henry. He could out-bluff an angel.

Polly played well enough for me to be sure she would never lose continually in ordinary company, and even William knew a running flush from a full house.

They had been at it for some time. Henry's pile of poker chips was, as usual, three times as big as anyone else's.

Polly said, 'Henry won all the chips a little while ago, so we had to share them out and start all over again.'

Henry grinned. Cards were an open book to him and he couldn't help reading.

I took ten of Henry's chips and sat in with them. Joan dealt. She gave me a pair of fives and I drew another one. Henry discarded and drew two cards only, and looked satisfied.

The others threw in during the first two rounds. Then I boldly advanced two more chips to join the two on the table. 'Raise you two, Henry,' I said.

Henry glanced at me to make sure I was looking at him, then made a great show of indecision, drumming his fingers on the table and sighing. Knowing his habit of bluffing, I suspected he had a whipper of a hand and was scheming how to get me to disgorge the largest possible number of chips.

'Raise you one,' he said at last.

I was just about to put another two chips firmly out, but I stopped and said, 'Oh no you don't, Henry. Not this time,' and I threw in my hand. I pushed the four chips across to him. 'This time you get four and no more.'

'What did you have, Alan?' Polly turned my cards over, showing the three fives.

Henry grinned. He made no attempt to stop Polly looking at his cards too. He had a pair of Kings. Just one pair.

27

'Got you that time, Alan,' he said happily.

William and Polly groaned heavily.

We played until I had won back my reputation and a respectable number of Henry's chips. Then it was the children's bedtime, and I went up to see Scilla.

She was awake, lying in the dark.

'Come in, Alan.'

I went over and switched on the bedside light. The first shock was over. She looked calm, peaceful.

'Hungry?' I asked. She had not eaten since lunch the day before.

'Do you know, Alan, I am,' she said as if surprised.

I went downstairs and with Joan rustled up some supper. I carried the tray up and ate with Scilla. Sitting propped up with pillows, alone in the big bed, she began to tell me about how she had met Bill, the things they had done together, the fun they had had. Her eyes shone with remembered happiness. She talked for a long time, all about Bill, and I did not stop her until her lips began to tremble. Then I told her about Henry and his pair of Kings, and she smiled and grew calm again.

I wanted very much to ask her whether Bill had been in any trouble or had been threatened in any way during the last few weeks, but it wasn't the right time to do it. So I got her to take another of the sedatives the hospital had given me for her, turned off her light, and said good night.

As I undressed in my own room the tiredness hit me. I had been awake for over forty hours, few of which could be called restful. I flopped into bed. It was one of those times when the act of falling asleep is a conscious, delicious luxury.

Half an hour later Joan shook me awake again. She was in her dressing-gown.

'Alan, wake up for goodness' sake. I've been knocking on your door for ages.'

'What's the matter?'

'You're wanted on the telephone. Personal call,' she said.

'Oh no,' I groaned. It felt like the middle of the night. I looked at my watch. Eleven o'clock.

I staggered downstairs, eyes bleary with sleep.

'Hello?'

'Mr Alan York?'

'Yes.'

'Hold on, please.' Some clicks on the line. I yawned.

'Mr York? I have a message for you from Inspector Lodge, Maidenhead police. He would like you to come here to the police station tomorrow afternoon, at four o'clock.'

'I'll be there,' I said. I rang off, went back to bed, and slept and slept.

*

Lodge was waiting for me. He rose, shook hands, pointed to a chair. I sat down. The desk was clear now of everything except a neat, quarto-sized folder placed squarely in front of him. Slightly behind me, at a small table in the corner, sat a constable in uniform, pencil in hand, shorthand notebook at the ready.

'I have some statements here,' Lodge tapped the file, 'which I will tell you about. Then I have some questions to ask.' He opened the file and took out two sheets of paper clipped together.

'This is a statement from Mr J. L. Dace, Clerk of the Course of Maidenhead racecourse. In it he says nine of the attendants, the men who stand by to make temporary repairs to the fences during the races, are regularly employed in that capacity. Three of them were new this meeting.'

Lodge laid down this statement, and took out the next.

'This is a statement from George Watkins, one of the regular attendants. He says they draw lots among themselves to decide which fence each of them shall stand by. There are two at some fences. On Friday they drew lots as usual, but on Saturday one of the new men volunteered to go down to the farthest fence. None of them likes having to go right down there, Watkins says, because it is too far to walk back between races to "have a bit" on a horse. So they were glad enough to let the stranger take that fence, and they drew lots for the rest.'

'What did this attendant look like?' I said.

'You saw him yourself,' said Lodge.

'No, not really,' I said. 'All he was to me was a man. I didn't look at him. There's at least one attendant at every fence. I wouldn't know any of them again.'

'Watkins says he thinks he'd know the man again, but he can't describe him. Ordinary, he says. Not tall, not short. Middle-aged, he thinks. Wore a cap, old grey suit, loose mackintosh.'

'They all do,' I said gloomily.

Lodge said, 'He gave his name as Thomas Cook. Said he was out of work, had a job to go to next week and was filling in time. Very plausible, nothing odd about him at all, Watkins says. He spoke like a Londoner though, not with a Berkshire accent.'

Lodge laid the paper down, and took out another.

'This is a statement from John Russell of the St John Ambulance Brigade. He says he was standing beside the first fence in the straight watching the horses go round the bottom of the course. Because of the mist he says he could see only three fences: the one he was standing beside, the next fence up the straight, and the farthest fence, where Major Davidson fell. The fence before that, which was opposite him on the far side of the course, was an indistinct blur.

'He saw Major Davidson race out of the mist after

he had jumped that fence. Then he saw him fall at the next. Major Davidson did not reappear, though his horse got up and galloped off riderless. Russell began to walk towards the fence where he had seen Major Davidson fall; then when you, Mr York, passed him looking over your shoulder, he began to run. He found Major Davidson lying on the ground.'

'Did he see the wire?' I asked eagerly.

'No. I asked him if he had seen anything at all unusual. I didn't mention wire specifically. He said there was nothing.'

'Didn't he see the attendant roll up the wire while he was running towards him?'

'I asked him if he could see either Major Davidson or the attendant as he ran towards them. He says that owing to the sharp bend and the rails round it he could not see them until he was quite close. I gather he ran round the course instead of cutting across the corner through the long rough grass because it was too wet.'

'I see,' I said despondently. 'And what was the attendant doing when he got there?'

'Standing beside Major Davidson looking down at him. He says the attendant looked frightened. This surprised Russell, because although he was knocked out Major Davidson did not appear to him to be badly injured. He waved his white flag, the next First-Aid man saw it and waved his, and the message was thus relayed through the fog all the way up the course to the ambulance.'

'What did the attendant do then?'

'Nothing particular. He stayed beside the fence after the ambulance had taken Major Davidson away, and Russell says he was there until the abandonment of the last race was announced.'

Clutching at straws, I said, 'Did he go back with the other attendants and collect his pay?'

Lodge looked at me with interest. 'No,' he said, 'he didn't.'

He took out another paper.

'This statement is from Peter Smith, head travelling lad for the Gregory stables, where Admiral is trained. He says that after Admiral got loose at Maidenhead he tried to jump a blackthorn hedge. He stuck in it and was caught beside it, scared and bleeding. There are cuts and scratches all over the horse's shoulders, chest and forelegs.' He looked up. 'If the wire left any mark on him at all, it is impossible to distinguish it now.'

'You have been thorough,' I said, 'and quick.'

'Yes. We were lucky, for once, to find everyone we wanted without delay.'

There was only one paper left. Lodge picked it up, spoke slowly.

'This is the report of the post mortem on Major Davidson. Cause of death with multiple internal injuries. Liver and spleen were both ruptured.'

He sat back in his chair and looked at his hands.

'Now, Mr York, I have been directed to ask you some questions which . . .' his dark eyes came up to mine suddenly, '. . . which I do not think you will like. Just answer them.' His half smile was friendly.

'Fire away,' I said.

'Are you in love with Mrs Davidson?'

I sat up straight, surprised.

'No,' I said.

'But you live with her?'

'I live with the whole family,' I said.

'Why?'

'I have no home in England. When I first got to know Bill Davidson he asked me to his house for a week-end. I liked it there, and I suppose they liked me. Anyway, they asked me often. Gradually the week-ends got longer and longer, until Bill and Scilla suggested I should make their house my headquarters. I spend a night or two every week in London.'

'How long have you lived at the Davidsons?' asked Lodge.

'About seven months.'

'Were your relations with Major Davidson friendly?'

'Yes, very.'

'And with Mrs Davidson?'

'Yes.'

'But you do not love her?'

'I am extremely fond of her. As an elder sister,' I

said, sitting tight on my anger. 'She is ten years older than I am.'

Lodge's expression said quite plainly that age had nothing to do with it. I was aware, just then, that the constable in the corner was writing down my replies.

I relaxed. I said, tranquilly, 'She was very much in love with her husband, and he with her.'

Lodge's mouth twitched at the corners. He looked, of all things, amused. Then he began again.

'I understand,' he said, 'that Major Davidson was the leading amateur steeplechase jockey in this country?'

'Yes.'

'And you yourself finished second to him, a year ago, after your first season's racing in England?'

I stared at him. I said, 'For someone who hardly knew steeplechasing existed twenty-four hours ago, you've wasted no time.'

'Were you second to Major Davidson on the amateur riders' list last year? And were you not likely to be second to him again? Is it not also likely that now, in his absence, you will head the list?'

'Yes, yes, and I hope so,' I said. The accusation was as plain as could be, but I was not going to rush unasked into protestations of my innocence. I waited. If he wanted the suggestion made that I had sought to injure or kill Bill in order to acquire either his wife or his racing prestige, or both, Lodge would have to make it himself.

35

But he didn't. A full minute ticked by, during which I sat still. Finally Lodge grinned.

'Well, I think that's all, then, Mr York. The information you gave us yesterday and your answers today will be typed together as one statement, and I shall be glad if you will read and sign it.'

The policeman with the notebook stood up and walked into the outer office. Lodge said, 'The coroner's inquest on Major Davidson is to be held on Thursday. You will be needed as a witness; and Mrs Davidson, too, for evidence of identification. We'll be getting in touch with her.'

He asked me questions about steeplechasing, ordinary conversational questions, until the statement was ready. I read it carefully and signed it. It was accurate and perfectly fair. I could imagine these pages joining the others in Lodge's tidy file. How fat would it grow before he found the accidental murderer of Bill Davidson.

If he ever did.

He stood up and held out his hand, and I shook it. I liked him. I wondered who had 'directed' him to find out if I might have arranged the crime I had myself reported.

CHAPTER THREE

I rode at Plumpton two days later.

The police had been very discreet in their enquiries, and Sir Creswell also, for there was no speculation in the weighing room about Bill's death. The grapevine was silent.

I plunged into the bustle of a normal racing day, the minor frustration of a lot of jockeys changing in a smallish space, the unprintable jokes, the laughter, the cluster of cold half-undressed men round the red-hot coke stove.

Clem gave me my clean breeches, some pants, a thin fawn under-jersey, a fresh white stock for my neck, and a pair of nylon stockings. I stripped and put on the racing things. On top of the nylon stockings (laddered, as always) my soft, light, close-fitting racing boots slid on easily. Clem handed me my racing colours, the thick woollen sweater of coffee and cream checks, and the brown satin cap. He tied my stock for me. I pulled on the jersey, and slid the cap on to my crash helmet, ready to put on later.

Clem said, 'Only the one ride today, sir?' He pulled two thick rubber bands from his large apron pocket and slipped them over my wrists. They were to anchor the sleeves of my jersey and prevent the wind blowing them up my arms.

'Yes,' I said. 'So far, anyway.' I was always hopeful.

'Will you be wanting to borrow a light saddle? The weight's near your limit, I should think.'

'No,' I said, 'I'd rather use my own saddle if I can. I'll get on the trial scales with that first, and see how much overweight I am.'

'Right you are, sir.'

I went over with Clem, picked up my six pound racing saddle with its girth and stirrup leathers wound round it, and weighed myself with it, my crash helmet perched temporarily and insecurely on the back of my head. The total came to ten stone, nine pounds, which was four pounds more than the handicapper thought my horse deserved.

Clem took back the saddle, and I put my helmet on the bench again.

'I'll think I'll carry the overweight, Clem,' I said.

'Right.' He hurried off to attend to someone else.

I could have got down to the proper weight – just – by using a three pound 'postage stamp' saddle and changing into silk colours and 'paper' boots.

But as I was riding my own horse I could please myself, and he was an angular animal whose ribs would probably have been rubbed raw by too small a saddle.

He, Forlorn Hope, my newest acquisition, was a strongly built brown gelding only five years old. He looked as though he would develop into a 'chaser in a year or two, but meanwhile I was riding him in novice hurdle races to give him some sorely needed experience.

His unreliability as a jumper had made Scilla, the evening before, beg me not to ride him at Plumpton, a course full of snares for the unwary.

Unbearably strung up, and facing her loss for the first time without the help of drugs, she was angry and pleading by turns.

'Don't, Alan. Not a novice hurdle at Plumpton. You know your wretched Forlorn Hope isn't safe. You haven't got to do it, so why do you?'

'I like it.'

'There never was a horse more aptly named,' she said, miserably.

'He'll learn,' I said. 'But not if I don't give him the opportunity.'

'Put someone else up. Please.'

'There isn't any point in having a horse if I don't ride it myself. That's really why I came to England at all, to race. You know that.'

'You'll be killed, like Bill.' She began to cry, helplessly, worn out. I tried to reason with her.

'No, I won't. If Bill had been killed in a motor crash you wouldn't expect me to stop driving. Steeple-chasing's just as safe and unsafe as motoring.' I paused, but she went on crying. 'There are thousands more people killed on the roads than on the race-track,' I said.

At this outrageous statement she recovered enough to point out acidly the difference in the number of people engaged in the two pursuits.

'Very few people are killed by steeplechasing,' I tried again.

'Bill was . . .'

'Only about one a year, out of hundreds,' I went on.

'Bill was the second since Christmas.'

'Yes.' I looked at her warily. There were still tears in her eyes.

'Scilla, was Bill in any sort of trouble recently?'

'Why ever do you ask?' She was astounded by my question.

'Was he?'

'Of course not.'

'Not worried about anything?' I persisted.

'No. Did he seem worried to you?'

'No,' I said. It was quite true. Until the moment of his fall Bill had been the same as I had always known him, cheerful, poised, reliable. He had had, and enjoyed, a pretty wife, three attractive children, a grey stone manor house, a considerable fortune and the best hunter 'chaser in England. A happy man. And rack my memory as I would, I could not recall the slightest ruffling of the pattern.

'Then why do you ask?' said Scilla, again.

I told her as gradually, as gently as I could, that Bill's fall had not been an ordinary accident. I told her about the wire and about Lodge's investigations.

She sat like stone, absolutely stunned.

'Oh no,' she said. 'Oh no. Oh no.'

As I stood now outside the weighing room at Plumpton I could still see her stricken face. She had raised no more objections to my racing. What I had told her had driven every other thought out of her head.

A firm hand came down on my shoulder. I knew it well. It belonged to Peter Gregory, racehorse trainer, a burly man nearly six feet tall, running to fat, growing bald, but in his day, I had been told, the toughest man ever to put his foot in a racing stirrup.

'Hello, Alan me lad. I'm glad to see you're here. I've already declared you for your horse in the second race.'

'How is he?' I asked.

'All right. A bit thin, still.' Forlorn Hope had only been in his stable for a month. 'I should give him an "easy", coming up the hill the first time, or he'll blow up before the finish. He needs more time before we can hope for much.'

'OK,' I said.

'Come out and see what the going is like,' said Pete. 'I want to talk to you.' He hitched the strap of his binoculars higher on his shoulder.

We walked down through the gate on to the course and dug our heels experimentally into the turf. They sank in an inch.

'Not bad, considering all the snow that melted into it a fortnight ago,' I said.

'Nice and soft for you to fall on,' said Pete with elementary humour.

We went up the rise to the nearest hurdle. The landing side had a little too much give in it, but we knew the ground at the other end of the course was better drained. It was all right.

Pete said abruptly, 'Did you see Admiral fall at Maidenhead?' He had been in Ireland buying a horse when it happened and had only just returned.

'Yes. I was about ten lengths behind him,' I said, looking down the course, concentrating on the hurdle track.

'Well?'

'Well, what?' I said.

'What happened? Why did he fall?' There was some sort of urgency in his voice, more than one would expect, even in the circumstances. I looked at him. His eyes were grey, unsmiling, intent. Moved by an instinct I didn't understand, I retreated into vagueness.

'He just fell,' I said. 'When I went over the fence he was on the ground with Bill underneath him.'

'Did Admiral meet the fence all wrong, then?' he probed.

'Not as far as I could see. He must have hit the top of it.' This was near enough to the truth.

'There wasn't ... anything else?' Pete's eyes were fierce, as if they would look into my brain.

'What do you mean?' I avoided the direct answer.

'Nothing.' His anxious expression relaxed. 'If you didn't see anything...' We began to walk back. It troubled me that I hadn't told Pete the truth. He had been too searching, too aware. I was certain he was not the man to risk destroying a great horse like Admiral, let alone a friend, but why was he so relieved now he believed I had noticed nothing?

I had just decided to ask him to explain his attitude, and to tell him what had really happened, when he began to speak.

'Have you got a ride in the Amateur 'Chase, Alan?' He was back to normal, bluff and smiling.

'No, I haven't,' I said. 'Pete, look ...'

But he interrupted. 'I had a horse arrive in my yard five or six days ago, with an engagement in today's Amateur 'Chase. A chestnut. Good sort of animal, I should say. He seems to be fit enough – he's come from a small stable in the West Country – and his new owner is very keen to run him. I tried

43

to ring you this morning about it, but you'd already left.'

'What's his name?' I asked, for all this preamble of Pete's was, I knew, his way of cajoling me into something I might not be too delighted to do.

'Heavens Above.'

'Never heard of him. What's he done?' I asked.

'Well, not much. He's young, of course . . .'

I interrupted. 'What *exactly* has he done?'

Pete sighed and gave in. 'He's only had two runs, both down in Devon last autumn. He didn't fall, but – er – he got rid of his jockey both times. But he jumped well enough over my schooling fences this morning. I don't think you'd have any difficulty getting him round safely, and that's the main thing at this stage.'

'Pete, I don't like to say no, but . . .' I began.

'His owner is so hoping you'll ride him. It's her first horse, and it's running for the first time in her brand new colours. I brought her to the races with me. She's very excited. I said I'd ask you . . .'

'I don't think . . .' I tried again.

'Well, at least meet her,' said Pete.

'If I meet her, you know it'll be far more difficult for me to refuse to ride her horse.'

Pete didn't deny it.

I went on, 'I suppose she's another of your dear old ladies about to go into a nursing home from which she is unlikely to return, and wants a final thrill before she meets her fate?'

This was the sad tale which Peter had used not long before to inveigle me on to a bad horse against my better judgement. And I often saw the old lady at the races afterwards. The nursing home and her fate were still presumably awaiting her.

'This one is not,' said Pete, 'a dear old lady.'

We came to a stop in the paddock, and Pete looked around him and beckoned to someone. Out of the corner of my eye I saw a woman begin to walk towards us. It was already, without unforgivable rudeness, too late to escape. I had time for one heart-felt oath in Pete's ear before I turned to be introduced to the new owner of the jockey-depositing Heavens Above.

'Miss Ellery-Penn, Alan York,' said Pete.

I was lost before she spoke a word. The first thing I said was, 'I'll be glad to ride your horse.'

Pete was laughing openly at me.

She was beautiful. She had clear features, wonderful skin, smiling grey eyes, dark glossy hair falling almost to her shoulders. And she was used to the effect she had on men: but how could she help it?

Pete said, 'Right, then. I'll declare you for the amateurs' – it's the fourth race. I'll give your colours to Clem.' He went off towards the weighing room.

'I am so glad you agreed to ride my horse,' the girl said. Her voice was low-pitched and unhurried. 'He's a birthday present. Rather a problem one, don't you think? My Uncle George, who is a dear fellow but just the slightest bit off the beat, *advertised* in *The Times* for a racehorse. My aunt says he received fifty replies and bought this horse without seeing it because he liked the name. He said it would be more amusing for me to have a horse for my birthday than the conventional string of pearls.'

'Your Uncle George sounds fascinating,' I said.

'But just a little devastating to live with.' She had a trick of lifting the last two or three words in a sentence so that they sounded like a question. As if she had added, 'Don't you agree?' to her remark.

'Do you in fact live with him?' I asked.

'Oh, yes. Parents divorced in the murky past. Scattered to the four winds, and all that.'

'I'm sorry.'

'Waste no sympathy. I can't remember either of them. They abandoned me on Uncle George's doorstep, figuratively speaking, at the tender age of two.'

'Uncle George has done a good job,' I said, looking at her with the frankest admiration.

She accepted this without gaucherie, almost as a matter of course.

'Aunt Deb, actually. She is faintly more on the ball than Uncle George. Absolute pets, the pair of them.'

'Are they here today?' I asked.

'No, they aren't,' said Miss Ellery-Penn. 'Uncle

George remarked that having given me a passport into a new world peopled entirely by brave and charming young men, it would defeat the object if my path were cluttered up with elderly relatives.'

'I am getting fonder of Uncle George every minute,' I said.

Miss Ellery-Penn gave me a heavenly smile which held no promises of any sort.

'Have you seen my horse? Isn't he a duck?' she said.

'I haven't seen him. I'm afraid I didn't know he existed until five minutes ago. How did Uncle George happen to send him to Pete Gregory? Did he pick the stable with a pin?'

She laughed. 'No, I don't think so. He had the stable all planned. He said I could get a Major Davidson to ride for me if the horse went to Mr Gregory's.' She reflected, wrinkling her brow. 'He was quite upset on Monday when he read in the paper that Major Davidson had been killed.'

'Did he know him?' I asked idly, watching the delicious curves at the corners of her red mouth.

'No, I'm sure he didn't know him personally. Probably he knew his father. He seems to know most people's fathers. He just said "Good God, Davidson's dead" in a shocked sort of way and went on eating his toast. But he didn't hear me or Aunt Deb until we had asked him four times for the marmalade!'

'And that was all?'

'Yes. Why do you ask?' said Miss Ellery-Penn, curiously.

'Oh, nothing special,' I said. 'Bill Davidson and I were good friends.'

She nodded. 'I see.' She dismissed the subject. 'Now what do I have to do in my new role as racehorse owner? I don't particularly want to make a frightful boob on my first day. Any comments and instructions from you will be welcome, Mr York.'

'My name is Alan,' I said.

She gave me an appraising look. It told me plainer than words that although she was young she was already experienced at fending off unwelcome attentions and not being rushed into relationships she was not prepared for.

But she finally smiled, and said, 'Mine is Kate.' She bestowed her name like a gift; I was pleased to receive it.

'How much do you know about racing?' I asked.

'Not a thing. Never set foot on the Turf before today.' She gave the capital letter its full value, ironically.

'Do you ride, yourself?'

'Positively not.'

'Perhaps your Uncle George is fond of horses? Perhaps he hunts?' I suggested.

'Uncle George is the most un-addicted man to horses I have ever met. He says one end kicks and the other bites, and as for hunting, he says that he has cosier

48

things to do than chase bushy tailed vermin in the gravest discomfort over waterlogged countryside in the depths of winter.'

I laughed. 'Perhaps he bets. Off the course?' I asked.

'Uncle George has been known to ask, on Cup Final day, what has won the Derby.'

'Then why Heavens Above?'

'Wider horizons for me, Uncle George says. My education has been along the well-tramped lines of boarding school, finishing school, and an over-chaperoned tour of Europe. I needed to get the smell of museums out of my nose, Uncle George said.'

'So he gave you a racehorse for your twenty-first birthday,' I stated matter-of-factly.

'Yes,' she said: then she looked at me sharply. I grinned. I had jumped her defences, that time.

'There's nothing special for you to do as an owner,' I said, 'except to go along to those stalls over there,' I pointed, 'before the fourth race, to see your horse being saddled up. Then you'll go into the parade ring with Pete, and stand around making intelligent remarks about the weather until I arrive and mount and go out for the race.'

'What do I do if he wins?'

'Do you expect him to win?' I asked. I was not sure how much she really knew about her horse.

'Mr Gregory says he won't.'

I was relieved. I did not want her to be disappointed.

'We'll all know much more about him after the race. But if he should come in the first three, he will be unsaddled down there opposite the weighing room. Otherwise, you'll find us up here on the grass.'

It was nearly time for the first race. I took the delectable Miss Ellery-Penn on to the stands and fulfilled Uncle George's design by introducing her to several brave and charming young men. I unfortunately realized that by the time I came back from riding in the novice hurdle, I should probably be an 'also ran' in the race for Miss Ellery-Penn's attentions.

I watched her captivating a group of my friends. She was a vivid, vital person. It seemed to me that she had an inexhaustible inner fire battened down tight under hatches, and only the warmth from it was allowed to escape into the amused, slow voice. Kate was going to be potently attractive even in middle age, I thought inconsequently, and it crossed my mind that had Scilla possessed this springing vitality instead of her retiring, serene passiveness, Inspector Lodge's implications might not have been very far off the mark.

After we had watched the first race I left Kate deciding which of her new acquaintances should have the honour of taking her to coffee, and went off to weigh out for the novice hurdle. Looking back, I saw her setting off to the refreshment room with a trail of admirers, rather like a comet with a tail. A flashing, bewitching comet.

For the first time in my life I regretted that I was going to ride in a race.

CHAPTER FOUR

In the changing room Sandy Mason stood with his hands on his hips and laid about him with his tongue. His red hair curled strongly, his legs, firmly planted with the feet apart, were as rigid as posts. From top to toe he vibrated life. He was a stocky man in his thirties, on the short side, very strong, with dark brown eyes fringed disconcertingly by pale, reddish lashes.

As a jockey, a professional, he was not among the top dozen, but he had had a good deal of success, mainly owing to his fighting spirit. Nothing ever frightened him. He would thrust his sometimes unwilling mounts into the smallest openings, even occasionally into openings which did not exist until he made them by sheer force. His aggressiveness in races had got him into hot water more than once with the Stewards, but he was not particularly unpopular with the other jockeys, owing to his irrepressible, infectious cheerfulness.

His sense of humour was as vigorous as the rest of

him, and if I thought privately that some of his jokes were too unkindly practical or too revoltingly obscene, I appeared to be in a minority.

'Which of you sods has half-inched my balancing pole?' he roared in a voice which carried splendidly above the busy chatter to every corner of the room. To this enquiry into the whereabouts of his whip, he received no reply.

'Why don't you lot get up off your fannies and see if you're hatching it,' he said to three or four jockeys who were sitting on a bench pulling on their boots. They looked up appreciatively and waited for the rest of the tirade. Sandy kept up a flow of invective without repeating himself until one of the valets produced the missing whip.

'Where did you find it?' demanded Sandy. 'Who had it? I'll twist his bloody arm.'

'It was on the floor under the bench, in your own place.'

Sandy was never embarrassed by his mistakes. He roared with laughter and took his whip. 'I'll forgive you all this time, then.' He went out into the weighing room carrying his saddle and whacking the air with his whip as if to make sure it was as pliable as usual. He always used it a good deal in the course of a race.

As he passed me where I stood just inside the changing room door, his eyes lifted to mine with one of the darting, laughing glances which made him likeable in spite of his faults. I turned and watched him go over and sit on the scales, parking the whip on the table beside him. He said something I couldn't hear, and both the Clerk of the Scales and the Judge, who was sitting there learning the colours so that he could distinguish them at the finish, laughed as they checked him against their lists and passed him for the race.

There had been rumours, a while back, that Sandy had 'stopped' a few horses and had been rewarded handsomely by bookmakers for the service. But nothing had been proved, and the official enquiry had lasted barely an hour. Those who had felt the rough edge of Sandy's practical jokes believed him capable of anything. Everyone else pointed out that stopping a horse was entirely out of character for one who had been in trouble for trying too ruthlessly to win.

Watching the free and easy way he handled the two racing officials, I could understand that in the face of that friendly, open manner, the Stewards at the enquiry must have found it impossible, in the absence of solidly convincing evidence, to believe him guilty. The general opinion among the jockeys was that Sandy had 'strangled' a couple at one stage, but not during the past few months.

'Stopping' a horse can be done by missing the start, setting off some lengths behind, and staying at the back. Then the crooked jockey can ride a fairly honest finish from the second last fence, when he is closely under the eyes of the crowd, secure in the knowledge that he had left the horse far too much to do and cannot possibly win. It is rare enough, because a jockey seen to do it regularly soon finds himself unemployed.

During my one and a half seasons' racing I had seen it happen only twice. It was the same man both times, a fair, round-faced youth called Joe Nantwich. On the second occasion, about two months ago, he had been lucky to escape with his licence, for he had been foolish enough to try it in a race where one of the jockeys was David Stampe, the tale-bearing younger son of the Senior Steward.

Joe, and, I was sure, Sandy too, had both gone to the lengths of deliberately holding back horses which, without their interference, would have been certain to win. They had, in fact, been guilty of criminal fraud. But was I so very much better, I wondered, as I tied on my helmet and took my saddle over to the scales. For I proposed to take Forlorn Hope sensibly over the hurdles, concentrating on getting round the course; and I had no intention of riding him all out in the faint possibility that he might finish in the first three. He was not properly fit, and too hard a race would do him great harm. Of course if by some unforeseen circumstances, such as a lot of falls among the other horses, I found myself placed with a winning chance, I intended to seize it. There is a world of difference between 'stopping' and 'not trying hard, but willing to win': but the result for disgruntled backers is the same. They lose their money.

I took my saddle out to the saddling boxes, where Pete was already waiting with Forlorn Hope. He saddled up, and Rupert, the tiny stable lad, led the horse out into the parade ring. Pete and I strolled in after him, discussing the other horses in the race. There was no sign of Kate.

When the time came I mounted and rode out on to the course. The familiar excitement was in my blood again. Not Bill's death, nor Scilla's mourning, nor the thought of Kate making progress with someone else, could affect the gripping happiness I always felt when cantering down to the starting gate. The speed of racing, the quick decisions, the risks, these were what I badly needed to counteract the safeties of civilization. One can be too secure. Adventure is good for the soul, especially for someone like me, whose father stopped counting after the fourth million.

And my father, with an understanding based on his own much wilder youth, had given me unconditionally a fast car and three good horses and turned me loose in a country five thousand miles from home. He said, however, as he dispatched me with his blessing, that he thought steeplechasing was rather mild for one who had been taken crocodile hunting on the Zambezi every year since he was ten. My father's annual month away from his trading empire usually meant for us a dash across the veldt and a plunge into the primeval forest, sometimes equipped with the absolute minimum of kit and no one but ourselves to carry it. And I, for whom the deep jungle was a familiar playground, found the challenge I needed in a tamed land, on friendly animals, in a sport hemmed all about with rules and regulations. It was very odd, when one came to consider it.

The starter called the roll to make sure everyone had arrived, while he circled round and checked the tightness of the girths. I found Joe Nantwich guiding his horse along beside me. He was wearing his usual unpleasant expression, half petulance, half swank.

'Are you going back to the Davidsons' after the races, Alan?' he asked. He always spoke to me with a familiarity I slightly resented, though I tried not to.

'Yes,' I said. Then I thought of Kate. 'I may not go at once, though.'

'Will you give me a lift as far as Epsom?'

'I don't go that way,' I said, very politely.

'But you go through Dorking. I could get a bus on from there if you don't want to go to Epsom. I came with someone who is going on to Kent, so I've got to find some transport home.' He was persistent, and although I thought he could find someone going directly to Epsom if he tried hard enough, I agreed in the end to take him.

We lined up for the start. Joe was on one side of me and Sandy on the other, and from the looks they gave each other across me, there was no love lost between them. Sandy's smile was a nasty one: Joe's round baby face puckered up like a child trying not to cry. I imagined that Sandy had been puncturing Joe's inflated ego with one of those famous practical jokes, such as filling the feet of his racing boots with jam.

Then we were off, and I gave all my attention to getting Forlorn Hope round as neatly, quickly, and safely as I could. He was still very green and inclined to waver as he met the clattering hurdles, but the basic spring was there. He was going so well that for over half of the race I lay in third place, staying slightly towards the outside, to give him a clear view of the obstacles. The last quarter mile coming up the hill was too much for him, though, and we finished sixth. I was satisfied; and Scilla would be reassured.

Sandy Mason finished ahead of me. Then Joe Nant-wich's horse galloped past loose, reins dangling, and looking back to the far end of the course I saw the tiny figure of Joe himself trudging back to the stands. No doubt I would be hearing a stride by stride account of the calamity all the way to Dorking.

I unsaddled, went back to the weighing-room, changed into Kate's brand new colours, got Clem to pack me a weight cloth with ten pounds of flat lead pieces, the weight I needed for the Amateur 'Chase, and went out to see what had become of Miss Ellery-Penn.

She was leaning on the parade ring rails, looking alternately at the horses and (with too much approval,

I thought) at Dane Hillman, one of the brave and charming young men I had introduced to her.

'Mr Hillman has been telling me,' said Kate, 'that that poor-looking bag of bones over there – the one with his head down by his knees and those floppy ears – is the fastest horse in the race. Am I to believe it, or is the mickey being gently taken?'

'No mickey,' I said. 'That's the best horse. Not on looks, I grant you, but he's a certainty today, in this company.'

Dane said, 'Horses who go along with their heads down like that are nearly always good jumpers. They look where they're going.'

'But I like this gorgeous creature coming round now,' said Kate, looking at a bay with an arched back and high head carriage. Most of his body was covered by a rug to keep out the February cold, but at the back his glossy rump swelled roundly.

'He's much too fat,' said Dane. 'He probably ate his head off during the snow and hasn't had enough exercise since. He'll blow up when he's asked to do anything.'

Kate sighed. 'Horses appear to be as full of paradoxes as G. K. Chesterton. The duds look good, and good looks duds.'

'Not always,' said Dane and I together.

'I shall be glad,' said Dane, 'to give you a prolonged course in racehorse recognition, Miss Ellery-Penn.'

'I am a slow learner, Mr Hillman.'

'All the better,' said Dane, cheerfully.

'Aren't you riding today, Dane?' I asked hopefully.

'In the last two, my lad. Don't worry, I shall be able to look after Miss Ellery-Penn for you while you ride her horse.' He grinned.

'Are you a jockey too, Mr Hillman?' asked Kate in a surprised voice.

'Yes,' said Dane, and left it at that. He was the rising star of the profession, clearly heading straight to the top. Pete Gregory had first claim on him, which, apart from natural affinity, brought us together a good deal. Strangers often mistook us for each other. We were the same age, both dark, both of middle height and medium build. On horseback the difference was greater; he was a better jockey than I would ever be.

'I thought all jockeys were instantly recognizable as having come straight from Lilliput,' said Kate, 'but you two are quite a decent size.' She had to look up to both of us, although she was tall enough herself.

We laughed. I said, 'Steeplechasing jockeys are nearly all a decent size. It's easier to stick on over big fences if you have long legs to grip with.'

'Several of the Flat chaps are as tall as us, too,' said Dane. 'But they are very skinny, of course.'

'All my illusions are being shattered,' said Kate.

Dane said, 'I like your new horse, Alan. He'll make a good 'chaser next year.'

'Are you riding your own horses today, too?' Kate asked Dane.

'No, I'm not. I haven't any,' said Dane. 'I'm a professional, so I'm not allowed to own racehorses.'

'A professional?' Kate's eyebrows went up. She had clearly taken in the superlative tailoring of the suit under the short camel overcoat, the pleasant voice, the gentle manners. Another illusion was being shattered, I was amused to see.

'Yes. I ride for my life,' said Dane, smiling. 'Unlike Alan, I haven't a stinking rich father. But I get paid for doing what I like best in the world. It's a very satisfactory state of affairs.'

Kate looked carefully from one to the other of us. 'Perhaps in time I shall understand what makes you want to risk your elegant necks,' she said.

'When you find out, please tell us,' said Dane. 'It's still a mystery to me.'

We wandered back to the stands and watched the third race. The poor-looking horse won in a canter by twenty lengths. Kate's fancy was tailed-off after a mile and refused at the third last fence.

'Don't imagine that we always know what's going to win,' said Dane. 'Jockeys are bad tipsters. But that one was a cert, a dead cert.'

A dead cert. The casual, everyday racing expression

jabbed in my mind like a needle. Bill Davidson's attacker had relied on Admiral's being a certainty.

A dead cert. Dead . . .

Kate's horse, for a pig in a poke, was not as bad as I feared. At the second fence he put in a short one and screwed in mid-air. I came clear out of the saddle and landed back in it more by luck than judgement. This was obviously the trick which had rid Heaven's Above of his former jockey, who now had all my sympathy. He did it again at the third open ditch, but the rest of our journey was uneventful. The horse even found an unsuspected turn of foot up the hill and, passing several tired animals, ran on into fourth place.

Kate was delighted.

'Bless Uncle George for a brainwave,' she said. 'I've never had such a happy day in my life.'

'I thought you were coming off at the second, Alan,' said Pete Gregory, as I undid the girth buckles.

'So did I,' I said, feelingly. 'It was sheer luck I didn't.'

Pete watched the way Heavens Above was breathing: the ribs were moving in and out a good deal, but not labouring. He said, 'He's remarkably fit, considering everything. I think we'll win a race or two with him before the end of the season.'

'Can't we all go and celebrate with the odd

magnum?' asked Kate. Her eyes were shining with excitement.

Pete laughed. 'Wait till you have a winner, for the magnum,' he said. 'I'd like to have drunk a more modest toast to the future with you, though, but I've a runner in the next. Alan will take you, no doubt.' He looked at me sideways, very amused still at my complete surrender to the charm of Miss Ellery-Penn.

'Will you wait for me, Kate?' I asked. 'I have to go and weigh in now, because we were fourth. I'll change and be out as quickly as I can.'

'I'll come down outside the weighing room,' promised Kate, nodding.

I weighed in, gave my saddle to Clem, washed, and changed back into ordinary clothes. Kate was waiting outside the weighing-room, looking at a group of girls standing near her chatting.

'Who are they?' asked Kate. 'They have been here all the time I have, just doing nothing.'

'Jockeys' wives, mostly,' I said, grinning. 'Waiting outside the weighing room is their chief occupation.'

'And jockeys' girl friends too, I suppose,' said Kate, wryly.

'Yes,' I said. 'And I've just found out how nice it is to know there is someone waiting for you outside.'

We went round to the bar, and settled for two cups of coffee.

'Uncle George will be shattered to hear we drank to

Heavens Above so non-alcoholically,' said Kate. 'Don't grain and grapes figure in your life?'

'Oh, yes, of course. But I've never got used to them at three o'clock in the afternoon. How about you?'

'Champers for breakfast is my passion,' said Kate, with smiling eyes.

I asked her then if she would spend the evening with me, but she said she could not. Aunt Deb, it appeared, was having a dinner party, and Uncle George would be agog to hear how the birthday present had got on.

'Tomorrow, then?'

Kate hesitated and looked down at her glass. 'I'm . . . er . . . I'm going out with Dane, tomorrow.'

'Blast him,' I said, exploding.

Kate positively giggled.

'Friday?' I suggested.

'That will be lovely,' said Kate.

We went up to the stands and watched Dane win the fifth race by a short head. Kate cheered him home uninhibitedly.

CHAPTER FIVE

A battle was raging in the car park. I walked out to the gate to go home after the last race, and came to a dead stop. In the open space between the gate and the first rank of parked cars, at least twenty men were fighting, and fighting to hurt. Even at first glance there was a vicious quality about the strictly non-Queensberry type blows.

It was astounding. Scuffles between two or three men are common on racecourses, but a clash of this size and seriousness had to be caused by more than a disagreement over a bet.

I looked closer. There was no doubt about it. Some of the men were wearing brass knuckles. A length of bicycle chain swung briefly in the air. The two men nearest to me were lying on the ground, almost motionless, but rigid with exertion, as if locked in some strange native ritual. The fingers of one were clamped round the wrist of the other, whose hand held a knife with a sharp three-inch blade. Not long enough to be readily lethal, it was designed to rip and disfigure.

There seemed to be two fairly equally matched sides fighting each other, but one could not distinguish which was which. The man with the knife, who was slowly getting the worst of it, I saw to be little more than a boy; but most of the men were in their full strength. The only older-looking fighter was on his knees in the centre with his arms folded over his head, while the fight raged on around him.

They fought in uncanny silence. Only their heavy breathing and a few grunts were to be heard. The semi-circle of open-mouthed homeward-bound racegoers watching them was growing larger, but no one felt inclined to walk into the mêlée and try to stop it.

I found one of the newspaper sellers at my elbow.

'What's it all about?' I asked. Nothing much to do with racing escapes the newsboys.

'It's the taxi-drivers,' he said. 'There's two rival gangs of 'em, one lot from London and one lot from Brighton. There's usually trouble when they meet.'

'Why?'

'Couldn't tell you, Mr York. But this isn't the first time they've been at it.'

I looked back at the struggling mob. One or two of them still had peaked caps on. Some pairs were rolling about on the ground, some were straining and heaving against the sides of the taxis. There were two rows of taxis parked there. All the drivers were fighting.

The fists and what they held in the way of iron-mongery were doing a lot of damage. Two of the men were bent over, clasping their bellies in agony. There was blood on nearly all their faces, and the clothes of some of them had been torn off to the skin.

They fought on with appalling fury, taking no notice at all of the swelling crowd around them.

'They'll kill each other,' said a girl standing next to me, watching the scene in a mixture of horror and fasci-nation.

I glanced up over her head at the man standing on the other side of her, a big man well over six feet tall, with a deeply tanned skin. He was watching the fight with grim disapproval, his strong profile bleak, his eyes narrowed. I could not remember his name, though I had a feeling I ought to know it.

The crowd was growing uneasy, and began looking round for the police. The girl's remark was not idle. Any of the men might die, if they were unlucky, from the murderous chopping, gouging, and slogging, which showed no signs of abating.

The fight had caused a traffic jam in the car park. A policeman came, took a look, and disappeared fast for reinforcements. He returned with four constables on foot and one on horseback, all armed with truncheons. They plunged into the battle, but it took them several minutes to stop it.

More police arrived. The taxi-drivers were dragged

and herded into two groups. Both lots appeared to be equally battered, and neither side seemed to have won. The battlefield was strewn with caps and torn pieces of coats and shirts. Two shoes, one brown, one black, lay on their sides ten feet apart. Patches of blood stained the ground. The police began making a small pile of collected weapons.

The main excitement over, people began drifting away. The little knot of prospective customers for the taxis moved across to ask the policeman how long the drivers would be detained. The tall sunburned man who had been standing near me went over to join them.

One of the racing journalists paused beside me, scribbling busily in his notebook.

'Who is that very big man over there, John?' I asked him. He looked up and focused his eyes. 'His name's Tudor, I think. Owns a couple of horses. A newly arrived tycoon type. I don't know much about him. He doesn't look too pleased about the transport situation.'

Tudor, in fact, looked heavily angry, his lower jaw jutting forward obstinately. I was still sure there was something about this man which I ought to remember, but I did not know what. He was not having any success with the policeman, who was shaking his head. The taxis remained empty and driverless.

'What's it all about?' I asked the journalist.

'Gang warfare, my spies tell me,' he said cheerfully.

Five of the taxi-drivers were now lying flat out on

the cold damp ground. One of them groaned steadily.

The journalist said, 'Hospital and police station in about equal proportions, I should say. What a story!'

The man who was groaning rolled over and vomited.

'I'm going back to phone this lot through to the office,' said the journalist. 'Are you off home now?'

'I'm waiting for that wretched Joe Nantwich,' I said. 'I promised him a lift to Dorking, but I haven't seen a sign of him since the fourth race. It would be just like him to get a lift right home with someone else and forget to let me know.'

'The last I saw of him, he was having a few unfriendly words with Sandy in the gents, and getting the worst of it.'

'Those two really hate each other,' I said.

'Do you know why?'

'No idea. Have you?' I asked.

'No,' said the journalist. He smiled good-bye and went back into the racecourse towards the telephone.

Two ambulances drove up to collect the injured drivers. A policeman climbed into the back of each ambulance with them, and another sat in front beside the driver. With full loads the ambulances trundled slowly up the road to the main gates.

The remaining drivers began to shiver as the heat of the battle died out of them and the raw February afternoon took over. They were stiff and bruised, but unrepentant. A man in one group stepped forward, gave the other group a sneer, and spat, insultingly, on the ground in their direction. His shirt was in ribbons and his face was swelling in lumps. The muscles of his forearm would have done credit to a blacksmith, and silky dark hair grew low on his forehead in a widow's peak. A dangerous-looking man. A policeman touched his arm to bring him back into the group and he jumped round and snarled at him. Two more policemen began to close in, and the dark-haired man subsided angrily.

I was just giving Joe up when he came out of the gate and hailed me with no apology for his lateness. But I was not the only person to notice his arrival.

The tall dark Mr Tudor strode towards us.

'Nantwich, be so good as to give me a lift into Brighton, will you?' he said, authoritatively. 'As you can see, the taxis are out of action, and I have an important appointment in Brighton in twenty minutes.'

Joe looked at the taxi-drivers with vague eyes.

'What's happened?' he said.

'Never mind that now,' said Tudor impatiently. 'Where is your car?'

Joe looked at him blankly. His brain seemed to be working at half speed. He said, 'Oh – er – it isn't here, sir. I've got a lift.'

'With you?' said Tudor to me. I nodded. Joe, typically, had not introduced us.

'I'll be obliged if you will take me into Brighton,' said Tudor, briskly. 'I'll pay you the regular taxi fare.'

He was forceful and in a hurry. It would have been difficult to refuse to do him a favour so small to me, so clearly important to him.

'I'll take you for nothing,' I said, 'but you'll find it a bit of a squeeze. I have a two-seater sports car.'

'If it's too small for all of us, Nantwich can stay here and you can come back for him,' said Tudor in a firm voice. Joe showed no surprise, but I thought that the dark Mr Tudor was too practised at consulting no one's convenience but his own.

We skirted the groups of battered taxi-drivers, and threaded our way to my car. Tudor got in. He was so large that it was hopeless to try to wedge Joe in as well.

'I'll come back for you, Joe,' I said, stifling my irritation. 'Wait for me up on the main road.'

I climbed into the car, nosed slowly out of the car park, up the racecourse road, and turned out towards Brighton. There was too much traffic for the Lotus to show off the power of the purring Climax engine, and going along at a steady forty gave me time to concentrate on my puzzling passenger.

Glancing down as I changed gear, I saw his hand resting on his knees, the fingers spread and tense. And suddenly I knew where I had seen him before. It was his hand, darkly tanned, with the faint bluish tint under the finger-nails, that I knew.

He had been standing in the bar at Sandown with his back towards me and his hand resting flat on the

counter beside him, next to his glass. He had been talking to Bill; and I had waited there, behind him, not
wanting to interrupt their conversation. Then Tudor
finished his drink and left, and I had talked with Bill.

Now I glanced at his face.

'It's a great shame about Bill Davidson,' I said.

The brown hand jumped slightly on his knee. He
turned his head and looked at me while I drove.

'Yes, indeed it is.' He spoke slowly. 'I had been
hoping he would ride a horse for me at Cheltenham.'

'A great horseman,' I said.

'Yes indeed.'

'I was just behind him when he fell,' I said, and on
an impulse added, 'There are a great many questions to
be asked about it.'

I felt Tudor's huge body shift beside me. I knew
he was still looking at me, and I found his presence
overpowering. 'I suppose so,' he said. He hesitated, but
added nothing more. He looked at his watch.

'Take me to the Pavilion Plaza Hotel, if you please. I
have to attend a business meeting there,' he said.

'Is it near the Pavilion?' I asked.

'Fairly. I will direct you when we get there.' His tone
relegated me to the status of chauffeur.

We drove for some miles in silence. My passenger
sat apparently in deep thought. When we reached
Brighton he told me the way to the hotel.

'Thank you,' he said, without warmth, as he lifted his

bulk clumsily out of the low-slung car. He had an air of accepting considerable favours as merely his due, even when done him by complete strangers. He took two steps away from the car, then turned back and said, 'What is your name?'

'Alan York,' I said. 'Good afternoon.' I drove off without waiting for an answer. I could be brusque too. Glancing in the mirror I saw him standing on the pavement looking after me.

I went back to the racecourse.

Joe was waiting for me, sitting on the bank at the side of the road. He had some difficulty opening the car door, and he stumbled into his seat, muttering. He lurched over against me, and I discovered that Joe Nantwich was drunk.

The daylight was almost gone. I turned on the lights. I could think of pleasanter things to do than drive the twisty roads to Dorking with Joe breathing alcohol all over me. I sighed, and let in the clutch.

Joe was nursing a grievance. He would be. Everything which went wrong for Joe was someone else's fault, according to him. Barely twenty, he was a chronic grumbler. It was hard to know which was worse to put up with, his grousing or his bragging, and that he was treated with tolerance by the other jockeys said much for their good nature. Joe's saving grace was his undoubted ability as a jockey, but he had put that to bad use already by his 'stopping' activities, and now he was threatening it altogether by getting drunk in the middle of the afternoon.

'I would have won that race,' he whined.

'You're a fool, Joe,' I said.

'No, honestly, Alan, I would have won that race. I had him placed just right. I had the others beat, I had 'em stone cold. Just right.' He made sawing motions with his hands.

'You're a fool to drink so much at the races,' I said.

'Eh?' He couldn't focus.

'Drink,' I said. 'You've had too much to drink.'

'No, no, no, no . . .' The words came dribbling out, as if once he had started to speak it was too much effort to stop.

'Owners won't put you on their horses if they see you getting drunk,' I said, feeling it was no business of mine, after all.

'I can win any race, drunk or not,' said Joe.

'Not many owners would believe it.'

'They know I'm good.'

'So you are, but you won't be if you go on like this,' I said.

'I can drink and I can ride and I can ride and I can drink. If I want to.' He belched.

I let it pass. What Joe needed was a firm hand applied ten years ago. He looked all set now on the road to ruin and he wasn't going to thank anyone for directions off it.

74

He was whining again. 'That bloody Mason . . .'

I didn't say anything. He tried again.

'That bloody Sandy, he tipped me off. He bloody well tipped me off over the bloody rails. I'd have won that race as easy as kiss your hand and he knew it and tipped me off over the bloody rails.'

'Don't be silly, Joe.'

'You can't say I wouldn't have won the race,' said Joe argumentatively.

'And I can't say you would have won it,' I said. 'You fell at least a mile from home.'

'I didn't fall. I'm telling you, aren't I? Sandy bloody Mason tipped me off over the rails.'

'How?' I asked idly, concentrating on the road.

'He squeezed me against the rails. I shouted at him to give me more room. And do you know what he did? Do you know? He laughed. He bloody well laughed. Then he tipped me over. He stuck his knee into me and gave a heave and off I went over the bloody rails.' His whining voice finished on a definite sob.

I looked at him. Two tears were rolling down his round cheeks. They glistened in the light from the dashboard, and fell with a tiny flash on to the furry collar of his sheepskin coat.

'Sandy wouldn't do a thing like that,' I said mildly.

'Oh yes he would. He told me he'd get even with me. He said I'd be sorry. But I couldn't help it, Alan, I really couldn't.' Two more tears rolled down.

I was out of my depth. I had no idea what he was talking about; but it began to look as though Sandy, if he had unseated him, had had his reasons.

Joe went on talking. 'You're always decent to me, Alan, you're not like the others. You're my friend . . .' He put his hand heavily on my arm, pawing, leaning over towards me and giving me the benefit of the full force of his alcoholic breath. The delicate steering of the Lotus reacted to his sudden weight on my arm with a violent swerve towards the curb.

I shook him off. 'For God's sake sit up, Joe, or you'll have us in the ditch,' I said.

But he was too immersed in his own troubles to hear me. He pulled my arm again. There was a lay-by just ahead. I slowed, turned into it, and stopped the car.

'If you don't sit up and leave me alone you can get out and walk,' I said, trying to get through to him with a rough tone.

But he was still on his own track, and weeping noisily now.

'You don't know what it's like to be in trouble,' he sobbed. I resigned myself to listen. The quicker he got his resentments off his chest, I thought, the quicker he would relax and go to sleep.

'What trouble?' I said. I was not in the least interested.

'Alan, I'll tell you because you're a pal, a decent pal.' He put his hand on my knee. I pushed it off.

Amid a fresh burst of tears Joe blurted, 'I was supposed to stop a horse and I didn't, and Sandy lost a lot of money and said he'd get even with me and he's been following me around saying that for days and days and I knew he'd do something awful and he has.' He paused for breath. 'Lucky for me I hit a soft patch or I might have broken my neck. It wasn't funny. And that bloody Sandy,' he choked on the name, 'was laughing. I'll make him laugh on the other side of his bloody face.'

That last sentence made me smile. Joe with his baby face, strong of body perhaps, but weak of character, was no match for the tough, forceful Sandy, more than ten years older and incalculably more self-assured. Joe's bragging, like his whining, sprang from feelings of insecurity. But the beginning of his outburst was something different.

'What horse did you not stop?' I asked. 'And how did Sandy know you were supposed to be going to stop one?'

For a second I thought action would silence him, but after the smallest hesitation he babbled on. The drink was still at the flood. So were the tears.

From the self-pitying, hiccuping, half incoherent voice I learned a sorry enough story. Shorn of blasphemy and reduced to essentials, it was this. Joe had been paid well for stopping horses on several occasions, two of which I had seen myself. But when David Stampe had told his father the Senior Steward about the last one, and Joe had nearly lost his licence, it gave him a steadying shock. The next time he was asked to stop a horse he said he would, but in the event, from understandable nerves, he had not done it thoroughly enough early in the race, and at the finish was faced with the plain knowledge that if he lost the race he would lose his licence as well. He won. This had happened ten days ago.

I was puzzled. 'Is Sandy the only person who has harmed you?'

'He tipped me over the rails . . .' He was ready to start all over again.

I interrupted. 'It wasn't Sandy, surely, who was paying you not to win?'

'No, I don't think so. I don't know,' he snivelled.

'Do you mean you don't know who was paying you? Ever?'

'A man rang up and told me when he wanted me to stop one, and afterwards I got a packet full of money through the post.'

'How many times have you done it?' I asked.

'Ten,' said Joe, 'all in the last six months.' I stared at him.

'Often it was easy,' said Joe defensively. 'The —s wouldn't have won anyway, even if I'd helped them.'

'How much did you get for it?'

'A hundred. Twice it was two-fifty.' Joe's tongue was still running away with him, and I believed him. It was big money, and anyone prepared to pay on that scale would surely want considerable revenge when Joe won against orders. But Sandy? I couldn't believe it.

'What did Sandy say to you after you won?' I asked.

Joe was still crying. 'He said he'd backed the horse I beat and that he'd get even with me,' said Joe. And it seemed that Sandy had done that.

'You didn't get your parcel of money, I suppose?'

'No,' said Joe, sniffing.

'Haven't you any idea where they come from?' I asked.

'Some had London postmarks,' said Joe. 'I didn't take much notice.' Too eager to count the contents to look closely at the wrappings, no doubt.

'Well, I said, 'surely now that Sandy has had his little revenge, you are in the clear? Can't you possibly stop crying about it? It's all over. What are you in such a state about?'

For answer Joe took a paper from his jacket pocket and gave it to me.

'You might as well know it all. I don't know what to do. Help me, Alan. I'm frightened.'

In the light of the dashboard I could see that this was true. And Joe was beginning to sober up.

I unfolded the paper and switched on the lights inside the car. It was a single sheet of thin, ordinary typing paper. In simple capital letters, written with a

ball-point pen, were five words: BOLINGBROKE, YOU WILL
BE PUNISHED.

'Bolingbroke is the horse you were supposed to stop
and didn't?'

'Yes.' The tears no longer welled in his eyes.

'When did you get this?' I asked.

'I found it in my pocket, today, when I put my jacket
on after I'd changed. Just before the fifth race. It wasn't
there when I took it off.'

'And you spent the rest of the afternoon in the bar,
in a blue funk, I suppose,' I said.

'Yes . . . and I went back there while you took Mr
Tudor to Brighton. I didn't think anything was going to
happen to me because of Bolingbroke, and I've been
frightened ever since he won. And just as I was thinking
it was all right Sandy pushed me over the rails and then
I found this letter in my pocket. It isn't fair.' The self-
pity still whined in his voice.

I gave him back the paper.

'What am I to do?' said Joe.

I couldn't tell him, because I didn't know. He had
got himself into a thorough mess, and he had good
reason to be afraid. People who manipulated horses
and jockeys to that extent were certain to play rough.
The time lag of ten days between Bolingbroke's win
and the arrival of the note could mean, I thought, that
there was a cat-and-mouse, rather than a straight-

forward, mentality at work. Which was little comfort to offer Joe.

Apart from some convulsive hiccups and sniffs, Joe seemed to have recovered from his tears, and the worst of the drunkenness was over. I switched off the inside lights, started the car up, and pulled back on the road. As I had hoped, Joe soon went to sleep. He snored loudly.

Approaching Dorking, I woke him up. I had some questions to ask.

'Joe, who is that Mr Tudor I took to Brighton? He knows you.'

'He owns Bolingbroke,' said Joe. 'I often ride for him.'

I was surprised. 'Was he pleased when Bolingbroke won?' I asked.

'I suppose so. He wasn't there. He sent me ten per cent afterwards, though, and a letter thanking me. The usual thing.'

'He hasn't been in racing long, has he?' I asked.

'Popped up about the same time you did,' said Joe, with a distinct return to his old brash manner. 'Both of you arrived with dark sun-tans in the middle of winter.'

I had come by air from the burning African summer to the icy reception of October in England: but after eighteen months my skin was as pale as an Englishman's. Tudor's, on the other hand, remained dark.

Joe was sniggering. 'You know why Mr Clifford

bloody Tudor lives at Brighton? It gives him an excuse to be sunburnt all the year round. Touch of the old tar, really.'

After that I had no compunction in turning Joe out at the bus stop for Epsom. Unloading his troubles on me seemed, for the present at least, to have restored his ego.

I drove back to the Cotswolds. At first I thought about Sandy Mason and wondered how he had got wind of Joe's intention to stop Bolingbroke.

But for the last hour of the journey I thought about Kate.

CHAPTER SIX

Scilla was lying asleep on the sofa with a rug over her legs and a half-full glass on a low table beside her. I picked up the glass and sniffed. Brandy. She usually drank gin and Campari. Brandy was for bad days only.

She opened her eyes. 'Alan! I'm so glad you're back. What time is it?'

'Half past nine,' I said.

'You must be starving,' she said, pushing off the rug. 'Why ever didn't you wake me? Dinner was ready hours ago.'

'I've only just got here, and Joan is cooking now, so relax,' I said.

We went in to eat. I sat in my usual place. Bill's chair, opposite Scilla, was empty. I made a mental note to move it back against the wall.

Half way through the steaks, Scilla said, breaking a long silence, 'Two policemen came to see me today.'

'Did they? About the inquest tomorrow?'

'No, it was about Bill.' She pushed her plate away.

'They asked me if he was in any trouble, like you did. They asked me the same questions in different ways for over half an hour. One of them suggested that if I was as fond of my husband as I said I was and on excellent terms with him, I ought to know if something was wrong in his life. They were rather nasty, really.'

She was not looking at me. She kept her eyes down, regarding her half-eaten, congealing steak, and there was a slight embarrassment in her manner, which was unusual.

'I can imagine,' I said, realizing what was the matter. 'They asked you, I suppose, to explain your relationship with me, and why I was still living in your house?'

She glanced up in surprise and evident relief. 'Yes, they did. I didn't know how to tell you. It seems so ordinary to me that you should be here, yet I couldn't seem to make them understand that.'

'I'll go tomorrow, Scilla,' I said. 'I'm not letting you in for any more gossip. If the police can think that you were cheating Bill with me, so can the village and the county. I've been exceedingly thoughtless, and I'm very very sorry.' For I, too, had found it quite natural to stay on in Bill's house after his death.

'You will certainly not leave tomorrow on my account, Alan,' said Scilla with more resolution that I would have given her credit for. 'I need you here. I shall do nothing but cry all the time if I don't have you to talk to, especially in the evenings. I can get through the days, with the children and the house to think about. But the nights . . .' And in her suddenly ravaged face I could read all the tearing, savage pain of a loss four days old.

'I don't care what anyone says,' she said through starting tears, 'I need you here. Please, please, don't go away.'

'I'll stay,' I said. 'Don't worry. I'll stay as long as you want me to. But you must promise to tell me when you are ready for me to go.'

She dried her eyes and raised a smile. 'When I begin to worry about my reputation, you mean? I promise.'

I had driven the better part of three hundred miles besides riding in two races, and I was tired. We went to our beds early, Scilla promising to take her sleeping pills.

But at two o'clock in the morning she opened my bedroom door. I woke at once. She came over and switched on my bedside light, and sat down on my bed.

She looked ridiculously young and defenceless. She was wearing a pale blue knee-length chiffon nightdress which flowed transparently about her slender body and fell like mist over the small round breasts.

I propped myself up on my elbow and ran my fingers through my hair.

'I can't sleep,' she said.

'Did you take the pills?' I asked.

But I could answer my own question. Her eyes

looked drugged, and in her right mind she would not have come into my room so unrevealingly undressed.

'Yes, I took them. They've made me a bit groggy, but I'm still awake. I took an extra one.' Her voice was slurred and dopey. 'Will you talk for a bit?' she said. 'Then perhaps I'll feel more sleepy. When I'm on my own I just lie and think about Bill . . . Tell me more about Plumpton . . . You said you rode another horse . . . Tell me about it. Please. . . .'

So I sat up in bed and wrapped my eiderdown round her shoulders, and told her about Kate's birthday present and Uncle George, thinking how often I had told Polly and Henry and William bedside stories to send them to sleep. But after a while I saw she was not listening, and presently the slow heavy tears were falling from her bent head on to her hands.

'You must think me a terrible fool to cry so much,' she said, 'but I just can't help it.' She lay down weakly beside me, her head on my pillow. She took hold of my hand and closed her eyes. I looked down at her sweet, pretty face with the tears trickling past her ears into her cloudy dark hair, and gently kissed her forehead. Her body shook with two heavy sobs. I lay down and slid my arm under her neck. She turned towards me and clung to me, holding me fiercely, sobbing slowly with her deep terrible grief.

And at last, gradually, the sleeping pills did their job. She relaxed, breathing audibly, her hand twisted into the jacket of my pyjamas. She was lying half on top of the bedclothes, and the February night was cold. I tugged the sheet and blankets gently from underneath her with my free hand and spread them over her, and pulled the eiderdown up over our shoulders. I switched off the light and lay in the dark, gently cradling her until her breath grew soft and she was soundly asleep.

I smiled to think of Inspector Lodge's face if he could have seen us. And I reflected that I should not have been content to be so passive a bedfellow had I held Kate in my arms instead.

During the night Scilla twisted uneasily several times, murmuring jumbled words that made no sense, seeming to be calmed each time by my hand stroking her hair. Towards morning she was quiet. I got up, wrapped her in the eiderdown and carried her to her own bed. I knew that if she woke in my room, with the drugs worn off, she would be unnecessarily ashamed and upset.

She was still sleeping peacefully when I left her.

A few hours later, after a hurried breakfast, I drove her to Maidenhead to attend the inquest. She slept most of the way and did not refer to what had happened in the night. I was not sure she even remembered.

Lodge must have been waiting for us, for he met us as soon as we went in. He was carrying a sheaf of papers, and looked businesslike and solid. I introduced him to Scilla, and his eyes sharpened appreciatively at the sight of her pale prettiness. But what he said was a surprise.

'I'd like to apologize,' he began, 'for the rather unpleasant suggestions which have been put to you and Mr York about each other.' He turned to me. 'We are now satisfied that you were in no way responsible for Major Davidson's death.'

'That's big of you,' I said lightly, but I was glad to hear it.

Lodge went on, 'You can say what you like to the Coroner about the wire, of course, but I'd better warn you that he won't be too enthusiastic. He hates anything fancy, and you've no evidence. Don't worry if you don't agree with his verdict – I think it's sure to be accidental death – because inquests can always be reopened, if need be.'

In view of this I was not disturbed when the coroner, a heavily moustached man of fifty, listened keenly enough to my account of Bill's fall, but dealt a little brusquely with my wire theory. Lodge testified that he had accompanied me to the racecourse to look for the wire I had reported, but that there had been none there.

The man who had been riding directly behind me when Bill fell was also called. He was an amateur rider who lived in Yorkshire, and he'd had to come a long way. He said, with an apologetic glance for me, that he had seen nothing suspicious at the fence, and that in his opinion it was a normal fall. Unexpected maybe, but not mysterious. He radiated common sense.

Had Mr York, the Coroner enquired in a doubtful voice, mentioned the possible existence of wire to anyone at all on the day of the race? Mr York had not.

The Coroner, summing up medical, police, and all other evidence, found that Major Davidson had died of injuries resulting from his horse having fallen in a steeplechase. He was not convinced, he said, that the fall was anything but an accident.

Owing to a mistake about the time, the local paper had failed to send a representative to the inquest, and from lack of detailed reporting the proceedings rated only small paragraphs in the evening and morning papers. The word 'wire' was not mentioned. This omission did not worry me one way or the other, but Scilla was relieved. She said she could not yet stand questions from inquisitive friends, let alone reporters.

Bill's funeral was held quietly in the village on Friday morning, attended only by his family and close friends. Bearing one corner of his coffin on my shoulder and bidding my private good-byes, I knew for sure that I would not be satisfied until his death was avenged. I didn't know how it was to be done, and, strangely enough, I didn't feel any urgency about it. But in time, I promised him, in time, I'll do it.

Scilla's sister had come to the funeral and was to stay

with her for two or three days, so, missing lunch out of deference to the light weight I was committed to ride at on the following day, I drove up to London to spend some long overdue hours in the office, arranging the details of insurance and customs duty on a series of shipments of copper.

The office staff were experts. My job was to discuss with Hughes, my second in command, the day-to-day affairs of the company, to make decisions and agree to plans made by Hughes, and to sign my name to endless documents and letters. It seldom took me more than three days a week. On Sunday it was my weekly task to write to my father. I had a feeling he skipped the filial introduction and the accounts of my racing, and fastened his sharp brain only on my report of the week's trade and my assessment of the future.

Those Sunday reports had been part of my life for ten years. School homework could wait, my father used to say. It was more important for me to know every detail about the kingdom I was to inherit; and to this end he made me study continually the papers he brought home from his office. By the time I left school I could appraise at a glance the significance of fluctuations in the world prices of raw materials, even if I had no idea when Charles I was beheaded.

On Friday evening I waited impatiently for Kate to join me for dinner. Unwrapped from the heavy overcoat and woolly boots she had worn at Plumpton, she was more ravishing than ever. She wore a glowing red dress, simple and devastating, and her dark hair fell smoothly to her shoulders. She seemed to be alight from within with her own brand of effervescence. The evening was fun and, to me at least, entirely satisfactory. We ate, we danced, we talked.

While we swayed lazily round the floor to some dreamy slow-tempo music Kate introduced the only solemn note of the evening.

'I saw a bit about your friend's inquest in this morning's paper,' she said.

I brushed my lips against her hair. It smelled sweet. 'Accidental death,' I murmured vaguely. 'I don't think.'

'Hm?' Kate looked up.

'I'll tell you about it one day, when I know the whole story,' I said, enjoying the taut line of her neck as she tilted her face up to mine. It was strange, I thought, that it was possible to feel two strong emotions at once. Pleasure in surrendering to the seduction of the music with a dancing Kate balanced in my arms, and a tugging sympathy for Scilla trying to come to terms with her loneliness eighty miles away in the windy Cotswold hills.

'Tell me now,' said Kate with interest. 'If it wasn't accidental death, what was it?'

I hesitated. I didn't want too much reality pushing the evening's magic sideways.

'Come on, come on,' she urged, smiling. 'You can't stop here. I'll die of suspense.'

So I told her about the wire. It shocked her enough to stop her dancing, and we stood flat-footed in the middle of the floor with the other couples flowing round and bumping into us.

'Dear heavens,' she said, 'how . . . how wicked.'

She wanted me to explain why the inquest verdict had been what it was, and after I had told her that with the wire gone there was no evidence of anything else, she said, 'I can't bear to think of anyone getting away with so disgusting a trick.'

'Nor can I,' I said, 'and they won't, I promise you, if I can help it.'

'That's good,' she said seriously. She began to sway again to the music, and I took her in my arms and we drifted back into the dance. We didn't mention Bill again.

It seemed to me for long periods that evening as if my feet were not in proper contact with the floor, and the most extraordinary tremors constantly shook my knees. Kate seemed to notice nothing: she was friendly, funny, brimming over with gaiety, and utterly unsentimental.

When at length I helped her into the chauffeur-driven car which Uncle George had sent up from Sussex to take her home, I had discovered how painful it is to love. I was excited, keyed up. And also anxious;

for I was sure that she did not feel as intensely about me as I about her.

I already knew I wanted to marry Kate. The thought that she might not have me was a bitter one.

The next day I went to Kempton Park races. Outside the weighing room I ran into Dane. We talked about the going, the weather, Pete's latest plans for us, and the horses. Usual jockey stuff. Then Dane said, 'You took Kate out last night?'

'Yes.'

'Where did you go?'

'The River Club,' I said. 'Where did you take her?'

'Didn't she tell you?' asked Dane.

'She said to ask you.'

'River Club,' said Dane.

'Damn it,' I said. But I had to laugh.

'Honours even,' said Dane.

'Did she ask you down to stay with Uncle George?' I asked suspiciously.

'I'm going today, after the races,' said Dane, smiling. 'And you?'

'Next Saturday,' I said gloomily. 'You know, Dane, she's teasing us abominably.'

'I can stand it,' said Dane. He tapped me on the shoulder. 'Don't look so miserable, it may never happen.'

'That's what I'm afraid of,' I sighed. He laughed and went into the weighing room.

It was an uneventful afternoon. I rode my big black mare in a novice 'chase and Dane beat me by two lengths. At the end of the day we walked out to the car park together.

'How is Mrs Davidson bearing up?' Dane asked.

'Fairly well, considering the bottom has dropped out of her world.'

'Jockeys' wives' nightmare come true.'

'Yes,' I said.

'It makes you pause a bit, before you ask a girl to put up with that sort of constant worry,' said Dane, thoughtfully.

'Kate?' I asked. He looked round sharply and grinned.

'I suppose so. Do you mind?'

'Yes,' I said, keeping my voice light. 'I mind very much.'

We came to his car first, and he put his race glasses and hat on the seat. His suitcase was in the back.

'So long, mate,' he said. 'I'll keep you posted.'

I watched him drive off, answered his wave. I seldom felt envious of anybody, but at that moment I envied Dane sorely.

I climbed into the Lotus and pointed its low blue nose towards home.

It was on the road through Maidenhead Thicket that I saw the horse-box. It was parked in a lay-by on the near side, with tools scattered on the ground round it and the bonnet up. It was facing me as I approached, as if it had broken down on its way into Maidenhead. A man was walking a horse up and down in front of it.

The driver, standing by the bonnet scratching his head, saw me coming and gestured me to stop. I pulled up beside him. He walked round to talk to me through the window, a middle-aged man, unremarkable, wearing a leather jacket.

'Do you know anything about engines, sir?' he asked.

'Not as much as you, I should think,' I said, smiling. He had grease on his hands. If a horse-box driver couldn't find the fault in his own motor, it would be a long job for whoever did. 'I'll take you back into Maidenhead, though, if you like. There's bound to be someone there who can help you.'

'That's extremely kind of you, sir,' he said, civilly. 'Thank you very much. But – er – I'm in a bit of a difficulty.' He looked into the car and saw my binoculars on the seat beside me. His face lightened up. 'You don't possibly know anything about horses, sir?'

'A bit, yes,' I said.

'Well, it's like this, sir. I've got these two horses going to the London docks. They're being exported. Well, that one's all right.' He pointed to the horse walking up and down. 'But the other one, he don't seem so good. Sweating hard, he's been, the last hour or so, and biting at his stomach. He keeps trying to lie down. Looks ill.

The lad's in there with him now, and he's proper worried, I can tell you.'

'It sounds as though it might be colic,' I said. 'If it is, he ought to be walking round, too. It's the only way to get him better. It's essential to keep them on the move when they've got colic.'

The driver looked troubled. 'It's a lot to ask, sir,' he said, tentatively, 'but would you have a look at him? Motors are my fancy, not horses, except to back 'em. And these lads are not too bright. I don't want a rocket from the boss for not looking after things properly.'

'All right,' I said, 'I'll have a look. But I'm not a vet, you know, by a long way.'

He smiled in a relieved fashion. 'Thank you, sir. Anyway, you'll know if I've got to get a vet at once or not, I should think.'

I parked the car in the lay-by behind the horse-box. The door at the back of the horse-box opened and a hand, the stable lad's, I supposed, reached out to help me up. He took me by the wrist.

He didn't leave go.

There were three men waiting for me inside the horse-box. And no horse, sick or otherwise. After a flurried ten seconds during which my eyes were still unused to the dim light, I ended up standing with my back to the end post of one of the partition walls.

The horse-box was divided into three stalls with two partition walls between them, and there was a space across the whole width of the box at the back, usually occupied by lads travelling with their horses.

Two of the men held my arms. They stood on each side of the partition and slightly behind me, and they had an uncomfortable leverage on my shoulders. The post of the partition was padded with matting, as it always is in racehorse boxes, to save the horses hurting themselves while they travel. The mattress tickled my neck.

The driver stepped up into the box and shut the door. His manner, still incredibly deferential, held a hint of triumph. It was entitled to. He had set a neat trap.

'Very sorry to have to do this, sir,' he said politely. It was macabre.

'If it's money you want,' I said, 'you're going to be unlucky. I don't bet much and I didn't have a good day at the races today. I'm afraid you've gone to a lot of trouble for a measly eight quid.'

'We don't want your money, sir,' he said. 'Though as you're offering it we might as well take it, at that.' And still smiling pleasantly he put his hand inside my jacket and took my wallet out of the inside pocket.

I kicked his shin as hard as I could, but was hampered because of my position against the post. As soon as they felt me move the two men behind me jerked my arms painfully backwards.

'I shouldn't do that, sir, if I was you,' said the friendly

driver, rubbing his leg. He opened my wallet and took out the money, which he folded carefully and stowed inside his leather coat. He peered at the other things in the wallet, then stepped towards me, and put it back in my pocket. He was smiling, faintly.

I stood still.

'That's better,' he said, approvingly.

'What's all this about?' I asked. I had some idea that they intended to ransom me to my distant millionaire parent. Along the lines of 'Cable us ten thousand pounds or we post your son back to you in small pieces.' That would mean that they knew all along who I was, and had not just stopped any random motorist in a likely-looking car to rob him.

'Surely you know, sir?' said the driver.

'I've no idea.'

'I was asked to give you a message, Mr York.'

So he did know who I was. And he had not this minute discovered it from my wallet, which contained only money, stamps, and a cheque book in plain view. One or two things with my name on were in a flapped pocket, but he had not looked there.

'What makes you think my name is York?' I asked, trying a shot at outraged surprise. It was no good.

'Mr Alan York, sir, was scheduled to drive along this road on his way from Kempton Park to the Cotswolds at approximately five fifteen p.m. on Saturday, February 27th, in a dark blue Lotus Elite, licence number KAB

890. I must thank you, sir, for making it easy for me to intercept you. You could go a month on the road without seeing another car like yours. I'd have had a job flagging you down if you'd been driving, say, a Ford or an Austin.' His tone was still conversational.

'Get on with your message. I'm listening,' I said.

'Deeds speak louder than words,' said the driver, mildly.

He came close and unbuttoned my jacket, looking at me steadily with wide eyes, daring me to kick him. I didn't move. He untied my tie, opened the neck of my shirt. We looked into each other's eyes. I hoped mine were as expressionless as his. I let my arms go slack in the grip of the two men behind me, and felt them relax their hold slightly.

The driver stepped back and looked towards the fourth man, who had been leaning against the horse-box wall, silently. 'He's all yours, Sonny. Deliver the message,' he said.

Sonny was young, with sideboards. But I didn't look at his face, particularly. I looked at his hands.

He had a knife. The hilt lay in his palms, and his fingers were lightly curled round it, not gripping. The way a professional holds a knife.

There was nothing of the driver's mock deference in Sonny's manner. He was enjoying his work. He stood squarely in front of me and put the point of his short blade on my breastbone. It scarcely pricked, so light was his touch.

Oh bloody hell, I thought. My father would not be at all pleased to receive ransom messages reinforced by pleas from me for my own safety. I would never be able to live it down. And I was sure that this little melodrama was intended to soften me up into a suitably frightened state of mind. I sagged against the post, as if to shrink away from the knife, Sonny's grim mouth smiled thinly in a sneer.

Using the post as a springboard I thrust forwards and sideways as strongly as I knew how, bringing my knee up hard into Sonny's groin and tearing my arms out of the slackened grasp of the men behind me.

I leaped for the door and got it open. In the small area of the horse-box I had no chance, but I thought that if only I could get out into the thicket I might be able to deal with them. I had learned a nasty trick or two about fighting from my cousin, who lived in Kenya and had taken lessons from the Mau Mau.

But I didn't make it.

I tried to swing out with the door, but it was stiff and slow. The driver grabbed my ankle. I shook his hand off, but the vital second had gone. The two men who had held me clutched at my clothes. Through the open door I glimpsed the man who had been leading the horse up and down. He was looking enquiringly at the horse-box. I had forgotten about him.

I lashed out furiously with feet, fists and elbows, but they were too much for me. I ended up where I began, against the matting-padded post with my arms pulled backwards. This time the two men were none too gentle. They slammed me back against the post hard and put their weight on my arms. I felt the wrench in my shoulders and down my chest to my stomach. I shut my teeth.

Sonny, clutching his abdomen, was half sitting, half kneeling in the corner. He watched with satisfaction.

'That hurt the bastard, Peaky,' he said. 'Do it again.'

Peaky and his mate did it again.

Sonny laughed. Not a nice laugh.

A little more pressure and I should have some torn ligaments and a dislocated shoulder. There didn't seem to be much I could do about it.

The driver shut the horse-box door and picked the knife up from the floor, where it had fallen. He was not looking quite so calm as before. My fist had connected with his nose and blood was trickling out of it. But his temper was intact.

'Stop it. Stop it, Peaky,' he said. 'The boss said we weren't to hurt him. He made quite a point of it. You wouldn't want the boss to know you disobeyed him, would you?' There was a threat in his voice.

The tension on my arms slowly relaxed. Sonny's smile turned to a sullen scowl. It appeared I had the boss to thank for something, even if not much.

'Now, Mr York,' said the driver reproachfully, wiping his nose on a blue handkerchief, 'all that was quite unnecessary. We only want to give you a message.'

'I don't like listening with knives sticking into me,' I said.

The driver sighed. 'Yes, sir, I can see that was a mistake. It was meant for you to understand that the warning is serious, see. Take no notice of it, and you'll find you're in real trouble. I'm telling you, real trouble.'

'What warning?' I said, mystified.

'You're to lay off asking questions about Major Davidson,' he said.

'*What?*' I goggled at him. It was so unexpected. 'I haven't been asking questions about Major Davidson,' I said weakly.

'I don't know about that, I'm sure,' said the driver, mopping away, 'but that's the message, and you'd do well to take heed of it, sir. I'm telling you for your own good. The boss don't like people poking into his affairs.'

'Who is the boss?' I asked.

'Now, sir, you know better than to ask questions like that. Sonny, go and tell Bert we've finished here. We'll load up the horse.'

Sonny stood up with a groan and went over to the door, his hand still pressed to his groin. He yelled something out of the window.

'Stand still, Mr York, and you'll come to no harm,' said the driver, his politeness unimpaired. He mopped, and looked at his handkerchief to see if his nose was still bleeding. It was. I took his advice, and stood still. He opened the door and climbed down out of the horse-box. A little time passed during which Sonny and I exchanged glares and nobody said anything.

Then there was the noise of bolts and clips being undone, and the side of the horse-box which formed the ramp was lowered to the ground. The fifth man, Bert, led the horse up the ramp and fastened him into the nearest stall. The driver raised the ramp again and fastened it.

I used the brief period while what was left of the daylight flooded into the box, to twist my head round as far as I could and take a clear look at Peaky. I saw what I expected, but it only increased my bewilderment.

The driver climbed into the cab, shut the door, and started the engine.

Bert said, 'Take him over to the door.' I needed no urging.

The horse-box began to move. Bert opened the door. Peaky and his pal let go of my arms and Bert gave me a push. I hit the ground just as the accelerating horse-box pulled out of the lay-by on to the deserted road. It was as well I had had a good deal of practice at falling off horses. Instinctively, I landed on my shoulder and rolled.

I sat on the ground and looked after the speeding

horse-box. The number plate was mostly obscured by thick dust, but I had time to see the registration letters. They were APX.

The Lotus still stood in the lay-by. I picked myself up, dusted the worst off my suit, and walked over to it. I intended to follow the horse-box and see where it went. But the thorough driver had seen to it that I should not. The car would not start. Opening the bonnet to see how much damage had been done, I found that three of the four sparking plugs had been taken out. They lay in a neat row on the battery. It took me ten minutes to replace them, because my hands were trembling.

By then I had no hope of catching the horse-box or of finding anyone who had noticed its direction. I got back into the car and fastened the neck of my shirt. My tie was missing altogether.

I took out the AA book and looked up the registration letters PX. For what it was worth, the horse-box was originally registered in West Sussex. If the number plate were genuine, it might be possible to discover the present owner. For a quarter of an hour I sat and thought. Then I started the car, turned it, and drove back into Maidenhead.

The town was bright with lights, though nearly all the shops were shut. The door of the police station was open wide. I went in and asked for Inspector Lodge.

'He isn't in yet,' said the policeman at the enquiry

desk, glancing up at the clock. It was ten past six. 'He'll be here any minute, if you care to wait, sir.'

'He isn't in yet? Do you mean he is just starting work for the day?'

'Yes, sir. He's on late turn. Busy evening here, Saturday,' he grinned. 'Dance halls, pubs, and car crashes.' I smiled back, sat down on the bench and waited. After five minutes Lodge came in quickly, peeling off his coat.

'Evening, Small, what's new?' he said to the policeman at the enquiry desk.

'Gentleman here to see you, sir,' said Small, gesturing to me. 'He's only been waiting a few minutes.'

Lodge turned round. I stood up. 'Good evening,' I said.

'Good evening, Mr York.' Lodge gave me a piercing look but showed no surprise at seeing me. His eyes fell to the neck of my shirt, and his eyebrows rose a fraction. But he said only, 'What can I do for you?'

'Are you very busy?' I asked. 'If you have time, I would like to tell you . . . how I lost my tie.' In mid-sentence I funked saying baldly that I had been man-handled. As it was, Small looked at me curiously, clearly thinking me mad to come into a police station to tell an inspector how I lost my tie.

But Lodge, whose perception was acute, said, 'Come into my office, Mr York.' He led the way. He hung up his hat and coat on pegs and lit the gas fire, but its glowing bars couldn't make a cosy place of the austere, square, filing-cabineted little room.

Lodge sat behind his tidy desk, and I, as before, faced him. He offered me a cigarette and gave me a light. As the smoke went comfortingly down into my lungs, I was wondering where to begin.

I said, 'Have you got any further with the Major Davidson business since the day before yesterday?'

'No, I'm afraid not. It no longer has any sort of priority with us. Yesterday we discussed it in conference and consulted your Senior Steward, Sir Creswell Stampe. In view of the verdict at the inquest, your story is considered, on the whole, to be the product of a youthful and overheated imagination. No one but you saw any wire. The grooves on the posts of the fence may or may not have been caused by wire, but there is no indication *when* they were made. I understand it is fairly common practice for groundsmen to raise a wire across a fence so that members of the riding public shall not try to jump it and make holes in the birch.' He paused, then went on, 'Sir Creswell says the view of the National Hunt Committee, several of whom he has talked to on the telephone, is that you made a mistake. If you saw any wire, they contend, it must have belonged to the groundsman.'

'Have they asked him?' I said.

Lodge sighed. 'The head groundsman says he didn't leave any wire on the course, but one of his staff is old and vague, and can't be sure that he didn't.'

We looked at each other in glum silence.

'And what do you think, yourself?' I asked finally.

Lodge said, 'I believe you saw the wire and that Major Davidson was brought down by it. There is one fact which I personally consider significant enough to justify this belief. It is that the attendant who gave his name as Thomas Cook did not collect the pay due to him for two days' work. In my experience there has to be a very good reason for a workman to ignore his pay packet.' He smiled sardonically.

'I could give you another fact to prove that Major Davidson's fall was no accident,' I said, 'but you'll have to take my word for it again. No evidence.'

'Go on.'

'Someone has been to great pains to tell me not to ask awkward questions about it.' I told him about the events in and around the horse-box, and added, 'And how's that for the product of a youthful and overheated imagination?'

'When did all this happen?' asked Lodge.

'About an hour ago.'

'And what were you doing between then and the time you arrived here?'

'Thinking,' I said, stubbing out my cigarette.

'Oh,' said Lodge. 'Well, have you given any thought to the improbabilities in your story? My chief isn't going to like them when I make my report.'

'Don't make it then,' I said, smiling. 'But I suppose

the most glaring improbability is that five men, a horse, and a horse-box should all be employed to give a warning which might much more easily have been sent by post.'

'That certainly indicates an organization of unusual size,' said Lodge, with a touch of irony.

'There are at least ten of them,' I said. 'One or two probably in hospital, though.'

Lodge sat up straighter.

'What do you mean? How do you know?'

'The five men who stopped me today are all taxi-drivers. Either from London or Brighton, but I don't know which. I saw them at Plumpton races three days ago, fighting a pitched battle against a rival gang.'

'What?' Lodge exclaimed. Then he said, 'Yes, I saw a paragraph about it in a newspaper. Do you recognize them positively?'

'Yes,' I said. 'Sonny had his knife out at Plumpton, too, but he was pinned down by a big heavy man, and didn't get much chance to use it. But I saw his face quite clearly. Peaky you couldn't mistake, with that dark widow's peak growing down his forehead. The other three were all rounded up into the same group at Plumpton. I was waiting to give someone a lift, and I had a long time to look at the taxi-drivers after the fight was over. Bert, the man with the horse, had a black eye today, and the man who held my right arm, whose name I don't know, he had some sticking plaster on his forehead. But why were they all free? The last I saw of them, they were bound for the cells, I thought, for disturbing the peace.'

'They may be out on bail, or else they were let off with a fine. I don't know, without seeing a report,' said Lodge. 'Now why, in your opinion, were so many sent to warn you?'

'Rather flattering, sending five, when you come to think of it,' I grinned. 'Perhaps the taxi business is in the doldrums and they hadn't anything else to do. Or else it was, like the driver said, to ram the point home.'

'Which brings me,' said Lodge, 'to another improbability. Why, if you were faced with a knife at your chest, did you throw yourself forward? Wasn't that asking for trouble?'

'I wouldn't have been so keen if he'd held the point a bit higher up; but it was against my breast bone. You'd need a hammer to get a knife through that. I reckoned that I'd knock it out of Sonny's hand rather than into me, and that's what happened.'

'Didn't it cut you at all?'

'Not much,' I said.

'Let's see,' said Lodge, getting up and coming round the desk.

I opened my shirt again. Between the second and third buttons there was a shallow cut an inch or so long in the skin over my breastbone. Some blood had clotted on the cut and there was a dried rusty trail down my chest where a few drops had run. My shirt was spotted here and there. Nothing. I hadn't felt it much.

Lodge sat down again. I buttoned my shirt.

'Now,' he said, picking up his pen and biting the end of it. 'What questions have you been asking about Major Davidson, and of whom have you asked them?'

'That is really what is most surprising about the whole affair,' I said. 'I've hardly asked anything of anybody. And I certainly haven't had any useful answers.'

'But you must have touched a nerve somewhere,' said Lodge. He took a sheet of paper out of the drawer. 'Tell me the names of everyone with whom you have discussed the wire.'

'With you,' I said promptly. 'And with Mrs Davidson. And everyone at the inquest heard me say I'd found it.'

'But I noticed that the inquest wasn't properly reported in the papers. There was no mention of wire in the press,' he said. 'And anyone seeing you at the inquest wouldn't have got the impression that you were hell-bent on unravelling the mystery. You took the verdict very calmly and not at all as if you disagreed with it.'

'Thanks to your warning me in advance what to expect,' I said.

Lodge's list looked short and unsatisfactory on the large sheet of paper.

'Anyone else?' he said.

'Oh . . . a friend . . . a Miss Ellery-Penn. I told her last night.'

'Girl friend?' he asked bluntly. He wrote her down.

'Yes,' I said.

'Anyone else?'

'No.'

'Why not?' he asked, pushing the paper away.

'I reckoned you and Sir Creswell needed a clear field. I thought I might mess things up for you if I asked too many questions. Put people on their guard, ready with their answers – that sort of thing. But it seems, from what you've said about dropping your enquiries, that I might as well have gone ahead.' I spoke a little bitterly.

Lodge looked at me carefully. 'You resent being considered youthful and hot-headed,' he said.

'Twenty-four isn't young,' I said. 'I seem to remember England once had a Prime Minister of that age. He didn't do so badly.'

'That's irrelevant, and you know it,' he said.

I grinned.

Lodge said, 'What do you propose to do now?'

'Go home,' I said, looking at my watch.

'No, I meant about Major Davidson.'

'Ask as many questions as I can think of,' I said promptly.

'In spite of the warning?'

'Because of it,' I said. 'The very fact that five men were sent to warn me off means that there is a good deal to find out. Bill Davidson was a good friend, you know. I can't tamely let whoever caused his death get away with it.' I thought a moment. 'First, I'll find out who owns the taxis which Peaky and Co. drive.'

'Well, unofficially, I wish you luck,' said Lodge. 'But be careful.'

'Sure,' I said standing up.

Lodge came to the street door of the police station and shook hands. 'Let me know how you get on,' he said.

'Yes, I will.'

He raised his hand in a friendly gesture, and went in. I resumed my interrupted journey to the Cotswolds. My wrenched shoulders were aching abominably, but as long as I concentrated on Bill's accident I could forget them.

It struck me that both the accident and the affair of the horse-box should give some clue to the mind which had hatched them. It was reasonable to assume it was the same mind. Both events were elaborate, where some simpler plan would have been effective, and the word 'devious' drifted into my thoughts and I dredged around in my memory chasing its echo. Finally I traced it to Joe Nantwich and the threatening letter which had reached him ten days late, but decided that Joe's troubles had nothing to do with Bill's.

Both the attack on Bill and the warning to me had been, I was certain, more violent in the event than in the plan. Bill had died partly by bad luck, and I would have been less roughly handled had I not tried to escape. I came to the conclusion that I was looking for someone with a fanciful imagination, someone prepared to be brutal up to a point, and whose little squibs, because of their complicated nature, were apt to go off with bigger bangs than were intended.

And it was comforting to realize that my adversary was not a man of superhuman intelligence. He could make mistakes. His biggest so far, I thought, was to go to great lengths to deliver an unnecessary warning whose sole effect was to stir me to greater action.

For two days I did nothing. There was no harm in giving the impression that the warning was being taken to heart.

I played poker with the children and lost to Henry because half my mind was occupied with his father's affairs.

Henry said, 'You aren't thinking what you're doing, Alan,' in a mock sorrowful tone as he rooked me of ten chips with two pairs.

'I expect he's in love,' said Polly, turning on me an assessing female eye. There was that, too.

'Pooh,' said Henry. He dealt the cards.

'What's in love?' said William, who was playing tiddly-winks with his chips, to Henry's annoyance.

'Soppy stuff,' said Henry. 'Kissing, and all that slush.'

'Mummy's in love with me,' said William, a cuddly child.

'Don't be silly,' said Polly loftily, from her eleven years. 'In love means weddings and brides and confetti and things.'

'Well, Alan,' said Henry, in a scornful voice, 'you'd better get out of love quick or you won't have any chips left.'

William picked up his hand. His eyes and mouth opened wide. This meant he had at least two aces. They were the only cards he ever raised on. I saw Henry give him a flick of a glance, then look back at his own hand. He discarded three and took three more, and at his turn, he pushed away his cards. I turned them over. Two queens and two tens. Henry was a realist. He knew when to give in. And William, bouncing up and down with excitement, won only four chips with three aces and a pair of fives.

Not for the first time I wondered at the quirks of heredity. Bill had been a friendly, genuine man of many solid virtues. Scilla, matching him, was compassionate and loving. Neither was at all intellectually gifted; yet they had endowed their elder son with a piercing, exceptional intelligence.

And how could I guess, as I cut the cards for Polly and helped William straighten up his leaning tower of chips, that Henry already held in his sharp eight-year-old brain the key to the puzzle of his father's death.

He didn't know it himself.

CHAPTER SEVEN

The Cheltenham National Hunt Festival meeting
started on Tuesday, 2 March.

Three days of superlative racing lay ahead, and the
finest 'chasers in the world crowded into the racecourse
stables. Ferries from Ireland brought them across by
boat and plane load; dark horses from the bogs whose
supernatural turn of foot was foretold in thick mysterious brogue, and golden geldings who had already
taken prizes and cups galore across the Irish Sea.

Horse-boxes from Scotland, from Kent, from Devon,
from everywhere, converged on Gloucestershire.
Inside, they carried Grand National winners, champion
hurdlers, all-conquering handicappers, splendid hunters: the aristocrats among jumpers.

With four big races in the three days reserved for
them alone, every amateur jockey in the country who
could beg, borrow, or buy a mount hurried to the
course. A ride at Cheltenham was an honour: a win at
Cheltenham an experience never to be forgotten. The

amateur jockeys embraced the Festival with passionate fervour.

But one amateur jockey, Alan York, felt none of this passionate fervour as he drove into the car park. I could not explain it to myself, but for once the hum of the gathering crowd, the expectant faces, the sunshine of the cold invigorating March morning, even the prospect of riding three good horses at the meeting, stirred me not at all.

Outside the main gate I sought out the newspaper seller I had spoken to at Plumpton. He was a short, tubby little Cockney with a large moustache and a cheerful temperament. He saw me coming, and held out a paper.

'Morning, Mr York,' he said. 'Do you fancy your horse today?'

'You might have a bit on,' I said, 'but not your shirt. There's the Irishman to be reckoned with.'

'You'll do him, all right.'

'Well, I hope so.' I waited while he sold a newspaper to an elderly man with enormous race glasses. Then I said, 'Do you remember the taxi-drivers fighting at Plumpton?'

'Couldn't hardly forget it, could I?' He beamed.

'You told me one lot came from London and one from Brighton.'

'Yes, that's right.'

'Which lot were which?' I said. He looked mystified.

I said, 'Which lot came from London and which came from Brighton?'

'Oh, I see.' He sold a paper to two middle-aged ladies wearing thick tweeds and ribbed woollen stockings, and gave them change. Then he turned back to me.

'Which lot was which, like? Hm . . . I see 'em often enough, you know, but they ain't a friendly lot. They don't talk to you. Not like the private chauffeurs, see? I'd know the Brighton lot if I could see 'em, though. Know 'em by sight, see?' He broke off to yell 'Midday Special' at the top of his lungs, and as a result sold three more papers. I waited patiently.

'How do you recognize them?' I asked.

'By their faces, o'course.' He thought it a foolish question.

'Yes, but which faces? Can you describe them?'

'Oh, I see. There's all sorts.'

'Can't you describe just one of them?' I asked.

He narrowed his eyes, thinking, and tugged his moustache. 'One of 'em. Well, there's one nasty-looking chap with sort of slitty eyes. I wouldn't like a ride in his taxi. You'd know him by his hair, I reckon. It grows nearly down to his eyebrows. Rum-looking cove. What do you want him for?'

'I don't want him,' I said. 'I just want to know where he comes from.'

'Brighton, that's it.' He beamed at me. 'There's

another one I see sometimes, too. A young ted with sideboards, always cleaning his nails with a knife.'

'Thanks a lot,' I said. I gave him a pound note and his beam grew wider. He tucked it into an inside pocket.

'Best of luck, sir,' he said. I left him, with 'Midday Special' ringing in my ears, and went in to the weighing room, pondering on the information that my captors with the horse-box came from Brighton. Whoever had sent them could not have imagined that I had seen them before, and could find them again.

Preoccupied, I suddenly realized that Pete Gregory was talking to me. '. . . Had a puncture on the way, but they've got here safely, that's the main thing. Are you listening, Alan?'

'Yes, Pete. Sorry. I was thinking.'

'Glad to hear you can,' said Pete with a fat laugh. Tough and shrewd though he was, his sense of humour had never grown up. Schoolboy insults passed as the highest form of wit for him; but one got used to it.

'How is Palindrome?' I asked. My best horse.

'He's fine. I was just telling you, they had a puncture . . .' He broke off, exasperated. He hated having to repeat things. 'Oh well . . . do you want to go over to the stables and have a look at him?'

'Yes, please,' I said.

We walked down to the stables. Pete had to come with me because of the tight security rules. Even owners could not visit their horses without the trainer to vouch for them, and stable boys had passes with their photographs on, to show at the stable gate. It was all designed to prevent the doping or 'nobbling' of horses.

In his box I patted my beautiful 'chaser, an eight-year-old bay with black points, and gave him a lump of sugar. Pete clicked his tongue disapprovingly and said, 'Not before the race,' like a nanny who had caught her charge being given sweets before lunch. I grinned. Pete had a phobia on the subject.

'Sugar will give him more energy,' I said, giving Palindrome another lump and making a fuss of him. 'He looks well.'

'He ought to win if you judge it right,' said Pete. 'Keep your eyes on that Irishman, Barney. He'll try to slip you all with a sudden burst as you go into the water so that he can start up the hill six lengths in front. I've seen him do it time and again. He gets everyone else chasing him like mad up the hill using up all the reserves they need for the finish. Now, either you burst with him, and go up the hill at his pace and no faster, or, if you lose him, take it easy up the hill and pile on the pressure when you're coming down again. Clear?'

'As glass,' I said. Whatever one might think of Pete's jokes, his advice on how to ride races was invaluable, and I owed a great deal to it.

I gave Palindrome a final pat, and we went out into the yard. Owing to the security system, it was the quietest place on the racecourse.

'Pete, was Bill in any trouble, do you know?' I said, plunging in abruptly.

He finished shutting the door of Palindrome's box, and turned round slowly, and stood looking at me vaguely for so long that I began to wonder if he had heard my question.

But at last he said, 'That's a big word, trouble. Something happened . . .'

'What?' I said, as he lapsed into silence again.

But instead of answering, he said, 'Why should you think there was any . . . trouble?'

I told him about the wire. He listened with a calm, unsurprised expression, but his grey eyes were bleak.

He said, 'Why haven't we all heard about it before?'

'I told Sir Creswell Stampe and the police a week ago,' I said, 'but with the wire gone they've nothing tangible to go on, and they're dropping it.'

'But you're not?' said Pete. 'Can't say I blame you. I can't help you much, though. There's only one thing . . . Bill told me he'd had a telephone call which made him laugh. But I didn't listen properly to what he said – I was thinking about my horses, you know how it is. It was something about Admiral falling. He thought it was a huge joke and I didn't go into it with him to find out what I'd missed. I didn't think it was important. When Bill was killed I did wonder if there could possibly be anything odd about it, but I asked you, and you said you hadn't noticed anything . . .' His voice trailed off.

121

'Yes, I'm sorry,' I said. Then I asked, 'How long before his accident did Bill tell you about the telephone call?'

'The last time I spoke to him,' Pete said. 'It was on the Friday morning just before I flew to Ireland. I rang him to say that all was ready for Admiral's race at Maidenhead the next day.'

We began to walk back to the weighing room. On an impulse I said, 'Pete, do you ever use the Brighton taxis?' He lived and trained on the Sussex Downs.

'Not often,' he said. 'Why?'

'There are one or two taxi-drivers there I'd like to have a few words with,' I said, not adding that I'd prefer to have the words with them one at a time in a deserted back alley.

'There are several taxi lines in Brighton, as far as I know,' he said. 'If you want to find one particular driver, why don't you try the railway station? That's where I've usually taken a taxi from. They line up there in droves for the London trains.' His attention drifted off as an Irish horse passed us on its way into the paddock for the first race.

'That's Connemara Pal or I'm a Dutchman,' said Pete enviously. 'I took one of my owners over and tried to buy him, last August, but they wanted eight thousand for him. He was tucked away in a broken-down hut behind some pigsties, so my owner wouldn't pay that price. And now look at him. He won the Leopardstown novice 'chase on Boxing Day by twenty lengths and would have blown a candle out afterwards. Best young horse we'll see this year.' Pete's mind was firmly back in its familiar groove, and we talked about the Irish raid until we were back in the weighing room.

I sought out Clem, who was very busy, and checked with him that my kit was all right, and that he knew the weight I was due to carry on Palindrome.

Kate had told me she was not coming to Cheltenham, so I went in search of the next best thing: news of her.

Dane's peg and section of bench were in the smaller of the two changing rooms, and he was sitting only one place away from the roaring stove, a sure sign of his rise in the jockeys' world. Champions get the warmest places by unwritten right. Beginners shiver beside the draughty doors.

He was clad in his shirt and pants, and was pulling on his nylon stockings. There was a hole in each foot and both his big toes were sticking comically out of them. He had long narrow feet, and long, narrow delicately strong hands to match.

'It's all very well for you to laugh,' said Dane, pulling the tops of the stockings over his knees. 'They don't seem to make nylons for size eleven shoes . . .'

'Get Walter to get you some stretching ones,' I suggested. 'Have you a busy day?'

'Three, including the Champion Hurdle,' said Dane.

'Pete has entered half the stable here.' He grinned at me. 'I might just find time to tell you about the Penn household, though, if that's what you're after. Shall I start with Uncle George, or Aunt Deb, or . . .' He broke off to pull on his silk breeches and his riding boots. His valet, Walter, gave him his under-jersey and some particularly vile pink and orange colours. Whoever had chosen them had paid no regard to their effect against a manly complexion. '. . . Or do you want to hear about Kate?' finished Dane, covering up the sickening jersey with a windproof jacket.

The changing room was filling up, packed with the extra Irish jockeys who had come over for the meeting and were in high spirits and robust voice. Dane and I went out into the crowded weighing room, where at least one could hear oneself speak.

'Uncle George,' he said, 'is a gem. And I'm not going to spoil him for you by telling you about him. Aunt Deb is the Honourable Mrs Penn to you and me, mate, and Aunt Deb to Kate alone. She has a chilly sort of charm that lets you know she would be downright rude if she were not so well bred. She disapproved of me, for a start. I think she disapproves on principle of everything to do with racing, including Heavens Above and Uncle George's idea of a birthday present.'

'Go on,' I urged, anxious for him to come to the most interesting part of the chronicle before someone else buttonholed him.

'Ah yes. Kate. Gorgeous, heavenly Kate. Strictly, you know, her name is Kate Ellery, not Penn at all. Uncle George added the hyphen and the Penn to her name when he took her in. He said it would be easier for her to have the same surname as him – save a lot of explanations. I suppose it does,' said Dane, musingly, knowing full well how he was tantalizing me. He relented, and grinned. 'She sent you her love.'

I felt a warm glow inside. The Cheltenham Festival meeting suddenly seemed not a bad place to be, after all.

'Thanks,' I said, trying not to smile fatuously and scarcely succeeding. Dane looked at me speculatively; but I changed the subject back to racing, and presently I asked him if he had ever heard Bill Davidson spoken of in connection with any sort of odd happenings.

'No, I never did,' he said positively. I told him about the wire. His reaction was typical.

'Poor Bill,' he said with anger. 'Poor old Bill. What a bloody shame.'

'So if you hear anything which might have even the faintest significance . . .'

'I'll pass it on to you,' he promised.

At that moment Joe Nantwich walked straight into Dane as if he hadn't seen him. He stopped without apology, took a step back, and then went on his way to the changing room. His eyes were wide, unfocused, staring.

'He's drunk,' said Dane, incredulously. 'His breath smells like a distillery.'

'He has his troubles,' I said.

'He'll have more still before the afternoon's much older. Just wait, till one of the Stewards catches that alcoholic blast.'

Joe reappeared at our side. It was true that one could smell his approach a good yard away. Without preamble he spoke directly to me.

'I've had another one.' He took a paper out of his pocket. It had been screwed up and straightened out again, so that it was wrinkled in a hundred fine lines, but its ball-pointed message was still abundantly clear.

BOLINGBROKE. THIS WEEK, it said.

'When did you get it?' I asked.

'It was here when I arrived, waiting for me in the letter rack.'

'You've tanked up pretty quickly, then,' I said.

'I'm not drunk,' said Joe indignantly. 'I only had a couple of quick ones in the bar opposite the weighing room.'

Dane and I raised our eyebrows in unison. The bar opposite the weighing room had no front wall, and anyone drinking there was in full view of every trainer, owner, and Steward who walked out of the weighing room. There might be a surer way for a jockey to commit professional suicide than to have 'a couple of quick ones' at that bar before the first race, but I couldn't think of it off-hand. Joe hiccuped.

'Double quick ones, I imagine,' said Dane with a smile, taking the paper out of my hand and reading it. 'What does it mean, Bolingbroke this week? Why are you so steamed up about it?'

Joe snatched the paper away and stuffed it back into his pocket. He seemed for the first time to be aware that Dane was listening.

'It's none of your business,' he said rudely.

I felt a great impulse to assure him it was none of mine either. But he turned back to me and said, 'What shall I do?' in a voice full of whining self-pity.

'Are you riding today?' I asked.

'I'm in the fourth and the last. Those bloody amateurs have got two races all to themselves today. A bit thick, isn't it, leaving us only four races to earn our living in? Why don't the fat-arsed gentlemen riders stick to the point-to-points where they belong? That's all they're – well, fit for,' he added, alliteratively.

There was a small silence. Dane laughed. Joe was after all not too drunk to realize he was riding his hobby horse in front of the wrong man. He said weakly, in his smarmiest voice, 'Well, Alan, of course I didn't mean you personally . . .'

'If you still want my advice, in view of your opinion of amateur jockeys,' I said, keeping a straight face, 'you should drink three cups of strong black coffee and stay out of sight as long as you can.'

'I mean, what shall I do about this note?' Joe had a thicker skin than a coach-hide cabin trunk.

'Pay it no attention at all,' I said. 'I should think that whoever wrote it is playing with you. Perhaps he knows you like to drown your sorrows in whisky and is relying on you to destroy yourself without his having to do anything but send you frightening letters. A neat, bloodless, and effective revenge.'

The sullen pout on Joe's babyish face slowly changed into a mulish determination which was only slightly less repellent.

'No one's going to do that to me,' he said, with an aggressiveness which I guessed would diminish with the alcohol level in his blood. He weaved off out of the weighing room door, presumably in search of black coffee. Before Dane could ask me what was going on, he received a hearty slap on the back from Sandy Mason, who was staring after Joe with dislike.

'What's up with that stupid little clot?' he asked, but he didn't wait for an answer. He said, 'Look, Dane, be a pal and gen me up on this horse of Gregory's I'm riding in the first. I've never seen it before, as far as I know. It seems the owner likes my red hair or something.' Sandy's infectious laugh made several people look round with answering smiles.

'Sure,' said Dane. They launched into a technical discussion and I turned away from them. But Dane touched my arm.

128

He said, 'Is it all right for me to tell people, say Sandy for instance, about the wire and Bill?'

'Yes, do. You might strike oil with someone I wouldn't have thought of asking about it. But be careful.' I thought of telling him about the warning in the horse-box, but it was a long story and it seemed enough to say, 'Remember that you're stirring up people who can kill, even if by mistake.'

He looked startled. 'Yes, you're right. I'll be careful.'

We turned back to Sandy together.

'What are you two so solemn about? Has someone swiped that luscious brunette you're both so keen on?' he said.

'It's about Bill Davidson,' said Dane, disregarding this.

'What about him?'

'The fall that killed him was caused by some wire being strung across the top of the fence, Alan saw it.'

Sandy looked aghast. 'Alan saw it,' he repeated, and then, as the full meaning of what Dane had said sank in, 'But that's murder.'

I pointed out the reasons for supposing that murder had not been intended. Sandy's brown eyes stared at me unwinkingly until I had finished.

'I guess you're right,' he said. 'What are you going to do about it?'

'He's trying to find out what is behind it all,' said Dane. 'We thought you might be able to help. Have you heard anything that might explain it? People tell you things, you know.'

Sandy ran his strong brown hands through his unruly red hair, and rubbed the nape of his neck. This brain massage produced no great thoughts, however. 'Yes, but mostly they tell me about their girl friends or their bets or such like. Not Major Davidson though. We weren't exactly on a bosom pals basis, because he thought I strangled a horse belonging to a friend of his. Well,' said Sandy with an engaging grin, 'maybe I did, at that. Anyway, we had words, as they say, a few months ago.'

'See if your bookmaker friends have heard any whispers, then,' said Dane. 'They usually have their ears usefully to the ground.'

'OK,' said Sandy. 'I'll pass the news along and see what happens. Now come on, we haven't much time before the first and I want to know what this sod of a horse is going to do.' And as Dane hesitated, he said, 'Come on, you don't have to wrap it up. Gregory only asks me to ride for him when it's such a stinker that he daren't ask any sensible man to get up on it.'

'It's a mare,' said Dane, 'with a beastly habit of galloping into the bottoms of fences as if they weren't there. She usually ends up in the open ditch.'

'Well, thanks,' said Sandy, apparently undaunted by this news. 'I'll tan her hide for her and she'll soon change her ways. See you later, then.' He went into the changing room.

Dane looked after him. 'The horse isn't foaled that could frighten that blighter Sandy,' he said with admiration.

'Nothing wrong with his nerve,' I agreed. 'But why ever is Pete running an animal like that here, of all places?'

'The owner fancies having a runner at Cheltenham. You know how it is. Snob value, and so on,' he said indulgently.

We were being jostled continually, as we talked, by the throng of trainers and owners. We went outside. Dane was immediately appropriated by a pair of racing journalists who wanted his views on his mount in the Gold Cup, two days distant.

The afternoon wore on. The racing began. With the fine sunny day and the holiday mood of the crowd, the excitement was almost crackling in the air.

Sandy got the mare over the first open ditch but disappeared into the next. He came back with a broad smile, cursing hard.

Joe reappeared after the second race, looking less drunk but more frightened. I avoided him shamelessly.

Dane, riding like a demon, won the Champion Hurdle by a head. Pete, patting his horse and sharing with the owner the congratulations of the great crowd round the unsaddling enclosure, was so delighted he could hardly speak. Large and red-faced, he stood there with his hat pushed back showing his baldness, trying to look as if this sort of thing happened every day, when it was in fact the most important winner he had trained.

He was so overcome that he forgot, as we stood some time later in the parade ring before the amateurs' race, to make his customary joke about Palindrome going backwards as well as forwards. And when I, following his advice to the letter, stuck like a shadow to the Irishman when he tried to slip the field, lay a scant length behind him all the way to the last fence, and passed him with a satisfying spurt fifty yards from the winning post, Pete said his day was complete.

I could have hugged him, I was so elated. Although I had won several races back in Rhodesia and about thirty since I had been in England, this was my first win at Cheltenham. I felt as high as if I had already drunk the champagne which waited unopened in the changing-room, the customary crateful of celebration for Champion Hurdle day. Palindrome was, in my eyes, the most beautiful, most intelligent, most perfect horse in the world. I walked on air to the scales to weigh in, and changed into my ordinary clothes, and had still not returned to earth when I went outside again. The gloom I had arrived in seemed a thousand years ago. I was so happy I could have turned cartwheels like a child. Such total, unqualified fulfilment comes rarely enough: and unexpectedly, I wished that my father were there to share it.

The problem of Bill had receded like a dot in the distance, and it was only because I had earlier planned to do it that I directed my airy steps down to the horse-box parking ground.

It was packed. About twenty horses ran in each race that day, and almost every horse-box available must have been pressed into service to bring them. I sauntered along the rows, humming light-heartedly, looking at the number plates with half an eye and less attention.

And there it was.

APX 708.

My happiness burst like a bubble.

There was no doubt it was the same horse-box. Regulation wooden Jennings design. Elderly, with dull and battered varnish. No name of owner or trainer painted anywhere on the doors or bodywork.

There was no one in the driver's cab. I walked round to the back, opened the door, and climbed in.

The horse-box was empty except for a bucket, a hay net, and a rug, the normal travelling kit for racehorses. The floor was strewn with straw, whereas three days earlier it had been swept clean.

The rug, I thought, might give me a clue as to where the box had come from. Most trainers and some owners have their initials embroidered or sewn in tape in large

133

letters on the corners of their horse rugs. If there were initials on this one, it would be easy.

I picked it up. It was pale fawn with a dark brown binding. I found the initials. I stood there as if turned to stone. Plainly in view, embroidered in dark brown silk, were the letters A.Y.

It was my own rug.

Pete, when I ran him to earth, looked in no mood to answer any questions needing much thought. He leaned back against the weighing-room wall with a glass of champagne in one hand and a cigar in the other, surrounded by a pack of friends similarly equipped. From their rosy smiling faces I gathered the celebration had already been going on for some time.

Dane thrust a glass into my hand.

'Where have you been? Well done on Palindrome. Have some bubbly. The owner's paying, God bless him.' His eyes were alight with that fantastic, top-of-the-world elation that I had so lately felt myself. It began to creep back into me too. It was, after all, a great day. Mysteries could wait.

I drank a sip of champagne and said, 'Well done yourself, you old son-of-a-gun. And here's to the Gold Cup.'

'No such luck,' said Dane. 'I haven't much chance in that.' And from his laughing face I gathered he didn't care, either. We emptied our glasses. 'I'll get another bottle,' he said, diving into the noisy, crowded changing room.

Looking around I saw Joe Nantwich backed up into a nearby corner by the enormous Mr Tudor. The big man was doing the talking, forcefully, his dark face almost merging with the shadows. Joe, still dressed in racing colours, listened very unhappily.

Dane came back with the bubbles fizzing out of a newly opened bottle and filled our glasses. He followed my gaze.

'I don't know whether Joe was sober or not, but didn't he make a hash of the last race?' he said.

'I didn't see it.'

'Brother, you sure missed something. He didn't try a yard. His horse damned nearly stopped altogether at the hurdle over on the far side, and it was second favourite, too. What you see now,' he gestured with the bottle, 'is, I should think, our Joe getting the well-deserved sack.'

'That man owns Bolingbroke,' I said.

'Yes, that's right. Same colours. What a fool Joe is. Owners with five or six goodish horses don't grow on bushes any more.'

Clifford Tudor had nearly done. As he turned away from Joe in our direction we heard the tail end of his remarks.

'. . . think you can make a fool of me and get away

with it. The Stewards can warn you off altogether, as far as I'm concerned.'

He strode past us, giving me a nod of recognition, which surprised me, and went out.

Joe leaned against the wall for support. His face was pallid and sweating. He looked ill. He took a few unsteady steps towards us and spoke without caution, as if he had forgotten that Stewards and members of the National Hunt Committee might easily overhear.

'I had a phone call this morning. The same voice as always. He just said, "Don't win the sixth race" and rang off before I could say anything. And then that note saying "Bolingbroke, this week" . . . I don't understand it . . . and I didn't win the race and now that bloody wog says he'll get another jockey . . . and the Stewards have started an inquiry about my riding . . . and I feel sick.'

'Have some champagne,' said Dane, encouragingly.

'Don't be so bloody helpful,' said Joe, clutching his stomach and departing towards the changing-room.

'What the hell's going on?' said Dane.

'I don't know,' I said, perplexed and more interested in Joe's troubles than I had been before. The phone call was inconsistent, I thought, with the notes. One ordered business as usual, the other promised revenge. 'I wonder if Joe always tells the truth,' I said.

'Highly unlikely,' said Dane, dismissing it.

One of the Stewards came and reminded us that even after the Champion Hurdle, drinking in the weighing room itself was frowned on, and would we please drift along into the changing room. Dane did that, but I finished my drink and went outside.

Pete, still attended by a posse of friends, had decided that it was time to go home. The friends were unwilling. The racecourse bars, they were saying, were still open.

I walked purposefully up to Pete, and he made me his excuse for breaking away. We went towards the gates.

'Whew, what a day!' said Pete, mopping his brow with a white handkerchief and throwing away the stub of his cigar.

'A wonderful day,' I agreed, looking at him carefully.

'You can take that anxious look off your face, Alan, my lad. I'm as sober as a judge and I'm driving myself home.'

'Good. In that case you'll have no difficulty in answering one small question for me?'

'Shoot.'

'In what horse-box did Palindrome come to Cheltenham?' I said.

'Eh? I hired one. I had five runners here today. The hurdler, the mare, and the black gelding came in my own box. I had to hire one for Palindrome and the novice Dane rode in the first.'

'Where did you hire it from?'

'What's the matter?' asked Pete. 'I know it's a bit old, and it had a puncture on the way, as I told you,

137

but it didn't do him any harm. Can't have done, or he wouldn't have won.'

'No, it's nothing like that,' I said. 'I just want to know where that horse-box comes from.'

'It's not worth buying, if that's what you're after. Too old by half.'

'Pete, I don't want to buy it. Just tell me where it comes from.'

'The firm I usually hire a box from, Littlepeths of Steyning.' He frowned. 'Wait a minute. At first they said all their boxes were booked up; then they said they could get me a box if I didn't mind an old one.'

'Who drove it here?' I asked.

'Oh, one of their usual drivers. He was swearing a bit at having to drive such an old hen coop. He said the firm had got two good horse-boxes out of action in Cheltenham week and he took a poor view of the administration.'

'Do you know him well?'

'Not exactly well. He often drives the hired boxes, that's all. He's always grousing about something. Now, what is all this in aid of?'

'It may have something to do with Bill's death,' I said, 'but I'm not sure what. Can you find out where the box really comes from? Ask the hire firm? And don't mention me, if you don't mind.'

'Is it important?' asked Pete.

'Yes, it is.'

'I'll ring 'em tomorrow morning, then,' he said.

As soon as he saw me the next day, Pete said, 'I asked about that horse-box. It belongs to a farm near Steyning. I've got his name and address here.' He tucked two fingers into his breast pocket, brought out a slip of paper, and gave it to me. 'The farmer uses the box to take his hunters around, and his children's show jumpers in the summer. He sometimes lets the hire firm use it, if he's not needing it. Is that what you wanted?'

'Yes, thank you very much,' I said. I put the paper in my wallet.

By the end of the Festival meeting I had repeated the story of the wire to at least ten more people, in the hope that someone might know why it had been put there. The tale spread fast round the racecourse.

I told fat Lew Panake, the well-dressed bookmaker who took my occasional bets. He promised to 'sound out the boys' and let me know.

I told Calvin Bone, a professional punter, whose nose for the smell of dirty work was as unerring as a bloodhound's.

I told a sly little tout who made his living passing on

stray pieces of information to anyone who would pay for them.

I told the newspaper seller, who tugged his moustache and ignored a customer.

I told a racing journalist who could scent a doping scandal five furlongs away.

I told an army friend of Bill's; I told Clem in the weighing-room; I told Pete Gregory's head travelling lad.

From all this busy sowing in the wind I learned absolutely nothing. And I would still, I supposed, have to reap the whirlwind.

CHAPTER EIGHT

On Saturday morning as I sat with Scilla and the children and Joan round the large kitchen table having a solidly domestic breakfast, the telephone rang.

Scilla went to answer it, but came back saying, 'It's for you, Alan. He wouldn't give his name.'

I went into the drawing-room and picked up the receiver. The March sun streamed through the windows on to a big bowl of red and yellow striped crocuses which stood on the telephone table. I said, 'Alan York speaking.'

'Mr York, I gave you a warning a week ago today. You have chosen to ignore it.'

I felt the hairs rising on my neck. My scalp itched. It was a soft voice with a husky, whispering note to it, not savage or forceful, but almost mildly conversational.

I didn't answer. The voice said, 'Mr York? Are you still there?'

'Yes.'

'Mr York, I am not a violent man. Indeed, I dislike

141

violence. I go out of my way to avoid it, Mr York. But sometimes it is thrust upon me, sometimes it is the only way to achieve results. Do you understand me, Mr York?'

'Yes,' I said.

'If I were a violent man, Mr York, I would have sent you a rougher warning last week. And I'm giving you another chance, to show you how reluctant I am to harm you. Just mind your own business and stop asking foolish questions. That's all. Just stop asking questions, and nothing will happen to you.' There was a pause, then the soft voice went on, with a shade, a first tinge, of menace, 'Of course, if I find that violence is absolutely necessary, I always get someone else to apply it. So that I don't have to watch. So that it is not too painful to me. You do understand me, I hope, Mr York?'

'Yes,' I said again. I thought of Sonny, his vicious grin, and his knife.

'Good, then that's all. I do so hope you will be sensible. Good morning, Mr York.' There was a click as he broke the connexion.

I jiggled the telephone rest to recall the operator. When she answered I asked if she could tell me where the call had come from.

'One moment, please,' she said. She suffered from enlarged adenoids. She came back. 'It was routed through London,' she said, 'but I can't trace it beyond there. So sorry.'

'Never mind. Thank you very much,' I said.

'Pleasure, I'm sure,' said the adenoids.

I put down the receiver and went back to my breakfast.

'Who was that?' asked Henry, spreading marmalade thickly on his toast.

'Man about a dog,' I said.

'Or in other words,' said Polly, 'ask no questions and you'll be told no thumping lies.'

Henry made a face at her and bit deeply into his toast. The marmalade oozed out of one corner of his mouth. He licked it.

'Henry always wants to know who's ringing up,' said William.

'Yes, darling,' said Scilla absently, rubbing some egg off his jersey. 'I wish you would lean over your plate when you eat, William.' She kissed the top of his blond head.

I passed my cup to Joan for more coffee.

Henry said, 'Will you take us out to tea in Cheltenham, Alan? Can we have some of those squelchy cream things like last time, and ice-cream sodas with straws, and some peanuts for coming home?'

'Oh, yes,' said William, blissfully.

'I'd love to,' I said, 'but I can't today. We'll do it next week, perhaps.' The day of my visit to Kate's house had come at last. I was to stay there for two nights, and I planned to put in a day at the office on Monday.

Seeing the children's disappointed faces I explained, 'Today I'm going to stay with a friend. I won't be back until Monday evening.'

'What a bore,' said Henry.

The Lotus ate up the miles between the Cotswolds and Sussex with the deep purr of a contented cat. I covered the fifty miles of good road from Cirencester to Newbury in fifty-three minutes, not because I was in a great hurry, but out of sheer pleasure in driving my car at the speed it was designed for. And I was going towards Kate. Eventually.

Newbury slowed me to a crawl, to a halt. Then I zipped briefly down the Basingstoke road, past the American air base at Greenham Common, and from the twisty village of Kingsclere onwards drove at a sedate pace which seldom rose above sixty.

Kate lived about four miles from Burgess Hill, in Sussex.

I arrived in Burgess Hill at twenty-past one, found my way to the railway station, and parked in a corner, tucked away behind a large shooting brake. I went into the station and bought a return ticket to Brighton. I didn't care to reconnoitre in Brighton by car: the Lotus had already identified me into one mess, and I hesitated to show my hand by taking it where it could be spotted by a cruising taxi driven by Peaky, Sonny, Bert, or the rest.

The journey took sixteen minutes. On the train I asked myself, for at least the hundredth time, what chance remark of mine had landed me in the horse-box hornet's nest. Whom had I alarmed by not only revealing that I knew about the wire, but more especially by saying that I intended to find out who had put it there? I could think of only two possible answers; and one of them I didn't like a bit.

I remembered saying to Clifford Tudor on the way from Plumpton to Brighton that a lot of questions would have to be answered about Bill's death; which was as good as telling him straight out that I knew the fall hadn't been an accident, and that I meant to do something about it.

And I had made the same thing quite clear to Kate. To Kate. To Kate. To Kate. The wheels of the train took up the refrain and mocked me.

Well, I hadn't sworn her to secrecy, and I hadn't seen any need to. She could have passed on what I had said to the whole of England, for all I knew. But she hadn't had much time. It had been after midnight when she left me in London, and the horse-box had been waiting for me seventeen hours later.

The train slowed into Brighton station. I walked up the platform and through the gate in a cluster of fellow passengers, but hung back as we came through the booking hall and out towards the forecourt. There were about twelve taxis parked there, their drivers standing outside them, surveying the out-pouring passengers for custom. I looked at all the drivers carefully, face by face.

They were all strangers. None of them had been at Plumpton.

Not unduly discouraged, I found a convenient corner with a clear view of arriving taxis and settled myself to wait, resolutely ignoring the cold draught blowing down my neck. Taxis came and went like busy bees, bringing passengers, taking them away. The trains from London attracted them like honey.

Gradually a pattern emerged. There were four distinct groups of them. One group had a broad green line painted down the wings, with the name Green Band on the doors. A second group had yellow shields on the doors, with small letters in black on the shields. A third group were bright cobalt blue all over. Into the fourth group I put the indeterminate taxis which did not belong to the other lines.

I waited for nearly two hours, growing stiffer and stiffer, and receiving more and more curious looks from the station staff. I looked at my watch. The last train I could catch and still arrive at Kate's at the right time was due to leave in six minutes. I had begun to straighten up and massage my cold neck, ready to go and board it, when at last my patience was rewarded.

Empty taxis began to arrive and form a waiting line, which I now knew meant that another London train was due. The drivers got out of their cars and clustered in little groups, talking. Three dusty black taxis arrived in minor convoy and pulled up at the end of the line. They had faded yellow shields painted on the doors. The drivers got out.

One of them was the polite driver of the horse-box. A sensible, solid citizen, he looked. Middle-aged, unremarkable, calm. I did not know the others.

I had three minutes left. The black letters were tantalizingly small on the yellow shields. I couldn't get close enough to read them without the polite driver seeing me, and I had not time to wait until he had gone. I went over to the ticket office, hovered impatiently while a woman argued about half fares for her teenage child, and asked a simple question.

'What is the name of the taxis with yellow shields on the doors?' The young man in the office gave me an uninterested glance.

'Marconicars, sir. Radio cabs, they are.'

'Thank you,' I said, and sprinted for the platform.

Kate lived in a superbly proportioned Queen Anne house which generations of Gothic-ruin-minded Victorians had left miraculously unspoilt. Its graceful symmetry, its creamy gravelled drive, its tidy lawns already mown in early spring, its air of solid serenity, all spoke of a social and financial security of such long standing that it was to be taken entirely for granted.

Inside, the house was charming, with just a saving touch of shabbiness about the furnishings, as if, though rich, the inhabitants saw no need to be either ostentatious or extravagant.

Kate met me at the door and took my arm, and walked me across the hall.

'Aunt Deb is waiting to give you tea,' she said. 'Tea is a bit of a ritual with Aunt Deb. You will be in her good graces for being punctual, thank goodness. She is very Edwardian, you'll find. The times have moved without her in many ways.' She sounded anxious and apologetic, which meant to me that she loved her aunt protectively, and wished me to make allowances. I squeezed her arm reassuringly, and said, 'Don't worry.'

Kate opened one of the white panelled doors and we went into the drawing-room. It was a pleasant room, wood panelled and painted white, with a dark plum-coloured carpet, good Persian rugs, and flower-patterned curtains. On a sofa at right angles to a glowing log fire sat a woman of about seventy. Beside her stood a low round table bearing a silver tray with Crown Derby cups and saucers and a Georgian silver teapot and cream jug. A dark brown dachshund lay asleep at her feet.

Kate walked across the room and said with some formality, 'Aunt Deb, may I introduce Alan York?'

Aunt Deb extended to me her hand, palm downwards. I shook it, feeling that in her younger days it would have been kissed.

'I am delighted to meet you, Mr York,' said Aunt Deb. And I saw exactly what Dane meant about her chilly, well-bred manner. She had no warmth, no genuine welcome in her voice. She was still, for all her years, or even perhaps because of them, exceedingly good-looking. Straight eyebrows, perfect nose, clearly outlined mouth. Grey hair cut and dressed by a first-class man. A slim, firm body, straight back, elegant legs crossed at the ankles. A fine shirt under a casual tweed suit, hand-made shoes of soft leather. She had everything. Everything except the inner fire which would make Kate at that age worth six of Aunt Deb.

She poured me some tea, and Kate handed it to me. There were pâté sandwiches and a home-made Madeira cake, and although tea was usually a meal I avoided if possible, I found my jinks in Brighton and no lunch had made me hungry. I ate and drank, and Aunt Deb talked.

'Kate tells me you are a jockey, Mr York.' She said it as if it were as dubious as a criminal record. 'Of course I am sure you must find it very amusing, but when I was a gel it was not considered an acceptable occupation in acquaintances. But this is Kate's home, and she may ask whoever she likes here, as she knows.'

I said mildly, 'Surely Aubrey Hastings and Geoffrey Bennett were both jockeys and acceptable when you were – er – younger?'

She raised her eyebrows, surprised. 'But they were gentlemen,' she said.

I looked at Kate. She had stuffed the back of her hand against her mouth, but her eyes were laughing.

'Yes,' I said to Aunt Deb, with a straight face. 'That makes a difference, of course.'

'You may realize then,' she said, looking at me a little less frigidly, 'that I do not altogether approve of my niece's new interest. It is one thing to own a racehorse, but quite another to make personal friends of the jockeys one employs to ride it. I am very fond of my niece. I do not wish her to make an undesirable . . . alliance. She is perhaps too young, and has led too sheltered a life, to understand what is acceptable and what is not. But I am sure you do, Mr York?'

Kate, blushing painfully, said, 'Aunt Deb!' This was apparently worse than she was prepared for.

'I understand you very well, Mrs Penn,' I said, politely.

'Good,' she said. 'In that case, I hope you will have an enjoyable stay with us. May I give you some more tea?'

Having firmly pointed out to me my place and having received what she took to be my acknowledgement of it, she was prepared to be a gracious hostess.

She had the calm authority of one whose wishes had been law from the nursery. She began to talk pleasantly enough about the weather and her garden, and how the sunshine was bringing on the daffodils.

Then the door opened and a man came in. I stood up.

Kate said, 'Uncle George, this is Alan York.'

He looked ten years younger than his wife. He had thick well-groomed grey hair and a scrubbed pink complexion with a fresh-from-the-bathroom moistness about it, and when he shook hands his palm was soft and moist also.

Aunt Deb said, without disapproval in her voice, 'George, Mr York is one of Kate's jockey friends.'

He nodded. 'Yes, Kate told me you were coming. Glad to have you here.'

He watched Aunt Deb pour him a cup of tea, and took it from her, giving her a smile of remarkable fondness.

He was too fat for his height, but it was not a bloated-belly fatness. It was spread all over him as though he were padded. The total effect was of a jolly rotundity. He had the vaguely good-natured expression so often found on fat people, a certain bland, almost foolish, looseness of the facial muscles. And yet his fat-lidded eyes, appraising me over the rim of the teacup as he drank, were shrewd and unsmiling. He reminded me of so many businessmen I had met in my work, the slap-you-on-the-back, come-and-play-golf men who would ladle out the Krug '49 and caviar with one hand while they tried to take over your contracts with the other.

He put down his cup and smiled, and the impression faded. 'I am very interested to meet you, Mr York,' he said, sitting down and gesturing to me to do the same. He looked me over carefully, inch by inch, while he asked me what I thought of Heavens Above. We discussed the horse's possibilities with Kate, which meant that I did most of the talking, as Kate knew little more than she had at Plumpton, and Uncle George's total information about racing seemed to be confined to Midday Sun's having won the Derby in 1937.

'He remembers it because of Mad Dogs and Englishmen,' said Kate. 'He hums it all the time. I don't think he knows the name of a single other horse.'

'Oh, yes I do,' protested Uncle George. 'Bucephalus, Pegasus, and Black Bess.'

I laughed. 'Then why did you give a racehorse to your niece?'

Uncle George opened his mouth and shut it again. He blinked. Then he said, 'I thought she should meet more people. She has no young company here with us, and I believe we may have given her too sheltered an upbringing.'

Aunt Deb, who had been bored into silence by the subject of horses, returned to the conversation at this point.

'Nonsense,' she said briskly. 'She has been brought up as I was, which is the right way. Gels are given too much freedom nowadays, with the result that they lose their heads and elope with fortune hunters or men-about-town of unsavoury background. Gels need strictness and guidance if they are to behave as ladies, and make suitable, well-connected marriages.'

She at least had the grace to avoid looking directly at me while she spoke. She leaned over and patted the sleeping dachshund instead.

Uncle George changed the subject with an almost audible jolt, and asked me where I lived.

'Southern Rhodesia,' I said.

'Indeed?' said Aunt Deb. 'How interesting. Do your parents plan to settle there permanently?' It was a delicate, practised, social probe.

'They were both born there,' I answered.

'And will they be coming to visit you in England?' asked Uncle George.

'My mother died when I was ten. My father might come some time if he is not too busy.'

'Too busy doing what?' asked Uncle George interestedly.

'He's a trader,' I said, giving my usual usefully non-committal answer to his question. 'Trader' could cover anything from a rag-and-bone man to what he actually was, the head of the biggest general trading concern in the Federation. Both Uncle George and Aunt Deb looked unsatisfied by this reply, but I did not add to it. It would have embarrassed and angered Aunt Deb to have had my pedigree and prospects laid out before her after her little lecture on jockeys, and in any case for Dane's sake I could not do it. He had faced Aunt Deb's social snobbery without any of the defences I could muster if I wanted to, and I certainly felt myself no better man than he.

I made instead a remark admiring an arrangement of rose prints on the white panelled walls, which pleased Aunt Deb but brought forth a sardonic glance from Uncle George.

'We keep our ancestors in the dining-room,' he said.

Kate stood up. 'I'll show Alan where he's sleeping, and so on,' she said.

'Did you come by car?' Uncle George asked. I nodded. He said to Kate, 'Then ask Culbertson to put Mr York's car in the garage, will you, my dear?'

'Yes, Uncle George,' said Kate, smiling at him.

As we crossed the hall again for me to fetch my suitcase from the car, Kate said, 'Uncle George's chauffeur's name is not really Culbertson. It's Higgins, or something like that. Uncle George began to call him Culbertson because he plays bridge, and soon we all did it. Culbertson seems quite resigned to it now. Trust Uncle George,' said Kate, laughing, 'to have a chauffeur who plays bridge.'

'Does Uncle George play bridge?'

'No, he doesn't like cards, or games of any sort. He says there are too many rules to them. He says he doesn't like learning rules and he can't be bothered to keep them. I should think bridge with all those conventions would drive him dotty. Aunt Deb can play quite respectably, but she doesn't make a thing of it.'

I lifted my suitcase out of the car, and we turned back.

Kate said, 'Why didn't you tell Aunt Deb you were an amateur rider and rich, and so on?'

'Why didn't you?' I asked. 'Before I came.'

She was taken aback. 'I . . . I . . . er . . . because . . .' She could not bring out the truthful answer, so I said it for her.

'Because of Dane?'

'Yes, because of Dane.' She looked uncomfortable.

'That's quite all right by me,' I said lightly. 'And I like you for it.' I kissed her cheek, and she laughed and turned away from me, and ran up the stairs in relief.

After luncheon – Aunt Deb gave the word three syllables – on Sunday I was given permission to take Kate out for a drive.

In the morning Aunt Deb had been to church with Kate and me in attendance. The church was a mile distant from the house, and Culbertson drove us there in a well-polished Daimler. I, by Aunt Deb's decree, sat beside him. She and Kate went in the back.

While we stood in the drive waiting for Aunt Deb to come out of the house, Kate explained that Uncle George never went to church.

'He spends most of his time in his study. That's the little room next to the breakfast room,' she said. 'He talks to all his friends on the telephone for hours, and he's writing a treatise or a monograph or something about Red Indians, I think, and he only comes out for meals and things like that.'

'Rather dull for your aunt,' I said, admiring the way the March sunlight lay along the perfect line of her jaw and lit red glints in her dark eyelashes.

'Oh, he takes her up to Town once a week. She has her hair done, and he looks things up in the library of the British Museum. Then they have a jolly lunch at the Ritz or somewhere stuffy like that, and go to a matinée or an exhibition in the afternoon. A thoroughly debauched programme,' said Kate, with a dazzling smile.

After lunch, Uncle George invited me into his study to see what he called his 'trophies'. These were a collection of objects belonging to various primitive or barbaric peoples, and, as far as I could judge, would have done credit to any small museum.

Ranks of weapons, together with some jewellery, pots, and ritual objects were labelled and mounted on shelves inside glass cases which lined three walls of the room. Among others, there were pieces from Central Africa and the Polynesian Islands, from the Viking age of Norway, and from the Maoris of New Zealand. Uncle George's interest covered the globe.

'I study one people at a time,' he explained. 'It gives me something to do since I retired, and I find it enthralling. Did you know that in the Fiji Islands the men used to fatten women like cattle and eat them.'

His eyes gleamed, and I had a suspicion that part of the pleasure he derived from primitive peoples lay in contemplation of their primitive violences. Perhaps he needed a mental antidote to those lunches at the Ritz, and the matinées.

I said, 'Which people are you studying now? Kate said something about Red Indians . . .?'

He seemed pleased that I was taking an interest in his hobby.

'Yes. I am doing a survey of all the ancient peoples of the Americas, and the North American Indians were my last subject. Their case is over here.'

He showed me over to one corner. The collection of feathers, beads, knives, and arrows looked almost ridiculously like those in Western films, but I had no doubt that these were genuine. And in the centre hung a hank of black hair with a withered lump of matter dangling from it, and underneath was gummed the laconic lable, 'Scalp'.

I turned round, and surprised Uncle George watching me with a look of secret enjoyment. He let his gaze slide past me to the case.

'Oh, yes,' he said. 'The scalp's a real one. It's only about a hundred years old.'

'Interesting,' I said non-committally.

'I spent a year on the North American Indians because there are so many different tribes,' he went on. 'But I've moved on to Central America now. Next I'll do the South Americans, the Incas and the Fuegians and so on. I'm not a scholar, of course, and I don't do any field work, but I do write articles sometimes for various publications. At the moment I am engaged on a series about Indians for the *Boys' Stupendous Weekly.*' His fat cheeks shook as he laughed silently at what appeared to be an immense private joke. Then he straightened his lips and the pink folds of flesh grew still, and he began to drift back towards the door.

I followed him, and paused by his big, carved, black oak desk which stood squarely in front of the window. On it, besides two telephones and a silver pen tray, lay several cardboard folders with pale blue stick-on labels marked Arapaho, Cherokee, Sioux, Navajo, and Mohawk.

Separated from these was another folder marked Mayas, and I idly stretched out my hand to open it, because I had never heard of such a tribe. Uncle George's plump fingers came down firmly on the folder, holding it shut.

'I have only just started on this nation,' he said

apologetically. 'And there's nothing worth looking at yet.'

'I've never heard of that tribe,' I said.

'They were Central American Indians, not North,' he said pleasantly. 'They were astronomers and mathematicians, you know. Very civilized. I am finding them fascinating. They discovered that rubber bounced, and they made balls of it long before it was known in Europe. At the moment I am looking into their wars. I am trying to find out what they did with their prisoners of war. Several of their frescos show prisoners begging for mercy.' He paused, his eyes fixed on me, assessing me. 'Would you like to help me correlate the references I have so far collected?' he said.

'Well ... er ... er ...' I began.

Uncle George's jowls shook again. 'I didn't suppose you would,' he said. 'You'd rather take Kate for a drive, no doubt.'

As I had been wondering how Aunt Deb would react to a similar suggestion, this was a gift. So three o'clock found Kate and me walking round to the big garage behind the house, with Aunt Deb's grudging consent to our being absent at tea-time.

'You remember me telling you, a week ago, while we were dancing, about the way Bill Davidson died?' I said casually, while I helped Kate open the garage doors.

'How could I forget?'

'Did you by any chance mention it to anyone the

next morning? There wasn't any reason why you shouldn't . . . but I'd like very much to know if you did.'

She wrinkled her nose. 'I can't really remember, but I don't think so. Only Aunt Deb and Uncle George, of course, at breakfast. I can't think of anyone else. I didn't think there was any secret about it, though.' Her voice rose at the end into a question.

'There wasn't,' I said, reassuringly, fastening back the door. 'What did Uncle George do before he retired and took up anthropology?'

'Retired?' she said. 'Oh, that's only one of his jokes. He retired when he was about thirty, I think, as soon as he inherited a whacking great private income from his father. For decades he and Aunt Deb used to set off round the world every three years or so, collecting all those gruesome relics he was showing you in the study. What did you think of them?'

I couldn't help a look of distaste, and she laughed and said, 'That's what I think too, but I'd never let him suspect it. He's so devoted to them all.'

The garage was a converted barn. There was plenty of room for the four cars standing in it in a row. The Daimler, a new cream coloured convertible, my Lotus, and after a gap, the social outcast, an old black eight-horse-power saloon. All of them, including mine, were spotless. Culbertson was conscientious.

'We use that old car for shopping in the village and so on,' said Kate. 'This georgeous cream job is mine.

Uncle George gave it to me a year ago when I came home from Switzerland. Isn't it absolutely rapturous?' She stroked it with love.

'Can we go out in yours, instead of mine?' I asked. 'I would like that very much, if you wouldn't mind.'

She was pleased. She let down the roof and tied a blue silk scarf over her head, and drove us out of the garage into the sunlight, down the drive, and on to the road towards the village.

'Where shall we go?' she asked.

'I'd like to go to Steyning,' I said.

'That's an odd sort of place to choose,' she said. 'How about the sea?'

'I want to call on a farmer in Washington, near Steyning, to ask him about his horse-box,' I said. And I told her how some men in a horse-box had rather forcefully told me not to ask questions about Bill's death.

'It was a horse-box belonging to this farm at Washington,' I finished. 'I want to ask him who hired it from him last Saturday.'

'Good heavens,' said Kate. 'What a lark.' And she drove a little faster. I sat sideways and enjoyed the sight of her. The beautiful profile, the blue scarf whipped by the wind, with one escaping wisp of hair blowing on her forehead, the cherry-red curving mouth. She could twist your heart.

It was ten miles to Washington. We went into the village and stopped, and I asked some children on their way home from Sunday school where farmer Lawson lived.

'Up by there,' said the tallest girl, pointing.

'Up by there' turned out to be a prosperous work-manlike farm with a mellow old farmhouse and a large new Dutch barn rising behind it. Kate drove into the yard and stopped, and we walked round through a garden gate to the front of the house. Sunday afternoon was not a good time to call on a farmer, who was probably enjoying his one carefree nap of the week, but it couldn't be helped.

We rang the door bell, and after a long pause the door opened. A youngish good-looking man holding a newspaper looked at us enquiringly.

'Could I speak to Mr Lawson, please?' I said.

'I'm Lawson,' he said. He yawned again.

I said I understood he had a horse-box for hire. He rubbed his nose with his thumb while he looked us over. Then he said, 'It's very old, and it depends when you want it.'

'Could we see it, do you think?' I asked.

'Yes,' he said. 'Hang on a moment.' He went indoors and we heard his voice calling out and a girl's voice answering him. Then he came back without the newspaper.

'It's round here,' he said, leading the way. The horse-box stood out in the open, sheltered only by the hay piled in the Dutch barn. APX 708. My old friend.

162

I told Lawson then that I didn't really want to hire his box, but I wanted to know who had hired it eight days ago. And because he thought this question decidedly queer and was showing signs of hustling us off at once, I told him why I wanted to know.

'It can't have been my box,' he said at once.

'It was,' I said.

'I didn't hire it to anyone eight days ago. It was standing right here all day.'

'It was in Maidenhead,' I said, obstinately.

He looked at me for a full half a minute. Then he said, 'If you are right, it was taken without me knowing about it. I and my family were all away last week-end. We were in London.'

'How many people would know you were away?' I asked.

He laughed. 'About twelve million, I should think. We were on one of those family quiz shows on television on Friday night. My wife, my eldest son, my daughter, and I. The younger boy wasn't allowed on because he's only ten. He was furious about it. My wife said on the programme that we were all going to the Zoo on Saturday and to the Tower of London on Sunday, and we weren't going home until Monday.'

I sighed. 'And how soon before you went up to the quiz show did you know about it?'

'A couple of weeks. It was all in the local papers, that we were going. I was a bit annoyed about it, really. It doesn't do to let every tramp in the neighbourhood know you'll be away. Of course, there are my cowmen about, but it's not the same.'

'Could you ask them if they saw anyone borrow your box?'

'I suppose I could. It's almost milking time, they'll be in soon. But I can't help thinking you've mistaken the number plate.'

'Have you a middleweight thoroughbred bay hunter, then,' I said, 'with a white star on his forehead, one lop ear, and a straggly tail?'

His scepticism vanished abruptly. 'Yes, I have,' he said. 'He's in the stable over there.'

'Surely your men would have missed him when they went to give him his evening feed?' I said.

'My brother – he lives a mile away – borrows him whenever he wants. The men would just assume he'd got him. I'll ask the cowmen.'

'Will you ask them at the same time if they found a necktie in the box?' I said. 'I lost one there, and I'm rather attached to it. I'd give ten bob to have it back.'

'I'll ask them,' said Lawson. 'Come into the house while you wait.' He took us through the back door, along a stone-flagged hall into a comfortably battered sitting-room, and left us. The voices of his wife and children and the clatter of teacups could be heard in the distance. A half-finished jigsaw puzzle was scattered on a table; some toy railway lines snaked round the floor.

At length Lawson came back. 'I'm very sorry,' he said, 'the cowmen thought my brother had the horse and none of them noticed the box had gone. They said they didn't find your tie, either. They're as blind as bats unless it's something of theirs that's missing.'

I thanked him all the same for his trouble, and he asked me to let him know, if I found out, who had taken his box.

Kate and I drove off towards the sea.

She said, 'Not a very productive bit of sleuthing, do you think? Anyone in the world could have borrowed the horse-box.'

'It must have been someone who knew it was there,' I pointed out. 'I expect it was because it was so available that they got the idea of using it at all. If they hadn't known it would be easy to borrow, they'd have delivered their message some other way. I dare say one of those cowmen knows more than he's telling. Probably took a quiet tenner to turn a blind eye, and threw in the horse for local colour. Naturally he wouldn't confess it in a hurry to Lawson this afternoon.'

'Well, never mind,' said Kate lightheartedly. 'Perhaps it's just as well Farmer Lawson had nothing to do with it. It would have been rather shattering if he had turned out to be the head of the gang. You would probably have been bopped behind the ear with a gun butt and dumped in a bag of cement out at sea and I would have been tied up on the railway lines in the path of oncoming diesels.'

I laughed. 'If I'd thought he could have possibly been the leader of the gang I wouldn't have taken you there.'

She glanced at me. 'You be careful,' she said, 'or you'll grow into a cosseting old dear like Uncle George. He's never let Aunt Deb within arm's length of discomfort, let alone danger. I think that's why she's so out of touch with modern life.'

'You don't think danger should be avoided, then?' I asked.

'Of course not. I mean, if there's something you've got to do, then to hell with the danger.' She gave an airy wave with her right hand to illustrate this carefree point of view, and a car's horn sounded vigorously just behind us. A man swept past glaring at Kate for her unintentional signal. She laughed.

She swung the car down to the sea in Worthing, and drove eastwards along the coast road. The smell of salt and seaweed was strong and refreshing. We passed the acres of new bungalows outside Worthing, the docks and the power stations of Shoreham, Southwick, and Portslade, the sedate façades of Hove, and came at length to the long promenade at Brighton. Kate turned deftly into a square in the town, and stopped the car.

'Let's go down by the sea,' she said. 'I love it.'

We walked across the road, down some steps, and

staggered across the bank of shingle on to the sand. Kate took her shoes off and poured out a stream of little stones. The sun shone warmly and the tide was out. We walked slowly along the beach for about a mile, jumping over the breakwaters, and then turned and went back. It was a heavenly afternoon.

As we strolled hand in hand up the road towards Kate's car, I saw for the first time that she had parked it only a hundred yards from the Pavilion Plaza Hotel, where I had driven Clifford Tudor from Plumpton ten days earlier.

And talk of the devil, I thought. There he was. The big man was standing on the steps of the hotel, talking to the uniformed doorman. Even at a distance there was no mistaking that size, that dark skin, that important carriage of the head. I watched him idly.

Just before we arrived at Kate's car a taxi came up from behind us, passed us, and drew up outside the Pavilion Plaza. It was a black taxi with a yellow shield on the door, and this time it was close enough for me to read the name: Marconicars. I looked quickly at the driver and saw his profile as he went past. He had a large nose and a receding chin, and I had never seen him before.

Clifford Tudor said a few last words to the doorman, strode across the pavement, and got straight into the taxi without pausing to tell the driver where he wanted to go. The taxi drove off without delay.

'What are you staring at?' said Kate, as we stood beside her car.

'Nothing much,' I said. 'I'll tell you about it if you'd like some tea in the Pavilion Plaza Hotel.'

'That's a dull dump,' she said. 'Aunt Deb approves of it.'

'More sleuthing,' I said.

'All right, then. Got your magnifying glass and bloodhound handy?'

We went into the hotel. Kate said she would go and tidy her hair. While she was gone I asked the young girl in the reception desk if she knew where I could find Clifford Tudor. She fluttered her eyelashes at me and I grinned encouragingly back.

'You've just missed him, I'm afraid,' she said. 'He's gone back to his flat.'

'Does he come here often?' I asked.

She looked at me in surprise. 'I thought you knew. He's on the board of governors. One of the chief shareholders. In fact,' she added with remarkable frankness, 'he very nearly owns this place and has more say in running it than the manager.' It was clear from her voice and manner that she thoroughly approved of Mr Tudor.

'Has he got a car?' I asked.

This was a very odd question, but she prattled on without hesitation. 'Yes, he's got a lovely big car with a long bonnet and lots of chromium. Real classy. But he

168

doesn't use it, of course. Mostly it's taxis for him. Why, just this minute I rang for one of those radio cabs for him. Real useful, they are. You just ring their office and they radio a message to the taxi that's nearest here and in no time at all it's pulling up outside. All the guests use them . . .'

'Mavis!'

The talkative girl stopped dead and looked round guiltily. A severe girl in her late twenties had come into the reception desk.

'Thank you for relieving me, Mavis. You may go now,' she said.

Mavis gave me a flirting smile and disappeared.

'Now, sir, can I help you?' She was polite enough, but not the type to gossip about her employers.

'Er – can we have afternoon tea here?' I asked.

She glanced at the clock. 'It's a little late for tea, but go along into the lounge and the waiter will attend to you.'

Kate eyed the resulting fishpaste sandwiches with disfavour. 'This is one of the hazards of detecting, I suppose,' she said, taking a tentative bite. 'What did you find out about what?'

I said I was not altogether sure, but that I was interested in anything that had even the remotest connexion with the yellow shield taxis or with Bill Davidson, and Clifford Tudor was connected in the most commonplace way with both.

'Nothing in it, I shouldn't think,' said Kate, finishing the sandwich but refusing another.

I sighed. 'I don't think so, either,' I said.

'What next, then?'

'If I could find out who owns the yellow shield taxis . . .'

'Let's ring them up and ask,' said Kate, standing up. She led the way to the telephone and looked up the number in the directory.

'I'll do it,' she said. 'I'll say I have a complaint to make and I want to write directly to the owners about it.'

She got through to the taxi office and gave a tremendous performance, demanding the names and addresses of the owners, managers and the company's solicitors. Finally, she put down the receiver and looked at me disgustedly.

'They wouldn't tell me a single thing,' she said. 'He was a really patient man, I must say. He didn't get ruffled when I was really quite rude to him. But all he would say was, "Please write to us with the details of your complaint and we will look into it fully." He said it was not the company's policy to disclose the names of its owners and he had no authority to do it. He wouldn't budge an inch.'

'Never mind. It was a darned good try. I didn't really think they would tell you. But it gives me an idea . . .'

I rang up the Maidenhead police station and asked

for Inspector Lodge. He was off duty, I was told. Would I care to leave a message? I would.

I said, 'This is Alan York speaking. Will you please ask Inspector Lodge if he can find out who owns or controls the Marconicar radio taxi cabs in Brighton? He will know what it is about.'

The voice in Maidenhead said he would give Inspector Lodge the message in the morning, but could not undertake to confirm that Inspector Lodge would institute the requested enquiries. Nice official jargon. I thanked him and rang off.

Kate was standing close to me in the telephone box. She was wearing a delicate flowery scent, so faint that it was little more than a quiver in the air. I kissed her, gently. Her lips were soft and dry and sweet. She put her hands on my shoulders, and looked into my eyes, and smiled. I kissed her again.

A man opened the door of the telephone box. He laughed when he saw us. 'I'm so sorry . . . I want to telephone . . .' We stepped out of the box in confusion.

I looked at my watch. It was nearly half-past six.

'What time does Aunt Deb expect us back?' I asked.

'Dinner is at eight. We've got until then,' said Kate. 'Let's walk through the Lanes and look at the antique shops.'

We went slowly down the back pathways of Brighton, pausing before each brightly lit window to admire the contents. And stopping, too, in one or two corners in the growing dusk, to continue where we had left off in the telephone box. Kate's kisses were sweet and virginal. She was unpractised in love, and though her body trembled once or twice in my arms, there was no passion, no hunger in her response.

At the end of one of the Lanes, while we were discussing whether to go any further, some lights were suddenly switched on behind us. We turned round. The licensee of The Blue Duck was opening his doors for the evening. It looked a cosy place.

'How about a snifter before we go back?' I suggested.

'Lovely,' said Kate. And in this casual inconsequential way we made the most decisive move in our afternoon's sleuthing.

We went into The Blue Duck.

CHAPTER NINE

The bar was covered with a big sheet of gleaming copper. The beer handles shone. The glasses sparkled. It was a clean, friendly little room with warm lighting and original oils of fishing villages round the walls.

Kate and I leaned on the bar and discussed sherries with the innkeeper. He was a military-looking man of about fifty with a bristly moustache waxed at the ends. I put him down as a retired sergeant-major. But he knew his stuff, and the sherry he recommended to us was excellent. We were his first customers, and we stood chatting to him. He had the friendly manner of all good innkeepers, but underlying this I saw a definite wariness. It was like the nostril cocked for danger in a springbok; uneasy, even when all appeared safe. But I didn't pay much attention, for his troubles, I thought erroneously, had nothing to do with me.

Another man and a girl came in, and Kate and I turned to take our drinks over to one of the small scattered tables. As we did so she stumbled, knocked her

173

glass against the edge of the bar and broke it. A jagged edge cut her hand, and it began to bleed freely.

The innkeeper called his wife, a thin, small woman with bleached hair. She saw the blood welling out of Kate's hand, and exclaimed with concern, 'Come and put it under the cold tap. That'll stop the bleeding. Mind you don't get it on your nice coat.'

She opened a hatch in the bar to let us through, and led us into her kitchen, which was as spotless as the bar. On a table at one side were slices of bread, butter, cooked meats, and chopped salads. We had interrupted the innkeeper's wife in making sandwiches for the evening's customers. She went across to the sink, turned on the tap, and beckoned to Kate to put her hand in the running water. I stood just inside the kitchen door looking round me.

'I'm so sorry to be giving you all this trouble,' said Kate, as the blood dripped into the sink. 'It really isn't a very bad cut. There just seems to be an awful lot of gore coming out of it.'

'It's no trouble at all, dear,' said the innkeeper's wife. 'I'll find you a bandage.' She opened a dresser drawer to look for one, giving Kate a reassuring smile.

I started to walk over from the doorway to take a closer look at the damage. Instantly there was a deadly menacing snarl, and a black Alsatian dog emerged from a box beside the refrigerator. His yellow eyes were fixed on me, his mouth was slightly open with the top lip drawn back, and the razor-sharp teeth were parted. There was a collar round his neck, but he was not chained up. Another snarl rumbled deep in his throat.

I stood stock still in the centre of the kitchen.

The innkeeper's wife took a heavy stick from beside the dresser and went over to the dog. She seemed flustered.

'Lie down, Prince. Lie down.' She pointed with the stick to the box. The dog, after a second's hesitation, stepped back into it and sat erect, still looking at me with the utmost hostility. I didn't move.

'I'm very sorry, sir. He doesn't like strange men. He's a very good guard dog, you see. He won't hurt you now, not while I'm here.' And she laid the stick on the dresser, and went over to Kate with cotton wool, disinfectant, and a bandage.

I took a step towards Kate. Muscles rippled along the dog's back, but he stayed in his box. I finished the journey to the sink. The bleeding had almost stopped, and, as Kate said, it was not a bad cut. The innkeeper's wife dabbed it with cotton wool soaked in disinfectant, dried it, and wound on a length of white gauze bandage.

I leaned against the draining board, looking at the dog and the heavy stick, and remembering the underlying edginess of the innkeeper. They added up to just one thing.

Protection.

Protection against what? Protection against Protection, said my brain, dutifully, in a refrain. Someone had been trying the Protection racket on mine host. Pay up or we smash up your pub ... or you ... or your wife. But this particular innkeeper, whether or not I was right about his sergeant-major past, looked tough enough to defy that sort of bullying. The collectors of Protection had been met, or were to be met, by an authentically lethal Alsatian. They were likely to need protection themselves.

The innkeeper put his head round the door.

'All right?' he said.

'It's fine, thank you very much,' said Kate.

'I've been admiring your dog,' I said.

The innkeeper took a step into the room. Prince turned his head away from me for the first time and looked at his master.

'He's a fine fellow,' he agreed.

Suddenly out of nowhere there floated into my mind a peach of an idea. There could not, after all, be too many gangs in Brighton, and I had wondered several times why a taxi line should employ thugs and fight pitched battles. So I said, with a regrettable lack of caution, 'Marconicars.'

The innkeeper's professionally friendly smile vanished, and he suddenly looked at me with appalling, vivid hate. He picked the heavy stick off the dresser and raised it to hit me. The dog was out of his box in one fluid stride, crouching ready to spring, with his ears flat and his teeth bared. I had struck oil with a vengeance.

Kate came to the rescue. She stepped to my side and said, without the slightest trace of alarm, 'For heaven's sake don't hit him too hard because Aunt Deb is expecting us for roast lamb and the odd potato within half an hour or so and she is very strict about us being back on the dot.'

This surprising drivel made the innkeeper hesitate long enough for me to say 'I don't belong to Marconi-cars. I'm against them. Do be a good chap and put that stick down, and tell Prince his fangs are not required.'

The innkeeper lowered the stick, but he left Prince where he was, on guard four feet in front of me.

Kate said to me, 'Whatever have we walked into?' The bandage was trailing from her hand, and the blood was beginning to ooze through. She wound up the rest of the bandage unconcernedly and tucked in the end.

'Protection, I think?' I said to the innkeeper. 'It was just a wild guess, about the taxis. I'd worked out why you need such an effective guard dog, and I've been thinking about taxi-drivers for days. The two things just clicked, that's all.'

'Some of the Marconicar taxi-drivers beat him up a bit a week ago,' said Kate conversationally to the innkeeper's wife. 'So you can't expect him to be quite sane on the subject.'

The innkeeper gave us both a long look. Then he

went to his dog and put his hand round its neck and fondled it under its chin. The wicked yellow eyes closed, the lips relaxed over the sharp teeth, and the dog leaned against his master's leg in devotion. The innkeeper patted its rump, and sent it back to its box.

'A good dog, Prince,' he said, with a touch of irony. 'Well now, we can't leave the bar unattended. Sue, dear, will you look after the customers while I talk to these young people?'

'There's the sandwiches not made yet,' protested Sue.

'I'll do them,' said Kate, cheerfully. 'And let's hope I don't bleed into them too much.' She picked up a knife and began to butter the slices of bread. The innkeeper and his wife looked less able to deal with Kate than with the taxi-drivers: but after hesitating a moment, the wife went out to the bar.

'Now, sir,' said the innkeeper.

I outlined for him the story of Bill's death and my close contact with the taxi-drivers in the horse-box. I said, 'If I can find out who's at the back of Marconicars, I'll probably have the man who arranged Major Davidson's accident.'

'Yes, I see that,' he said. 'I hope you have more luck than I've had. Trying to find out who owns Marconicars is like running head on into a brick wall. Dead end. I'll tell you all I can, though. The more people sniping at them, the sooner they'll be liquidated.' He leaned over and picked up two sandwiches. He gave one to me, and bit into the other.

'Don't forget to leave room for the roast lamb,' said Kate, seeing me eating. She looked at her watch. 'Oh, dear, we'll be terribly late for dinner and I hate to make Aunt Deb cross.' But she went on placidly with her buttering.

'I bought The Blue Duck eighteen months ago,' said the innkeeper. 'When I got out into civvy street.'

'Sergeant-major?' I murmured.

'Regimental,' he said, with justifiable pride. 'Thomkins, my name is. Well, I bought The Blue Duck with my savings and my retirement pay, and dead cheap it was too. Too cheap. I should have known there'd be a catch. We hadn't been here more than three weeks, and taking good money too, when this chap comes in one night and says as bold as brass that if we didn't pay up like the last landlord it'd be just too bad for us. And he picked up six glasses off the bar and smashed them. He said he wanted fifty quid a week. Well, I ask you, fifty quid! No wonder the last landlord wanted to get out. I was told afterwards he'd been trying to sell the place for months, but all the locals found out they would be buying trouble and left it alone for some muggins like me straight out of the army and still wet behind the ears to come along and jump in with my big feet.'

Innkeeper Thomkins chewed on his sandwich while he thought.

'Well, then, I told him to eff off. And he came back the next night with about five others and smashed the place to bits. They knocked me out with one of my own bottles and locked my wife in the heads. Then they smashed all the bottles in the bar and all the glasses, and all the chairs. When I came round I was lying on the floor in the mess, and they were standing over me in a ring. They said that was just a taste. If I didn't cough up the fifty quid a week they'd be back to smash every bottle in the store-room and all the wine in the cellar. After that, they said, it would be my wife.'

His face was furious, as he relived it.

'What happened?' I asked.

'Well, my God, after the Germans and the Japs I wasn't giving in meekly to some little runts at the English seaside. I paid up for a couple of months to give myself a bit of breathing space, but fifty quid takes a bit of finding, on top of overheads and taxes. It's a good little business, see, but at that rate I wasn't going to be left with much more than my pension. It wasn't on.'

'Did you tell the police?' I asked.

A curious look of shame came into Thomkins' face. 'No,' he said hesitantly, 'not then I didn't. I didn't know then where the men had come from, see, and they'd threatened God knows what if I went to the police. Anyway, it's not good army tactics to re-engage an enemy who has defeated you once, unless you've got reinforcements. That's when I started to think about a dog. And I did go to the police later,' he finished, a little defensively.

'Surely the police can close the Marconicar taxi line if it's being used for systematic crime,' I said.

'Well, you'd think so,' he said, 'but it isn't like that. It's a real taxi service, you know. A big one. Most of the drivers are on the up and up and don't even know what's going on. I told a couple of them once that they were a front for the protection racket and they refused to believe me. The crooked ones look so plausible, see? Just like the others. They drive a taxi up to your door at closing time, say, all innocent like, and walk in and ask quietly for the money; and as like as not they'll pick up a customer in the pub and drive him home for the normal fare as respectable as you please.'

'Couldn't you have a policeman in plain clothes sitting at the bar ready to arrest the taxi driver when he came to collect the money?' suggested Kate.

The innkeeper said bitterly, 'It wouldn't do no good, miss. It isn't only that they come in on different days, at different times, so that a copper might have to wait a fortnight to catch one, but there aren't any grounds for arrest. They've got an IOU with my signature on it for fifty pounds, and if there was any trouble with the police, all they'd have to do would be show it, and they couldn't be touched. The police'll help all right if you can give them something they can use in court, but when it's just one man's word against another, they can't do much.'

'A pity you signed the IOU,' I sighed.

'I didn't,' he said, indignantly, 'but it looks like my signature, even to me. I tried to grab it once, but the chap who showed it to me said it wouldn't matter if I tore it up, they'd soon make out another one. They must have had my signature on a letter or something, and copied it. Easy enough to do.'

'You do pay them, then,' I said, rather disappointed.

'Not on your nellie, I don't,' said the innkeeper, his moustache bristling. 'I haven't paid them a sou for a year or more. Not since I got Prince. He chewed four of them up in a month, and that discouraged them, I can tell you. But they're still around all the time. Sue and I daren't go out much, and we always go together and take Prince with us. I've had burglar alarm bells put on all the doors and windows and they go off with an awful clatter if anyone tries to break in while we're out or asleep. It's no way to live, sir. It's getting on Sue's nerves.'

'What a dismal story,' said Kate, licking chutney off her fingers. 'Surely you can't go on like that for ever?'

'Oh, no, miss, we're beating them now. It isn't only us, see, that they got money from. They had a regular round. Ten or eleven pubs like ours – free houses. And a lot of little shops, tobacconists, souvenir shops, that sort of thing, and six or seven little cafés. None of the big places. They only pick on businesses run by people who own them, like us. When I cottoned on to that I went round to every place I thought they might be putting the screws on and asked the owners straight out if they were paying protection. It took me weeks, it's such a big area. The ones that were paying were all dead scared, of course, and wouldn't talk, but I knew who they were, just by the way they clammed up. I told them we ought to stop paying and fight. But a lot of them have kids and they wouldn't risk it, and you can't blame them.'

'What did you do?' asked Kate, enthralled.

'I got Prince. A year old, he was then. I'd done a bit of dog handling in the army, and I trained Prince to be a proper fighter.'

'You did, indeed,' I said, looking at the dog who now lay peacefully in his box with his chin on his paws.

'I took him round and showed him to some of the other victims of the protection racket,' Thomkins went on, 'and told them that if they'd get dogs too we'd chase off the taxi-drivers. Some of them didn't realize the taxis were mixed up in it. They were too scared to open their eyes. Anyway, in the end a lot of them did get dogs and I helped to train them, but it's difficult, the dog's only got to obey one master, see, and I had to get them to obey someone else, not me. Still, they weren't too bad. Not as good as Prince, of course.'

'Of course,' said Kate.

The innkeeper looked at her suspiciously, but she was demurely piling sandwiches on to a plate.

'Go on,' I said.

'In the end I got some of the people with children to join in too. They bought Alsatians or bull terriers, and we arranged a system for taking all the kiddies to school by car. Those regular walks to school laid them wide open to trouble, see? I hired a judo expert and his car to do nothing but ferry the children and their mothers about. We all club together to pay him. He's expensive, of course, but nothing approaching the protection money.'

'How splendid,' said Kate warmly.

'We're beating them all right, but it isn't all plain sailing yet. They smashed up the Cockleshell Café a fortnight ago, just round the corner from here. But we've got a system to deal with that, too, now. Several of us went round to help clear up the mess, and we all put something into the hat to pay for new tables and chairs. They've got an Alsatian bitch at that café, and she'd come into season and they'd locked her in a bedroom. I ask you! Dogs are best,' said the innkeeper, seriously.

Kate gave a snort of delight.

'Have the taxi-drivers attacked any of you personally, or has it always been your property?' I asked.

'Apart from being hit on the head with my own bottle, you mean?' The innkeeper pulled up his sleeve and showed us one end of a scar on his forearm. 'That's about seven inches long. Three of them jumped me one evening when I went out to post a letter. It was just after Prince had sent one of their fellows off, and silly like, I went out without him. It was only a step to the pillar box, see? A mistake though. They made a mess of me, but I got a good look at them. They told me I'd get the same again if I went to the police. But I rang the boys in blue right up, and told them the lot. It was a blond young brute who slashed my arm and my evidence got him six months,' he said with satisfaction. 'After that I was careful not to move a step without Prince, and they've never got near enough to have another go at me.'

'How about the other victims?' I asked.

'Same as me,' he said. 'Three or four of them were beaten up and slashed with knives. After I'd got them dogs I persuaded some of them to tell the police. They'd had the worst of it by then, I thought, but they were still scared of giving evidence in court. The gang have never actually killed anyone, as far as I know. It wouldn't be sense, anyhow, would it? A man can't pay up if he's dead.'

'No,' I said, thoughtfully. 'I suppose he can't. They might reckon that one death would bring everyone else to heel, though.'

'You needn't think I haven't that in my mind all the time,' he said sombrely, 'but there's a deal of difference between six months for assault and a life sentence or a hanging, and I expect that's what has stopped 'em. This isn't Chicago after all, though you'd wonder sometimes.'

I said, 'I suppose if they can't get money from their old victims, the gang try "protecting" people who don't know about your systems and your dogs . . .'

The innkeeper interrupted, 'We've got a system for that, too. We put an advertisement in the Brighton paper every week telling anyone who has been threatened with Protection to write to a Box number and they will get help. It works a treat, I can tell you.'

Kate and I looked at him with genuine admiration.

'They should have made you a general,' I said, 'not a sergeant-major.'

'I've planned a few incidents in my time,' he said modestly. 'Those young lieutenants in the war, straight out of civvy street and rushed through an officer course, they were glad enough now and then for a suggestion from a regular.' He stirred. 'Well, how about a drink now?'

But Kate and I thanked him and excused ourselves, as it was already eight o'clock. Thomkins and I promised to let each other know how we fared in battle, and we parted on the best of terms. But I didn't attempt to pat Prince.

Aunt Deb sat in the drawing-room tapping her foot. Kate apologized very prettily for our lateness, and Aunt

Deb thawed. She and Kate were clearly deeply attached to each other.

During dinner it was to Uncle George that Kate addressed most of the account of our afternoon's adventures. She told him amusingly and lightly about the wandering horse-box and made a rude joke about the Pavilion Plaza's paste sandwiches, which drew a mild reproof from Aunt Deb to the effect that the Pavilion Plaza was the most hospitable of the Brighton hotels. I gave a fleeting thought to the flighty Mavis, whom I had suspected, perhaps unjustly, of dispensing her own brand of hospitality on the upper floors.

'And then we had a drink in a darling little pub called The Blue Duck,' said Kate, leaving out the telephone box and our walk through the Lanes. 'I cut my hand there—' she held it out complete with bandage, '—but not very badly of course, and we went into the kitchen to wash the blood off, and that's what made us late. They had the most terrifying Alsatian there that I'd ever seen in my life. He snarled a couple of times at Alan and made him shiver in his shoes like a jelly . . .' She paused to eat a mouthful of roast lamb.

'Do you care for dogs, Mr York?' said Aunt Deb, with a touch of disdain. She was devoted to her dachshund.

'It depends,' I said.

Kate said, 'You don't exactly fall in love with Prince. I expect they call him Prince because he's black. The

187

Black Prince. Anyway, he's useful if any dog is. If I told you two dears what the man who keeps The Blue Duck told Alan and me about the skulduggery that goes on in respectable little old Brighton, you wouldn't sleep sound in your beds.'

'Then please don't tell us, Kate dear?' said Aunt Deb. 'I have enough trouble with insomnia as it is.'

I looked at Uncle George to see how he liked being deprived of the end of the story, and saw him push his half-filled plate away with a gesture of revulsion, as if he were suddenly about to vomit.

He noticed I was watching, and with a wry smile said, 'Indigestion, I'm afraid. Another of the boring nuisances of old age. We're a couple of old crocks now, you know.'

He tried to raise a chuckle, but it was a poor affair. There was a tinge of grey in the pink cheeks, and fine beads of sweat had appeared on the already moist-looking skin. Something was deeply wrong in Uncle George's world.

Aunt Deb looked very concerned about it, and as sheltering her from unpleasant realities was for him so old and ingrained a habit, he made a great effort to rally his resources. He took a sip of water and blotted his mouth on his napkin, and I saw the tremor in his chubby hands. But there was steel in the man under all that fat, and he cleared his throat and spoke normally enough.

He said, 'It quite slipped my mind, Kate my dear, but while you were out Gregory rang up to talk to you about Heavens Above. I asked him how the horse was doing and he said it had something wrong with its leg and won't be able to run on Thursday at Bristol as you planned.'

Kate looked disappointed. 'Is he lame?' she asked.

Uncle George said, 'I could swear Gregory said the horse had thrown out a splint. He hadn't broken any bones though, has he? Most peculiar.' He was mystified, and so, I saw, was Kate.

'Horses' leg-bones sometimes grow knobs all of a sudden, and that is what a splint is,' I said. 'The leg is hot and tender while the splint is forming, but it usually lasts only two or three weeks. Heavens Above will be sound again after that.'

'What a pest,' said Kate. 'I was so looking forward to Thursday. Will you be going to Bristol, Alan, now that my horse isn't running?'

'Yes,' I said. 'I'm riding Palindrome there. Do try and come Kate, it would be lovely to see you.' I spoke enthusiastically, which made Aunt Deb straighten her back and bend on me a look of renewed disapproval.

'It is not good for a young gel's reputation for her to be seen too often in the company of jockeys,' she said.

*

At eleven o'clock, when Uncle George had locked the study door on his collection of trophies, and when Aunt Deb had swallowed her nightly quota of sleeping pills, Kate and I went out of the house to put her car away in the garage. We had left it in the drive in our haste before dinner.

The lights of the house, muted by curtains, took the blackness out of the night, so that I could still see Kate's face as she walked beside me.

I opened the car door for her, but she paused before stepping in.

'They're getting old,' she said, in a sad voice, 'and I don't know what I'd do without them.'

'They'll live for years yet,' I said.

'I hope so . . . Aunt Deb looks very tired sometimes, and Uncle George used to have so much more bounce. I think he's worried about something now . . . and I'm afraid it's Aunt Deb's heart, though they haven't said . . . They'd never tell me if there was anything wrong with them.' She shivered.

I put my arms round her and kissed her. She smiled.

'You're a kind person, Alan.'

I didn't feel kind. I wanted to throw her in the car and drive off with her at once to some wild and lonely hollow on the Downs for a purpose of which the cave men would thoroughly have approved. It was an effort for me to hold her lightly, and yet essential.

'I love you, Kate,' I said, and I controlled even my breathing.

'No,' she said, 'Don't say it. Please don't say it.' She traced my eyebrows with her finger. The dim light was reflected in her eyes as she looked at me, her body leaning gently against mine, her head held back.

'Why not?'

'Because I don't know . . . I'm not sure . . . I've liked you kissing me and I like being with you. But love is so big a word. It's too important. I'm . . . I'm not . . . ready . . .'

And there it was. Kate the beautiful, the brave, the friendly, was also Kate the unawakened. She was not aware yet of the fire that I perceived in her at every turn. It had been battened down from childhood by her Edwardian aunt, and how to release it without shocking her was a puzzle.

'Love's easy to learn,' I said. 'It's like taking a risk. You set your mind on it and refuse to be afraid, and in no time you feel terrifically exhilarated and all your inhibitions fly out of the window.'

'And you're left holding the baby,' said Kate, keeping her feet on the ground.

'We could get married first,' I said, smiling at her.

'No. Dear Alan. No. Not yet.' Then she said, almost in a whisper, 'I'm so sorry.'

She got into the car and drove slowly round to the barn garage. I followed behind the car and helped her shut the big garage doors, and walked back with her to the house. On the doorstep she paused and squeezed my hand, and gave me a soft, brief, sisterly kiss.

I didn't want it.

I didn't feel at all like a brother.

CHAPTER TEN

On Tuesday it began to rain, cold slanting rain which lashed at the opening daffodils and covered the flowers with splashed-up mud. The children went to school in shining black capes with sou'-westers pulled down to their eyes and gum boots up to their knees. All that could be seen of William was his cherubic mouth with milk stains at the corners.

Scilla and I spent the day sorting out Bill's clothes and personal belongings. She was far more composed than I would have expected, and seemed to have won through to an acceptance that he was gone and that life must be lived without him. Neither of us had mentioned, since it happened, the night she had spent in my bed, and I had become convinced that when she woke the next morning she had had no memory of it. Grief and drugs had played tricks with her mind.

We sorted Bill's things into piles. The biggest section was to be saved for Henry and William, and into this pile Scilla put not only cuff links and studs and two gold watches, but dinner jackets and a morning suit and grey top hat. I teased her about it.

'It isn't silly,' she said. 'Henry will be needing them in ten years, if not before. He'll be very glad to have them.' And she added a hacking jacket and two new white silk shirts.

'We might just as well put everything back into the cupboards and wait for Henry and William to grow,' I said.

'That's not a bad idea,' said Scilla, bequeathing to the little boys their father's best riding breeches and his warmly lined white mackintosh.

We finished the clothes, went downstairs to the cosy study, and turned our attention to Bill's papers. His desk was full of them. He clearly hated to throw away old bills and letters, and in the bottom drawer we found a bundle of letters that Scilla had written to him before their marriage. She sat on the window seat reading them nostalgically while I sorted out the rest.

Bill had been methodical. The bills were clipped together in chronological order, and the letters were in boxes and files. There were some miscellaneous collections in the pigeon-holes, and a pile of old, empty, used envelopes with day-to-day notes on the backs. They were reminders to himself, mostly, with messages like 'Tell Simpson to mend fence in five-acre field,' and 'Polly's birthday Tuesday.' I looked through them quickly, hovering them over the heap bound for the wastepaper basket.

I stopped suddenly. On one of them, in Bill's loopy sprawling handwriting, was the name Clifford Tudor, and underneath, a telephone number and an address in Brighton.

'Do you know anyone called Clifford Tudor?' I asked Scilla.

'Never heard of him,' she said without looking up.

If Tudor had asked Bill to ride for him, as he had told me when I drove him from Plumpton to Brighton, it was perfectly natural for Bill to have his name and address. I turned the envelope over. It had come from a local tradesman, whose name was printed on the top left-hand corner, and the postmark was date-stamped January, which meant that Bill had only recently acquired Tudor's address.

I put the envelope in my pocket and went on sorting. After the old envelopes I started on the pigeon-holes. There were old photographs and some pages the children had drawn and written on with straggly letters in their babyhood, address books, luggage labels, a birthday card, school reports, and various notebooks of different shapes and sizes.

'You'd better look through these, Scilla,' I said.

'You look,' she said, glancing up from her letters with a smile. 'You can tell me what's what, and I'll look at them presently.'

Bill had had no secrets. The notebooks mainly contained his day-to-day expenses, jotted down to help his accountant at the annual reckoning. They went back some years. I found the latest, and leafed through it.

School fees, hay for the horses, a new garden hose, a repair to the Jaguar's head-lamp in Bristol, a present for Scilla, a bet on Admiral, a donation to charity. And that was the end. After that came the blank pages which were not going to be filled up.

I looked again at the last entries. A bet on Admiral. Ten pounds to win, Bill had written. And the date was the day of his death. Whatever had been said to Bill about Admiral's falling, he had taken it as a joke and had backed himself to win in spite of it. I would dearly have liked to know what the 'joke' had been. He had told Pete, whose mind was with the horses. He had not told Scilla, nor any of his friends as far as I could find out. Possibly he had thought it so unimportant that after he spoke to Pete it had wholly slipped his mind.

I stacked up the notebooks and began on that last pigeon-hole full of oddments. Among them were fifteen or twenty of the betting tickets issued by bookmakers at race meetings. As evidence of bets lost, they are usually torn up or thrown away by disappointed punters, not carefully preserved in a tidy desk.

'Why did Bill keep these betting tickets?' I asked Scilla.

'Henry had a craze for them not long ago, don't you

remember?' she said. 'And after it wore off Bill still brought some home for him. I think he kept them in case William wanted to play bookmakers in his turn.'

I did remember. I had backed a lot of horses for halfpennies with Henry the bookmaker, the little shark. They never won.

The extra tickets Bill had saved for him were from several different bookmakers. It was part of Bill's pleasure at the races to walk among the bookmakers' stands in Tattersall's and put his actual cash on the best odds, instead of betting on credit with a bookmaker on the rails.

'Do you want to keep them for William still?' I asked.

'May as well,' said Scilla.

I put them back in the desk, and finished the job. It was late in the afternoon. We went into the drawing-room, stoked up the fire, and settled into armchairs.

She said, 'Alan, I want to give you something which belonged to Bill. Now, don't say anything until I've finished. I've been wondering what you'd like best, and I'm sure I've chosen right.'

She looked from me to the fire and held her hands out to warm them.

She said, 'You are to have Admiral.'

'No.' I was definite.

'Why not?' She looked up, sounding disappointed.

'Dearest Scilla, it's far too much,' I said. 'I thought

you meant something like a cigarette case, a keepsake. You can't possibly give me Admiral. He's worth thousands. You must sell him, or run him in your name if you want to keep him, but you can't give him to me. It wouldn't be fair to you or the children for me to have him.'

'He might be worth thousands if I sold him – but I couldn't sell him, you know. I couldn't bear to do that. He meant so much to Bill. How could I sell him as soon as Bill's back was turned? And if I keep him and run him, I'll have to pay the bills, which might not be easy for a while with death duties hanging over me. If I give him to you, he's in hands Bill would approve of, and you can pay for his keep. I've thought it all out, so you're not to argue. Admiral is yours.'

She meant it.

'Then let me lease him from you,' I said.

'No, he's a gift. From Bill to you, if you like.'

And on those terms I gave in, and thanked her as best I could.

The following morning, early, I drove to Pete Gregory's stables in Sussex to jump my green young Forlorn Hope over the schooling hurdles. A drizzling rain was falling as I arrived, and only because I had come so far did we bother to take the horses out. It was not a very satisfactory session, with Forlorn Hope slipping on the wet grass as we approached the first hurdle and not taking on the others with any spirit after that.

We gave it up and went down to Pete's house. I told him Admiral was to be mine and that I would be riding him.

He said, 'He's in the Foxhunters' at Liverpool, did you know?'

'So he is!' I exclaimed delightedly. I had not yet ridden round the Grand National course, and the sudden prospect of doing it a fortnight later was exciting.

'You want to have a go?'

'Yes, indeed,' I said.

We talked over the plans for my other horses, Pete telling me Palindrome was in fine fettle after his Cheltenham race and a certainty for the following day at Bristol. We went out to look at him and the others, and I inspected the splint which Heavens Above was throwing out. His leg was tender, but it would right itself in time.

When I left Pete's I went back to Brighton, parking the Lotus and taking a train as before. I walked out of Brighton station with a brief glance at the three taxis standing there (no yellow shields) and walked briskly in the direction of the headquarters of the Marconicars as listed in the telephone directory.

I had no particular plan, but I was sure the core of the mystery was in Brighton, and if I wanted to discover it, I would have to dig around on the spot. My feelers on the racecourse had still brought me nothing but a husky warning on the telephone.

The Marconicars offices were on the ground floor of a converted Regency terrace house. I went straight into the narrow hall.

The stairs rose on the right, and on the left were two doors, with a third, marked Private, facing me at the far end of the passage. A neat board on the door nearest the entrance said 'Enquiries'. I went in.

It had once been an elegant room and even the office equipment could not entirely spoil its proportions. There were two girls sitting at desks with typewriters in front of them, and through the half-open folded dividing doors I could see into an inner office where a third sat in front of a switchboard. She was speaking into a microphone.

'Yes, madam, a taxi will call for you in three minutes,' she said. 'Thank you.' She had a pleasant high voice of excellent carrying quality.

The two girls in the outer office looked at me expectantly. They wore tight sweaters and large quantities of mascara. I spoke to the one nearest the door.

'Er . . . I'm enquiring about booking some taxis . . . for a wedding. My sister's,' I added, improvising and inventing the sister I never had. 'Is that possible?'

'Oh, yes, I think so,' she said. 'I'll ask the manager. He usually deals with big bookings.'

I said, 'I'm only asking for an estimate . . . on behalf of my sister. She has asked me to try all the firms, to find out which will be most – er – reasonable. I can't give you a definite booking until I've consulted her again.'

'I see,' she said. 'Well, I'll ask Mr Fielder to see you.' She went out, down the passage, and through the door marked Private.

While I waited I grinned at the other girl, who patted her hair, and I listened to the girl at the switchboard.

'Just a minute, sir. I'll see if there's a taxi in your area,' she was saying. She flipped a switch and said, 'Come in, any car in Hove two. Come in, any car in Hove two.'

There was a silence and then a man's voice said out of the radio receiving set, 'It looks as though there's no one in Hove two, Marigold. I could get there in five minutes. I've just dropped a fare in Langbury Place.'

'Right, Jim.' She gave him the address, flipped the switch again, and spoke into the telephone. 'A taxi will be with you in five minutes, sir. I am sorry for the delay, we have no cars available who can reach you faster than that. Thank you, sir.' As soon as she had finished speaking the telephone rang again. She said, 'Marconicars. Can I help you?'

Down the hall came the clip clop of high heels on linoleum, and the girl came back from Mr Fielder. She said, 'The manager can see you now, sir.'

'Thank you,' I said. I went down the hall and through the open door at the end.

The man who rose to greet me and shake hands was a heavy, well-tailored, urbane man in his middle forties. He wore spectacles with heavy black frames, had smooth black hair and hard blue eyes. He seemed a man of too strong a personality to be sitting in the back office of a taxi firm, too high-powered an executive for the range of his job.

I felt my heart jump absurdly, and I had a moment's panic in which I feared he knew who I was and what I was trying to do. But his gaze was calm and business-like, and he said only, 'I understand you wish to make a block booking for a wedding.'

'Yes,' I said, and launched into fictitious details. He made notes, added up some figures, wrote out an esti-mate, and held it out to me. I took it. His writing was strong and black. It fitted him.

'Thank you,' I said. 'I'll give this to my sister, and let you know.'

As I went out of his door and shut it behind me, I looked back at him. He was sitting behind his desk staring at me through his glasses with unwinking blue eyes. I could read nothing in his face.

I went back into the front office and said, 'I've got the estimate I wanted. Thank you for your help.' I turned to go, and had a second thought. 'By the way, do you know where I can find Mr Clifford Tudor?' I asked.

The girls, showing no surprise at my enquiry, said they did not know.

'Marigold might find out for you,' said one of them. 'I'll ask her.'

Marigold, finishing her call, agreed to help. She pressed the switch. 'All cars. Did anyone pick up Mr Tudor today? Come in please.'

A man's voice said, 'I took him to the station this morning, Marigold. He caught the London train.'

'Thanks, Mike,' said Marigold.

'She knows all their voices,' said one of the girls, admiringly. 'They never have to tell her the number of their car.'

'Do you all know Mr Tudor well?' I asked.

'Never seen him,' said one girl, and the others shook their heads in agreement.

'He's one of our regulars. He takes a car whenever he wants one, and we book it here. The driver tells Marigold where he's taking him. Mr Tudor has a monthly account, and we make it up and send it to him.'

'Suppose the driver takes Mr Tudor from place to place and fails to report it to Marigold?' I asked conversationally.

'He wouldn't be so silly. The drivers get commission on regulars. Instead of tips, do you see? We put ten per cent on the bills to save the regulars having to tip the drivers every five minutes.'

'A good idea,' I said. 'Do you have many regulars?'

'Dozens,' said one of the girls. 'But Mr Tudor is about our best client.'

'And how many taxis are there?' I asked.

'Thirty-one. Some of them will be in the garage for servicing, of course, and sometimes in the winter we only have half of them on the road. There's a lot of competition from the other firms.'

'Who actually owns the Marconicars?' I asked casually.

They said they didn't know and couldn't care less.

'Not Mr Fielder?' I asked.

'Oh, no,' said Marigold. 'I don't think so. There's a Chairman, I believe, but we've never seen him. Mr Fielder can't be all that high up, because he sometimes takes over from me in the evenings and at week-ends. Though another girl comes in to relieve me on my days off, of course.'

They suddenly all seemed to realize that this had nothing to do with my sister's wedding. It was time to go, and I went.

I stood outside on the pavement wondering what to do next. There was a café opposite, across the broad street, and it was nearly lunch-time. I went over and into the café, which smelled of cabbage, and because I had arrived before the rush there was a table free by the window. Through the chaste net curtains of the Olde Oake Café I had a clear view of the Marconicar office. For what it was worth.

A stout girl with wispy hair pushed a typed menu card in front of me. I looked at it, depressed. English home cooking at its very plainest. Tomato soup, choice of fried cod, sausages in batter, or steak and kidney pie, with suet pudding and custard to follow. It was all designed with no regard for an amateur rider's weight. I asked for coffee. The girl said firmly I couldn't have coffee by itself at lunch-time, they needed the tables. I offered to pay for the full lunch if I could just have the coffee, and to this she agreed, clearly thinking me highly eccentric.

The coffee, when it came, was surprisingly strong and good. I was getting the first of the brew, I reflected, idly watching the Marconicar front door. No one interesting went in or out.

On the storey above the Marconicars a big red neon sign flashed on and off, showing little more than a flicker in the daylight. I glanced up at it. Across the full width of the narrow building was the name L. C. PERTH. The taxi office had 'Marconicars' written in bright yellow on black along the top of its big window, and looking up I saw that the top storey was decorated with a large blue board bearing in white letters the information 'Jenkins, Wholesale Hats'.

The total effect was colourful indeed, but hardly what the Regency architect had had in mind. I had a mental picture of him turning in his grave so often that he made knots in his winding sheet, and I suppose I smiled, for a voice suddenly said, 'Vandalism, isn't it?'

A middle-aged woman had sat down at my table, unnoticed by me as I gazed out of the window. She had a mournful horsey face with no make-up, a hideous brown hat which added years to her age, and an earnest look in her eyes. The café was filling up, and I could no longer have a table to myself.

'It's startling, certainly,' I agreed.

'It ought not to be allowed. All these old houses in this district have been carved up and turned into offices, and it's really disgraceful how they look now. I belong to the Architectural Preservation Group,' she confided solemnly, 'and we're getting out a petition to stop people descrating beautiful buildings with horrible advertisements.'

'Are you having success?' I asked.

She looked depressed. 'Not very much, I'm afraid. People just don't seem to care as they should. Would you believe it, half the people in Brighton don't know what a Regency house looks like, when they're sur-rounded by them all the time? Look at that row over there, with all those boards and signs. And that neon,' her voice quivered with emotion, 'is the last straw. It's only been there a few months. We've petitioned to make them take it down, but they won't.'

'That's very discouraging,' I said, watching the Mar-conicar door. The two typists came out and went chattering up the road, followed by two more girls whom I supposed to have come down from the upper floors.

My table companion chatted on between spoonfuls of tomato soup. 'We can't get any satisfaction from Perth's at all because no one in authority there will meet us, and the men in the office say they can't take the sign down because it doesn't belong to them, but they won't tell us who it does belong to so that we can petition him in person.' I found I sympathized with Perth's invisible ruler in his disinclination to meet the Architectural Preservation Group on the warpath. 'It was bad enough before, when they had their name just painted on the windows, but neon . . .' Words failed her, at last.

Marigold left for lunch. Four men followed her. No one arrived.

I drank my coffee, parted from the middle-aged lady without regret, and gave it up for the day. I took the train back to my car and drove up to London. After a long afternoon in the office, I started for home at the tail end of the rush-hour traffic. In the hold-ups at crossings and roundabouts I began, as a change from Bill's mystery, to tackle Joe Nantwich's.

I pondered his 'stopping' activities, his feud with Sandy Mason, his disgrace with Tudor, his obscure threatening notes. I thought about the internal workings of the weighing-room, where only valets, jockeys, and officials are allowed in the changing rooms, and trainers and owners are confined to the weighing room itself: while the press and the public may not enter at all.

If the 'Bolingbroke, this week' note was to be believed, Joe would already have received his punishment, because 'this. week' was already last week. Yet I came to the conclusion that I would see him alive and well at Bristol on the following day, even if not in the best of spirits. For, by the time I reached home, I knew I could tell him who had written the notes, though I wasn't sure I was going to.

Sleep produces the answers to puzzles in the most amazing way. I went to bed on Wednesday night thinking I had spent a more or less fruitless morning in Brighton. But I woke on Thursday morning with a name in my mind and the knowledge that I had seen it before, and where. I went downstairs in my dressing-gown to Bill's desk, and took out the betting tickets he had saved for Henry. I shuffled through them, and found what I wanted. Three of them bore the name L. C. PERTH.

I turned them over. On their backs Bill had pencilled the name of a horse, the amount of his bet, and the date. He was always methodical. I took all the tickets up to my room, and looked up the races in the form book. I remembered many casual snatches of conversation. And a lot of things became clear to me.

But not enough, not enough.

CHAPTER ELEVEN

It poured with rain at Bristol, a cold, steady unrelenting wetness which took most of the pleasure out of racing.

Kate sent a message that she was not coming because of the weather, which sounded unlike her, and I wondered what sort of pressure Aunt Deb had used to keep her at home.

The main gossip in the weighing-room concerned Joe Nantwich. The Stewards had held an inquiry into his behaviour during the last race on Champion Hurdle day, and had, in the official phrase, 'severely cautioned him as to his future riding'. It was generally considered that he was very lucky indeed to have got off so lightly, in view of his past record.

Joe himself was almost as cocky as ever. From a distance his round pink face showed no traces of the fear or drunkenness which had made a sodden mess of him at Cheltenham. Yet I was told that he had spent the preceding Friday and Saturday and most of Sunday in the Turkish baths, scared out of his wits. He had drunk himself silly and sweated it off alternately during the whole of that time, confiding to the attendants in tears that he was safe with them, and refusing to get dressed and go home.

The authority for this story, and one who gave it its full flavour, was Sandy, who had happened, he said, to go into the Turkish baths on Sunday morning to lose a few pounds for Monday's racing.

I found Joe reading the notices. He was whistling through his teeth.

'Well, Joe,' I said, 'what makes you so cheerful?'

'Everything.' He smirked. At close quarters I could see the fine lines round his mouth and the slightly bloodshot eyes, but his experiences had left no other signs of strain. 'I didn't get suspended by the Stewards. And I got paid for losing that race.'

'You what?' I exclaimed.

'I got paid. You know, I told you. The packet of money. It came this morning. A hundred quid.' I stared at him. 'Well, I did what I was told, didn't I?' he said aggrievedly.

'I suppose you did,' I agreed, weakly.

'And another thing, those threatening notes. I fooled them you know. I stayed in the Turkish baths all over the week-end, and they couldn't harm me there. I got off scot free,' said Joe triumphantly, as if 'this week' could not be altered to 'next week'. He did not realize either that he had already taken his punishment, that there are other agonies than physical ones. He had suffered a week of acute anxiety, followed by three days of paralysing fear, and he thought he had got off scot free.

'I'm glad you think so,' I said, mildly. 'Joe, answer me a question. The man who rings you up to tell you what horse not to win on, what does his voice sound like?'

'You couldn't tell who it is, not by listening to him. It might be anybody. It's a soft voice, and sort of fuzzy. Almost a whisper, sometimes, as if he were afraid of being overheard. But what does it matter?' said Joe. 'As long as he delivers the lolly he can croak like a frog for all I care.'

'Do you mean you'll stop another horse, if he asks you to?' I said.

'I might do. Or I might not,' said Joe, belatedly deciding that he had been speaking much too freely. With a sly, sidelong look at me he edged away into the changing room. His resilience was fantastic.

Pete and Dane were discussing the day's plans not far away, and I went over to them. Pete was cursing the weather and saying it would play merry hell with the going, but that Palindrome, all the same, should be able to act on it.

'Go to the front at half way, and nothing else will be able to come to you. They're a poor lot. As far as I can see, you're a dead cert.'

'That's good,' I said, automatically, and then

211

remembered with a mental wince that Admiral had been a dead cert at Maidenhead.

Dane asked me if I had enjoyed my stay with Kate and did not look too overjoyed by my enthusiastic answer.

'Curses on your head, pal, if you have cut me out with Kate.' He said it in a mock ferocious voice, but I had an uncomfortable feeling that he meant it. Could a friendship survive between two men who were in love with the same girl? Suddenly at that moment, I didn't know; for I saw in Dane's familiar handsome face a passing flash of enmity. It was as disconcerting as a rock turning to quicksand. And I went rather thoughtfully into the changing-room to find Sandy.

He was standing by the window, gazing through the curtain of rain which streamed down the glass. He had changed into colours for the first race, and was looking out towards the parade ring, where two miserable-looking horses were being led round by dripping, mackintoshed stable lads.

'We'll need windscreen wipers on our goggles in this little lot,' he remarked, with unabashed good spirits. 'Anyone for a mud bath? Blimey, it's enough to discourage ducks.'

'How did you enjoy your Turkish bath on Sunday?' I asked, smiling.

'Oh, you heard about that, did you?'

'I think everyone has heard about it,' I said.

'Good. Serve the little bastard right,' said Sandy, grinning hugely.

'How did you know where to find him?' I asked.

'Asked his mother . . .' Sandy broke off in the middle of the word, and his eyes widened.

'Yes,' I said. 'You sent him those threatening Bolingbroke notes.'

'And what,' said Sandy, with good humour, 'makes you think so?'

'You like practical jokes, and you dislike Joe,' I said. 'The first note he received was put into his jacket while it hung in the changing-room at Plumpton, so it had to be a jockey or a valet or an official who did it. It couldn't have been a bookmaker or a trainer or an owner or any member of the public. So I began to think that perhaps the person who planted the note in Joe's pocket was not the person who was paying him to stop horses. That person has, strangely enough, exacted no revenge at all. But I asked myself who else would be interested in tormenting Joe, and I came to you. You knew before the race that Joe was not supposed to win on Bolingbroke. When he won you told him you'd lost a lot of money, and you'd get even with him. And I guess you have. You even tracked him down to enjoy seeing him suffer.'

'Revenge is sweet, and all that. Well, it's a fair cop,' said Sandy. 'Though how you know such a lot beats me.'

'Joe told me most of it,' I said.

'What a blabbermouth. That tongue of Joe's will get him into a right mess one of these days.'

'Yes, it will,' I said, thinking of the incautious way Joe had spoken of his 'stopping' and its rewards.

'Did you tell him I had sent him those notes?' asked Sandy, with his first show of anxiety.

'No, I didn't. It would only stir up more trouble,' I said.

'Thanks for that, anyway.'

'And in reward for that small service, Sandy,' I said, 'will you tell me how you knew in advance that Bolingbroke was not supposed to win?'

He grinned widely, rocking gently on his heels, but he didn't answer.

'Go on,' I said. 'It isn't much to ask, and it might even give me a lead to that other mystery, about Bill Davidson.'

Sandy shook his head. 'It won't help you any,' he said. 'Joe told me himself.'

'What?' I exclaimed.

'He told me himself. In the washroom when we were changing before the race. You know how he can't help swanking? He wanted to show off, and I was handy, and besides, he knew I'd stopped a horse or two in my time.'

'What did he say?' I asked.

'He said if I wanted a lesson in how to choke a horse I'd better watch him on Bolingbroke. Well, a nod's as good as a wink to Sandy Mason. I got a punter to put fifty quid on Leica, which I reckoned was bound to win with Bolingbroke not trying. And look what happened. The little sod lost his nerve and beat Leica by two lengths. I could have throttled him. Fifty quid's a ruddy fortune, mate, as far as I'm concerned.'

'Why did you wait as long as ten days before you gave him that first note?' I asked.

'I didn't think of it until then,' he said, frankly. 'But it was a damn good revenge, wasn't it? He nearly got his licence suspended at Cheltenham, and he sweated his guts out for three days at the week-end, all in the screaming heeby-jeebies worked up by yours truly.' Sandy beamed. 'You should have seen him in the Turkish baths. A sodden, whining, clutching wreck. In tears, and begging me to keep him safe. Me! What a laugh. I was nearly sick, trying not to laugh. A cracking good revenge, that was.'

'And you put him over the rails at Plumpton, too,' I said.

'I never did,' said Sandy, indignantly. 'Did he tell you that? He's a bloody liar. He fell off, I saw him. I've a good mind to frighten him again.' His red hair bristled and his brown eyes sparkled. Then he relaxed. 'Oh, well . . . I'll think of something, sometime. There's no rush. I'll make his life uncomfortable – ants in his pants, worms in his boots, that sort of thing. Harmless,' and Sandy began to laugh. Then he said, 'As you're such a roaring success as a private eye, how are you getting on with that other business?'

'Not fast enough,' I said. 'But I know a lot more than I did at this time last week, so I haven't lost hope. You haven't heard anything useful?' He shook his head.

'Not a squeak anywhere. You're not giving it up, then?'

'No,' I said.

'Well, the best of British luck,' said Sandy, grinning.

An official poked his head round the door. 'Jockeys out, please,' he said. It was nearly time for the first race.

Sandy put his helmet on and tied the strings. Then he took out his false teeth, the two centre incisors of the upper jaw, wrapped them in a handkerchief and tucked them into the pocket of the coat hanging on his peg. He, like most jockeys, never rode races wearing false teeth, for fear of losing them, or even swallowing them if he fell. He gave me a gap-toothed grin, sketched a farewell salute, and dived out into the rain.

It was still raining an hour later when I went out to ride Palindrome. Pete was waiting for me in the parade ring, the water dripping off the brim of his hat in a steady stream.

'Isn't this a God-awful day?' he said. 'I'm glad it's you that's got to strip off and get soaked, and not me. I had a bellyful when I was riding. I hope you're good at swimming.'

'Why?' I asked, mystified.

'If you are, you'll know how to keep your eyes open under water.' I suspected another of Pete's rather feeble jokes, but he was serious. He pointed to the goggles slung round my neck. 'You won't need those, for a start. With all the mud that's being kicked up today, they'd be covered before you'd gone a furlong.'

'I'll leave them down, then,' I said.

'Take them off. They'll only get in your way,' he said.

So I took them off, and as I turned my head to ease the elastic over the back of my helmet, I caught a glimpse of a man walking along outside the parade ring. There were few people standing about owing to the rain, and I had a clear view of him.

It was Bert, the man in charge of the horse in the lay-by on Maidenhead Thicket. One of the Marconicar drivers.

He was not looking at me, but the sight of him was as unpleasant as an electric shock. He was a long way from base. He might have travelled the hundred and forty miles solely to enjoy an afternoon's racing in the rain. Or he might not.

I looked at Palindrome, plodding slowly round the parade ring in his waterproof rug.

A dead cert.

I shivered.

I knew I had made some progress towards my quarry, the man who had caused Bill's death, even though he himself was as unknown to me as ever. I had disregarded his two emphatic warnings and I feared I had left a broad enough trail for him to be well aware of my pursuit. Bert would not be at Bristol alone, I thought, and I could guess that a third deterrent message was on its way.

There are times when one could do without an intuition, and this was one of them. Palindrome, the dead cert. What had been done once would be tried again, and somewhere out on the rain-swept racecourse another strand of wire could be waiting. For no logical reason, I was certain of it.

It was too late to withdraw from the race. Palindrome was an odds-on favourite, and clearly in the best of health; he showed no lameness, no broken blood-vessels, none of the permitted excuses for a last minute cancellation. And if I myself were suddenly taken ill and couldn't ride, another jockey would be quickly found to take my place. I couldn't send someone out in my colours to take a fall designed for me.

If I refused point-blank, without explanation, to let Palindrome run in the race, my permit to ride would be withdrawn, and that would be the end of my steeple-chasing.

If I said to the Stewards, 'Someone is going to bring Palindrome down with wire,' they might possibly send an official round the course to inspect the fences: but he wouldn't find anything. I was quite sure that if a wire were rigged, it would be, as in Bill's case, a last minute job.

If I rode in the race, but kept Palindrome reined in behind other horses the whole way, the wire might not be rigged at all. But my heart sank as I regarded the faces of the jockeys who had already ridden, and remembered in what state they had come back from their previous race. Mud was splashed on their faces like thick khaki chicken-pox, and their jerseys were soaked and muddied to such an extent that their colours were almost unrecognizable from a few steps away, let alone the distance from one fence to the next. My own coffee and cream colours would be particularly indistinct. A man waiting with wire would not be able to tell for certain which horse was in front, but he would expect me and act accordingly.

I looked at the other jockeys in the parade ring, now reluctantly taking off their raincoats and mounting their horses. There were about ten of them. They were men who had taught me a lot, and accepted me as one of themselves, and given me a companionship I enjoyed almost as much as the racing itself. If I let one of them crash in my place, I couldn't face them again.

It was no good. I'd have to ride Palindrome out in front and hope for the best. I remembered Kate saying, 'If there's something you've go to do, then to hell with the danger.'

To hell with the danger. After all, I could fall any

day, without the aid of wire. If I fell today, with it, that would be just too bad. But it couldn't be helped. And I might be wrong; there might be no wire at all.

Pete said, 'What's the matter? You look as if you'd seen a ghost.'

'I'm all right,' I said, taking off my coat. Palindrome was standing beside me, and I patted him, admiring his splendid intelligent head. My chief worry from then on was that he, at least, should come out of the next ten minutes unscathed.

I swung up on to his back and looked down at Pete, and said, 'If . . . if Palindrome falls in this race, please will you ring up Inspector Lodge at Maidenhead police station, and tell him about it?'

'What on earth . . .?'

'Promise,' I said.

'All right. But I don't understand. You could tell him yourself, if you want to, and anyway, you won't fall.'

'No, perhaps not,' I said.

'I'll meet you in the winner's enclosure,' he said, slapping Palindrome's rump as we moved off.

The rain was blowing into our faces as we lined up for the start in front of the stands, with two circuits of the course to complete. The tapes went up, and we were off.

Two or three horses jumped the first fence ahead of me, but after that I took Palindrome to the front, and stayed there. He was at his best, galloping and jumping with the smooth flow of a top class 'chaser. On any other day, the feel of this power beneath me would have pleased me beyond words. As it was, I scarcely noticed it.

Remembering Bill's fall, I was watching for an attendant to walk across behind a fence as the horses approached it. He would be uncoiling the wire, raising it, fixing it . . . I planned when I saw that to try to persuade Palindrome to take off too soon before the fence, so that he would hit the wire solidly with his chest when he was already past the height of his spread. That way, I hoped he might break or pull down the wire and still stay on his feet; and if we fell, it should not be in a shattering somersault like Admiral's. But it is easier to plan than to do, and I doubted whether a natural jumper like Palindrome *could* be persuaded to take off one short stride too soon.

We completed the first circuit without incident, squelching on the sodden turf. About a mile from home, on the far side of the course, I heard hoofbeats close behind, and looked over my shoulder. Most of the field were bunched up some way back, but two of them were chasing me with determination and they were almost up to Palindrome's quarters.

I shook him up and he responded immediately, and we widened the gap from our pursuers to about five lengths.

No attendant walked across the course.

I didn't see any wire.

But Palindrome hit it, just the same.

It wouldn't have been too bad a fall but for the horses behind me. I felt the heavy jerk on Palindrome's legs as we rose over the last fence on the far side of the course, and I shot off like a bullet, hitting the ground with my shoulder several yards ahead. Before I had stopped rolling the other horses were jumping the fence. They would have avoided a man on the ground if they possibly could, but in this case, I was told afterwards, they had to swerve round Palindrome, who was struggling to get up, and found me straight in their path.

The galloping hooves thudded into my body. One of the horses kicked my head and my helmet split so drastically that it fell off. There were six seconds of bludgeoning, battering chaos, in which I could neither think nor move, but only feel.

When it was all over I lay on the wet ground, limp and growing numb, unable to get up, unable even to stir. I was lying on my back with my feet towards the fence. The rain fell on my face and trickled through my hair, and the drops felt so heavy on my eyelids that opening them was like lifting a weight. Through a slit, from under my rain-beaded lashes, I could see a man at the fence.

He wasn't coming to help me. He was very quickly coiling up a length of wire, starting on the outside of the course and working inwards. When he reached the inner post he put his hand in his raincoat pocket, drew out a tool, and clipped the wire where it was fastened eighteen inches above the fence. This time, he had not forgotten his wire cutters. He finished his job, hooked the coil over his arm, and turned towards me.

I knew him.

He was the driver of the horse-box.

The colour was going out of everything. The world looked grey to me, like an under-exposed film. The green grass was grey, the box driver's face was grey . . .

Then I saw that there was another man at the fence, and he was walking towards me. I knew him, too, and he was not a taxi-driver. I was so glad to find I had some help against the box driver that I could have wept with relief. I tried to tell him to look at the wire, so that this time there should be a witness. But the words could get no farther than my brain. My throat and tongue refused to form them.

He came over and stood beside me, and stooped down. I tried to smile and say hello, but not a muscle twitched. He straightened up.

He said, over his shoulder, to the box driver, 'He's been knocked out.' He turned back to me.

He said, 'You nosey bastard,' and he kicked me. I heard the ribs crack, and I felt the hot stab in my side. 'Perhaps that'll teach you to mind your own business.' He kicked me again. My grey world grew darker. I was nearly unconscious, but even in that dire moment some part of my mind went on working, and I knew why the attendant had not walked across with the wire. He had not needed to. He and his accomplice had stood on opposite sides of the course and had raised it between them.

I saw the foot drawn back a third time. It seemed hours, in my disjointed brain, until it came towards my eyes, growing bigger and bigger until it was all that I could see.

He kicked my face, and I went out like a light.

CHAPTER TWELVE

Hearing came back first. It came back suddenly, as if someone had pressed a switch. At one moment no messages of any sort were getting through the swirling, distorted dreams which seemed to have been going on inside my head for a very long time, and in the next I was lying in still blackness, with every sound sharp and distinct in my ears.

A woman's voice said, 'He's still unconscious.'

I wanted to tell her it was not true, but could not.

The sounds went on; swishing, rustling, clattering, the murmur of distant voices, the thump and rattle of water in pipes of ancient plumbing. I listened, but without much interest.

After a while I knew I was lying on my back. My limbs, when I became aware of them, were as heavy as lead and ached persistently, and ton weights rested on my eyelids.

I wondered where I was. Then I wondered who I

was. I could remember nothing at all. This seemed too much to deal with, so I went to sleep.

The next time I woke up the weights were gone from my eyes. I opened them, and found I was lying in a dim light in a room whose fuzzy lines slowly grew clear. There was a wash-basin in one corner, a table with a white cloth on it, an easy chair with wooden arms, a window to my right, a door straight ahead. A bare, functional room.

The door opened and a nurse came in. She looked at me in pleased surprise and smiled. She had nice teeth.

'Hello there,' she said. 'So you've come back at last. How do you feel?'

'Fine,' I said, but it came out as a whisper, and in any case it wasn't strictly true.

'Are you comfortable?' she asked, holding my wrist for the pulse.

'No,' I said, giving up the pretence.

'I'll go and tell Dr Mitcham you've woken up, and I expect he will come and see you. Will you be all right for a few minutes?' She wrote something on a board which lay on the table, gave me another bright smile, and swished out of the door.

So I was in hospital. But I still had no idea what had happened. Had I, I wondered, been run over by a steam roller? Or a herd of elephants?

Dr Mitcham, when he came, would solve only half the mystery.

'Why am I here?' I asked, in a croaky whisper.

'You fell off a horse,' he said.

'Who am I?'

At this question he tapped his teeth with the end of his pencil and looked at me steadily for some seconds. He was a blunt-featured young man with fluffy, already receding, fair hair, and bright intelligent pale blue eyes.

'I'd rather you remember that for yourself. You will, soon, I'm sure. Don't worry about it. Don't worry about anything. Just relax, and your memory will come back. Not all at once, don't expect that, but little by little you'll remember everything, except perhaps the fall itself.'

'What is wrong with me, exactly?' I asked.

'Concussion is what has affected your memory. As to the rest of you,' he surveyed me from head to foot, 'you have a broken collar-bone, four cracked ribs and multiple contusions.'

'Nothing serious, thank goodness,' I croaked.

He opened his mouth and gasped, and then began to laugh. He said, 'No, nothing serious. You lot are all the same. Quite mad.'

'Which lot?' I said.

'Never mind, you'll remember soon,' he said. 'Just go to sleep for a while, if you can, and you'll probably understand a great deal more when you wake up.'

I took his advice, closed my eyes and drifted to sleep. I dreamed of a husky voice which came from the centre of a bowl of red and yellow crocuses, whispering menacing things until I wanted to scream and run away, and then I realized it was my own voice whispering, and the crocuses faded into a vision of deep green forests with scarlet birds darting in the shadows. Then I thought I was very high up, looking to the ground, and I was leaning farther and farther forward until I fell, and this time what I said made perfect sense.

'I fell out of the tree.' I knew it had happened in my boyhood.

There was an exclamation beside me. I opened my eyes. At the foot of the bed stood Dr Mitcham.

'What tree?' he said.

'In the forest,' I said. 'I hit my head, and when I woke my father was kneeling beside me.'

There was an exclamation again at my right hand. I rolled my head over to look.

He sat there, sunburnt, fit, distinguished, and at forty-six looking still a young man.

'Hi, there,' I said.

'Do you know who this is?' asked Dr Mitcham.

'My father.'

'And what is your name?'

'Alan York,' I said at once, and my memory bounded back. I could remember everything up to the morning I was going to Bristol races. I remembered setting off, but what happened after that was still a blank.

'How did you get here?' I asked my father.

'I flew over. Mrs Davidson rang me up to tell me you had had a fall and were in hospital. I thought I'd better take a look.'

'How long . . .' I began, slowly.

'How long were you unconscious?' said Dr Mitcham. 'This is Sunday morning. Two and a half days. Not too bad, considering the crack you had. I kept your crash-helmet for you to see.' He opened a locker and took out the shell which had undoubtedly saved my life. It was nearly in two pieces.

'I'll need a new one,' I said.

'Quite mad. You're all quite mad,' said Dr Mitcham.

This time I knew what he meant. I grinned, but it was a lopsided affair, because I discovered that half my face was swollen as well as stiff and sore. I began to put up my left hand to explore the damage, but I changed my mind before I had raised it six inches, owing to the sudden pain which the movement caused in my shoulder. In spite of the tight bandages which arched my shoulders backwards, I heard and felt the broken ends of collar-bone grate together.

As if they had been waiting for a signal, every dull separate ache in my battered body sprang to vicious, throbbing life. I drew in a deep breath, and the broken ribs sharply rebelled against it. It was a bad moment.

I shut my eyes. My father said anxiously, 'Is he all right?' and Dr Mitcham answered, 'Yes, don't worry. I rather think his breakages have caught up with him. I'll give him something to ease it, shortly.'

'I'll be out of bed tomorrow,' I said. 'I've been bruised before, and I've broken my collar-bone before. It doesn't last long.' But I added ruefully to myself that *while* it lasted it was highly unpleasant.

'You will certainly not get up tomorrow,' said Dr Mitcham's voice. 'You'll stay where you are for a week, to give that concussion a chance.'

'I can't stay in bed for a week,' I protested. 'I shouldn't have the strength of a flea when I got up, and I'm going to ride Admiral at Liverpool.'

'When is that?' asked Dr Mitcham suspiciously.

'March twenty-fourth,' I said.

There was a short silence while they worked it out.

'That's only a week on Thursday,' said my father.

'You can put it right out of your head,' said Dr Mitcham severely.

'Promise me,' said my father.

I opened my eyes and looked at him, and when I saw the anxiety in his face I understood for the first time in my life how much I meant to him. I was his only child, and for ten years, after my mother died, he had reared me himself, not delegating the job to a succession of housekeepers, boarding schools, and tutors as many a rich man would have done, but spending time playing with me and teaching me, and making sure I learned in my teens how to live happily and usefully under the burden of extreme wealth. He himself had taught me how to face all kinds of dangers, yet I realized that it must seem to him that if I insisted on taking my first tilt at Liverpool when I was precariously unfit, I was risking more than I had any right to do.

'I promise,' I said. 'I won't ride at Liverpool this month. But I'm going on racing afterwards.'

'All right. It's a deal.' He relaxed, smiling, and stood up. 'I'll come again this afternoon.'

'Where are you staying? Where are we now?' I asked.

'This is Bristol Hospital, and I'm staying with Mrs Davidson,' he said.

I said, 'Did I get this lot at Bristol races? With Palindrome?' My father nodded. 'How is he? Was he hurt? What sort of fall did he have?'

'No, he wasn't hurt,' he said. 'He's back in Gregory's stables. No one saw how or why he fell because it was raining so hard. Gregory said you had a premonition you were going to fall, and he asked me to tell you he had done what you wanted.'

'I don't remember anything about it, and I don't know what it was I wanted him to do.' I sighed. 'It's very irritating.'

Dr Mitcham and my father went away and left me puzzling over the gap in my memory. I had an elusive feeling that I had known for a few seconds a fact of paramount significance, but grope as I would, my conscious life ended on the road to Bristol races and began again in Bristol Hospital.

The rest of the day passed slowly and miserably, with each small movement I made setting up a chorus of protest in every crushed muscle and nerve. I had been kicked by horses before, but never in so many places all at once, and I knew, though I couldn't see it, that my skin must be covered with large angry crimson patches which had spread and were turning black and finally yellow as the blood underneath congealed and dispersed. My face, I knew, must be giving the same rainbow performance, and I undoubtedly had two lovely black eyes.

The pills Dr Mitcham had sent via the nurse with pretty teeth made less difference than I would have liked, so I lay with my eyes shut and pretended I was floating on the sea in the sunshine, with my grating bones and throbbing head cushioned by a gentle swell. I filled in the scene with sea-gulls and white clouds and children splashing in the shallows, and it worked well each time until I moved again.

Late in the evening my headache grew worse and I slid in and out of weird troubled dreams in which I imagined that my limbs had been torn off by heavy weights, and I woke soaked in sweat to wiggle my toes and fingers in an agony of fear that they were missing. But no sooner had the feel of them against the sheets sent relief flooding over me than I was drifting away into the same nightmare all over again. The cycle of short awakenings and long dreams went on and on, until I was no longer sure what was real and what was not.

So shattering was the night passed in this fashion that when Dr Mitcham came into my room in the morning I implored him to show me that my hands and feet were in fact still attached to me. Without a word he stripped back the bedclothes, grasped my feet firmly, and lifted them a few inches so that I could see them. I raised my hands and looked at them, and laced my fingertips together over my stomach: and felt a complete idiot to have been so terrified over nothing.

'There's no need to be embarrassed,' said Mitcham. 'You can't expect your brain to be in perfect working order when you've been unconscious for so long. I promise you that you have no injuries you don't know about. No internal damage, no bits missing. You'll be as good as new in three weeks.' His steady pale blue eyes were reliable. 'Only,' he added, 'you'll have a scar on your face. We stitched up a cut over your left cheekbone.'

As I had not been exactly handsome before, this news did not disturb me. I thanked him for his forbearance, and he pulled the sheet and blankets over me again. His blunt face suddenly lit up with a mischievous smile, and he said, 'Yesterday *you* told *me* there was nothing seriously wrong with you and you'd be out of bed today, if I remember correctly.'

'Blast you,' I said weakly. 'I'll be out of bed tomorrow.'

In the end it was Thursday before I made it on my feet, and I went home to Scilla's on Saturday morning feeling more tottery than I cared to admit, but in good spirits nevertheless. My father, who was still there but planning to leave early the next week, came to fetch me.

Scilla and Polly clicked their tongues and made sympathetic remarks as I levered myself out of the Jaguar at one quarter my usual speed and walked carefully up the front steps. But young Henry, giving me a sweeping, comprehensive glance which took in my black and yellow face and the long newly healed cut across one cheek, greeted me with, 'And how's the horrible monster from outer space?'

'Go and boil your head,' I said, and Henry grinned delightedly.

At seven o'clock in the evening, just after the children had gone upstairs to bed, Kate rang up. Scilla and my father decided to bring some wine up from the cellar, and left me alone in the drawing-room to talk to her.

'How are the cracks?' she asked.

'Knitting nicely,' I said. 'Thank you for your letter, and for the flowers.'

'The flowers were Uncle George's idea,' she said. 'I said it was too much like a funeral, sending you flowers, and he thought that was so funny that he nearly choked. It didn't seem all that funny to me, actually, when I knew from Mrs Davidson that it very nearly was your funeral.'

'It was nowhere near that,' I said. 'Scilla was exaggerating. And whether it was your idea or Uncle George's, thank you anyway for the flowers.'

'Lilies, I expect I should have sent, not tulips,' Kate teased.

'You can send lilies next time,' I said, taking pleasure in hearing her slow attractive voice.

'Good heavens, is there going to be a next time?'

'Bound to be,' I said cheerfully.

'Well all right,' said Kate, 'I'll place a standing order with Interflora, for lilies.'

'I love you, Kate,' I said.

'I must say,' she said happily, 'it's nice hearing people say that.'

'People? Who else has said it? And when?' I asked, fearing the worst.

'Well,' she said, after a tiny pause. 'Dane, as a matter of fact.'

'Oh.'

'Don't be jealous,' she said. 'And Dane's just as bad

235

as you. He glowers like a thunderstorm if he hears your name. You're both being childish.'

'Yes, ma'am,' I said. 'When will I see you again?'

We fixed a luncheon date in London, and before she rang off I told her again that I loved her. I was about to put down my own receiver, when I heard the most unexpected sound on the telephone.

A giggle. A quickly suppressed, but definite giggle.

I knew she had disconnected; but I said into the dead mouthpiece in front of me, 'Hang on a minute, Kate, I – er – want to read you something . . . in the paper. Just a minute while I get it.' I put my receiver down on the table, went carefully out of the drawing-room, up the stairs, and into Scilla's bedroom.

There stood the culprits, grouped in a guilty huddle round the extension telephone. Henry, with the receiver pressed to his ear; Polly, her head close against his; and William, looking earnestly up at them with his mouth open. They were all in pyjamas and dressing-gowns.

'And just what do you think you're doing?' I asked, with a severe expression.

'Oh golly,' said Henry, dropping the receiver on to the bed as if it were suddenly too hot to hold.

'Alan!' said Polly, blushing deeply.

'How long have you been listening?' I demanded.

'Actually, right from the beginning,' said Polly shamefacedly.

'Henry always listens,' said William, proud of his brother.

'Shut up,' said Henry.

'You little beasts,' I said.

William looked hurt. He said again. 'But Henry always listens. He listens to everyone. He's checking up, and that's good, isn't it? Henry checks up all the time, don't you Henry?'

'Shut up William,' said Henry, getting red and furious.

'So Henry checks up, does he?' I said, frowning crossly at him. Henry stared back, caught out, but apparently unrepentant.

I advanced towards them, but the homily on the sacredness of privacy that I was about to deliver suddenly flew out of my mind. I stopped and thought.

'Henry, how long have you been listening to people on the telephone?' I asked mildly.

He looked at me warily. Finally he said, 'Quite some time.'

'Days? Weeks? Months?'

'Ages,' said Polly, taking heart again as I no longer seemed angry with them.

'Did you ever listen to your father?' I asked.

'Yes, often,' said Henry.

I paused, studying this tough, intelligent little boy. He was only eight, but if he knew the answers to what I was going to ask him, he would understand their

237

significance and be appalled by his knowledge all his life. But I pressed on.

'Did you by any chance ever hear him talking to a man with a voice like this?' I asked. Then I made my voice husky and whispering, and said, 'Am I speaking to Major Davidson?'

'Yes,' said Henry without hesitation.

'When was that?' I asked, trying to show nothing of the excitement I felt. I was sure now that he had listened in to the telephone call which Bill had mentioned as a joke to Pete, who had not taken in what he said.

'It was that voice the last time I listened to Daddy,' said Henry, matter-of-factly.

'Do you remember what the voice said?' I forced myself to speak slowly, gently.

'Oh yes, it was a joke. It was two days before he was killed,' said Henry, without distress. 'Just when we were going to bed, like now. The phone rang and I scooted in here and listened as usual. That man with the funny voice was saying, "Are you going to ride Admiral on Saturday, Major Davidson?" and Daddy said he was.' Henry paused. I waited, willing him to remember.

He screwed up his eyes in concentration and went on. 'Then the man with the funny voice said, "You are not to win on Admiral, Major Davidson." Daddy just laughed, and the man said, "I'll pay you five hundred pounds if you promise not to win." And Daddy said, "Go to hell" and I nearly snorted because he was always telling me not to say that. Then the whispery man said he didn't want Daddy to win, and that Admiral would fall if Daddy didn't agree not to win, and Daddy said "You must be mad." And then he put down the telephone, and I ran back to my room in case he should come up and find me listening.'

'Did you say anything to your father about it?' I asked.

'No,' said Henry frankly, 'That's the big snag about listening. You have to be awfully careful not to know too much.'

'Yes, I can see that,' I said, trying not to smile.

Then I saw the flicker in Henry's eyes as the meaning of what he had heard grew clearer to him. He said jerkily, 'It wasn't a joke after all, was it?'

'No, it wasn't,' I said.

'But that man didn't make Admiral fall, did he? He couldn't . . . could he? Could he?' said Henry desperately, wanting me to reassure him. His eyes were stretched wide open and he was beginning to realize that he had listened to the man who had caused his father's death. Although he would have to know one day about the strand of wire, I didn't think I ought to tell him at that moment.

'I don't really know. I don't expect so,' I lied calmly. But Henry's wide eyes stared blindly at me as if he were looking at some inward horror.

'What's the matter?' said Polly. 'I don't understand

why Henry is so upset. Just because someone told Daddy they didn't want him to win is no reason for Henry to go off in a fit.'

'Does he always remember so clearly what people say?' I asked Polly. 'It's a month ago, now, since your father died.'

'I expect Daddy and that man said a lot of things that Henry has forgotten,' said Polly judiciously, 'but he doesn't make things up.' And I knew this was true. He was a truthful child.

He said stonily, 'I don't see how he could have done it.'

I was glad at least that Henry was dealing with his revelation practically and not emotionally. Perhaps I had not done him too much harm, after all, in making him understand what he had heard and disregarded.

'Come along to bed and don't worry about it, Henry,' I said, holding out my hand to him. He took it, and uncharacteristically held on to it all the way along the landing and into his bedroom.

CHAPTER THIRTEEN

While I was dressing myself at tortoise pace the following morning the front door bell rang downstairs, and presently Joan came up to say that an Inspector Lodge would like to see me, please.

'Tell him I'll be down as soon as possible,' I said, struggling to get my shirt on over the thick bracing bandage round my shoulders. I did up most of the buttons, but decided I didn't need a tie.

The strapping round my ribs felt tight and itched horribly, my head ached, large areas of flesh were black still and tender, I had slept badly, and I was altogether in a foul mood. The three aspirins I had swallowed in place of breakfast had not come up to scratch.

I picked up my socks, tried to bend to put them on with my one useful arm, found how far away my feet had become, and flung them across the room in a temper. The day before, in the hospital, the nurse with nice teeth had helped me to dress. Today perverseness stopped me asking my father to come and do it for me.

The sight of my smudgy, yellow, unshaven face in the looking-glass made matters no better. Henry's 'horrible monster from outer space' was not so far off the mark. I longed to scratch the livid scar on my cheek, to relieve its irritation.

I plugged in my electric razor and took off the worst, brushed my hair sketchily, thrust my bare feet into slippers, put one arm into my hacking jacket and swung it over the other shoulder, and shuffled gingerly downstairs.

Lodge's face when he saw me was a picture.

'If you laugh at me I'll knock your block off. Next week,' I said.

'I'm not laughing,' said Lodge, his nostrils twitching madly as he tried to keep a straight face.

'It's not funny,' I said emphatically.

'No.'

I scowled at him.

My father said, glancing at me from behind his Sunday newspaper in the depths of an armchair by the fire, 'You sound to me as if you need a stiff brandy.'

'It's only half-past ten,' I said crossly.

'Emergencies can happen at any time of the day,' said my father, standing up, 'and this would appear to be a grave one.' He opened the corner cupboard where Scilla kept a few bottles and glasses, poured out a third of a tumbler full of brandy, and splashed some soda into it. I complained that it was too strong, too early, and unnecessary.

My father handed me the glass. 'Drink it and shut up,' he said.

Furious, I took a large mouthful. It was strong and fiery, and bit into my throat. I rolled the second mouthful round my teeth so that the scarcely diluted spirit tingled on my gums, and when I swallowed I could feel it slide warmly down to my empty stomach.

'Did you have any breakfast?' asked my father.

'No,' I said.

I took another, smaller gulp. The brandy worked fast. My bad temper began draining away, and in a minute or two I felt reasonably sane. Lodge and my father were looking at me intently as though I were a laboratory animal responding to an experiment.

'Oh very well then,' I admitted grudgingly, 'I feel better.' I took a cigarette from the silver box on the table and lit it, and noticed the sun was shining.

'Good.' My father sat down again.

It appeared that he and Lodge had introduced themselves while they waited for me, and Lodge had told him, among other things, about my adventures in the horse-box outside Maidenhead, a detail I had omitted from my letters. This I considered to be treachery of the basest sort, and said so; and I told them how Kate and I had tracked down the horse-box, and that that particular line of enquiry was a dead end.

243

I took my cigarette and glass across the room and sat on the window seat in the sun. Scilla was in the garden, cutting flowers. I waved to her.

Lodge, dressed today not in uniform but in grey flannels, fine wool shirt, and sports jacket, opened his briefcase, which lay on the table, and pulled out some papers. He sat down beside the table and spread them out.

He said, 'Mr Gregory rang me up at the station on the morning after your fall at Bristol to tell me about it.'

'Why on earth did he do that?' I asked.

'You asked him to,' said Lodge. He hesitated, and went on, 'I understand from your father that your memory is affected.'

'Yes. Most bits of that day at Bristol have come back now, but I still can't remember going out of the weighing room to ride Palindrome, or the race or the fall, or anything.' My last mental picture was of Sandy walking out into the rain. 'Why did I ask Pete to tell you I fell?'

'You asked him before the race. You apparently thought you were likely to fall. So, unofficially, I checked up on that crash of yours.' He smiled suddenly. 'You've accounted for all my free time lately, and today is really my day off. Why I bother with you I really don't know!' But I guessed that he was as addicted to detecting as an alcoholic to drink. He couldn't help doing it.

He went on, 'I went down to Gregory's stables and

took a look at Palindrome. He had a distinct narrow wound across his front on those two pads of flesh . . .'

'Chest,' I murmured.

'. . . Chest, then; and I'll give you one guess at what cut him.'

'Oh, no,' I said, guessing, but not believing it.

'I checked up on the attendants at the fences,' he said. 'One of them was new and unknown to the others. He gave his name as Thomas Butler and an address which doesn't exist, and he volunteered to stand at the farthest fence from the stands, where you fell. His offer was readily accepted because of the rain and the distance of the fence from the bookmakers. The same story as at Maidenhead. Except that this time Butler collected his earnings in the normal way. Then I got the clerk of the course to let me inspect the fence, and I found a groove on each post, six feet six inches from the ground.'

There was a short silence.

'Well, well, well,' I said blankly. 'It looks as though I was luckier than Bill.'

'I wish you could remember something about it . . . anything. What made you suspect you would fall?' asked Lodge.

'I don't know.'

'It was something that happened while you were in the parade ring waiting to mount.' He leaned forward, his dark eyes fixed intently on my face, willing my sluggish memory to come to life. But I remembered nothing, and I still felt weary from head to foot. Concentration was altogether too much of an effort.

I looked out into the peaceful spring garden. Scilla held an armful of forsythia, golden yellow against her blue dress.

'I can't remember,' I said flatly. 'Perhaps it'll come back when my head stops aching.'

Lodge sighed and sat back in his hard chair.

'I suppose,' he said, a little bitterly, 'that you do at least remember sending me a message from Brighton, asking me to do your investigating for you?'

'Yes, I do,' I said. 'How did you get on?'

'Not very well. No one seems to know who actually owns the Marconicar taxi line. It was taken over just after the war by a business man named Clifford Tudor . . .'

'What?' I said in astonishment.

'Clifford Tudor, respectable Brighton resident, British subject. Do you know him?'

'Yes,' I said. 'He owns several racehorses.'

Lodge sorted out a paper from his briefcase. 'Clifford Tudor, born Khroupista Thasos, in Trikkala, Greece. Naturalized nineteen thirty-nine, when he was twenty-five. He started life as a cook, but owing to natural business ability he acquired his own restaurant that same year. He sold it for a large profit after the war, went to Brighton, and bought for next to nothing an old taxi business that had wilted from wartime restrictions and lack of petrol. Four years ago he sold the taxis, again at a profit, and put his money into the Pavilion Plaza Hotel. He is unmarried.'

I leaned my head back against the window and waited for these details to mean something significant, but all that happened was that my inability to think increased.

Lodge went on. 'The taxi line was bought from Tudor by nominees, and that's where the fog begins. There have been so many transfers of ownership from company to company, mostly through nominees who can't be traced, that no one can discover who is the actual present owner. All business matters are settled by a Mr Fielder, the manager. He says he consults with a person he calls "the Chairman" by telephone, but that "the Chairman" rings him up every morning, and never the other way round. He says the Chairman's name is Claud Thiveridge, but he doesn't know his address or telephone number.'

'It sounds very fishy to me,' said my father.

'It is,' said Lodge. 'There is no Claud Thiveridge on the electoral register, or in any other official list, including the telephone accounts department, in the whole of Kent, Surrey, or Sussex. The operators in the telephone exchange are sure the office doesn't receive a long distance call regularly every morning, yet the morning call has been standard office routine for the last four years.

As this means that the call must be a local one, it seems fairly certain that Claud Thiveridge is not the gentleman's real name.'

He rubbed the palm of his hand round the back of his neck and looked at me steadily. 'You know a lot more than you've told me, amnesia or not,' he said. 'Spill the beans, there's a good chap.'

'You haven't told me what the Brighton police think of the Marconicars,' I said.

Lodge hesitated. 'Well, they were a little touchy on the subject, I would say. It seems they have had several complaints, but not much evidence that will stand up in court. What I have just told you is the result of their inquiries over the last few years.'

'They would not seem,' said my father dryly, 'to have made spectacular progress. Come on, Alan, tell us what's going on.'

Lodge turned his head towards him in surprise. My father smiled.

'My son is Sherlock Holmes reincarnated, didn't you know?' he said. 'After he went to England I had to employ a detective to do the work he used to do in connexion with frauds and swindles. As one of my head clerks put it, Mr Alan has an unerring instinct for smelling out crooks.'

'Mr Alan's unerring instinct is no longer functioning,' I said gloomily. Clouds were building up near the sun, and Scilla's back disappeared through the macro-carpa hedge by the kitchen door.

'Don't be infuriating, Alan,' said my father. 'Elucidate.'

'Oh, all right.' I stubbed out my cigarette, began to scratch my cheek, and dragged my fingers away from the scar with a strong effort of will. It went on itching.

'There's a lot I don't know,' I said, 'but the general gist appears to be this. The Marconicars have been in the protection racket for the last four years, intimidating small concerns like cafés and free house pubs. About a year ago, owing to the strongmindedness of one particular publican, mine host of The Blue Duck, business in the protection line began to get unexpectedly rough for the protectors. He set Alsatians on them, in fact.' I told my fascinated father and an aghast Lodge what Kate and I had learned in The Blue Duck's kitchen, carefully watched by the yellow-eyed Prince.

'Ex-Regimental Sergeant-Major Thomkins made such serious inroads into the illicit profits of Marconicars,' I continued, 'that as a racket it was more or less defunct. The legitimate side hasn't been doing too well during the winter either, according to the typists who work in the office. There are too many taxis in Brighton for the number of fares at this time of year, I should think. Anyway, it seems to me that the Marconicar boss – the Chairman, your mysterious Claud Thiveridge – set about mending his fortunes by branching out into another form of crime. He bought, I think, the shaky bookmaking business on the floor above the Marconicars, in the same building.'

I could almost smell the cabbage in the Olde Oake Café as I remembered it. 'An earnest lady told me the bookmakers had been taken over by a new firm about six months ago, but that its name was still the same. L. C. Perth, written in neon. She was very wrought up about them sticking such a garish sign on an architectural gem, and she and her old buildings society, whose name I forget, had tried to reason with the new owners to take down what they had just put up. Only they couldn't find out who the new owner was. It's too much of a coincidence to have two businesses, both shady, one above the other, both with invisible and untraceable owners. They must be owned by the same person.'

'It doesn't follow, and I don't see the point,' said my father.

'You will in a minute,' I said. 'Bill died because he wouldn't stop his horse winning a race. I know his death wasn't necessarily intended, but force was used against him. He was told not to win by a husky-voiced man on the telephone. Henry, Bill's elder son, he's eight—' I explained to Lodge, 'has a habit of listening on the extension upstairs, and he heard every word. Two days before Bill died, Henry says, the voice offered him five hundred pounds to stop his horse winning, and when

Bill laughed at this, the voice told him he wouldn't win because his horse would fall.'

I paused, but neither Lodge nor my father said anything. Swallowing the last of the brandy, I went on. 'There is a jockey called Joe Nantwich who during the last six months, ever since L. C. Perth changed hands, has regularly accepted a hundred pounds, sometimes more, to stop a horse winning. Joe gets his instructions by telephone from a husky-voiced man he has never met.'

Lodge stirred on his hard, self-chosen chair.

I went on. 'I, as you know, was set upon by the Marconicar drivers, and a few days later the man with the husky voice rang me up and told me to take heed of the warning I had been given in the horse-box. One doesn't have to be Sherlock Holmes to see that the crooked racing and the Marconicar protection racket were being run by the same man.' I stopped.

'Finish it off, then,' said my father impatiently.

'The only person who would offer a jockey a large sum to lose a race is a crooked bookmaker. If he *knows* a well-fancied horse is not going to win, he can accept any amount of money on that horse without risk.'

'Enlarge,' said Lodge.

'Normally bookmakers try to balance their books so that whichever horse wins they come out on the winning side,' I said. 'If too many people want to back one horse, they accept the bets, but they back the horse themselves with another bookmaker; then if that horse wins, they collect their winnings from the second bookmaker, and pay it out to their customers. It's a universal system known as "laying off". Now suppose you were a crooked bookmaker and Joe Nantwich is to ride a fancied horse. You tip Joe the wink to lose. Then however much is betted with you on that horse, you do no laying off, because you know you won't have to pay out.'

'I would have thought that a hundred pounds would have been more than it was worth,' said Lodge, 'since bookmakers normally make a profit anyway.'

'Your friend wasn't satisfied with the legitimate gains from the taxis,' my father pointed out.

I sighed, and shifted my stiff shoulders against the frame of the window.

'There's a bit more to it, of course,' I said. 'If a bookmaker knows he hasn't got to pay out on a certain horse, he can offer better odds on it. Not enough to be suspicious, but just enough to attract a lot of extra custom. A point better than anyone else would go to – say eleven to four, when the next best offer was five to two. The money would roll in, don't you think?'

I stood up and went towards the door, saying, 'I'll show you something.'

The stairs seemed steeper than usual. I went up to my room and fetched the racing form book and the little bunch of bookmakers' tickets, and shuffled back to the drawing-room. I laid the tickets out on the table in front of Lodge, and my father came over to have a look.

'These,' I explained, 'are some tickets Bill kept for his children to play with. Three of them, as you see, were issued by L. C. Perth, and all the others are from different firms, no two alike. Bill was a methodical man. On the backs of all the tickets he wrote the date, the details of his bet, and the name of the horse he'd put his money on. He used to search around in Tattersall's for the best odds and bet in cash, instead of betting on credit with Tote Investors or one of the bookmakers on the rails – those,' I added for Lodge's benefit, as I could see the question forming on his lips, 'are book-makers who stand along the railing between Tattersall's and the Club enclosures, writing down bets made by Club members and other people known to them. They send out weekly accounts, win or lose. Bill didn't bet in large amounts, and he thought credit betting wasn't exciting enough.'

Lodge turned over the three Perth tickets.

Bill's loopy writing was clear and unmistakable. I picked up the first ticket, and read aloud, ' "Peripatetic. 7 November. Ten pounds staked at eleven to ten." So he stood to win eleven pounds for his money.' I opened the detailed form book and turned to 7 November.

'Peripatetic,' I said, 'lost the two mile hurdle at Sandown that day by four lengths. He was ridden by

Joe Nantwich. The starting price was eleven to ten on –
that is, you have to stake eleven pounds to win ten –
and had earlier been as low as eleven to eight on. L. C.
Perth must have done a roaring trade at eleven to ten
against.'

I picked up the second card and read, 'Sackbut. 10
October. Five pounds staked at six to one.' I opened
the form book for that day. 'Sackbut was unplaced at
Newbury and Joe Nantwich rode it. The best price generally offered was five to one, and the starting price was
seven to two.'

I put the Sackbut ticket back on the table, and read
the third card where it lay. 'Malabar. 2 December. Eight
pounds staked at fifteen to eight.' I laid the form book
beside it, opened at 2 December. 'Malabar finished
fourth at Birmingham. Joe Nantwich rode him. The
starting price was six to four.'

Lodge and my father silently checked the book with
the ticket.

'I looked up all the other cards as well,' I said. 'Of
course, as Bill still had the tickets, all the horses lost;
but on only one of them did he get better odds than
you'd expect. Joe didn't ride it, and I don't think it's
significant, because it was an outsider at a hundred to
six.'

'I wish the racing fraternity would use only whole
numbers and halves,' said Lodge plaintively.

'Haven't you heard,' I asked, 'about the keen gambler who taught his baby son to count? One, six-to-four, two . . .'

Lodge laughed, his dark eyes crinkling at the corners. 'I'll have to write down these figures on the Perth tickets alongside the form book information, and get it straightened out in my mind,' he said, unscrewing his pen and settling to the task.

My father sat down beside him and watched the telltale list grow. I went back to the window seat and waited.

Presently Lodge said, 'I can see why your father misses you as a fraud spotter.' He put his pen back in his pocket.

I smiled and said, 'If you want to read a really blatant fraud, you should look up the Irish racing in that form book. It's fantastic.'

'Not today. This is quite enough to be going on with,' said Lodge, rubbing his hand over his face and pinching his nose between thumb and forefinger.

'All that remains, as far as I'm concerned, is for you to tell us who is organizing the whole thing,' said my father with a touch of mockery, which from long understanding I interpreted as approval.

'That, dear Pa, I fear I cannot do,' I said.

But Lodge said seriously, 'Could it be anyone you know on the racecourse? It must be someone connected with racing. How about Perth, the bookmaker?'

'It could be. I don't know him. His name won't

actually be Perth of course. That name was sold with the business. I'll have a bet on with him next time I go racing and see what happens,' I said.

'You will do no such thing,' said my father emphatically, and I felt too listless to argue.

'How about a jockey, or a trainer, or an owner?' asked Lodge.

'You'd better include the Stewards and the National Hunt Committee,' I said, ironically. 'They were almost the first to know I had discovered the wire and was looking into it. The man we are after knew very early on that I was inquisitive. I didn't tell many people I suspected more than an accident, or ask many pointed questions, before that affair in the horse-box.'

'People you know . . .' said Lodge, musingly. 'How about Gregory?'

'No,' I said.

'Why not? He lives near Brighton, near enough for the Marconicar morning telephone call.'

'He wouldn't risk hurting Bill or Admiral,' I said.

'How can you be sure?' asked Lodge. 'People aren't always what they seem, and murderers are often fond of animals, until they get in the way. One chap I saw at the assizes lately killed a nightwatchman and showed no remorse at all. But when evidence was given that the nightwatchman's dog had had his head bashed in too, the accused burst into tears and said he was sorry.'

'Pathetic,' I said. 'But no dice. It isn't Pete.'

'Faith or evidence?' persisted Lodge.

'Faith,' I said grudgingly, because I was quite sure.

'Jockeys?' suggested Lodge, leaving it.

'None of them strikes me as being the type we're looking for,' I said, 'and I think you're overlooking the fact that racing came second on the programme and may even have been adopted solely because a shaky bookmaking business existed on the floor above the Marconicars. I mean, that in itself may have turned the boss of Marconicars towards racing.'

'You may be right,' admitted Lodge.

My father said, 'It's just possible that the man who originally owned Marconicars decided to launch out into crime, and faked a sale to cover his tracks.'

'Clifford Tudor, née Thasos, do you mean?' asked Lodge with interest. My father nodded, and Lodge said to me, 'How about it?'

'Tudor pops up all over the place,' I said. 'He knew Bill, and Bill had his address noted down on a scrap of paper.' I put my hand into my jacket pocket. The old envelope was still there. I drew it out and looked at it again. 'Tudor told me he had asked Bill to ride a horse for him.'

'When did he tell you that?' asked Lodge.

'I gave him a lift from Plumpton races into Brighton, four days after Bill died. We talked about him on the way.'

'Anything else?' asked Lodge.

'Well . . . Tudor's horses have been ridden – up until lately – by our corrupted friend Joe Nantwich. It was on Tudor's horse Bolingbroke that Joe won once when he had been instructed to lose . . . but at Cheltenham he threw away a race on a horse of Tudor's, and Tudor was very angry about it.'

'Camouflage,' suggested my father.

But I rested my aching head against the window, and said, 'I don't think Tudor can possibly be the crook we're looking for.'

'Why not?' asked Lodge. 'He has the organizing ability, he lives in Brighton, he owned the taxis, he employs Joe Nantwich, and he knew Major Davidson. He seems the best proposition so far.'

'No,' I said tiredly. 'The best lead we've had is the taxis. If I hadn't recognized that the men who stopped me in the horse-box were also taxi-drivers, I'd never have found out anything at all. Whoever put them on to me can't possibly have imagined I would know them, or he wouldn't have done it. But if there's one person who knew I would recognize them, it's Clifford Tudor. He was standing near me while the taxi-drivers fought, and he knew I'd had time to look at them after the police had herded them into two groups.'

'I don't rule him out altogether, even so,' said Lodge, gathering his papers together, and putting them back into his briefcase. 'Criminals often make the stupidest mistakes.'

I said, 'If we ever do find your Claud Thiveridge, I think he will turn out to be someone I've never met and never heard of. A complete stranger. It's far more likely.'

I wanted to believe it.

I did not want to have to face another possibility, one that I shied away from so uncomfortably that I could not bring myself even to lay it open for Lodge's inspection.

Who, besides Tudor, knew before the horse-box incident that I wanted Bill's death avenged? Kate. And to whom had she passed this on? To Uncle George. Uncle George, who, I suspected, housed a lean and hungry soul in his fat body, behind his fatuous expression.

Uncle George, out of the blue, had bought a horse for his niece. Why? To widen her interests, he had said. But through her, I thought, he would learn much of what went on at the races.

And Uncle George had sent Heavens Above to be trained in the stable which housed Bill's horse. Was it a coincidence . . . or the beginning of a scheme which Bill's unexpected death had cut short?

It was nebulous, unconvincing. It was based only on supposition, not on facts, and bolstered only by memory of the shock on Uncle George's face when Kate told him we had been to The Blue Duck – shock which he had called indigestion. And perhaps it had been indigestion, after all.

And all those primitive weapons in his study, the ritual objects and the scalp . . . were they the playthings of a man who relished violence? Or who loathed it? Or did both at the same time?

Scilla came into the drawing-room, carrying a copper bowl filled with forsythia and daffodils. She put it on the low table near me, and the spring sun suddenly shone on the golden flowers, so that they seemed like a burst of light, reflecting their colour upwards on to her face as she bent over them, tweaking them into order.

She gave me a sharp glance, and turned round to the others.

'Alan looks very tired,' she said. 'What have you been doing?'

'Talking,' I said, smiling at her.

'You'll find yourself back in hospital if you're not careful,' she scolded mildly, and without pausing offered mid-morning coffee to Lodge and my father.

I was glad of the interruption, because I had not wished to discuss with them what was to be done next in pursuit of Mr Claud Thiveridge. Every small advance I had made in his direction had brought its retribution, it was true; yet in each of his parries I had found a clue. My faulty memory was still cheating me of the information I had paid for with the drubbing at Bristol, but it did not deter me from wanting to see the business through.

I would get closer to Thiveridge. He would hit out again, and in doing it show me the next step towards him, like the flash of a gunshot in the dark revealing the hiding-place of a sniper.

CHAPTER FOURTEEN

Joe Nantwich found the sniper first.

Eight days after Lodge's visit I drove down to West Sussex races, having put in a short morning at the office. My bruises had faded and gone; the ribs and collar-bone were mended and in perfect working order, and even my stubborn headache was losing its grip. I whistled my way into the changing-room and presented to Clem my brand new crash-helmet, bought that morning from Bates of Jermyn Street for three guineas.

The weighing room was empty, and distant oohs and ahs proclaimed that the first race was in progress. Clem, who was tidying up the changing-room after the tornado of getting a large number of jockeys out of their ordinary clothes, into racing colours, past the scales, and out to the parade ring, greeted me warmly and shook hands.

'Glad to see you back, sir,' he said, taking the helmet. With a ball-point pen he wrote my name on a piece of adhesive tape and stuck it on to the shiny shell. 'Let's hope you won't be needing another new one of these in a hurry.' He pressed his thumb firmly on to the adhesive tape.

'I'm starting again tomorrow, Clem,' I said. 'Can you bring my gear? Big saddle. There's no weight problem, I'm riding Admiral.'

'Top flipping weight,' said Clem, resignedly. 'And a lot of lead, which Admiral isn't used to. Major Davidson hardly ever needed any.' Clem gave me an assessing sideways look and added, 'You've lost three or four pounds, I shouldn't wonder.'

'All the better,' I said cheerfully, turning to the door.

'Oh, just a minute, sir,' said Clem. 'Joe Nantwich asked me to let you know, if you came, that he has something to tell you.'

'Oh, yes?' I said.

'He was asking for you on Saturday at Liverpool, but I told him you'd probably be coming here, as Mr Gregory mentioned last week that you'd be riding Admiral tomorrow,' said Clem, absent-mindedly picking up a saddle and smoothing his hand over the leather.

'Did Joe say what it was he wanted to tell me?' I asked.

'Yes, he wants to show you a bit of brown wrapping paper with something written on it. He said you'd be interested to see it, though I can't think why – the word I saw looked like something to do with chickens. He had the paper out in the changing-room at Liverpool,

and folded it up flat on the bench into a neat shape,
and tucked it into the inside pocket of his jacket.
Giggling over it, he was. He'd had a drink or two I
reckon, but then most people had, it was after the
National. He said what was written on the paper was
double Dutch to him, but it might be a clue, you never
knew. I asked him a clue to what? But he wouldn't
say, and anyway, I was too busy to bother with him
much.'

'I'll see him, and find out what it's all about,' I said.
'Has he still got the paper with him, do you know?'

'Yes, he has. He patted his pocket just now when
he asked me if you were here, and I heard the paper
crackle.'

'Thanks, Clem,' I said.

I went outside. The race was over, the winner was
being led towards the unsaddling enclosure in front of
the weighing-room, and down from the stands
streamed the hundreds of chattering racegoers. I stood
near the weighing-room door, waiting for Joe and
catching up with the latest gossip. Liverpool, I learned,
had been disappointing, fabulous, bloody, a dead loss,
and the tops, according to who told it. I had not been
there. I had been too busy getting intensive treatment
on my shoulder muscles to help my strength back.

Sandy clapped me soundly on the back as he passed,
remarking that it was 'Bloody good to see your old
physog on the horizon again, even if you do look like

an understudy for Scarface.' He went on, 'Have you seen Joe? The little drip's been squealing for you.'

'So I hear,' I said. 'I'm waiting for him now.'

A couple of press men asked me my riding plans, and made notes about Admiral for their morning edition. Sir Creswell Stampe noticed my existence with a nod of his distinguished head and the characteristic puffing up of his top lip which passed with him for a smile.

My content at being back in my favourite environment was somewhat marred by the sight of Dane strolling across the grass, talking intently to a slender, heart-catchingly beautiful girl at his side. Her face was turned intimately towards his, and she was laughing. It was Kate.

When they saw me they quickened their steps and approached me smiling, a striking pair evenly matched in grace and dark good looks.

Kate, who had got used to my battered face over lunch some days earlier, greeted me with a brisk 'Hi, there,' from which all undertones of love and longing were regrettably absent. She put her hand on my arm and asked me to walk down the course with her and Dane to watch the next race from beside the water jump.

I glanced at Dane. His smile was faint, and his dark eyes looked at me inscrutably, without welcome. My own muscles had tensed uncontrollably when I saw him and Kate together; so now I knew exactly how he felt about me.

It was as much unease over the low ebb of our friendship as desire to chase Claud Thiveridge which made me say, 'I can't come at this instant. I must find Joe Nantwich first. How about later on ... if you'd like to walk down again?'

'All right, Alan,' she said. 'Or maybe we could have tea together?' She turned away with Dane and said, 'See you later,' over her shoulder with a mischievous grin, in which I read her mockery of the jealousy she could arouse in me.

Watching them go, I forgot to look out for Joe, and went in to search for him through the weighing- and changing-rooms again. He wasn't there.

Pete towered over me as I returned to my post outside the door and greeted me like a long-lost friend. His hat tipped back on his big head, his broad shoulders spreading apart the lapels of his coat, he gazed with good humour at my face, and said, 'They've made a good job of sewing you up, you know. You were a very gory sight indeed last time I saw you. I suppose you still can't remember what happened?'

'No,' I said, regretfully. 'Sometimes I think ... but I can't get hold of it ...'

'Perhaps it's just as well,' he said comfortingly, hitching the strap of his race glasses higher on to his shoulder and preparing to go into the weighing-room.

'Pete,' I said, 'have you seen Joe anywhere? I think he's been asking for me.'

'Yes, he said. 'He was looking for you at Liverpool, too. He was very keen to show you something, an address I think, written on some brown paper.'

'Did you see it?' I asked.

'Yes, as a matter of fact I did, but he annoys me and I didn't pay much attention. Chichester, I think the place was.'

'Do you know where Joe is now?' I asked. 'I've been waiting for him for some time, but there isn't a sign of him.'

Pete's thin lips showed contempt. 'Yes, I saw the little brute going into the bar, about ten minutes ago.'

'Already!' I exclaimed.

'Drunken little sod,' he said dispassionately. 'I wouldn't put him up on one of my horses if he was the last jockey on earth.'

'Which bar?' I pressed.

'Eh? Oh, the one at the back of Tattersall's, next to the Tote. He and another man went in with that dark fellow he rides for . . . Tudor, isn't that his name?'

I gaped at him. 'But Tudor finished with Joe at Cheltenham . . . and very emphatically, too.'

Pete shrugged. 'Tudor went into the bar with Joe and the other chap a few steps behind him. Maybe it was only coincidence.'

'Thanks, anyway,' I said.

It was only a hundred yards round one corner to the bar where Joe had gone. It was a long wooden hut backing on to the high fence which divided the race-course from the road. I wasted no time, but nonetheless when I stepped into the building and threaded my way through the overcoated, beer-drinking customers, I found that Joe was no longer there. Nor was Clifford Tudor.

I went outside again. The time for the second race was drawing near, and long impatient queues waited at the Tote next door to the bar, eyes flickering between racecards and wrist watches, money clutched ready in hopeful hands. The customers from the bar poured out, hurrying past me. Men were running across the grass towards the stands, coat-tails flapping. Bells rang loudly in the Tote building, and the queues squirmed with the compulsion to push their money through the little windows before the shutters came down.

I hovered indecisively. There was no sign of Joe in all this activity, and I decided to go up to the jockeys' box in the stands and look for him there. I put my head into the bar for a final check, but it was now empty except for three ageing young ladies mopping up the beer-slopped counter.

It was only because I was moving so slowly that I found Joe at all.

Owing to the curve of the road behind them, the Tote and bar buildings did not stand in a perfectly straight line. The gap between the two was narrow at the front, barely eighteen inches across; but it widened farther back until, by the high fence itself, the Tote and bar walls were four or five feet apart.

I glanced into this narrow area as I passed. And there was Joe. Only I did not know it was Joe until I got close to him.

At first I saw only a man lying on the ground in the corner made by the boundary fence and the end wall of the Tote, and thinking he might be ill, or faint, or even plain drunk, went in to see if he needed help.

He lay in shadow, but something about his shape and rag-doll relaxedness struck me with shocking recognition as I took the five or six strides across to him.

He was alive, but only just. Bright red frothy blood trickled from his nose and the corner of his mouth, and a pool of it lay under his cheek on the weedy gravel. His round young face still wore, incredibly, a look of sulky petulance, as if he did not realize that what had happened to him was more than a temporary inconvenience.

Joe had a knife in his body. Its thick black handle protruded incongruously from his yellow and white checked shirt, slanting downwards from underneath his breastbone. A small patch of blood stained the cloth round it, a mild enough indication of the damage the blade was doing inside.

His eyes were open, but vague and already glazing.

I said, urgently, 'Joe!'

His eyes came round to mine and I saw them sharpen into focus and recognize me. A muscle moved in his cheek and his lips opened. He made a great effort to speak.

The scarlet blood suddenly spilled in a gush from his nostrils and welled up in a sticky, bottomless pool in his open mouth. He gave a single choking sound that was almost indecently faint, and over his immature face spread a look of profound astonishment. Then his flesh blanched and his eyes rolled up, and Joe was gone. For several seconds after he died his expression said clearly, 'It's not fair.' The skin settled in this crisis into the lines most accustomed to it in life.

Fighting nausea at the sweet smell of his blood, I shut the eyes with my fingers, and sat back on my heels, looking at him helplessly.

I knew it was useless, but after a moment or two I opened his coat and felt in his pockets for the brown paper he had wanted to show me. It was not there, and his death would not have made sense if it had been. The brown paper was, I thought, the wrapping from Joe's last payment for stopping a horse. It had to be. With something about it which he thought would disclose who had sent it. A postmark? An address? Something to do with chickens, Clem had said; and Pete said it was Chichester. Neither of these held any significance at all for me. According to Clem it meant nothing to Joe either, and he was simply going to show it to me because he had said he would.

He had always been too talkative for his own good. Not quick or quiet. Prudently and privately he could have telephoned to tell me his discovery as soon as he made it. But instead he had flourished the paper at Liverpool. Someone had taken drastic steps to make sure he did not show it to me.

'Poor, silly blabbermouth,' I said softly, to his still body.

I got to my feet, and went back to the narrow entrance of the little area. There was no one about. The voice of the commentator boomed over the loud-speakers that the horses were approaching the second open ditch, which meant that the race was already half over and that I would have to hurry.

I ran the last fifty yards to the Clerk of the Course's office and thrust open the door. A nondescript, grey-haired man in glasses, sitting at a desk, looked up, startled, his pen in mid-air and the paper he was writing on pressed under the palm of his hand. He was the Clerk of the Course's secretary.

'Mr Rollo isn't here?' I asked unnecessarily, glancing round the otherwise empty office.

'He's watching the race. Can I help you?' A dry voice, a dry manner. Not the sort of man one would choose to announce a murder to. But it had to be done. Suppressing all urgency from my voice I told him plainly and quietly that Joe Nantwich was lying dead between the Tote and the bar with a knife through his lungs. I suggested that he send for a canvas screen to put across the gap between the two buildings, as when the crowds began to stream towards the bar and the paying-out Tote windows after the race, someone would be certain to see him. The ground round his body would be well trodden over. Clues, if there were any, would be lost.

The eyes behind the spectacles grew round and disbelieving.

'It's not a joke,' I said desperately. 'The race is nearly over. Tell the police then. I'll find a screen.' He still did not move. I could have shaken him, but I could not spare the time. 'Hurry,' I urged. But his hand had still not gone out to his telephone when I shut the door.

The ambulance room was attached to the end of the weighing-room building. I went in in a hurry, to find two motherly St John's nurses drinking tea. I spoke to the younger one, a middle-aged soul of ample proportions.

'Put that down and come with me quickly,' I said, hoping she would not argue. I picked up a stretcher which was standing against the wall, and as she put her cup down slowly, I added, 'Bring a blanket. There's a man hurt. Please hurry.'

The call to duty got my nurse moving without demur,

and picking up a blanket she followed me across the paddock, though at under half speed.

The commentator's voice rose slightly as he described the race from the last fence, and crisply into the silence when the cheers died away came another voice announcing the winner. I reached the gap by the Tote building as he spoke the names of the second and third horses.

The first stalwart punters began to drift back towards the bar. I looked in at Joe. He had not been disturbed.

I set the stretcher up on end on its handles, to make a sort of screen across the gap. The nurse came up to me, breathing audibly. I took the blanket from her and hung it over the stretcher so that no one could see into the area at all.

'Listen,' I said, trying to speak slowly. 'There is a man between these two buildings. He is dead, not hurt. He has been killed with a knife. I am going to make sure that the police are coming, and I want you to stand here holding the stretcher up like this. Don't let anyone past you until I come back with a policeman. Do you understand?'

She did not answer. She twisted the stretcher a little so that she could peer through the gap. She took a long look. Then, drawing up her considerable bosom and with the light of battle in her eyes, she said firmly, 'No one shall go in, I'll see to that.'

I hurried back to the Clerk of the Course's office. Mr

Rollo was there himself this time, and after I had told him what had happened things at last began to move.

It is always difficult to find a place to be alone at the races. After I had taken a policeman along to where Joe lay, and seen the routine bustle begin, I needed a pause to think. I had had an idea while I crouched beside Joe's body, but it was not one to be acted upon headlong.

People thronged everywhere in the paddock and the racecourse buildings, and to get away from them I walked out on to the course and over the rough grass in the centre until the stands were some way behind. Distance, I hoped, would give me a sense of proportion as well as solitude.

I thought about Bill and Scilla, and also about what I owed to my father, now back in Rhodesia. I thought about the terrorized pub-keepers in Brighton and the bloody face of Joe Nantwich.

It was no use pretending that Joe's murder had not made a great deal of difference to the situation, for until now I had blithely pursued Mr Claud Thiveridge in the belief that though he might arrange for people to be beaten up, he did not purposely kill. Now the boundary was crossed. The next killing would come easier, and the next easier still. The plucky, dog-owning rebels against protection were in greater danger than before, and I was probably responsible.

Joe had shown his brown paper to several people, and no one, including apparently himself, had immediately seen the meaning of what was written on it. Yet he had been killed before he could show it to me. To me, then, the words would have told their tale. Perhaps to me alone.

I watched the rising wind blowing the grass in flattening ripples across the course, and heard the distant voices of the bookmakers as they shouted the odds for the next race.

The question to be answered was simple. Was I, or was I not, going on with the chase? I'm no hero. I did not want to end up dead. And there was no doubt that the idea I had had beside Joe's body was as safe as a stick of dynamite in a bonfire.

The horses for the third race came out and cantered down to the start. Idly I watched them. The race was run: the horses returned to the paddock: and still I stood in the centre of the course, dithering on top of my mental fence.

At last I walked back to the paddock. The jockeys were already out in the parade ring for the fourth race, and as I reached the weighing-room one of the racecourse officials grabbed my arm, saying the police had been looking everywhere for me. They wanted me to make a statement, he said, and I would find them in the Clerk of the Course's office.

I went along there, and opened the door.

Mr Rollo, spare and short, leaned against the window wearing a worried frown. His grey-haired bespectacled secretary still sat at his desk, his mouth slightly open as if even yet he had not grasped the reality of what had happened.

The police inspector, who introduced himself as Wakefield, had established himself at Mr Rollo's table, and was attended by three constables, one of them armed with shorthand notebook and pencil. The race-course doctor was sitting on a chair by the wall, and a man I did not know stood near him.

Wakefield was displeased with me for what he called my irresponsibility in disappearing for over half an hour at such a time. Big and thick, he dominated the room. Authority exuded from his short upspringing grey hair, his narrow eyes, his strong stubby fingers. A policeman to put the fear of God into evildoers. His baleful glare suggested that at the moment I should be included in this category.

'If you're quite ready, Mr York,' he began sarcastic-ally, 'we'll take your statement.'

I looked round the crowded little office, and said, 'I prefer to make my statement to you alone.'

The inspector growled and erupted and argued; but finally everyone left except Wakefield, myself, and the notebook constable, to whom I agreed as a compro-mise. I told Wakefield exactly what had happened. The whole truth, and nothing but the truth.

Then I went back to the weighing-room, and to every one of the dozens who clustered round asking for an eye-witness account, I said I had found Joe alive. Yes, I agreed steadily, he had spoken to me before he died. What did he say? Well, it was only two or three words, and I preferred not to discuss it at present, if they did not mind. I added that I had not actually mentioned it to the police yet, but of course I would if I thought it would be important. And I put on a puzzled, thoughtful expression, hoping I looked as if I had a key in my hand and was on the point of finding the right lock to put it in.

I took Kate to tea, and Pete, catching sight of us, came over to join us. To them, too, I told the same story, feeling ashamed, but not caring to risk their broadcasting the truth, that Joe had died without uttering a syllable.

Shortly before the sixth race I left the meeting. The last thing I saw, as I glanced back from the gate, was Wakefield and Clifford Tudor standing outside the door of the Clerk of the Course's office, shaking hands. Tudor, who had been with Joe so soon before his death, had apparently been 'assisting the police with their investigations'. Satisfactorily, it seemed.

I went through the car park to the Lotus, started up, and drove out towards the west, and along the straight secondary roads of the South Downs I opened up the engine and sent the little car along at over a hundred. No Marconicars, I thought with satisfaction, could compete with that. But to make quite certain I was not being followed I stopped once at a vantage point on top of a rise, and studied the road behind me with raceglasses. It was deserted. There was nothing on my tail.

About thirty miles from the racecourse I stopped at an undistinguished roadhouse and booked a room for the night. I insisted also on a lock-up garage for the car. It was too far from Brighton to be within the normal reach of the Marconicars, but I was taking no chances. I wanted to be invisible. It is one thing to stick your neck out; but quite another to go to sleep in full view of the axe.

After a dull dinner I went to my room and wrote a letter to my father. A difficult one. I told him about Joe's death, and that I was trying to use it to entice Mr Thiveridge out of his lair. I asked him, as lightly as I could, to forgive me. I am, I wrote, only hunting another crocodile.

I finished the letter, sealed it, went early to bed, and lay awake for a long time before I slept.

On the way back to the racecourse in the morning I stopped at a post office and air-mailed my letter. I also acquired four shillings' worth of pennies, which I stacked into a paper-wrapped roll. I took the spare pair of socks out of my overnight case and slid the roll of pennies down into the foot of one of them, knotting them there securely. I swung my little cosh experiment-ally on to the palm of my hand. It was heavy enough, I thought, to knock a man out. I put it in my trouser pocket and finished the journey to the course.

I asked a constable on duty in the paddock where I could find Inspector Wakefield if I wanted him. The constable said that Wakefield was at the station, he thought, and was not coming to the course that afternoon, although he had been there in the morning. I thanked him, and went into the weighing-room, and asked several people in a loud voice to tell me if they saw Inspector Wakefield about, as I wanted to have a word with him about what Joe had said to me before he died.

The awareness of danger, though I had brought it on myself, had a noticeable effect on my nerves. The wrought-up, quickened pulse I always felt to some extent when cantering down to the start of a race was unduly magnified, so that I could hear my own heart beating. Every noise seemed louder, every chance remark more significant, every light brighter. But I was not so much afraid as excited.

I was careful only about what I turned my back to, having no intention of being attacked from behind. It was more likely, I thought, that someone would try to cajole me into an out-of-the-way place as they must have done with Joe, because most of the racecourse was too public for murder.

A knife in the ribs seemed what I should be most wary of. Effective in Joe's case, it had the advantages – to its wielder – of being silent and accurate. Moreover the weapon was left with the body, so that there was no subsequent difficulty in getting rid of it. The black handle protruding from Joe had had the familiar knobbed shape of the sort of French steel cooking knife on sale in any hardware shop. Too common to be a clue of any kind, I suspected, and easy to replace with another to stick into the guts of a second victim. If anyone tried that I intended to be ready. My fingers closed comfortably on the pennies in my pocket.

I hoped to be able to deliver an attacker (unconscious from a four-shilling bump behind the ear) to Inspector Wakefield, to be charged with attempted murder. I had great faith that Wakefield's bulldog personality would shake information out of the toughest criminal in those circumstances, and that with reasonable luck a firm clue to Thiveridge's identity might disclose itself. It was too much to hope that Thiveridge would appear himself. I believed his husky avowal to me on the telephone that he hated personal violence and ordered others to do his dirty work for him, out of his squeamish sight.

I changed, and weighed on the trial scales, and chatted, and went about my ordinary business, and waited.

Nothing happened.

No one asked me to step into dim corners to discuss private business. No one showed any particular interest in what Joe was supposed to have told me before he died. Naturally his murder was still the chief topic of conversation, but it lost ground as the day wore on, and the living horses became more interesting to the inmates of the weighing-room than the dead jockey.

Admiral was to run in the fifth race. By the time the fourth was over my nerves had calmed down and my tense readiness had evaporated. I had expected action before this. I had been at the meeting for nearly three hours, a man with essential information inviting to have his mouth permanently shut, and no move had been made against me.

It crossed my mind, not for the first time, that cause and effect in the Thiveridge organization never followed closely on each other. Joe's death happened two whole days after he showed his brown paper at Liverpool. The warning to me on the telephone was delivered two days after I had spread at Cheltenham the news of the wire which had killed Bill. The horse-box affair had taken at least a day to arrange. The Bristol wire was rigged to bring me down two days after my excursion into the Marconicar office.

I had begun to suspect that the whole organization was still geared to the telephone call Thiveridge made every morning to Fielder, and that Fielder had no other way of getting urgent messages to his 'Chairman', or of receiving instructions from him. Presumably Thiveridge still felt the delay in his news service was a lesser evil than providing an address or telephone number at which he could be reached and perhaps discovered.

Depressed, I was coming to believe that my carefully acted lies had not at all reached the ears for which they were meant, and felt that offering myself as bait to a predator who did not know he should be hunting me was a bit idiotic.

Trying to shake off this deflation, I went out to the parade ring to join Pete and mount Admiral. Bill's horse, now mine, looked as splendid as ever. With his intelligent head, deep chest, straight hocks, and good bone below the knee, he was a perfect example of what a top class steeplechaser should be.

'Even though he hasn't been on a racecourse since that ghastly day at Maidenhead, he's at the top of his form,' said Pete, admiring him beside me. 'You can't lose the race, so go along quietly for a while, getting used to him. You'll find he has plenty in reserve. You'll never get to the bottom of him. Bill used to take him to the front early on, as you know, but you don't need to. He's got a terrific turn of foot from the last.'

'I'll do as you say,' I said.

Pete gave me a leg-up. 'Admiral's odds-on, again,' he said. 'If you make a mess of this race the crowd'll murder you. So will I.' He grinned.

'I'll try to stay alive,' I said, grinning back cheerfully.

Admiral was as superb to ride as he looked. He put himself right before every fence, making his spring at exactly the right moment and needing no help from the saddle. He had the low, flowing galloping stride of the really fast mover, and from the first fence onward I found racing on his back an almost ecstatic pleasure. Following Pete's advice I went round the whole course without forcing the pace, but riding into the last fence alongside two others, I gave Admiral a kick in the ribs and shook up the reins. He took off from just inside the wings and landed as far out on the other side, gaining two lengths in the air and shedding the other two horses like dead leaves. We came home alone, easy winners, to warm cheers from the stands.

In the winner's unsaddling enclosure, where I dismounted and undid the girths, Admiral behaved as if he had only been out for an exercise gallop, his belly hardly moving as he breathed. I patted his glossy chestnut neck, noticed that he was hardly sweating at all, and asked Pete, 'What on earth can he do if he really tries?'

'The National, no less,' said Pete, rocking back on his heels, and tipping his hat off his face, as he collected his due congratulations from all around.

I grinned, pulled the saddle off over my arm, and went into the weighing-room to weigh-in and change. The familiar joy of winning flushed through my limbs, as warming as a hot bath, and I could have done handsprings down the changing-room if I hadn't known it was the horse to whom all credit was due, not the jockey.

Pete called to me to hurry up and we'd have a celebration drink together, so I changed quickly and went outside to join him. He steered me towards the bar next to the Tote building, and we stopped at the gap, looking in to where Joe had died. There was a shoulder-high wooden fence across the entrance now, to keep sensation seekers out. A rusty brown stain on the gravel was all that was left of Joe.

'A terrible thing, that,' Pete said, as we stepped into the bar. 'What did he say to you before he died?'

'I'll tell you sometime,' I said idly. 'But just now I'm more interested in where Admiral runs next.' And over our drinks we talked solely about horses.

Returning to the weighing-room we found two men in belted raincoats waiting for us near the door. They wore trilby hats and large shoes, and gave off that indefinable aura of solid menace which characterizes many plain-clothes policemen.

One of them put his hand inside his coat, drew out a folded warrant and flipped it in my direction.

'Mr York?'

'Yes.'

'Inspector Wakefield's compliments, and will you come down to the police station to help his inquiries, please.' The 'please' he tacked on as an afterthought.

'Very well,' I said, and asked Pete to see Clem about my kit.

'Sure,' he said.

I walked with the two men across to the gate and through the car park.

'I'll get my car and follow you to the station,' I said.

'There's a police car waiting for us in the road, sir,' said the larger of the two. 'Inspector Wakefield did say to bring you in it, and if you don't mind, sir, I'd rather do as the Inspector says.'

I grinned. If Inspector Wakefield were my boss I'd do as he said, too. 'All right,' I agreed.

Ahead of us the sleek black Wolseley was parked outside the gate, with a uniformed driver standing beside it and another man in a peaked cap in the front passenger's seat.

Away towards my right, in front of the ranks of parked horse-boxes, several of the runners from Admiral's race were being led up and down to get the stiffness out of their limbs before they were loaded up for the journey home. Admiral was among them, with Victor, his lad, walking proudly at his head.

I was telling the man on my right, the smaller of the two, that there was my horse and wasn't he a beauty, when I got a shock which knocked the breath out of me as thoroughly as a kick in the stomach.

To cover myself I dropped my race glasses on to the turf and bent slowly to pick them up, my escort stopping a pace ahead of me to wait. I grasped the strap and slung it over my shoulder, straightening and looking back at the same time to where we had come from. Forty yards of grass separated us from the last row of cars. There was no one about except some distant people going home. I looked at my watch. The last race was just about to begin.

I turned round unhurriedly, letting my eyes travel blankly past the man on my right and on towards Admiral, now going away from me. As usual after a race, he was belted into a rug to avoid cooling down too quickly, and he still wore his bridle. Victor would change that for a head collar when he put him in the horse-box.

Victor's great drawback was his slow wits. Endowed with an instinctive feeling for horses and an inborn skill in looking after them, he had never risen above 'doing his two' in forty years of stable life, and never would. I would have to do without much help from him.

'Victor,' I shouted, and when he turned round I signalled to him to bring Admiral over.

'I just want to make sure the horse's legs are all right,' I explained to the two men. They nodded and waited beside me, the larger one shifting from foot to foot.

I did not dare to take a third look, and in any case I knew I was not mistaken.

The man on my right was wearing the tie I had lost in the horse-box on Maidenhead Thicket.

It was made from a piece of silk which had been specially woven and given to me on my twenty-first birthday by a textile manufacturer who wanted to do business with my father. I had two other ties like it, and a scarf, and the pattern of small red and gold steamships interlaced with the letter Y on a dark green background was unique.

How likely was it that a junior CID officer should have come honestly by my tie, I asked myself urgently. Farmer Lawson had not found it, and none of his men admitted to having seen it. It was too much of a coincidence to be innocent that it should reappear round the throat of a man who was asking me to step into a car and go for a ride with him.

Here was the attack I had been waiting for, and I had damn nearly walked meekly into the trap. Getting out of it, when it was so nearly sprung, was not going to be easy. The 'police' car was parked across the gateway barely twenty paces ahead, with the driver standing by the bonnet and looking in our direction. The menacing aura of my two tough escorts now revealed itself to be something a great deal more sinister than a manner assumed to deal with crooks. One of them, perhaps, had killed Joe.

If I gave the slightest sign of doubting them, I was sure the three of them would hustle me into the car and drive off in a cloud of dust, leaving only Victor to report doubtfully what he had seen. And that, as far as I was concerned, would be that. It was to be one of those rides from which the passenger did not return.

My plan to present Wakefield with an attempted

murderer was no good. One, I could have managed.
But not three, and another sitting in the car.

When Victor was within fifteen paces of me I let the
strap of my race-glasses slip from my shoulder, down
my arm and into my hand. Abruptly, with all my
strength, I swung the glasses like a scythe round the
legs of the larger man and overbalanced him, tripped
the smaller man with the one elementary judo throw I
knew, and sprinted for Admiral.

The five seconds it took them to recover from the
unexpected assault were enough. As they started after
me with set faces I leaped on to Admiral's back, picked
up the reins which lay loosely on his neck, and turned
him round sharply out of Victor's grasp.

The third man was running towards me from the car.
I kicked Admiral into a canter in two strides, swerving
round the advancing chauffeur, and set him towards the
hedge which formed the boundary of the car park. He
cleared it powerfully, landing on the grass verge of the
road a few yards in front of the black car. The fourth
man had the door open and was scrambling out. I
looked back quickly.

Victor was standing stock-still with his mouth open.
The three men were all running towards the gate with
purposeful strides. They had nearly reached it. I had
barely time to hope they were not carrying guns, since I
presented a large and close target, when I saw the sun
glint on something bright in the hand of the man who

was wearing my tie. It hardly seemed the moment to stop and discover whether the glint came from a black-handled chef's knife: but I nearly found out the hard way, because he drew back his arm and threw it at me. I flung myself flat on the horse's neck and it missed, and I heard it clatter on to the road beyond.

I urged Admiral straight across the road, ignoring the squeal of brakes from a speeding lorry, and jumped him into the field opposite. The land sloped upwards, so that when I reined-in about halfway up it and turned round to see what was happening, the road and the car park were spread out below like a map.

The men were making no attempt to follow. They had moved the Wolseley away from the gate and were now drawing to a halt some yards further along the verge. It looked as if all four were inside the car.

Victor still stood in the car park, scratching his head as he looked up towards me. I could imagine his bewilderment. I wondered how long it would be before he went to tell Pete what had happened.

Once the last race was over the car park would be buzzing with people, and the cars would pour out of the now unobstructed gateway. I thought that then I would be able to return safely to the racecourse without being abducted.

At this point another black car drew up behind the Wolseley, and then another, and several others, until a line of eight or more stretched along the side of the road. There was something rather horribly familiar about the newcomers.

They were Marconicars.

CHAPTER FIFTEEN

All the drivers climbed out of the taxis and walked along towards the Wolseley. With its low expensive lines and its efficient-looking aerial on top, it sill looked every inch a police car; but the reinforcements it had called up dispelled any last doubts it was possible to have about the nature of the 'CID officers'.

The men stood in a dark group on the road, and I sat on Admiral half-way up the field watching them. They seemed to be in no hurry, but having seen their armoury of bicycle chains, knives, and assorted knuckledusters when they fought the London gang at Plumpton, and with Joe's fate constantly in mind, I had no doubt what would happen if I let them catch me.

I was in a good position. They could not drive the taxis up the field because there was no gate into it from the road, nor could they hope to reach me on foot, and I was still confident that when the race crowd flocked out I could evade the enemy and return to the course.

Two things quickly happened to change the picture.

First, the men began looking and pointing towards
the side of the field I was in. Turning my head to the
right I saw a car driving downhill on the farther side of
the hedge, and realized that there was a road there.
Twisting round, I now took note for the first time that
a large house with out-buildings and gardens spread
extensively across the skyline.

Three of the taxis detached themselves from the line
and drove round into the road on my right, stopping at
intervals along it. I now had taxi drivers to the right and
ahead, and the big house at my back, but I was still not
unduly dismayed.

Then yet another Marconicar came dashing up and
stopped with a jerk in front of the Wolseley. A stocky
man swung open the door and raised himself out of the
driver's seat. He strode across the road to the hedge,
and stood there pointing up at me with his arm
extended. I was still wondering why when I heard the
low whine of a bullet passing at the level of my feet.
There was no sound of a shot.

As I turned Admiral to gallop off across the field, a
bullet hit the ground with a phut in front of me. Either
the range was too far for accurate shooting with a gun
fitted with a silencer, or ... I began to sweat ... the
marksman was aiming deliberately low, not at me but
at Admiral.

It was only an eight or ten acre field, nothing like big
enough for safety. I used precious moments to pull the

horse up and take a look at the ragged sprawling hedge on the far side of the field. It was threaded half-way up with barbed wire. Over my shoulder I could see the man with the gun running along the road parallel to the course I had just taken. He would soon be within range again.

I took Admiral back a little way, faced him towards the hedge and urged him to jump. He cleared the whole thing, wire and all, without bending so much as a twig. We landed in another field, this time occupied by a herd of cows but again small and much too open to the road. Also, I discovered, trotting along the top boundary, that barbed wire had been laid lavishly in three strong strands all round it. All pastures have a gate, however, and I came to it in the farthest corner. I opened it, guided Admiral through into the next field, and shut it behind me.

This field was fenced with posts and wire only, and it was the extent of the barbed wire which decided me then to put as much space as I could between me and my pursuers in the shortest possible time. If I let the taxi-drivers follow me slowly from field to field I might find myself in a corner that even Admiral could not jump out of.

I was glad the sun was shining, for at least I could tell in which direction I was going. Since I was already headed towards the east, and because it seemed sensible to have a definite destination to aim for, I decided to take Admiral back to his own stable in Pete's yard.

I reckoned I had about twelve miles to cover, and I racked my brains to remember what the country was like in between. I knew the patchwork farmland which I was then grappling with gave way at some point ahead to Forestry Commission plantations. Then there would be a short distance of bare downland before I reached the hollow and the small village where Pete trained. Of the roads which crossed this area I had but the vaguest idea, and on any of them I could be spotted by a cruising Marconicar.

With this thought uncomfortably in mind, I found another by-road ahead. I let myself out on to it through a gate, and was trotting down it, looking for an opening in the neglected growth on the other side, when a squat black car swept round a distant bend and sped uphill towards me. Without giving Admiral a good chance to sight himself I turned him sharply towards the over-grown hedge and kicked his ribs.

It was too high for him, and too unexpected, but he did his best. He leaped straight into the tangle of sagging wire and beech saplings, crashed his way heavily through, and scrambled up almost from his knees on to the higher ground of the next field. It had been ploughed and planted with mangolds and made heavy going, but I urged him into a canter, hearing behind me the screech of brakes forcefully applied. A glance showed me the driver thrusting through the hole Admiral had made, but he did not try to chase me and I realized thankfully that he was not the man with the gun.

All the same, he had his radio. My whereabouts would be known to all the Marconicars within a minute.

I put another field between us and the taxi before pulling up and dismounting to see what damage Admiral had done himself. To my relief there were only a few scratches and one jagged cut on his stifle from which a thread of blood was trickling. I left it to congeal.

Patting his neck and marvelling at how he retained his calm sensible nature in very upsetting circumstances, I grasped the leather roller he wore round his middle, and sprang up again on to his back. The rug he was wearing now gaped in a right-angled tear on one side, but I decided not to take it off as it gave more purchase for my legs than riding him completely bareback.

Three or four fields farther on the arable land began to give way to bracken, and ahead lay the large enclosures of the Forestry Commission.

The trees, mostly conifers, were being grown in large orderly expanses with rough tracks between each section. These acted both as convenient roadways for the foresters and as breaks in case of fire. They occurred about one in each half-mile, and were crossed at intervals by tracks leading in the opposite direction.

I wanted to set a course towards the south-east, but by consulting my watch and the sun in conjunction, found that the tracks ran from almost due north to south, and from east to west. Fretting at the extra mileage this was going to cost me, I steered Admiral into an eastbound track, took the next turning right to the south, then the next left to the east, and so on, crabwise across the forest.

The sections of trees were of varying ages and stages of growth, and turning again to the south, I found the area on my left was planted with trees only two feet high. This did not specially alarm me until I saw, a hundred yards to my left, a red and white motor coach speeding along apparently through the middle of the plantation.

I pulled Admiral up. Looking carefully I could see the posts and the high wire fence which formed the boundary between the little trees and the road beyond. If I turned east at the next track according to schedule, I would be facing straight down to the road.

The far side of the road looked similar to the section I was in: regular rows of conifers, put there by careful design.

At some point, I knew, I would have to cross a road of some sort. If I retreated back into the part of the forest I had crossed and took no risks, I would have to stay there all night. All the same, I thought, as I cantered Admiral along the southbound track and turned into the east one, I could have wished for more cover just at that moment.

Ahead of me the wire gates to the road were open, but before going through them I stopped and took a look at the other side of the road. Not all the plantations were surrounded by high mesh wire like the one I was in, and opposite only three strands of plain wire threaded through concrete posts barred the way.

The road had to be crossed quickly because where I was I felt as sheltered as a cock pheasant on a snow field. The heads in all the passing cars turned curiously towards me. But I saw nothing which looked like a Marconicar, and waiting only for a gap in the traffic, I clicked my tongue and set Admiral towards the wire fence opposite. His hooves clattered loudly on the tarmac, drummed on the firm verge, and he lifted into the air like a bird. There was no track straight ahead, only some fairly sparsely growing tall pines, and as Admiral landed I reined him in to a gentle trot before beginning to thread a way through them.

Coming eventually to another track I checked again with my watch and the sun to make sure it was still running from east to west, which it was, and set off along it at a good pace. The going underfoot was perfect, dry and springy with loam and pine needles, and Admiral, though he had completed a three mile race and covered several miles of an unorthodox cross-country course, showed no signs of flagging.

We made two more turns and the sky began to cloud over, dulling the brilliant spring afternoon; but it was not the fading of beauty which bothered me so much as the fact that you cannot use a wrist watch as a compass unless the sun is shining. I would have to be careful not to get lost.

Just ahead, to my right, a small grass-grown hill rose sharply to its little rounded summit, the conifer forest flowing round its edges like sea round a rock. I had now left the bigger trees and was cantering through sections of young feathery pines only slightly taller than the top of my head, and I could see the hill quite clearly. A man, a black distant silhouetted man, was standing on the top, waving his arms.

I did not connect him with myself at all because I thought I had slipped my pursuers, so that what happened next had the full shock of a totally unexpected disaster.

From a track to the right, which I had not yet reached and could not see, a sleek black shape rolled out across my path and stopped, blocking the whole width of the track. It was the Wolseley.

The young pines on each side of me were too thick and low-growing to be penetrated. I flung a look over my shoulder. A squat black Marconicar was bumping up the track behind me.

I was so close to the Wolseley that I could see one of the men looking out of the rear window with a gloating grin on his face, and I decided then that even if I broke Admiral's neck and my own in trying to escape, it would be a great deal better than tamely giving in.

There was scarcely a pause between the arrival of the Wolseley and my legs squeezing tight into Admiral's sides.

I had no reason to suppose he would do it. A horse can dare just so much and no more. He had had a hard day already. He might be the best hunter-'chaser in England, but ... The thoughts flickered through my brain in a second and were gone. I concentrated wholly, desperately, on getting Admiral to jump.

He scarcely faltered. He put in a short stride and a long one, gathered the immense power of his hind-quarters beneath him, and thrust himself into the air. Undeterred even by the opening doors and the threatening shouts of the men scrambling out of the Wolseley, he jumped clear over its gleaming black bonnet. He did not even scratch the paint.

I nearly came off when we landed. Admiral stumbled, and I slipped off the rug round on to his shoulder, clinging literally for dear life to the leather roller with one hand and Admiral's plaited mane with the other. The reins hung down, swaying perilously near his galloping feet, and I was afraid he would put his foot through them and trip. I still had one leg half across his rump, and, bumping heavily against his side, I hauled myself inch by inch on to his back. A warning twinge in my shoulder told me my newly mended collar-bone could not be relied upon for too much of this, but leaning along his neck and holding on with all my strength, I reached the reins, gathered them up, and finally succeeded in reducing Admiral to a less headlong pace.

When I got my breath back I looked to see if the Wolseley was following, but it was so far behind that I was not sure whether it was moving or not. I could not spare time to stop and find out.

I realized that I had underestimated the Marconi-cars, and that it was only thanks to Admiral's splendid courage that I was still free. They had had an advantage in knowing the lie of the land, and had used the little hill as a spotting point. I suspected that its summit commanded quite a large area, and that as soon as I had entered the young pines I had been seen.

I was forced to admit that they had guessed which direction I would take and had circled round in front of me. And that being so, they probably knew I had been making for Pete's stable. If I went on I should find them in my way again, with perhaps as little warning and less chance of escape.

I had left the hill behind me, and turned right again on the next track, seeing in the distance a section of taller trees. The horse cantered along tirelessly, but he could not keep it up for ever. I had to reach shelter as quickly as I could, out of sight of the man still standing on the hill-top, and out of the danger of being ambushed on another of the straight and suddenly uninviting tracks. Once we were hidden in the big trees, I promised Admiral, he should have a rest.

The light was dim under the tall pines. They had been allowed to grow close together to encourage their bare trunks to height, and the crowns of foliage far above were matted together like a roof, shutting out most of the daylight. I was glad for the obscurity. I slowed Admiral to a walk and dismounted as we entered the trees, and we went quietly and deeply into them. It was like walking through a forest of telegraph poles. Which of course, I thought fleetingly, perhaps they were destined to be.

The forest felt like home, even though it was different from those I was schooled in. It was very quiet, very dark. No birds at all. No animals. The horse and I went steadily on, silent on the thick pine needles, relying on instinct to keep us on a straight course.

I did not find our situation particularly encouraging. Whichever way I went in this extensive plantation I would have to come to a road in the end, and within three or four square miles the Marconicars knew exactly where I was. They had only to stand round the forest like hounds waiting for the fox to break cover, then it would be view tally-ho over the radio intercoms and the hunt would be on again.

There was a track ahead. A narrow one. I tied the reins round a tree and went forward alone. Standing still on the edge of the track and giving, I hoped, a good imitation of a tree trunk in my tweed suit, I slowly turned my head both ways. The daylight was much stronger on the track owing to the gap in the trees overhead, and I could see quite clearly for several hundred yards. There was no one in sight.

I went back for Admiral, made a final check, and led him across the track. There was no alarm. We walked steadily on. Admiral had begun to sweat long ago and had worked up a lather after our dash away from the Wolseley, damping large patches of the rug. Now that he was cooling down it was not good for him to keep it on, but I hadn't a dry one to give him. I decided that a damp rug was better than no rug, and trudged on.

Eventually I began to hear the hum of traffic and the occasional toot of a horn, and as soon as I could see the road in the distance I tied Admiral to a tree and went on alone again.

The end of the plantation was marked by a fence made of only two strands of stout wire, looking as if it were designed mainly to prevent picnickers driving their cars farther in than the verge. I chose a tree as near to the fence as I could get, dropped down on to my belly behind it, and wriggled forward until I could look along the road. There was only sporadic traffic on it.

On the far side of the road there were no plantations, and no fence either. It was unorganized woodland, a mixture of trees, rhododendrons, and briars. Perfect cover, if I could reach it.

A heavy lorry ground past five feet from my nose, emitting a choking cloud of diesel fumes. I put my face down into the pine needles and coughed. Two saloon cars sped by in the other direction, one trying to pass the other, followed by a single-decker country bus full of carefree people taking home their Tuesday afternoon's shopping. A pair of schoolgirls in green uniform cycled past without noticing me, and when their high twittering voices had faded into the distance and the road was empty, I put my hands under my chest to heave myself up and go back for Admiral.

At that moment two Marconicars came into sight round a bend. I dropped my face down again and lay absolutely still. They drove past my head slowly, and though I did not look at them, I guessed they must be staring keenly into the forest. I hoped wholeheartedly that I had left Admiral far enough back to be invisible, and that he would not make a noise.

The Marconicars swerved across the road and pulled up on the opposite verge barely twenty-five yards away. The drivers got out of the taxis and slammed the doors. I risked a glance at them. They were lighting cigarettes, leaning casually against the taxis, and chatting. I could hear the mumble of their voices, but not what they were saying.

They had not seen me, or Admiral. Yet. But they

seemed to be in no hurry to move on. I glanced at my watch. It was six o'clock. An hour and a half since I had jumped off the racecourse. More important, there was only one hour of full daylight left. When it grew dark my mobility on Admiral would end and we should have to spend the night in the forest, as I could not get him to jump a fence if he could not see it.

There was a sudden clattering noise from one of the taxis. A driver put his hand through the window and brought out a hand microphone attached to a cord. He spoke into it distinctly, and this time I could make out what he said.

'Yeah, we got the road covered. No, he ain't crossed it yet.' There was some more clattering on the taxi radio, and the driver answered, 'Yeah, I'm sure. I'll let you know the second we see him.' He put the microphone back in the taxi.

I began to get the glimmerings of an idea of how to use the manhunt I had caused.

But first things first, I thought; and slowly I started to slither backwards through the trees, pressing close to the ground and keeping my face down. I had left Admiral a good way inside the forest, and I was now certain that the taxi-drivers could not see him. It was uncomfortable travelling on my stomach, but I knew if I stood up the drivers would see me moving among the bare tree trunks. When finally I got to my feet my suit was filthy peat brown, clogged with prickling pine

needles. I brushed off the dirt as best I could, went over
to Admiral and untied his reins.

Out in the daylight on the road I could still catch
glimpses, between the tree trunks, of the two taxis and
their drivers, but knowing that they could not see me, I
set off towards the west, keeping parallel with the road
and at some distance from it. It was, I judged, a little
more than a quarter of a mile before I saw another
Marconicar parked at the side of the road. I turned
back and, as I went along, began to collect an armful of
small dead branches. About half way between the
parked taxis, where they were all out of my sight, I took
Admiral right up to the wire fence to give him a look at
it. Although extremely simple in construction, it was
difficult to see in the shade of the trees. I set the dead
branches up on end in a row to make it appear more
solid; then jumped on to Admiral's back, and taking
him back a few paces, faced him towards the fence and
waited for a heavy vehicle to come along. In still air the
sound of hooves on tarmacadam would carry clearly,
and I did not want the taxi-drivers round the nearby
bends to hear me crossing the road. The longer they
believed I was still in the pine forest, the better. But
how long the taxis would *remain* parked I did not know,
and the palms of my hands grew damp with tension.

A motor bike sped past, and I stayed still with an
effort; but then, obligingly, a big van loaded with empty
milk bottles came rattling round the bend on my right.

It could not have been better. As it went past me I trotted Admiral forward. He made nothing of the dead-wood patch of fence, popped over on to the grass verge, took three loping strides over the tarmac, and in an instant was safely in the scrub on the far side. The milk lorry rattled out of sight.

I pulled up behind the first big rhododendron, dismounted, and peered round it.

I had not been a second too soon. One of the Marconicars was rolling slowly along in the wake of the milk lorry, and the driver's head was turned towards the forest I had left.

If one driver believed me still there, they all did. I walked Admiral away from the road until it was safe to mount, then jumped on to his back and broke him into a slow trot. The ground now was unevenly moulded into little hillocks and hollows and overgrown with brambles, small conifers, and the brown remains of last year's bracken, so I let the horse pick his own footing to a great extent while I worked out what I was going to do. After a little way he slowed to a walk and I left him to it, because if his limbs felt as heavy and tired as mine he was entitled to crawl.

As nearly as I could judge I travelled west, back the way I had come. If there is one thing you can be sure of in England, it is that a straight line in any direction will bring you to a road without much delay, and I had covered perhaps a mile when I came to the next one. Without going too close I followed it to the north.

I was hunting a prey myself, now. A taxi, detached from the herd.

Admiral was picking his way silently across a bare patch of leaf-moulded earth when I suddenly heard the now familiar clatter of a Marconicar radio, and the answering voice of its driver. I pulled up in two strides, dismounted, and tied Admiral to a nearby young tree. Then I climbed up into the branches.

Some way ahead I saw a white four-fingered sign-post, and beside it stood a Marconicar, of which only the roof and the top half of the windows were visible. The rest was hidden from me by the rhododendrons, trees, and undergrowth which crowded the ground ahead. My old friend the pine forest rose in a dark green blur away to the right.

I climbed down from the tree and felt in my pocket for the roll of pennies. I also found two lumps of sugar, which I fed to Admiral. He blew down his nostrils and nuzzled my hand, and I patted his neck gently and blessed Scilla for giving him to me.

With so much good cover it was easy enough to approach the cross-roads without being seen, but when, from the inside of an old rhododendron, I at length had a clear view of the taxi, the driver was not in it. He was a youngish sallow-faced man in a bright blue suit, and he was standing bareheaded in the middle of the cross-roads with his feet well apart, jingling some coins in his pocket. He inspected all four directions, saw nothing, and yawned.

The radio clattered again, but the driver took no notice. I had intended to creep up to his taxi and knock him out before he could broadcast that I was there; but now I waited, and cursed him, and he stood still and blew his nose.

Suddenly he began to walk purposefully in my direction.

For an instant I thought he had seen me, but he had not. He wheeled round a large patch of brambles close in front of me, turned his back towards my hiding place, and began to relieve himself. It seemed hardly fair to attack a man at such a moment, and I know I was smiling as I stepped out of the rhododendron, but it was an opportunity not to be missed. I took three quick steps and swung, and the sock-wrapped roll of pennies connected solidly with the back of his head. He collapsed without a sound.

I put my wrists under his shoulders and dragged him back to where I had left Admiral. Working as quickly as I could I ripped all the brown binding off the edge of the horse rug and tested it for strength. It seemed strong enough. Fishing my penknife out of my trouser pocket I cut the binding into four pieces and tied together the driver's ankles and knees with two of them. Then I dragged him closer to the tree and tied his wrists behind him. The fourth piece of binding knotted him securely to the trunk.

I patted his pockets. His only weapon was a spiked metal knuckleduster, which I transferred to my own jacket. He began to wake up. His gaze wandered fuzzily from me to Admiral and back again, and then his mouth opened with a gasp as he realized who I was.

He was not a big man in stature, nor, I now discovered, in courage. The sight of the horse looming so close above him seemed to worry him more than his trussed condition or the bump on the head.

'He'll tread on me,' he yelled, fright drawing back his lips to show a nicotine-stained set of cheap artificial teeth.

'He's very particular what he walks on,' I said.

'Take him away. Take him away,' he shouted. Admiral began to move restlessly at the noise.

'Be quiet and he won't harm you,' I said sharply to the driver, but he took no notice and shouted again. I stuffed my handkerchief unceremoniously into his mouth until his eyes bulged.

'Now shut up,' I said. 'If you keep quiet he won't harm you. If you screech you'll frighten him and he might lash out at you. Do you understand?'

He nodded. I took out the handkerchief, and he began to swear vindictively, but fairly quietly.

I soothed Admiral and lengthened his tether so that

he could get his head down to a patch of grass. He began munching peacefully.

'What is your name?' I asked the taxi driver.

He spat and said nothing.

I asked him again, and he said, 'What the ruddy hell has it got to do with you?'

I needed particularly to know his name and I was in a hurry.

With no feelings of compunction I took hold of Admiral's reins and turned him round so that the driver had a good close view of a massive pair of hindquarters. My captive's newfound truculence vanished in a flash. He opened his mouth to yell.

'Don't,' I said. 'Remember he'll kick you if you make a noise. Now, what is your name?'

'John Smith.'

'Try again,' I said, backing Admiral a pace nearer.

The taxi-driver gave in completely, his mouth trembling and sweat breaking out on his forehead.

'Blake.' He stumbled on the word.

'First name?'

'Corny. It's a nickname, sort of.' His eyes flickered fearfully between me and Admiral's hind legs.

I asked him several questions about the working of the radio, keeping the horse handy. When I had learned all I wanted I untied the reins from the tree and fastened them to a sapling a few feet away, so that when it grew dark the horse would not accidentally tread on the taxi-driver.

Before leaving them I gave Blake a final warning. 'Don't start yelling for help. For one thing there's no one to hear you, and for another, you'll upset the horse. He's a thoroughbred, which means nervous, from your point of view. If you frighten him by yelling he's strong enough to break his reins and lash out at you. Shut up and he'll stay tied up. Get it?' I knew if Admiral broke his reins he would not stop to attack the man, but luckily, Blake did not. He nodded, his body sagging with fear and frustration.

'I won't forget you're here,' I said. 'You won't have to stay here all night. Not that I care about you, but the horse needs to be in a stable.'

Admiral had his head down to the grass. I gave his rump a pat, made sure the knots were still tight on the demoralized driver, and picked my way quickly through the bushes to the taxi.

The signpost was important, for I would have to come back and find it in the dark in miles of haphazard woodland. I wrote down all the names and mileages on all of its four arms, just to make sure. Then I got into the taxi and sat in the driver's seat.

Inside the taxi one could hear the radio as a voice and not as a clatter. The receiver was permanently tuned in so that each driver could hear all messages and replies going from taxis to base and base to taxis.

A man was saying, 'Sid, here. No sign of him. I've got a good mile and a half of the road in view from up here, nearly the whole side of that wood he's in. I'll swear he hasn't got across here. The traffic's too thick for him to do it quickly. I'm sure to see him if he tries it.' Sid's voice came out of the radio small and tinny, like a voice on the telephone, and he spoke casually, as if he were looking for a lost dog.

While he spoke I started the engine, sorted out the gears, and drove off along the road going south. The daylight was just beginning to fade. Half an hour of twilight, I calculated, and perhaps another ten minutes of dusk. I put my foot down on the accelerator.

There was a short silence on the radio. Then someone said, 'He has got to be found before dark.'

Even though I had been half-hoping, half-expecting it, the husky timbre-less whisper made me jerk in my seat. I gripped the steering wheel tightly and the muscles round my eyes contracted. The voice was so close it seemed suddenly as if the danger it spelled for me were close as well, and I had to reassure myself by looking out sideways at the deserted heathland, and backwards in the driving mirror at the empty road astern.

'We're doing our best, sir,' said a quiet voice, respectfully. 'I've been driving up and down this ruddy road for nearly an hour. Two miles up and two miles back. All the parked cars in my section are still in position.'

'How many of you have guns?' said the whisper.

'Four altogether, sir. We could do with more, to be sure of him.'

There was a pause. Then the husky voice said, 'I have one here, but you haven't time to come in for it. You'll have to manage with what you've got.'

'Yes, sir.'

'Pay attention, all drivers. Aim for the horse. Shoot the horse. The man is not to be found with bullets in him. Do you understand?'

There was a chorus of assent.

'Fletcher, repeat your orders.'

The polite taxi-driver said, 'As soon as we spot him either in the trees or breaking cover, we shoot, aiming for the horse. Call up all drivers, chase and catch the man. We are to – er – restrain him as necessary, place him in one of the taxis, and wait for your instructions.'

Half-way through this recital of plans for my disposal, I recognized his voice. The polite tone, in the first instance, gave him away. I had heard it on the Maidenhead road, luring me with its false respectability into a waiting trap: he was the driver of the horse-box. Fletcher. I made a note of it.

Suddenly, as if someone had pressed a switch, a light flooded into my brain and I remembered the fence at Bristol. I remembered the pouring rain on my face and the greyness of everything, and now clearly I remembered the horse-box driver cutting the wire down from the fence, rolling it up, and hanging it over his arm.

There was something else, too . . . but before I could pin it down I came to a halt sign at a main road. I turned left from my empty by-road into a stream of traffic, and began to look for a signpost which would tell my how far away I was from Brighton. After half a mile I found one. Eleven miles. Say, twenty minutes to my destination.

I thought back to the Bristol fence, but the shade had come down again in my memory, and now I was not even sure that any gaps in it remained. My fingers wandered of their own accord to the scar on my cheek and traced along it gently, but it was a gesture I had caught myself in once or twice before, and I attached no importance to it. Besides, the immediate future needed all my thought.

All the way to Brighton I listened to the husky voice. Its tone grew both more urgent and more violent. I found it weird at first to eavesdrop on a man-hunt of which I was myself the quarry, but after a few minutes I got used to it and paid it less and less attention, and this could have been a catastrophic mistake.

'Have you anything to report, twenty-three?' said the husky whisper. There was no reply on the radio. I was only half aware of it. More sharply the voice said, 'Twenty-three, Blake, have you anything to report?'

I came back to the present with a jerk. I picked up the microphone, clicked over the switch, and said 'No' in as bored and nasal a tone as I could muster.

314

'Answer more quickly next time,' said the husky voice severely. He was apparently checking that all the outlying taxis were still in position, for he went on to ask three more drivers whether they had anything to report. I thanked heaven, as I switched off the microphone, that I had not had to impersonate Blake's voice for more than one second, for any attempt at conversation would have found me out. As it was, I listened more intently than before to the exchanges on the radio.

The whispering voice began to acquire tone and characteristics as I became more familiar with it, until it formed a pattern of phrasing and emphasis which tantalized me at first because I could not remember its origin.

Then I knew. I knew for sure, at last.

You can start on a plan that you think touches the limit of what you can do; and then you have to do much, much more. Once more into the breach . . . only the breach had got bigger. Stiffen the sinews, summon up the blood . . . and bend up every spirit to his full height. There was no one like Bill Shakespeare for bounding things in a nutshell.

I drove into the outskirts of Brighton very thoughtfully indeed.

CHAPTER SIXTEEN

A taxi-driver asking the way to the main police station would be enough to arouse suspicion in a moron. I parked the taxi in a side street and hurried round the corner to ask directions in the nearest shop.

It was a tobacconist's, and busy, so I buttonholed one of the customers, an elderly man with watery eyes and a cloth cap. He told me the way quite clearly, though with frequent sniffs.

'You in trouble, mate?' he enquired inquisitively, eyeing my dirty, dishevelled appearance as I thanked him.

'Lost my dog,' I said, smiling, pulling out the most unexciting reason I could think of for wanting the police.

The watery-eyed man lost interest. I walked quickly back to the taxi and found two small boys listening open-mouthed to the radio. I got into the taxi, winked at them, and said, 'It's a thrilling story on children's hour, isn't it?' Their little faces cleared and they grinned.

I drove off. The husky voice was saying, '... at all costs. I don't care how you do it. He must not get away. If you can't catch him alive you must kill him. No bullets, though.'

'It would be more certain if you would let us shoot him sir,' said the polite voice of Fletcher.

Following the watery-eyed man's instructions I found the police station without trouble. Lights shone inside it as I drove past. The daylight was going quickly.

I circled the police station until I found a quiet side turning a hundred yards away. There I stopped, close to the kerb. I turned on the side-lights and shut the windows. The radio was still chattering, and the man with the husky voice could no longer keep his fury in control. For a last moment I listened to him conceding, now that time was running out, to Fletcher's plea that they should be allowed to shoot on sight. Then with a grimace I got out of the taxi, shut the door, and walked away from it.

The Marconicars office, I reckoned, was not more than half a mile off. I half-walked, half-ran towards it, looking, as I went, for a telephone. The street lamps were suddenly turned on, the bulbs glowing palely in the fading light.

The red telephone box outside a sub-post-office was lit up inside, too, and although my reason told me I was in no danger, instinct would have made me stay in darkness. The whispering voice had done my nerves no good.

Though I knew I was still out of sight of the Marconi-car office, I went into the telephone box with a conscious effort. I asked Enquiries for the number of the Maidenhead police station, and without delay was put through to the desk sergeant. Inspector Lodge, he told me, had left an hour earlier, but after some urging he parted with Lodge's home number. I thanked him and rang off.

Fumbling with haste, I fed more coins into the machine, and gave the operator the new number. It rang and rang. My heart sank, for if I couldn't get hold of Lodge quickly I did not stand nearly so good a chance of cleaning up the Marconicars the way I wanted. But at last a voice answered. A woman's.

'Inspector Lodge? Just a minute, I'll see if I can find him.'

A pause. And, finally, Lodge's voice.

'Mr York?'

I explained briefly what had happened. I said, 'I've left the taxi in Melton Close, a hundred yards back from the main police station here. I want you to ring the Brighton police and get them to send someone responsible to fetch it in. Tell them to listen carefully to the radio in the taxi. Our friend with the husky voice is speaking on it, inciting all the drivers to kill me. That should settle the Marconicars once and for all, I should think. One of the drivers out looking for me is called Fletcher. He's the one who drove the horse-box at Maidenhead, and he also rigged that wire for me at Bristol. I've remembered about it. It's likely he did the same for Bill Davidson, don't you think?'

'Yes, I do. Where are you now?' asked Lodge.

'In a 'phone box,' I said.

'Well, go back to the taxi and wait there while I telephone the Brighton police. I don't really understand why you didn't go straight to them and explain it at first hand yourself.'

'I thought it would have more weight, coming from you. And anyway . . .' I broke off, realizing just in time that I could not tell Lodge what I was going to do next. I said instead, 'Don't tell the Brighton police to expect me back at the taxi. I've a few phone calls to make . . . er . . . I must tell Scilla I'll be late, and things like that. But you won't waste any time, will you? Mr Claud Thiveridge won't go on talking for ever, especially after it gets dark.'

'I'll ring at once,' promised Lodge, disconnecting. I put down the receiver and pushed out into the street.

I went on my way, totting up the time I could count on before Lodge sent the Brighton police to the Marconicar office. He had to ring them up and give them a fairly lengthy account of what was going on. Then they had to find the taxi, listen to the radio, and make a shorthand record of what they heard, to be used as proof a court would accept that the whole organization was illegal. Very shortly after that they would come chasing round to apprehend the owner of the voice. Ten minutes altogether perhaps, if they hustled; perhaps a quarter of an hour.

When the Marconicar office was in sight I stayed close to the buildings so that I should not be seen from the Marconicar window. The street was nearly empty, and across the road the Olde Oake Café had closed its doors for the night. Through the glass I could see the plump waitress tiredly piling the old oak chairs on to the old oak tables.

A small black car was parked by the kerb ahead. I glanced at it cursorily, and then with sudden recognition, I stopped. I purposely had not told Lodge whose face I had attached to the husky voice, though I knew I ought to have done. The sight of his car, parked flagrantly barely twenty yards from the Marconicar door, gave me a chance to square things with my conscience. I lifted the bonnet, unclipped the distributor lid, and took off the rocker arm, which I put in my pocket. Whatever happened now, there would be no quick getaway for Mr Thiveridge.

There were no lights on in the Marconicar office, nor in any of the floors above. The neon sign, L. C. Perth, was flashing steadily on and off at two-second intervals, wasting its message on the empty road. The only gambler in sight, I reflected, was myself.

Reaching the Marconicar window I bent double below the sill and edged past as close to the wall as I could press. The street door was closed, but opened readily at a touch. I stepped very quietly into the hall, leaving the door open behind me. The silence in the house was tensely oppressive, and for a cowardly instant I was tempted to go out into the street again and wait like a sensible citizen for the police.

Stepping cautiously I went down the hall and pressed my ear to the door of Fielder's room. I could hear nothing. I opened the door gently and looked in. The room was tidy and empty. Next I tried the door on my left, which led into the back office where Marigold by day presided over her radio switchboard.

Through the thick door I could hear nothing, but when I opened it an inch a faint hum reached my ears. There was no one in the office. I went quietly in.

The hum was coming from the radio equipment. A small red brightly glowing circle in the control panel indicated that it was switched on, and through a crack in the casing the tiny light of a valve shone blue-white. The microphone lay casually on its side on its ledge.

For a sickening moment I thought that my bird had flown during the time it had taken me to ring Lodge and travel the half mile from the taxi; then I remembered the car outside, and at the same time, looking for wires leading out of the radio, saw a narrow plastic-covered cable running up the far wall and into the ceiling.

Praying that the stairs in the old house would not creak, I went up them lightly and quickly, and pressed my ear to the panels of the door of the main office of L. C. Perth. There were some large painted capital letters beside my nose. I squinted across at them while I listened. They said PLEASE ENTER.

Owing to the solidity of the Regency door I could hear only a fierce hissing sound, but by this time the whisper was so familiar to me that an inch of mahogany could not disguise it.

He was there.

The hair on the back of my neck began to itch.

I judged it must have been seven or eight minutes since I spoke to Lodge. As I had to give the Brighton police time to find the taxi and record something of what they would hear on its radio, I could not risk interrupting the husky voice too soon. But neither did I intend to hover where I was until the police arrived. I made myself count one hundred slowly, and it seemed the longest three minutes of my life. Then I rubbed the palm of my hand on my trousers, and gingerly took hold of the ornate glass doorknob.

It turned silently and I eased the door open a few inches. It made no noise at all. I could see straight into that unlit room.

He was sitting at a desk with his back turned squarely towards me, and he seemed to be looking out into the street. The neon sign flashed off and on outside the window, illuminating the whole of the room and lighting up his dusky outline with a red glow. Red reflections winked on chromium ashtrays and slid along the metal edges of filing cabinets. A row of black telephones, ranked like an army on a long desk, threw curious angular shadows on the wall.

At close quarters the husky whisper lost some of its disembodied menace, even though what it was saying was now almost hysterically violent.

The open door can have stirred no current of air, for the man at the desk went on talking into his microphone, completely unaware that I was standing behind him.

'Kill him,' he said. 'Kill him. He's in that wood somewhere. He's an animal. Hunt him. Turn your cars towards the wood and put the headlights on. You'd better start beating through the trees. Fletcher, organize it. I want York dead, and quickly. Shoot him down. Smash him.'

The man paused and drew in so sharp a breath that it gagged in his throat. His hand stretched out for a glass of water, and he drank.

Fletcher's voice came tinnily into the room through an extension loud-speaker on the desk. 'We haven't seen a sign of him since he went into the wood. I think he might have got past us.'

The man at the desk shook with fury. He began to whisper again with a rough burring rasp.

'If he escapes, you'll pay for it. You'll pay, I tell you. I want him dead. I want him smashed. You can do what you like with him. Use those chains to good purpose, and the spiked knuckles. Tear him to pieces. If he lives it will be the end for all of us, remember that.' The whisper rose in tone to a thin sound like a strangled shriek. 'Rip his guts out . . . smash . . . destroy . . .'

He went on for some time elaborating on the way I should be killed, until it was clear that his mind was very nearly unhinged.

Abruptly I had heard enough. I opened the door wide, and put my hand on the light switch, and pressed it down. The room was suddenly brilliantly flooded with light.

The man at the desk whirled round and gaped at me.

'Good evening, Uncle George,' I said softly.

CHAPTER SEVENTEEN

His eyes scorched with hate. The vacuous expression was torn away, the hidden personality now out in the open and as mean and savage as any crocodile. He was still Kate's amusing Uncle George in corpulent outline and country-gentleman tweeds, the Uncle George who had written for boys' magazines and taken his wife to matinées, but the face was the one which had had a knife stuck into Joe Nantwich and had urged a blood-thirsty mob to tear me to bits.

His hand snaked out across the desk and came up with a gun. It was a heavy, old-fashioned pistol, cumbersome, but deadly enough, and it was pointing straight at my chest. I resolutely looked at Uncle George's eyes, and not at the black hole in the barrel. I took a step towards him.

Then it came, the instant on which I had gambled my safety.

Uncle George hesitated.

I saw the flicker, the drawing back. For all his sin, for

all the horror he had spread into the lives of others, he had never himself committed an act of violence. When he had delivered his threatening warning to me on the telephone on the very morning that I went to stay in his house, he had told me that he hated even to watch violence; and in spite of, or perhaps because of, his vicarious pleasure in the brutalities of primitive nations, I believed him. He was the sort of man, I thought, who liked to contemplate atrocities he could never inflict himself. And now, in spite of the fury he felt against me, he couldn't immediately, face to face, shoot me down.

I gave him no time to screw himself up. One fast stride and I had my hand on his wrist. He was trying to stand up. Too late he found the power to kill and squeezed the trigger; but the bullet smashed harmlessly into the wall. I bent his arm outwards with force, and twisted the gun out of his grasp. His muscles were soft and without strength, and he didn't know how to fight.

I flung him back hard into his chair, knocking the wind out of him, and then I reached over and switched off his microphone. I wasn't anxious that either the police or the taxi-drivers should overhear what I was going to say.

There was a crackle as I brushed against his coat. I pulled it open. A folded piece of brown paper protruded from an inner pocket, and I tugged it out and spread it open on the desk. He was gasping for breath and didn't try to stop me. I read what was on it.

Joe's address.

I turned it over. In one corner on the other side, scribbled carelessly as if someone were not sure of the spelling and had used the nearest piece of paper to try them out on, were the words:

Chichen Itza;
Chitchen Itsa
Chitsen

Not chickens, not Chichester. Chichen Itza. I had the vaguest memory of having heard it before. It was the name of an emperor I thought; and it meant nothing to me, nothing. Yet Joe had died for it.

I left the paper on the desk, and hoped that the police would find it useful.

The hysteria had drained out of Uncle George. He looked suddenly ill and old, now that his day was done. I could summon no compassion for him, all the same: but then it was not regard for Kate's uncle that had brought me into the Marconicar office, but love for Kate herself.

'The police will be here in less than a minute,' I said, speaking slowly and distinctly. He shifted in his seat and made a sharp helpless gesture with his pudgy hands. I went on, 'They have been listening in to what you have been saying on the radio.'

Uncle George's eyes widened. 'Twenty-three,' he

said, with a remnant of anger. 'Twenty-three hasn't answered my last few calls.'

I nodded. I said, 'You will be charged with incitement to murder. Gaol for life, at least.' I paused. 'Think,' I said with emphasis. 'Think of your wife. You did it all for her, didn't you, so that she could go on living in the luxury she was used to?' I was guessing, but I felt sure it was true, and he didn't deny it.

'You have shielded her from reality too long,' I said. 'What will it do to her, if you are arrested and tried, and maybe hanged?'

Or to Kate either, I added hopelessly to myself.

Uncle George listened and stared at me, and slowly his gaze fell to the pistol I still held in my hand.

'It's quicker,' I said.

There was a short silence.

Very faintly in the distance I heard an alarm bell. Uncle George heard it too. He looked up. He hated me still, but he had come to the end of the line, and he knew it.

'The police,' I said. The bell grew perceptibly louder.

I took the three steps across to the door, turned, and tossed the gun back into Uncle George's lap. As his stubby fingers fumbled and clutched it I went through the door, closed it, and ran down the stairs. The front door was still open. I hurried through that and pulled it shut behind me. The police alarm bells were no longer ringing.

In the shadow of the building I slipped along into the dark porch of the next-door house; and I was only just in time. Two police cars slowed, crawled, and halted in front of the Marconicar building.

Over in the Olde Oake Café the lights were out. The plump waitress had gone home.

There had been no sound from upstairs. I shivered, struck by the horrifying thought that Uncle George, having already screwed himself once to pull the trigger, might just possibly shoot a policeman instead of himself. With the gun I had so thoughtfully given back to him.

As the doors of the police cars slammed open and the black figures poured out I took the first step towards them to warn them that their quarry was armed. But Uncle George's devotion to Aunt Deb's interests remained steadfast after all. I thought that the single crashing shot in the room behind the neon sign was the best thing he had ever done for her sake.

I waited for a few minutes in my dark doorway, and while I stood there a small crowd began to collect on the pavement, drawn by the noise of the shots and the presence of the police cars. I slipped unhurriedly among them, and after a little while walked quietly away.

Round two or three turnings I found a telephone box and stepped inside, feeling in my pocket for coins. The calls to Lodge had taken all my small change, and

329

for a moment I looked blankly at the threepenny piece and two halfpennies which were all I could dredge from my trouser pocket. Then I remembered my cosh. I untied the sock, tipped some of the pennies out on to my hand, pushed four of them into the slot, and asked the operator for Pete's number.

He answered at the second ring.

He said, 'Thank God you've rung. Where the hell have you been?'

'Touring Sussex.'

'And where's Admiral?'

'Well . . . I left him tied to a tree somewhere in the heathland,' I said.

Pete began to splutter, but I interrupted him.

'Can you send the horse-box to collect him? Get the driver to come down to Brighton and pick me up on the sea-front, near the main pier. And Pete . . . have you got a decent map of Sussex?'

'A map? Are you mad? Don't you know where you left him? Have you really just tied the best hunter-'chaser in the country to a tree and forgotten where?' He sounded exasperated.

'I'll find him easily if you send a map. Don't be too long, will you? I'll tell you all about it later. It's a bit complicated.'

I put down the receiver, and after some thought, rang up The Blue Duck. Ex-Regimental Sergeant-Major Thomkins answered the phone himself.

'The enemy is routed, Sergeant-Major,' I said. 'The Marconicars are out of business.'

'A lot of people will be thankful to hear it,' said the strong deep voice, with a good deal of warmth.

I went on, 'However, the mopping up operations are still in progress. Would you be interested in taking charge of a prisoner and delivering him to the police?'

'I would indeed,' he said.

'Meet me down at the main pier, then, at the double, and I'll gen you up.'

'I'm on my way,' said the sergeant-major.

He joined me by the sea wall soon after I got there myself. It was quite dark by then, and the lights along the front barely lit the ghostly grey lines of the breaking waves.

We had not long to wait for the horse-box, and when it came, Pete himself poked his big bald head out of the passenger seat and called to me. He, I and the sergeant-major got into the back and sat on a couple of straw bales, and as we swayed to the movement of the box on its way west I told them all that had happened since the day Bill died at Maidenhead. All, that is, up to my last conversation with Lodge. Of my visit to the Marconicar office and the true identity of Claud Thiveridge, I said nothing. I didn't know how English law viewed the crime of inciting to suicide, and for various reasons had decided to tell no one about it.

Parts of the story Pete already knew, and part Thomkins knew, but I had to go over the whole thing for them both to get it clear from first to last.

The horse-box driver had been given my note of the all-important signpost, and by comparing it with the map Pete had brought, he drove us back to it in remarkably short time.

Both Admiral and Corny Blake were still attached to their various trees, and we led one and frog-marched the other into the horse-box. Admiral was overjoyed to see us, but Blake's emotions seemed slightly mixed, especially when he recognized Thomkins. It appeared that it was Blake who had bashed the sergeant-major on the head with one of his own bottles.

With a grin I fished Blake's brass knuckleduster out of my pocket and handed it to Thomkins. 'The prisoner's armoury,' I said.

Thomkins tossed the wicked-looking weapon in his hand and tried it on for size, and Blake gave one agonized look at it and rolled off his bale of straw in a dead faint.

'We had better go round by West Sussex racecourse, if you don't mind,' I said. 'My car is still in the car park there; I hope.'

It was there, all alone in the big field, the rising moon glinting on its low dark shape. I stepped down into the road, shook hands with Thomkins and Pete, wished them luck, and watched the red tail-lights of the horse-box until they disappeared into the darkness.

Then I went over and started my car, turned my back firmly on what was doubtless my duty – the answering of interminable questions in Brighton police station – and with a purring roar set off for the Cotswolds.

Driven by an irresistible curiosity, I made a detour along the coast to Portsmouth, taking a chance that the public library would still be open there; and it was. In the reference department I hefted out a volume of an encyclopedia and looked up Chichen Itza. The first spelling on the paper was the right one.

Chichen Itza, I found, was not an emperor; it was a capital city. It was the ancient Yucatán capital of the Mayas, an Indian nation who had flourished in Central America fifteen hundred years ago.

I stared at the page until the words faded into a blur.

What happened next was partly, I supposed, delayed reaction from the abysmal fear I felt when I looked into the barrel of Uncle George's gun; and partly it was hunger and a wave of deathly tiredness, and the sudden letting up of the stresses of the past weeks. My hands, my whole body, began to shake. I braced my foot against the leg of the table I was sitting at and gripped the big book hard to stop it. It went on for minutes, until I could have cried with weakness, but gradually the spasm lessened, and the tension went out of my muscles, and I was just plain cold.

Chichen Itza. I stood up stiffly and closed the book

and put it back on the shelf, and went soberly out to the car. I had set a better trap than I knew, pretending to be on the point of understanding what Joe might have said before he died.

I remembered clearly the study lined with glass cases. I could see the heavy carved oak desk, the folders devoted to Indian tribes, and the one separate folder clearly marked 'Mayas'. Uncle George had told me too much about the Mayas: and he'd known that Chichen Itza would lead me conclusively to him.

CHAPTER EIGHTEEN

What I had not managed to do for Kate by loving her, I had done by tearing her world apart.

She stood in front of me, rigidly controlling herself, with a look of such acrid unrelenting hatred that I tasted my misery literally as a bitterness in the mouth. The banked fires were burning fiercely at last. There was a new depth and maturity in her face, as if in two weeks she had become wholly a woman. It made her more desirable than ever.

The inquest and inquiry into the life and death of George Penn had been adjourned twice, and had just ended; and police, witnesses, and Kate and I were standing in the hall of the Brighton court buildings, preparing to leave.

The verdict of temporary insanity was merciful, but there had been no hiding from news-scenting journalists the extent of Uncle George's criminal activities, and L. C. Perth and Marconicars had been front page news, on and off, for a fortnight.

My getting Uncle George to kill himself had been no help after all to Aunt Deb. It had been impossible to keep the truth from her, and shock and distress had brought on a series of heart attacks, of which the fourth was fatal. But for Kate, though she knew nothing about it, it was still the best thing. She had had to face the knowledge of his guilt, but not his trial and punishment.

But my letters of condolence had been unanswered. My telephone calls had regularly found her 'out'. And now I saw why. She blamed me alone for the sorrows which had come to her.

'I loathe you,' she said implacably. 'You nauseate me. You wormed your way into our house and accepted everything we gave you . . .' I thought of those gentle kisses, and so, from the extra flash in her eyes, did Kate . . . 'and all you have done in return is to hound a poor old man to his death, and kill a defenceless old woman as a result. I have no uncle and no aunt. I have no one anywhere at all. I have no one.' She spoke in anguish. 'Why did you do it? Why couldn't you leave them alone? Why did you have to destroy my home? You knew how much I loved them. I can't bear to look at you, I loathe you so much . . .'

I swallowed, and tried to work some saliva into my dry mouth. I said, 'Do you remember the children who had to be driven to school by a judo expert to keep them safe?'

But Kate stared blackly back as if she hadn't heard.

'You are the most beastly person I have ever known, and although you have made it impossible for me to forget you, I shall never think of you without... without...' Her throat moved convulsively as if she were going to be sick. She turned away abruptly and walked unsteadily out through the big main door into the street.

The flash of camera bulbs met her and caught her unawares, and I saw her throw up her arm in a forlorn attempt to hide her face. The vulnerability and the loneliness in the droop of her shoulders cried out for comfort, and I, who most wanted to give it, was the only person she wouldn't accept it from. I watched her walk quickly through the questioning newspapermen and get into the hired car which was waiting for her.

It drove off. I stared after it, numbly.

Presently I became aware that Lodge was standing at my elbow and had been talking for some seconds. I hadn't heard a word he said, and he appeared to be waiting for a reply.

'I beg your pardon,' I said. 'What did you say?'

Lodge glanced out through the door where Kate had gone and sighed. 'It wasn't very important... Look, she'll see things more reasonably in a little while, when she begins to think straight again. I heard a good deal of what she said... but you aren't to blame because her uncle took to crime.'

'If I had known...' I stopped, on the verge of adding

the give-away words 'for sure': 'If I had known that George Penn was Claud Thiveridge, I would have done things differently.'

'Things worked out well for the Penns, I think,' said Lodge. 'A quick end has its merits.'

His tone was loaded with meaning, and I knew that he half guessed what part I had played in Uncle George's death. He had several times earlier remarked that my disappearance from Brighton at the moment of success was out of character, and had shown polite scepticism over my excuse that I was growing anxious about my horse. He had mentioned pointedly that the Brighton police, listening in the Marconicar taxi to Uncle George's ravings, had heard a faint murmur (indistinguishable) in the background, a single shot, and nothing more. They had not been able to account for this, apart from later finding the microphone switched off and a bullet in the wall, and had come to the conclusion that Uncle George had been testing the old pistol to see if it were in working order. The shot had, however, brought them in haste to the Marconicar buildings.

'You may be right,' I said non-committally to Lodge. His eyelids flickered, and he smiled and changed the subject.

'The Marconicar drivers come up in court again this week. You'll be there to give evidence, I suppose,' he said.

'Yes,' I agreed, not liking the prospect.

All the drivers who had been looking for me had been alarmed by the shot and the silence on their radios. Some had begun to drive back to Brighton, some had made for London, and one or two had left their taxis and started out on foot. But all had quickly been rounded up, as following the rather vague directions I had phoned to Lodge, the police had begun making road blocks round them while they were still listening to Uncle George. Now the drivers faced charges ranging from intimidation and grievous bodily harm to murder itself.

Records discovered in Uncle George's study, inside a folder marked with gory humour 'Notes on Human Sacrifices', made it clear that Joe Nantwich had indeed been knifed by the man who had been wearing my tie.

And Uncle George's motives were now clear too. Keeping up old standards of luxury had been too much for his income after the war, and instead of making Aunt Deb face reality, or facing it himself, he had gradually spent most of his capital. With almost the last of it he had bought Marconicars and launched into crime. He had directed everything through Fielder and had apparently never seen with his own eyes the brutal results of his orders. I doubted whether his misdeeds had seemed either more or less real to him than the primitive barbarities he spent his time studying.

The police had found neat lists, in files going back

four years, of the money he had collected from the little terrorized businesses; and occasionally against the name of a café or a shop or a pub, Lodge told me, was written the single word, 'Persuaded'.

The racing record was shorter and contained lists of sums of money which the police did not know the purpose of; but one sheet headed 'Joe Nantwich' was clear enough. It was a list of dates and amounts, of which the smallest was one hundred pounds. And underneath was drawn a thick line, with the words: 'Account closed' printed in Uncle George's neat handwriting.

With Kate gone, the press men had drifted away. Their fun was over.

'Are you ready to go?' I asked Lodge. I had picked him up in Maidenhead on my way down. He nodded, and we went out to my car.

I drive faster when I'm happy. That day I had no trouble at all in keeping within the speed limit through all the twisty Sussex villages; and Lodge endured my gloomy silence without comment half the way back to Maidenhead.

Finally he said, 'Miss Ellery-Penn was very useful to her uncle. Everything you did in pursuing him went straight back to him through her. No wonder he was so well informed about your movements.'

I had lived with this thought for a long time now; but hearing someone else speak it aloud had a most extraordinary effect. A tingle ran up my spine and set my brain suddenly alive, as if an alarm bell were ringing in my subconscious.

We were running through shrub and heathland. I slowed, swung the car off the road on to the peaty verge, and stopped. Lodge looked at me questioningly.

'What you said . . . I want to think,' I said.

He waited a while in silence, and then said, 'What's worrying you? The case is over. There are no more mysteries.'

I shook my head. 'There's someone else,' I said.

'What do you mean?'

'There's someone else we don't know about. Someone in Uncle George's confidence.' In spite of everything, I still thought of him as Uncle George.

Lodge said, 'Fielder, the manager, was rounded up. So were all the L. C. Perth operators, though they have been freed again. Only two of the clerks had any idea of what was going on, one who went to the race tracks and one in the office. They received their instructions through Fielder about which horses to accept unlimited money on. There are no niggers left in the woodpile.'

'Joe was stopping horses for months before Uncle George gave Heavens Above to Kate, and she had never been racing before that. Someone else who goes racing must have been working for Uncle George,' I said with conviction.

'Penn would need only the morning paper and a form book for choosing a horse to stop. He wouldn't need to go to the races himself. He didn't need an accomplice at the races apart from his bookmaker – Perth. You're imagining things.'

'Uncle George didn't know enough about horses,' I said.

'So he made out,' said Lodge sceptically.

'Kate told me that for as long as she remembers he was a dead loss on the subject. He started the Marconi-car Protection racket only four years ago, and the racing racket less than a year ago. Before that he had no reason to pretend. Therefore his ignorance of horses was genuine.'

'I'll give you that,' he said, 'But I don't see that it proves anything.'

'He *must* have had a contact on the racecourse. How else did he manage to pick on the one jockey who could most easily be corrupted?' I said.

'Perhaps he tried several, until he found a taker,' suggested Lodge.

'No. Everyone would have talked about it, if he had.'

'He tried Major Davidson,' said Lodge. 'That looks like a very bad mistake from your mythical adviser.'

'Yes,' I conceded. I changed to another tack. 'There have been one or two things which have been relayed recently to Uncle George which Kate herself didn't know. How do you explain that?'

'What things?'

'Joe's bit of brown wrapping paper, for instance. He

told everyone in the weighing-room at Liverpool about it. Kate wasn't at the meeting. But two days later, on Uncle George's instructions, Joe was killed and the paper taken away from him.'

Lodge pondered. 'Someone might have rung her up on the Sunday and mentioned it in passing.'

I thought fleetingly of Dane. I said, 'Even then, it was surely not interesting enough for her to have told Uncle George.'

'You never know,' he said.

I started up and drove on in silence for some miles. I was loath to produce for his scepticism the most deep-rooted of my reasons for believing an enemy still existed: the near-certainty that in the concussed gap in my memory I already knew who it was.

When at last I tentatively told him this, he treated it more seriously than I expected. And after some minutes of thought he pierced and appalled me by saying, 'Perhaps your subconscious won't let you remember who this enemy of yours is *because you like him*.'

I dropped Lodge at Maidenhead and went on to the Cotswolds.

Entering the old stone house with the children noisily tumbling through the hall on their way to tea was like stepping into a sane world again. Scilla was coming down the stairs with her arms full of Polly's summer dresses: I went over and met her on the bottom step and kissed her cheek.

'Joan and I will have to lengthen all these,' she said, nodding at the dresses. 'Polly's growing at a rate of knots.'

I followed her into the drawing-room and we sat down on the hearthrug in front of a newly lit fire.

'Is it all over?' asked Scilla, pushing the dresses off her lap on to the floor.

'Yes, I think so.' Too much was all over.

I told her about the inquest and the verdict. I said, 'It was only because of Bill that George Penn was ever found out. Bill didn't die for nothing.'

She didn't answer for a long time, and I saw the yellow flames glinting on the unshed tears in her eyes. Then she sniffed and shook her head as if to free herself from the past, and said, 'Let's go and have tea with the children.'

Polly wanted me to mend a puncture on her bicycle. Henry said he'd worked out some gambits in chess and would I play against him after tea. William gave me a sticky kiss and pressed an aged fruit drop into my palm as a present. I was home again.

CHAPTER NINETEEN

The almost unbearable belief that I had lost Kate grew very little easier as the days passed. I couldn't get her out of my mind. When I woke in the morning the ache rushed in to spoil the day: when I slept I dreamed continually that she was running away down a long dark tunnel. I thought it unlikely I would ever see her again, and tried to make myself be sensible about it.

Then, a week after the inquest on Uncle George, I went to ride at Banbury races, and Kate was there. She was dressed in dark navy blue and there were big grey hollows round her eyes. Her face was pale and calm, and her expression didn't change when she saw me. She was waiting outside the weighing-room, and spoke to me as soon as I drew near.

'Alan, I think I should apologize for what I said to you the other day.' The words were clearly an effort.

'It's all right,' I said.

'No . . . it's not. I thought about what you said . . . about those children going to school with the judo expert . . . and I realize Uncle George had got to be stopped.' She paused. 'It was not your fault Aunt Deb died. I'm sorry I said it was.' She let out a breath as if she had performed an intolerable duty.

'Did you come all the way here especially to say that?' I asked.

'Yes. It has been worrying me that I was so unjust.'

'My dear precious Kate,' I said, the gloom of the past week beginning to vanish like morning mist, 'I would have given anything for it not to have been Uncle George, believe me.' I looked at her closely. 'You look very hungry. Have you had anything to eat today?'

'No,' she said, in a small voice.

'You must have some lunch,' I said, and giving her no chance to refuse, took her arm and walked her briskly to the luncheon-room. There I watched her eat, pecking at first but soon with ravenous appetite, until some colour came back into her cheeks and a faint echo of her old gaiety to her manner.

She was well into her second helping of hot game pie when she said in a friendly tone, 'I wish you'd eat something too.'

I said, 'I'm riding.'

'Yes, I know, I saw in the paper. Forlorn Hope, isn't it?' she asked between forkfuls.

'Yes,' I said.

'You will be careful, won't you? He's not a very good jumper, Pete says.'

346

I looked at her with delighted astonishment, and she blushed deeply.

'Kate!' I said.

'Well . . . I thought you'd never forgive me for being so abysmally beastly. I've spent the most vile week of my life regretting every word I said. But at least it brought me to my senses about you. I tried to tell myself I'd be delighted never to see you again and instead I got more and more miserable. I . . . I didn't think you'd come back for a second dose, after the way you looked at Brighton. So I thought if I wanted you to know I was sorry I'd have to come and tell you, and then I could see how . . . how you reacted.'

'How did you expect me to react?'

'I thought you'd be rather toffee-nosed and cool, and I wouldn't have blamed you.' She stuffed an inelegant amount of pie-crust into her mouth.

'Will you marry me, then, Kate?' I asked.

She said, 'Yes' indistinctly with her mouth full and went on uninterruptedly cutting up her food. I waited patiently while she finished the pie and made good time with a stack of cheese and biscuits.

'When did you eat last?' I asked, as she eventually put down her napkin.

'Can't remember.' She looked across at me with a new joy in her face and the old sadness beneath it, and I knew from that and from her remark about Forlorn

347

Hope – the first concern she had ever shown for my safety – that she had indeed grown up.

I said, 'I want to kiss you.'

'Racecourses were not designed for the convenience of newly affianced lovers,' she said. 'How about a horse-box?'

'We've only got ten minutes,' I said. 'I'm riding in the second race.'

We borrowed Pete's horse-box without more ado. I took her in my arms, and found this time on Kate's lips a satisfactorily unsisterly response.

The ten minutes fled in a second, and the races wouldn't wait. We walked back, and I went into the weighing room and changed into colours, leaving Kate, who looked a bit dazed and said she felt it, sitting on a bench in the sun.

It was the first time I had been racing since Uncle George's inquest. I glanced uneasily round the changing room at the well-known faces, refusing to believe that any was the go-between who had brought death to Joe. Perhaps Lodge was right, and I didn't want to find out. I had liked Uncle George himself, once. Did I shrink from seeing the façade stripped from another friend to reveal the crocodile underneath?

Clem handed me my lead-packed weight cloth. I looked at his patient wrinkled face, and thought, 'Not you, not you.'

It was a sort of treachery to reflect that Clem heard

348

all that went on and that no event of any significance ever escaped his ears. 'The oracle,' some of the lads called him . . .

A hearty thump on the back cut off my speculations.

'Wotcher, me old cock sparrow, how's the sleuthing business?' bellowed Sandy, pausing and balancing his saddle on one knee while he looped up the girths. 'How's Sherlock these days?'

'Retired,' I said, grinning.

'No, really? After such grade A results?'

'I'll stick to steeplechasing, I think. It's less risky.'

Sandy's friendly gaze strayed to the scar on my cheek.

'You're welcome to your little illusions, chum,' he said. 'You'll change your mind when you've broken as many bones as I have.' He wound the girths round the saddle, tucked in the buckles, and with his helmet pushed far back on his head and his cheerful voice drawing heads round like a magnet, made his way out to the scales.

From across the changing room I had a good view of Dane's back solidly and deliberately turned towards me. Talking to someone by the gate, he had unfortunately seen Kate and me returning from the horse-box parking ground. He had had a good look at our radiant faces before we knew he was there, and he didn't need to have things spelled out for him. He had congratulated Kate in two clipped sentences, but to me he had still spoken not a word.

I went past his unyielding back and out to the paddock. He followed. Pete trained both the horses we were riding, and we both had to join him.

Pete jumped in with both feet.

'Alan, Kate's told me your news. Well done.'

He received a fierce glower from Dane, and hastily began to assess the race. He was talking about Dane's mount, and my attention wandered.

There, ten yards away, stood the craggy Clifford Tudor, opulently rolling a cigar round his mouth and laying down the law to his trainer and jockey. Odd, I thought, how often I had come across that man. I watched him make heavy chopping motions with his dark hands to emphasize his points, and caught the young jockey, Joe's substitute, wrinkling his forehead in acute anxiety.

My gaze slid beyond him to where Sir Creswell Stampe was superintending the raising of his unamiable son David into the saddle, before going to take his judicial position in the Stewards' box. Beyond him again were other groups of owners and trainers planning their plans, hoping their hopes, giving their jockeys instructions (and counter-instructions) and calculating their last-minute bets.

So many people I knew. So many people I liked.

Which of them . . . which of them was not what he seemed?

Pete gave me a leg up on to Forlorn Hope's narrow back, and I waved to Kate, who was standing by the parade ring rails, and cantered down towards the start.

On the way Dane came past briskly, turning his head in my direction as he drew level. With cold eyes he said, 'Blast you,' giving both words equal punch, and shook up his horse to get away from me and give me no chance to reply. I let him go. Either he would get over it or he wouldn't; and in either case there wasn't much I could do about it.

There were eleven runners in the race. We circled round while the starter's assistant tightened girths and the starter himself called the roll. Sandy asked his permission to dismount in order to straighten his saddle, which had slipped forwards on the way down to the gate. The starter nodded, looking at his wristwatch and telling Sandy not to be too long. This particular starter hated to start his races late and grew fidgety over every minor delay.

Sandy unbuckled the girths, pulling his saddle straight, and tightened it up again. I was watching him instead of concentrating wholly on Forlorn Hope, so that what happened was entirely my own fault.

An attendant flapped open under my horse's nose the white flag which it was his job to wave aloft, to signal to the stands that the horses were about to start.

My green young hurdler took fright, reared up like a circus horse, twisted sideways, and threw me off. I hit the ground almost flat on my back, winding myself, and I saw Forlorn Hope kick up his heels and depart at a smart pace up the course.

For a few seconds I lay there trying to get my breath back, and Sandy walked over with his hand outstretched to help me up, laughing and making some rude remarks about my sudden descent.

The most extraordinary dizziness suddenly swept over me, and my senses began to play fantastic tricks. Lying in the spring sun, I felt rain on my face. Winded but unhurt, my body was momentarily invaded by shocking pain. In my whirling brain it seemed as if past and present had become confused, and that two completely different events were somehow happening at the same time.

I stared up into Sandy's face. There was the familiar wide gap-toothed grin, the false incisors removed for safety; there were the devil-may-care expression. The sunshine bathed his face in light. And what I saw as well was the same face looming towards me in pouring rain, with cruel eyes and a grim mouth. I heard a voice say, 'You nosey bastard, perhaps that'll teach you to mind your own business;' and I threw up my hand to shield my cheek against the kick which was coming . . .

My sight cleared and steadied, and Sandy and I were

looking straight into each other's eyes as if a battle were being fought there. He dropped the hand outstretched to help me, and the friendliness went out of his face with the completeness of an actor shedding a role when the play is over.

I found my palm was still pressed against my cheek. I let it drop away, but the gesture had told its tale. I had remembered what had happened by the fence at Bristol, and Sandy knew it.

Strength returned to my limbs, and I stood up. The starter, consulting his watch in barely concealed annoyance, asked if I was all right. I replied that I was, and apologized for holding up the race. Some way down the course someone had caught Forlorn Hope, and as I watched he was turned round to be led back to the starting gate.

Sandy, showing no haste to remount, stood his ground in front of me.

'You can't prove a thing,' he said, characteristically taking the bull by the horns. 'No one can connect me with Penn.'

'Fletcher,' I said at once.

'He'll keep his mouth shut,' said Sandy, with conviction. 'He is my cousin.'

Uncle George's racing venture, I now saw, had not been inspired solely by the availability of a shaky bookmaking business. The existence of an easily recruited ally on the racecourse might have been the very factor which decided him, in the first place, to buy L. C. Perth.

I mentally reviewed the rest of the gang.

'How abut Fielder?' I suggested after a short pause.

'I'm a voice on the phone to him. A voice called Smith. He doesn't know me from Adam,' said Sandy.

Temporarily, I gave up. I said, 'What did you do it for?'

'Money. What else?' he said scornfully, clearly thinking the question foolish.

'Why didn't you stop the horses yourself? Why let Joe collect the big fat fees for losing?'

Sandy seemed perfectly willing to explain. 'I did stop a couple myself. The Stewards had me in over the second one, and I got off by the skin of my bloody teeth. I saw the red light, mate. I tipped the boss to try that little bastard Joe instead. Let him lose his licence, not me, I told him. But mind you, I was on to a bloody good percentage every time he strangled one.'

'Which made you all the more angry when he won against orders on Bolingbroke,' I said.

'That's right.'

'Then Joe didn't tell you in the washroom he was going to pull Bolingbroke. You knew already.'

'Proper little Sherlock,' mocked Sandy.

'And you put him over the rails at Plumpton, I suppose?'

'He bloody well deserved it. He lost me fifty quid on Leica as well as my bonus from the boss.'

'Did he deserve to die, as well?' I asked bitterly.

The man leading Forlorn Hope back was now only a hundred yards away.

'The stupid little sod couldn't keep his mouth shut,' said Sandy violently. 'Waving that brown paper at Liverpool and yelling for you. I saw what was written on it, and told Fielder, that's all. I didn't know what it meant, but it was a ton to a tanner the boss wouldn't like it. Joe was asking for it.'

'And after he'd got it, you rang Fielder and told him the job had been bungled, and Joe had lived long enough to talk to me?'

'Yes,' said Sandy morosely. 'I heard you telling every bloody body in the weighing-room.'

I couldn't resist it. I said, 'I was lying. Joe died without saying a word.'

As the full significance of this slowly dawned on him, his jaw dropped, and I saw him waver in some secret inner place as if an axe had hacked into the roots of his colossal self-confidence. He turned on his heel, strode across to where the starter's assistant held his horse, and swung abruptly into the saddle.

I went to meet Forlorn Hope, thanked the man who had brought him back, and remounted. The starter's patience had run out.

'Get into line, please,' he said, and the circling horses began to straighten out across the course. I came up from behind and took a place alongside Sandy. I had one more question to ask.

'Tell me,' I said, 'why on earth did you get Penn to try to bribe Major Davidson? You must have known he wouldn't have stopped Admiral winning for all the money in the world.'

'It was the boss's idea, not mine,' said Sandy roughly. 'I warned Fielder to tell him it wouldn't work, but the boss knew bee-all about horses and was pig-headed besides. Fielder said he wouldn't listen, because he thought if he fixed a cert it would be worth a fortune. He made a packet out of it, all right. He thought up the wire himself. And I'd be a ruddy sight better off if the wire had killed you too,' he added, with a sudden spurt of venom.

The starter's hand swept down on the lever. The tape flew up, and, five minutes late, the horses bounded forwards towards the first hurdle.

I don't know exactly when Sandy decided to put me over the rails. Perhaps the thought of all the money he would not be getting overwhelmed him, and perhaps I had brought it on myself by recalling that he had done it to Joe when Joe, as he saw it, had cheated him.

In any case, as we approached the second hurdle, he swerved his horse towards me. We were both in the group just behind the leaders, and I was on the inside, with the rails on my left.

I glanced at Sandy's face. His slitted eyes were concentrated on the jump ahead, but with every stride his horse drew nearer to mine. He wasn't leaving me much room, I thought.

Only just in time did I realize that he intended to leave me no room at all. He was aiming to crowd my horse so closely that I would be thrust into the six foot high wing leading up to the hurdles. A crash through the wings, I had been told, was one of the most dangerous of all falls. The time had clearly come for rapid evasive action if I were not to find this out for myself.

I literally hauled on the reins. Forlorn Hope lost impetus dramatically, and as soon as the quarters of Sandy's horse were past his shoulder I pulled his head unceremoniously to the right. It was only just in time. The hurdles were beneath his feet before he had time to see them, and he knocked one flat with his forelegs. The horse following us, going faster, bumped hard into the back of him, and the jockey yelled at me to mind what I was doing.

Forlorn Hope was too much of a novice to stand this sort of thing, and I decided that if I were not to ruin his nerve for good, I would have to keep him out of Sandy's way for the rest of the race.

But Sandy was not content with that. Along the straight in front of the stands he gradually worked himself back to my side. He was a better jockey than I and his horse was more experienced. When I tried to go faster, he kept pace, and when I slowed down, he slowed too. I could not shake him off. In front of the crowds, apart from keeping pace with me, he rode fairly enough; but round the next bend lay the long curved leg out into the comparatively deserted country, and what he might do there I hated to think.

I did consider pulling up and dropping out of the race altogether, but that seemed an even more ignominious defeat than being put over the rails.

As the field swept round the bend in a bunch, Sandy tried again. He closed his horse tight up against mine and very slightly behind. On my left I was jammed against Dane. He glanced across and shouted, 'Get over, Sandy. Give us some room.'

Sandy did not answer. Instead I felt his knee slide along under my thigh until he was pressing fiercely on my hamstrings. Then he gave a sudden violent jerk forwards and upwards with his whole leg.

My foot flew out of the stirrup and I lost my balance completely. I swayed wildly over to the left, my head tipping down beside my horse's neck, my fingers clutching frantically at his mane. I looked down and saw the blur of hooves pounding tight-packed round the bend, and I struggled to prevent myself slipping off among them. But all my weight was too far forward, and the jolt of the horse's galloping stride tended to tip me farther forward still. I knew that in a few seconds I would be off.

It was Dane who saved me. He put his hand on my side and literally pushed me back into my saddle.

'Thanks,' I gasped, feeling with my right foot for the dangling stirrup.

Not far round the bend lay the next flight of hurdles, and I fought to get myself and the horse properly balanced before we met it. As we came round the bend the sun had shone straight into our faces, but swinging out towards the country it lay on our right. Glancing to see if Sandy was still beside me I caught the sunshine full in the eyes and was for a second dazzled. He was there. He appeared to me as a black silhouette against the sun.

I remembered then that on such bright days on this course the sun shone straight into the eyes of the crowds on the stands also, and that it was difficult for them to distinguish what was happening on the far side of the course. Whatever Sandy did, he could be fairly sure the Stewards would not be able to see.

I gained a yard or two on Sandy and Dane at the next hurdle, but over my shoulder I could hear Sandy clicking with his tongue to hurry his horse, and in a few more strides he was beside me again. His shadow lay across my horse's withers.

Suddenly he swung his arm; and had I not been so acutely ready he would have had me. He swung his right arm round his body in a chop at my face, slashing with his riding whip. I ducked in a reflex, without actually seeing the whip at all. The heavy blow landed across my helmet just above the peak, and knocked it clean off my head. It bounced away on the turf.

I felt, rather than saw, Sandy draw back his arm for another try. I slipped my own whip and the reins into my left hand, and when he struck, threw up my right. More by luck than design my fingers fastened on the stick and I gripped and twisted and pulled with the strength of desperation.

I had him half out of his saddle and I almost exulted; but at the vital moment he let go of his stick and regained his balance. Rebounding, his horse swerved away from me, leaving a gap, and I looked hopefully over my shoulder for one of the other runners to come up between us. But most of them had gone on in front, and there was no one close. I threw Sandy's stick away.

The next hurdle lay ahead. I kept well away from the rails and tried to steady Forlorn Hope so that he should have a fair chance at it, but I was all too aware that Sandy was beginning to close on me again with a burst of extra speed.

My horse jumped the hurdle in reasonable style. Sandy kicked his horse into a tremendous leap, and as he landed he pulled straight across in front of me.

Forlorn Hope crashed into the rails.

By some miracle he did not fall. He bounced off, staggered, faltered, and galloped on. My leg, which had been crushed just below the knee between his body and the rails, was completely numb. I looked down at it: it appeared to be doing its job all right, even though I no longer seemed to be connected to it. My silk breeches were ripped open across the knee, and in my new extremely - expensive made-to-measure racing boots flapped a large triangular tear.

Illogically, this made me very angry.

Sandy was some lengths ahead and had not so far managed to pull back again. Dane came up on my right, and I was glad to see him there.

He yelled, 'What the hell's going on? What the blazes does Sandy think he's playing at?'

'He's not playing,' I shouted. 'He wants to get me off.'

'Why?' yelled Dane.

'He was working for George Penn. He was making a lot of money. Now he isn't. He blames me,' I shouted in snatches, the wind picking the words out of my mouth and blowing them back over my shoulder.

'With reason,' shouted Dane.

'Yes,' I agreed. I glanced at him, but now it was he who was outlined against the sun, and I could not see his expression clearly. If he felt badly enough about Kate to carry on where Sandy had for the moment left off, I should have no chance at all. He could ride rings round me, and Sandy, too.

We raced in silence towards the next hurdle, the last on the far side. Sandy was gradually slowing to wait for me.

361

Then Dane said, 'Alan?'

'Yes?' I shouted back.

'Do you want to give Sandy some of his own medicine?'

'Yes.' I suddenly had no reservations. It was a terrible thing to do, and if the Stewards saw me I'd lose my permit; but I had taken just about enough from Uncle George's assorted strong-arm boys.

Dane shouted, 'I'll go up on his outside. You come outside me. Then I'll get away and leave him between you and the rails. OK?'

I nodded. I tried to foresee the future. If I unseated Sandy he would not dare to complain to the Stewards; and I, as he said, could give no tangible evidence against him to the police. There could be an uneasy truce between us. And fall for fall, the score would be equal.

'Come on, then,' Dane shouted.

He kicked his horse and began to take his place on Sandy's right. I pulled away from the rails and urged Forlorn Hope to the outside. There was nearly a mile to go to the finish, and as no one had yet begun to put on the pressure the field was still fairly closely bunched just ahead of us. There was no one behind. After the hurdle lay the long oval bend leading round into the straight. If either Sandy or I were to get the other off, it would have to be done on the bend, once we were round into the straight the Stewards would have too clear a view of our behaviour.

Dane jumped the hurdle alongside Sandy with me not far behind. As soon as I was level with them both, Dane shook up his horse and sped clear away from us, leaving me, as he had promised, with Sandy between me and the rails.

I swung Forlorn Hope over roughly on to Sandy's horse, bumping him against the rails. Sandy yelled and lashed out with his fist. I hit his arm sharply with my stick.

I had got to unseat him without hurting his horse. I was being unfair enough already to the owner in trying to lose him the race by dislodging his jockey: if I could not do it without damaging the horse, I must not do it at all.

Shifting the reins into my right hand, I planted my left abruptly on Sandy's boot just behind his armpit, and shoved. But I was too far away to get enough force behind it. He swayed in his saddle, but kept his balance. He began to swear at me.

We were on the crown of the bend. It had to be now or never. I pushed Sandy's horse harder against the rails. He yelled again. His leg, I knew, must be being crushed, pounded, even torn by the white-painted wood. With my own leg numb from the same treatment, I had no sympathy for him. Then his foot crashed into one of the uprights with an audible snap.

He screamed.

I gritted my teeth, shot out my arm, and pushed him with all my might. I knew if he had not gone then I would not have had the resolution to try again. But he began to topple, slowly, it seemed, at first, and then with an accelerating rush, as if he had been sucked away by a slipstream.

I caught a final glimpse of his face, eyes staring widely, mouth twisted with agony, as he fell into the long grass on the other side of the rails. Then I was round the bend into the straight, bruised, breathless, tattered, and helmetless, but still on board.

Sandy's loose horse, relieved of his weight, spurted forward through the other runners.

Dane saw him, and turned round in his saddle and grinned at me, and jerked up his thumb.